PRAISE FOR

PROFESSOR FEELGOOD

"This book resonated with me so deeply, I felt it in my soul. A beautiful story that I can't begin to say enough good things about. 6 STARS!"

– About That Story

"I LOVED it. It was breathtaking, stunning, and emotional. I absolutely cannot recommend it highly enough!"

– Bookgasms Book Blog

"Rayven's poetry is BEYOND WORDS and had me wishing for my very own Professor Feelgood who would write me epic, heart-stirring poetry. Reading his words made my heart sing."

- Ssh Moms Reading

"I totally fell for these two people fighting a losing battle against a connection that was beyond words. Leisa Rayven's skill is undeniable. Her gift shines through this roller-coaster ride."

– Up All Night Book Blog

~

"I devoured this book from cover to cover and never looked up until I was done. Some of the story was hilarious, some of it was heartbreaking, and the rest was nothing short of outstanding."

– The Heathers Blog

"The writing was phenomenal! The characters, completely unforgettable! This sexy new standalone has what it takes to make every hopeless romantic swoon, sigh, and blush for days."

– Shayna's Spicy Reads

"The characters in Professor Feelgood are special, they will burrow into your heart and remain there. The unique poetry heightens the heat and the swoon-factor of the story."

– Book Angel Booktopia

"A tortured swoony hero with a broken heart. He was divine. It's not often we get heroes that compel us emotionally the way he did. Bravo Leisa Rayven for writing that 'perfect' male character we fell in utter book-love with."

– Totally Booked Blog

"The ultimate romance novel. It was the kind of book that made me think, it affected me deeply, and I fell in love with it wholeheartedly. It was truly a masterpiece."

– A Hopeless Romantic's Booklandia

"You know that feeling when you find a new author you love and you immediately want to read their entire backlist? That's how I felt after reading Professor Feelgood by Leisa Rayven."

– A Novel Glimpse

"The kind of book that captivates you and sweeps you off your feet. From entertaining banter to intense chemistry, and moments that made my heart ache. I'm telling you, this book hit all the marks."

– Once Upon a Bookblog

"Both hilarious and heart wrenching. With a wonderful premise, intriguing plot, great characters and both laughter and tears, this story had it all, and this author has a new fan. 5+ stars."

– B2B Kelly

Leisa Rayven has delivered another winner with this book. A smart, fun, emotional and gorgeously romantic read with a love story that is as surprising as it is beautiful, and so damn *right*. I was captivated from beginning to end.

– The Escapist Book Blog

DOCTOR LOVE

LEISA RAYVEN

AUTHOR'S NOTE & DEDICATION

For those readers new to my Masters of Love series, please note that although you can read this book as a standalone, it contains MAJOR SPOILERS for the other two books: *MISTER ROMANCE* and *PROFESSOR FEELGOOD*. If that's important to you, feel free to read the others first then come back to this one.

For those continuing the series, this book's timeline *overlaps* with events from *PROFESSOR FEELGOOD*, so keep an eye out for indicators. (For example, this book starts *before* the beginning of *PROFESSOR FEELGOOD*. Just an FYI so you can keep everything straight.)

As always, this book is dedicated to my amazing family who puts up with so much to enable me to do this crazy writing venture, and to my beautiful parents who have gone through so much recently, I adore you all with my whole heart.

Now, darling readers, onward! See you at the end.

DOCTOR
LOVE

TOBIAS

We all want to be remembered for something great. To leave our mark on the world and have people raise a glass in our honor and say things like, "Here's to Bob. He was one helluva guy." Or "Remember Bob? I sure do, because he was grrrrrreat."

I always thought I had greatness on a lock. After all, I was valedictorian at high school, got a full ride to MIT for computer science, lost my virginity before any of my geek friends, and graduated with a perfect GPA. And yet, here I am ... not great. I'm sure there are a few generous souls who'd disagree, but there's no arguing with solid facts.

My *List of Reasons Greatness Eludes Me* is a work in progress, but these are the current frontrunners:

1. I've failed to live up to my true potential. You may say, "Haven't we all?" but let's get real. When I graduated college, I was on top of the world. Blue chip job offers from Fortune 500 companies, and yeah, even one from NASA. But I said no to all of it. Would I have upped my cred working for the FBI or writing code for probes that would, and this isn't hyperbole, map our galaxy? Hell yeah. I'm a geek, and I'm breathing. But just before I graduated college, my father had a severe accident that left him partially paralyzed, and "normal" went out the window. I waved goodbye to my dreams as my mom, my little sister, and I got on with the business of surviving. A year later, when I was offered a job writing about video games and cutting-edge tech for an online

magazine, I took it. No, it wasn't going to change the world, but it was easy, and after working my ass off for so many years and taking over from Dad as the head of the family, easy sounded pretty damn good for a change.

2. I have a knack for trusting the wrong people. Out of the handful of girlfriends I've had over the years, all but one have betrayed me in some way. I don't know why I seem to be blind to a person's ability to lie straight to my face, but it always ends up kicking me in the balls. I'm working on changing that.

3. I'm nice. Not a character flaw, but to be super-successful, a certain level of assholishness is required, and I'm more of an if-I-can-help-you-I-will-or-die-trying kind of guy. That's probably one of the reasons I'm so fucking exhausted all the time, but we'll come back to that.

Of course, I do have some good traits to help balance out the bad: I have a decent sense of humor; I'm kind to animals; I can solve a Rubik's cube in each hand in under a minute; I can pretty much hack into any computer network on the planet; and if anyone hurts the people I love, I will hunt them to the ends of the earth and deliver a karmic bitch-slap of epic proportions.

Oh, and I also have a kickass collection of cardigans, so there's that.

Despite all of this, I really thought that by the time I turned twenty-five, I'd be living my best life, but clearly, that hasn't happened. Instead, I'm in a bar in Brooklyn on a Saturday night, stuck between a rock and a hard place. And when I say rock, I mean the staggering amount of work I still have to complete before I can relax for the evening, and when I say hard place, I mean a very soft, attractive female body.

"Toby, come onnnn. Let's get out of here. My roommate is away, and we have the whole apartment to ourselves."

There are arms around my waist and breasts pressed against me, and while I usually wouldn't complain about either of those things, the person doing the holding and pressing is someone I'm trying to stay away from.

"Jackie …" I gently pull her arms down. "We've talked about this."

"Yeah, we talked about not dating, and that's totally cool." She steps forward and judging by the smell of her breath and the way she hangs off me, she's had about three too many whiskey sours tonight.

"I'm just saying you should come back to my place and …" She trails her fingers across my chest, until she feels my nipple beneath my shirt. "... see what happens."

I shudder involuntarily. This is seriously the last thing I need tonight.

It's doesn't take a genius to figure out what Jackie wants. We got together in the first place because she gets horny as hell when she drinks, but our initial arrangement was for no-strings-attached sex. Turns out, there were strings. Lots of them. Without any warning, she went from zero to let's-spend-every-waking-moment-together-and-possibly-buy-a-cat in less than a month. And now, I don't know how many more ways I can tell her I don't want to be her boyfriend without learning a second language.

"Jackie ..." I take her hands in mine to prevent them from roaming anywhere else on my body without permission. "I'm pretty sure more meaningless sex is not what you're after, and I've been honest in letting you know I can't offer anything else."

"Then let's just have sex." She makes a whining sound. "You're so good at it, Toby, and the last couple of guys I've slept with haven't been." She lowers her voice. "I need a Tobygasm. Please. I'm so uptight right now, I feel like you could use my muscles to re-cable the Golden Gate bridge. Just give me one more night, and then I'll leave you alone."

"That's what you said a week ago, and also the week before that; and yet, here we are again."

"Yes, but I *mean* it this time. I promise." She tries to press against me again, but I step back and slide a stool between us. How is it that this woman seems to grow several extra sets of arms when she drinks?

I gesture for Joe the Bartender to get her some water.

Dammit, when will I learn? I knew sleeping with someone from work was a bad idea, and what's more, I knew damn well that Jackie was high maintenance before it happened. She writes the gossip column for *Pulse*, the online magazine for which we both work, and that alone should have been a red flag. The reason she's so good at turning the merest eyebrow raise between two celebrities into a three-act opera is that she thrives on drama. I found that out the hard way after the first time I told her we shouldn't hang out anymore. I thought I was nice about it. She gave me the impression she understood and felt the same way. However, a few hours later when I returned from lunch to find the entire contents of my desk shoved into a urinal, along with a note that read, "Screw you, asshole!", I realized she may have been a tad more upset than she'd let on.

Tonight, I have to finish things once and for all. It's been dragging on for way too long.

On the other side of the bar, I see my best friend, Eden Tate, looking at me in concern. I give her a head tilt, and she mouths, "Cut the cord, loser." I shoot her my middle finger as I guide a swaying Jackie onto a stool.

"Toby, I don't wanna sit down." She leans in and whispers, "Unless it's on your face."

I give her a patient smile. As annoying as Eden is with her constant, unsolicited advice, I really should have listened to her about Jackie. When she'd first seen us flirting, she warned me that I was making a mistake, but I ignored her. I was horny and lonely, and sometimes, being intimate with the wrong person is better than stubbornly holding out for the right one.

Since there's not even a hint of a soul mate on my romantic horizon, fleeting physical connections help stave off the terrifying, creeping certainty that I'm going to die alone. Now, I'm paying for my pathetic need for human contact. If I could go back and make a different choice, I would, partly to avoid extricating myself from Jackie's vice-like embrace, but mostly because as lonely as I am, I can tell Jackie is too. Maybe even more than I am. That's why consistently rejecting her makes me feel like a total prick.

"Listen, Jackie." I take her phone from her hand. "You deserve more than what I can offer, and there's something that might be able to help." I type a URL into her browser and download the latest beta version of the app I've been working on.

"What are you doing?" Jackie leans over to get a better look.

"You know how I've been moonlighting as the IT manager at Romance Central for a while now?"

She blinks. "Sure. That's where you can pay for fabulously unrealistic romantic experiences with people who are a thousand percent out of your league, right?"

I smile. Not the most flattering description, but certainly accurate. "That's the one."

"Eden's boyfriend runs it." She points over to the stupidly handsome man next to Eden. "What is it that they call him? Major Romance?"

I try not to laugh. "That may very well be what Eden calls him in the bedroom, but no. He was known as Mister Romance, and his real name is Max."

For years, Mister Romance was considered to be an urban legend among New York's social elite. When Eden found out that the mythical creature who charged lonely women thousands of dollars for dream dates was a real man, her investigative-journalism instincts kicked in, and she hunted him down with the singular focus of a Schnauzer sniffing out a pound of sausages. Despite her determination to expose him for the sleazy conman she believed him to be, she ended up falling in love with him instead. Because of course she did.

After that, he became a one-woman man and created Romance Central, a hub where people in need of quality companionship can hire perfect dates, minus the sex. When Max asked me to moonlight as his part-time tech guru, I found it impossible to say no. The truth is, as much as I resent him for being handsome, funny, intelligent, and stealing my best friend, he's also a pretty decent human being, and I believe in his mission to bring romance to the masses.

I hold the phone out to show Jackie what I've brought up on the screen. "This is what I'm working on for Max right now. It's a matchmaking app."

Jackie squints at it. "So, like, Tinder?"

I almost choke on my disgust. "No, not like Tinder. There's zero goddamn finesse in that program. It's literally the laziest fucking app I've ever seen. A monkey could have programmed an app that lets you swipe right on people you find vaguely attractive in your immediate vicinity. You want to get laid without paying for cab fare? Sure, go use Tinder. You want something more meaningful? You use my app."

Jackie takes the phone and studies the startup screen. "It's called HEA?"

"It stands for Happily Ever After. Look." I tap the screen. "This questionnaire will analyze everything about you. Sexuality, what you look for in a partner, what turns you on in the bedroom, likes, dislikes, hobbies, music, books, movies, politics, religion, and food. Then all that info is fed through my state-of-the-art algorithm, and you'll be matched with guys who are going to be the most compatible. Guys who'll want to *date* you, not just have sex with you."

She scrolls through the questions. "God, how long is this list?"

"Longer than Santa's. There are over three-hundred questions. But that's why the matches are so successful. When you're done, the app knows you better than you know yourself."

And that's the whole point.

Dating is a nightmare. That isn't my personal opinion, it's a stone-cold fact. The hard-wired human compulsion to form meaningful connections is one of the most ridiculous evolutionary traits in the living world. What the hell other species tortures themselves with the impossible task of finding their perfect other half? Sure, there are other creatures who mate for life, but you don't see them getting in screaming matches over one of them ogling the hot beefcake penguin neighbor they friended on Facebook, or coveting the sensuously limber lobster friend they follow on Instagram. Humans' innate capacity for distrust and self-sabotage is breathtaking in its scope.

That's where the HEA app comes in.

My theory is that dating would be more bearable if you knew the odds of the relationship before you started. Would you doubt your partner all the time if you knew that they were about as close to a perfect match as was statistically possible? Likewise, would you waste your time slugging away at a relationship that had zero chance of working out?

"Unlike crappy Tinder," I say. "HEA is for people who want to skip all the shallow bullshit dating brings and just find someone to love."

I scroll through the app to show Jackie how it works. "I've analyzed thousands of questionnaires from couples in successful, long-term relationships, and I've formulated a predictive algorithm that will give you a realistic compatibility percentage. If the percentage is low, you know the relationship is doomed, so don't waste your time. If it's high …" I let her fill in the blanks, and by the way her expression changes, I can tell I have her interest.

I point to the huge crowd in the bar. "All of these people here tonight? They're our latest batch of app testers. If you like, I could get you on the list for the next event. You never know. You might meet your one true love."

Jackie looks up at me and then scans the faces in the crowd. "That's a whole lot of good-looking people."

She's not wrong. Among the attractive app testers, I spy the stunning collection of Romance Central employees. Following Max's initial idea for selling fantasy dates, he now has around twenty people working for him, all from differing backgrounds, ethnicities, and sexual orientations. Some of them are students, some are actors. All look like they've walked straight out of a lab specializing in genetic perfection. Jackie is also gorgeous, so she'll fit right in.

I pass back her phone and urge her to stand. "Come on. You can fill out your questionnaire when you get home, and then we'll add you to the database." Perhaps my gentle encouragement will be the push she needs to move on to a guy more suitable than me. "But first, how about I call you a cab?"

I put my arm around her and move toward the exit on the other side of the bar.

"Wait a minute," she says, pointing to the guys we're passing. "I don't get to go home with one of these pretty men *or* you?"

When we step out into the street, I hope the cool night air will sober her up a little.

"Jackie, you've had too much to drink to make informed choices tonight. Why don't you just go home and get some rest? Tomorrow we can chat more about the whole HEA thing."

She stares at my chest and nods. "You're trying to get rid of me."

I cup her cheek and tilt her head up. "That's not what this is about. I'm not right for you. But I promise, I'm going to help you find a guy who is, okay?"

Moisture pools in her eyes, and for a moment, I think I'm a bastard for hurting her. But then she gives me a shaky smile and pulls me down for a gentle kiss.

"You're a really good guy, you know that, Toby Jenner? Why couldn't you have liked me the way I like you?"

And there it is. As much advanced calculus has gone into the production of my algorithm, the only equation that means anything when it comes to dating is that one plus zero equals one. If you like someone, you're a one. If they don't like you back, they're a zero. Doesn't matter which side the zero is on, it results in someone being alone and wishing they weren't. I've been on the receiving end of zeroes more times than I can count, so I hate that I'm Jackie's zero tonight.

After she climbs into a waiting cab, I watch until it disappears into the relentless New York traffic.

Okay, one fire out. Several hundred to go.

"Hey, Tobias, my dude." I turn to see my tech assistant Raj holding open the door to the bar. "You done with your woman dramas, home boy?" Like me, Raj is working at both *Pulse* and Romance Central. Unlike me, he believes he's a gangsta rap artist trapped in the body of a small Indian man. As passionate as I am about cardigans, he's more so about oversized track suits. It makes him look like he's been zapped by a shrink ray that left his clothes unaffected.

"Soooo," Raj says, indicating the direction in which Jackie's cab disappeared. "If you're done riding the bone train with the hot brunette, is it okay if I —?"

I hold up my hand to cut him off. "Dude, what have I told you about talking about women like that? Don't make me headbutt you." I walk past him back into the bar.

"Cool, cool. I dig you. No bother, my brother." He follows behind me, and we head to the back to the end of the bar where he's set up my laptop into a makeshift workstation. I bring up the latest list of error codes and scan through them.

"But for the record," he says, leaning in a little. "You two are done, right?"

"Yes."

"Cool, cool. She's just my type, you know? Long legs. Boobs you can sink your face into, and a booty that would make Beyoncé want to cut a bitch."

I sigh and hit him over the top of the head.

"Ow, shit man!"

"For fuck's sake, Raj. Women aren't just a collection of physical traits. What about how she graduated from NYU with a double degree in journalism and business? Or how she volunteers at a homeless shelter every month? Or how she can scale the hardest wall at the indoor rock-climbing center faster than most men?"

"Well, fuck, Tobias, you think she's all that, why the hell did you break up with her?"

I tackle the first few errors, fixing them within seconds. "I didn't. We were never really together."

"But I thought you wanted a girlfriend."

"I do. She and I just weren't a good fit."

"That's not what she was telling her friends in the break room the other day. According to her, you have a swingin' dick and know how to use it."

I rub my eyes. "Raj, I know you'll find this hard to understand, but what I want in a girlfriend extends beyond just sex. I want someone who stimulates me mentally as well as physically. I want someone who sets my whole goddamn world on fire."

"And you didn't have that with Jackie?"

"No."

He frowns for a second, completely perplexed. "But she's smokin'. With a slammin' body like that, how could she not light you up like a California wildfire?"

I have an urge to bang my head against the mahogany bar, but it would probably be more useful to bang his head. When it comes to understanding women, it's like his brain is titanium, and all the advice I give about how to treat them is just a collection of wet cotton balls that stick to his consciousness for a few seconds before sliding right off.

"Fuck's sake, Raj, you have a relationship with a *person*, not a *body*."

He leans on the bar. "Yeah, well, Jackie can have relations with my body all she likes."

I clench my jaw and type harder. "Okay. Good talk. Now, unless you have something better to do, let's get things rolling for this event, okay? Go work with Ming-Lee on mobile tech support and making sure the testers understand the full functionality of the app."

He gives me a thumbs up. "All over it like a stripper grindin' a pole." I give him a withering stare. "Shit. Sorry, man. I mean, sure. I got this."

As he scurries off, I finish ironing out the last few kinks in the operating system and save the latest version of the app to the server.

It seems I'm in the nick of time, because I see Ming-Lee gathering the whole group together in preparation for introducing Max and laying out how the night is going to work.

I throw back the last of my disgusting light beer, burp quietly, and then squeeze my hands together until my knuckles crack.

Okay, Toby. Here we go. Time to make everybody but you feel the love.

An hour later, I'm blasting through my compilation screens so fast, my fingers are starting to cramp. As couples get to know each other and submit feedback to the app about their compatibility, the data sets on the other side of the screen continue to morph and update. I write equations on the fly, determined to analyze and incorporate as much information as possible in real time. Unfortunately, there's a slew of shiny new error reports flashing at the top of the screen, and attempting to stay on top of everything has made the space behind my left eyeball ache.

I'm way too sober for this.

Like the masochist I am, I sip my second light beer for the night and grunt in disgust. This is a different brand, but it's still like making love in a canoe. In other words, fucking close to water.

"Well, Doctor Love, what's the prognosis?" A feminine hand comes down on my shoulder, and I look up to see Eden smiling at me. "Are they shot through the heart, and you're to blame? Do you, in fact, give love a bad name?"

"My last nerve, Eden Marigold," I say, going back to the screen. "You're wearing out my very last nerve."

She gives me a patient look. "Well now, that's not even close to an articulate response to my question."

I nod to the bartender, indicating he should serve Eden her usual drink, which is more than she deserves right now. "The prognosis is that if you insist on using that fucking hideous moniker, my blood pressure is going to pop all the capillaries in my eyes."

"What, you mean Doctor Looooove?" she asks, innocently. "Why on earth would a love doctor such as yourself object to being called Doctor Love? I mean, honestly. It's a term of endearment."

Her smile grows. So does my glower.

"If that thing catches on, you know I'm going to hack into every social media account you own and post the love letter you wrote to Justin Timberlake when you were thirteen."

She goes white. "You wouldn't."

"Oh, but I would." I clear my throat and do my most idiosyncratic teenaged-Eden voice. 'Dear Justin, you're so cute! I don't want a boyfriend, but if I did, it would be you. Every time you dance, you make my heart happy."

Her cheeks turn bright pink. "He's a fabulous dancer, okay? Lots of people think that!" I laugh as she slides onto the stool next to me. "Anyway, even if I stopped calling you Doctor Love, it's out there now. It's taken on a life of its own, and there's no going back." The bartender slides a glass of red wine to her, and she sips it. "Besides, what else are we going to call you?"

"Toby? Or Mr. Jenner if you're nasty?"

"Pfft. Boring. We need something more exciting for the man who's developed the most successful dating app of all time."

"*Potentially* most successful," I say, scanning my statistics tab. "If I can't get these functionality anomalies sorted out, it'll be the most glitchy app of all time. Right now, it has more bugs than a freaking bait shop." I fiddle with a line of code I've already rewritten six times today. My determination to beat it is fierce and petty.

"Toby, there are a few minor bugs. You'll get them sorted before the launch."

"Maybe. Also, I need to come up with a way to factor in the completely random outlier of people's lust. Unlike personality compatibility, there's no way to predict physical attraction, so I'm going to have to start thinking outside the box on this one. I mean, if I can just—"

Eden waves a hand in front of my screen. "Okay, yes, you still have some work to do. But you've been staring at that screen for hours. You need to take a break."

"Eden ..."

"A *tiny* break," she insists. "Throw away that beer-flavored water and have a real drink with me. Then I'll let you get back to being the only person in here not having a good time. We've barely spent any time together for weeks because of this app."

"Yeah, well then talk to your boyfriend about his production deadlines, because he's the one who wants this thing done in record time." Sure, that means I'm working eighteen-hour days, but at least it distracts me from my pathetic loneliness.

"Toby, come on." Eden tugs at the sleeve of my cardigan. "Take a moment to appreciate what you've achieved." When I ignore her, she grabs my face and forces me to take in what's happening around me. "Look at all these people. They're here because of you. They're chatting and laughing and flirting because of you. Several of them will probably get laid tonight *because of you*, Doctor Love."

With a grunt of frustration, I turn and observe the dozens of mating rituals taking place within the bar. "Don't you think people would be horrified if they knew that the architect behind their perfect matches is useless in finding his own Miss Right?"

Eden tilts her head. "Come on, now. You're making it sound worse than it is."

"Not possible. In the Venn diagram of my dating history, there's a circle for the women I like and an entirely separate circle for the women who like me, and let me tell you, there's zero goddamn overlap of those two things."

"So, you've *never* had a relationship where you've been attracted to each other equally?"

"Never. My love life is like that game where you flip cards over to try and make a match, but the cards are on fire, and the table's on fire, and everyone is in hell. That's why I'm not wasting any more time on dating, until I find a woman who has a kickass compatibility score."

Eden's eyes light up. "Oooh, okay. So, I assume you've gone through the HEA database and noted your best matches. Give me a rundown of your shortlist."

"There isn't one." I go back to my screen.

"Well, come on, Tobes, get onto that. I want to see you paired off and happy."

"No," I say, "I don't have a short list, because I'm not compatible with *any* of the women in the HEA database."

She frowns. "What the actual hell? There must be close to fifty-thousand women in there by now."

I tap a formula into a data field. "As of yesterday, over sixty-six thousand, and yet the highest score I got with any of them was twenty-eight percent." I hit enter harder than I mean to. "*Twenty-goddamn-eight percent*, Eden. Cats and dogs have a higher compatibility score. Gluten and Millennials are more likely to get along. Superman and Kryptonite will have a more harmonious relationship than me and most single women in the greater Tri-State area."

"Tobes, that has to be wrong."

I give her a deadpan look. "You've just told me how accurate my app is. You can't just change your tune to make me feel better."

She seems about to protest but thinks better of it. "But I want to."

The one thing that drives me to make this matchmaking app the best it can be is the thought that it may help people avoid feeling like every romantic road they travel is a dead end. When it comes to love, the one thing on which I'm an expert is rejection. I've lost track of the times I've been given the "It's not you, it's me" speech. The thing is, if you hear it enough times, you come to believe it is you. If you were clever enough, or good-looking enough, or funny enough, you wouldn't still be alone. When rejection is a way of life, you learn not to want anything too much, because you know without a doubt that you're not going to get it.

"So, what's the solution?" Eden asks. "When the app goes live, there'll be women using it all over the world. That could help."

"It could, but knowing my luck, my perfect woman will live in Siberia." Eden makes a face to let me know she thinks I'm being overly pessimistic, but I've seen the stats. I know I'm not.

"Anyway," I say, "I'll worry about dating when this whole launch drama is over. And even then, I'm not going to bother with anyone who's lower than a seventy-five. I'm done getting tangled up in messy connections that lead nowhere."

"Like Jackie?"

"Exactly like Jackie." I make a mental note to check my compatibility with Jackie after she fills out her questionnaire. I'd be interested to see how low it is.

Eden watches as I try to type in a line of code, but I'm so tired, I screw it up three times in a row. When I start verbally abusing the keyboard, she makes an impatient noise and pulls my hands away.

"Okay, this isn't even a request anymore; it's an intervention. Your eyes are so dark from staring at that screen, you look like you're wearing guyliner. One drink. No arguments. I'm buying."

I rub my eyes and sigh. I can't deny I'm exhausted. Between my day job at *Pulse*, working on this app in my off-hours, and the giant pit of quicksand surrounding my personal life, I feel like I'm always about three seconds away from total disaster. As much as I like to think I'm superhuman and can keep juggling an infinite number of bowling balls, I know that sometime soon, they're all going to come crashing down.

"Fine," I say, with a resigned sigh. "One drink."

"Excellent!" Eden beams as she beckons to the bartender. "Joe! Give me a shot of your most expensive whiskey."

Joe frowns and points to a fancy bottle on the top shelf. "That would be the Royal Solute. It's fifty bucks a glass."

Eden's smile fades. "Uh, okay, then." She pulls out her purse and counts out a bunch of crumpled bills. "In that case, give me your eighteen-dollarist glass of whiskey."

Joe nods. "You got it, big spender."

"You spoil me," I say to Eden and then stand so I can stretch. I've been sitting down so long, my ass has gone numb.

She pats my arm. "Nothing but the most mediocre for my bestie."

After I roll my neck and press my back to the bar, Eden leans against me, and we stand in silence for a while, watching the action around us.

My stomach twists when I see all the connections being made. Lately, I've been feeling increasingly isolated, and there's nothing that heightens that like witnessing people experience the kind of intense chemistry that seems to elude me.

Joe delivers my whiskey as I watch a cute brunette chat with a blond guy with glasses. Seeing how easy they are with each other, I get a pang of jealousy. I'm not easy with girls. Well, I'm easy in that I'll take sex when it's offered, but in terms of relationships, I tend to overthink things and then find new and impressive ways to fuck things up.

The kind of comfortable relationship I have with Eden is goals for my future girlfriend. Maybe that's why I crush on her sister Asha. Ash is similar to Eden but also completely different. Alas, she's just one in a long line of women who doesn't want me in the same way I want them.

"How's Ash doing?" I ask. I may have given up on her ever going out with me, but I still care.

Eden shrugs. "She's okay. Slugging away at work, counting the days until she gets her shot at being made an editor."

"She still with that guy she met in France?"

"Yeah, but we're fast approaching her breakup deadline. If she couldn't make it with beautiful perfect Peter who lived four blocks away, there's zero chance she's going to make it with a dude who lives in Paris." She sighs. "Dammit, now I remember how much I liked Peter."

"Remind me why she broke up with him."

"He manscaped too much."

I nod. "Okay. Understandable."

Manscaping is something I can never be accused of. I've been growing a beard on and off for the past five years, and I've cut my own hair since high school, which is why it falls in shaggy curls around my face. I don't have much hair to speak of on my chest and stomach, and what's there is so light, it's practically invisible. I certainly don't understand why some guys get haircuts every four weeks and wax their junk until they seem pre-pubescent. Apart from how bizarre it looks, it must hurt like a sonuvabitch. Forgive my cowardice, but there's no way I'm letting someone with hot wax near my balls. That's a special kind of torture reserved for insane men and masochists.

I down more of my drink. For an eighteen-dollarish glass of whiskey, it's not bad.

When I glance at Eden, I see her eyes have glazed over. I follow her gaze across the room to where her boyfriend is talking to one of the test couples. As if he feels her staring, Max turns, and the expression he gets makes me shake my head. Pretty sure I've never looked at a girl like that, but I'd like to.

I wonder what it must be like to be that much in love. The way they're looking at each other … the chemistry is so thick, you can almost see it shimmering in the air. It's like there's no one else in this entire place but them. Whenever I witness the passion between Eden and Max, I wonder if that sort of depth of emotion is reserved for a lucky few. Will everyone get to feel something that powerful during their lifetimes? Or is it some kind of cosmic lottery that most of us never get to win?

"Out of interest," I say. "Did you and Max fill out your compatibility questionnaires?"

Eden drags herself away from her man and leans one elbow on the bar. "Of course. Max wanted to make sure your algorithm was working."

"So, what did you score?"

She gives me a smug smile. "Ninety-two."

I almost choke on my own saliva. "Are you fucking kidding me?"

She looks confused. "No. Why?"

I stand up straighter. "Just haven't seen a score that high before. New record." Up until now, the highest was eighty-six, and that was one of my research couples who'd been together for thirty years. "Guess it must feel good to know you chose right."

She smiles wistfully into her wine. "I don't need a score to tell me Max is my soul mate. When you know, you know."

I roll my neck again to try and relieve the tension in my shoulders. "So I hear."

She touches my forearm, and I can feel the sympathy she's exuding.

"Toby, you're a six-foot-five, totally ripped, scruffily handsome genius. I have zero doubt you'll meet your perfect match someday soon."

I shrug her off. "Doesn't bother me." I'm such a liar. I want a soul mate just as much as the next person. I just doubt it's something I'm ever going to have.

Eden frowns for a second, before turning to me with an excited expression. "Well smack my ass and call me stupid, why didn't I think of it before? I have a single friend who'd be great for you."

Oh, Jesus, here we go. "Yeah, I don't think so."

"Just hear me out. She's gorgeous, intelligent, quirky as hell—"

"Eden, I'm the professional matchmaker here. How about we leave potential dates to the expert instead of just hooking me up with some random woman you know."

"She's not random. She's Asha's best friend."

I cringe. "Are you talking about that Joanna chick you mentioned ages ago? The one who first told you about Mister Romance? Didn't you say she was a compulsive liar?"

"That was before I got to know her. She's actually remarkably cool."

"I'm sure. Still not interested. Plus, I've already made it clear that until this app is out in the big, bad world, I have zero time to scratch myself, let alone date."

She nods like she understands, but knowing Eden, this subject is not being dropped any time soon. "Okay. Sure. I hear you. But just know that one day, you'll meet someone amazing and forget all about how busy you are. When your soul mate shows up, you can try to deny them, or ignore them, but it won't work. They'll bully their way into your life whether you want them to or not. Take it from someone who knows."

I down the dregs of my whiskey and put the empty glass on the bar. I love Eden like a sister, and I'm grateful that she looks out for me, but I'm really not in the mood for this conversation tonight. She's working on the assumption that there's someone out there for everyone, and the more I study the numbers, the more certain I am that most of us are destined to stagger from one bad relationship to the next, until we die, miserable and alone.

"Well, thanks for the drink," I say as I pat her shoulder. "But I really need to get back to work." Without waiting for permission, I sit back down in front of my laptop and open it.

She rubs my back. "Okay, then, Doctor Love. Go matchmake your little heart out. I have to head home to finish up a story, but I'll see you at work on Monday, okay?"

"Yep, see you then."

As she heads across the room to kiss Max goodbye, I watch them for a few seconds before taking a deep breath and diving back into the dizzying labyrinth of code on the screen in front of me.

2

FATE CAN'T WAIT

I wipe my hand over my face and yawn. I've officially reached the portion of the night when I'm so fucking tired, I can't see straight. I'd love nothing more than to put my head down on the bar and grab some ZZ's, but it'll be another few hours before I'll get to study the inside of my eyelids.

I'm surprised when a generous glass of whiskey slides into my line of vision. I look up to see bartender-Joe staring at me.

"On the house, man. I haven't seen someone who needs to get trashed more than you for a long time."

"Do I look that bad?"

"Not bad. Wiped. If you were a phone battery, you'd be on one percent."

Sounds about right.

I give him a grateful nod and down half the glass. The burn helps wake me up a little.

I glance around and wipe a hand over my beard. Things have definitely progressed for some couples. The dance floor is packed with people writhing to the slow hypnotic beat, and in dark corners of the bar, I can see at least three couples making out.

Mission accomplished, I guess. Good job, Doctor Love.

Fuck, now I'm saying it, too? Unacceptable.

I push the laptop away from me, and then stand and gesture to Raj, who's standing a few feet away. "I have to pee. Keep an eye on these stats while I'm gone."

"You got it, boss."

After he gives me the thumbs up, I stalk through the loved-up couples on the dancefloor to get to the bathrooms at the back of the bar.

When I push through the door, I catch a glimpse of myself in the mirror. I look like a crazy man. My hair is everywhere, my beard is long and unruly, and there's a kind of exhausted mania lurking behind my eyes. I'm also thinner than I've been for years.

As a kid, I spent a lot of time paying my dues in the social wasteland due to my appearance. I guess that's what happens when some freakish, latent, Viking DNA triggers a growth spurt that's rapid and mammoth. Between the ages of eleven and thirteen, I went from a normal-sized kid to a six-foot-five weirdo who looked like he'd just stepped out of a comic about a mysterious stretching boy. And to make matters worse, my massive change in height turned me from normal weight to being stick-thin. I can't remember when the kids started calling me Bean Pole, but it stuck for years. Even when I started eating like a horse and worked out morning and night to put some meat on my bones, the name-calling continued.

These days, I look more like a bouncer than a beanpole, but if I drop my calorie count or stop going to the gym for even a few days, it's alarming how fast I lose weight. Keeping my muscle mass requires constant vigilance. And yeah, some of it has to do with vanity, but mostly it's because was beaten up for being different by so many assholes in high school, I'm never allowing that to happen again. The next person who tries to pound the crap out of me is going to be on the receiving end of two-hundred-pounds of residual teenage rage.

Apart from not being in peak physical shape right now, my financial and living situations are also what I'd call 'not-ideal', but I have no time to dwell on them tonight.

I exhale and head to the urinals. When I'm done, I wash up before leaning my hands on the vanity and dropping my head. Then I take some deep breaths and try to release some tension. The whiskey has made everything blurry but not soft.

There's a thump to my left. When I glance over, the door slams open, and the most attractive woman I've ever laid eyes on rushes in. She pushes the door shut and leans back against it.

When I look at her, every ounce of anxiety and apathy in my body melts away, and I'm launched into a state of hyperawareness I've never felt before. It's almost like time slows down as I take her in. Out of nowhere, my heart falters and then speeds up, making me feel like I've been stabbed with a cardiac needle full of adrenaline.

Jesus. What the hell?

Sure, she's gorgeous, but I've been around a bunch of attractive women all night. Exactly zero of them had this effect.

I frown as I stare at her and try to decipher why I'm currently being bombarded by an inexplicable rush of hormones.

The gorgeous one looks at me, breathing hard. "Hey. How's it going? You busy? Wanna give a girl a hand?"

"You realize you're in the men's room, right?"

"Yeah. I was hoping to find someone big and burly and lucky me, here you are. Can I borrow you for a second?"

She beckons me over, and I hesitate, only because if someone as stunning as she is wants something from me, there's an unwritten guarantee it's going to get me into trouble. Nevertheless, I straighten up and walk to her. As she takes in my full height, her eyes widen.

"Whoa. You really are a big one. Okay, excellent." She grabs my arm and pushes me around, so our positions are reversed, and my back is to the door.

"Do me a favor and just lean on that thing, okay?" She places her hand on my chest and pushes gently. I take in a sharp breath when my whole body lights up at the contact. I don't know what she's feeling, but something sparks behind her eyes, too, and when she looks at me again it's with surprise. There are a few moments when we just stare at each other in awkward silence, and then I give into the pressure on my chest and lean against the door.

"Thanks. You're perfect." Her voice is breathy, and when she notices, she shakes her head. "I mean, that position is perfect. Don't move."

I'm about to ask her what the hell is going on, when someone bangs on the door.

"Liza, come on. It was a joke. Don't freak out. Let's go back to dancing."

I give the goddess a questioning look. "Friend of yours?"

"More like an acquaintance. Just met him tonight."

"You're one of the testers for the Romance Central event?"

She half shrugs in an "I can't believe I'm here" kind of way. "I came as a favor for a friend, and now, here I am, hiding in the men's room to get away from a drunk, handsy creep. So, things are pretty much going as I expected."

"Liza!" The dude knocks so hard, the door vibrates into my back. *"You're being ridiculous! Let me in, please!"*

A flash of anger hits me, and I hitch a thumb at the door. "You sure you don't want me to let him in? He did say 'please.'"

"Oh, sure," she says with a bitter smile. "He was super polite, right up to the point when he grabbed my ass while we were dancing, and then said it was my own fault, because my dress 'practically begged him' to do it."

That knowledge ignites a vicious fire in a part of me reserved for the assholes that give all men a bad name. How dare he lay his filthy, douche-bag hands on this angel?

"He groped you?" I try to sound less manic than I feel. "Are you okay?"

She nods, but I don't miss the expression that passes over her face.

"I should be used to these sorts of things by now," she says, trying to smile. "And yet every time it happens, I'm surprised and disappointed all over again." She gestures to the door. "He's drunk and clearly not in the mood to handle any kind of rejection, hence me hiding in here. I figure he'll get bored soon and move on. I've seen his type before."

Me, too. I know exactly the kind of 'man' he is, and it boils my freaking blood.

More knocking. *"Open the goddamn door, Liza! Stop being such a stuck-up bitch. I've apologized, for fuck's sake. What the hell do you want?"*

The second he calls her a bitch, something inside me snaps. I've known assholes like him my whole life. Men who victimize others, and then play the victim. During high school, it was guys like him who beat me up every damn day. They think they can treat people however they like and get away with it. Well, not on my fucking watch, they can't.

I yank on the door handle and find the douche in question with his hand raised, about to pound the wood again. He's tall, but not as tall as I am, and he looks at me in surprise as I size him up.

"What are you looking at, stretch?" He glances behind me to where Liza's standing. "Liza, what are you doing? Come out of there so we can talk."

He goes to move past me, but I sidestep to block his way.

"If you didn't get the hint from her barricading herself inside the men's room, she doesn't want to talk to you, asshole. So how about you apologize for putting your hands on her, and then get the fuck out of here."

"And who the hell are you?"

"The guy whose had a spectacularly shitty night and is itching to do something stupid."

He squares up to me with the bravado of someone who's too drunk to register I'm over a head taller and sixty pounds heavier than he is. "Is that right? Well, bring it on, pal."

He punctuates 'pal' by poking me in the chest. I clench my jaw and tighten my hands into fists. He doesn't understand what a monumental mistake he's making by taking me on tonight. I don't think I've ever felt this on edge. Apart from the anxiety of my life right now, I have a savage need to defend the integrity of a woman I've just met, and both those things together mean I'm about half-second away from going all John Cena on his ass.

"Is this a regular thing for you?" I ask, leaning forward enough to get in his face. "Groping women and then getting pissed when they reject you? Do I need to explain the finer points of consent?" Maybe he'll consent to me groping his face with my fist.

"You think I'm intimidated by a dick in a cardigan? Please. I'd destroy you."

What he doesn't know is that because of the dicks who beat me up in high school, I've been training in mixed martial arts since I was fourteen. "You're welcome to try."

"Okay, guys," Liza says behind me, and an electrical current jolts through my spine when I feel her hand on my lower back. "There's no need for this. Henry, go home. You're an angry, handsy drunk, and I never want to see you again. And in the future, when you're trying to convince a woman to take a chance on dating you, perhaps don't treat her like a piece of meat within an hour of meeting her. That's reason number one you're still single."

He scoffs and rolls his eyes, and goddammit, I want to reach into his ocular cavities and squeeze his eyeballs, just a little.

He points at Liza. "And you're single because you're a fucking know-it-all bitch who has no sense of humor."

I don't make a conscious decision to move, but before I know it, I'm holding a fistful of his shirt and have almost lifted him off the floor.

"That's it. We're done here." His legs flail in protest as I drag him down the corridor and into the main area, where I can see Max's best friend Dyson. He's almost as big as I am and is the default security guard tonight.

"Dyson!"

Henry struggles to pull free as I continue to yank him forward, and just before Dyson gets to us, the drunken idiot starts swinging.

"Fucking asshole!" His fist slams into my mouth, and I growl in anger when my lip splits and I taste blood. Whatever expression he sees on my face makes him immediately freeze, and thank God Dyson wrestles him away from me, because otherwise I have no clue what I might have done. Right now, some part of me is itching for a fight. I make a mental note to go to the gym tomorrow and do some sparring to let go of the tension that's threatening to boil over in non-constructive ways.

Before things can escalate further, Dyson wraps his giant hand around the back of Henry's neck and squeezes, and then another couple of guys from Romance Central are there, helping to 'escort' him out of the bar.

I shake out the tension in my hands and roll my neck. I'd give anything to head back to my old apartment right now and sink into the ugly corduroy couch before eating a tray of therapy brownies, but considering I was evicted a month ago and now have no fixed address, that's no longer an option.

"You okay?"

I wipe my mouth and turn to see our event director, Ming-Lee, looking at me with concern.

"I'm fine. But take that fucker off our tester list. He won't be back." I also make a mental note to find out his full name, so I can track him down on any other dating apps. I think Handsy Henry is about to have all of his dating profiles inexplicably deleted. He might also make some embarrassing statements on his social media accounts about the size of his dick and how his inferiority issues lead to him treating women like trash. The extent to which I'm going to destroy him will depend on how much I can calm down before getting back to my computer.

~

WHEN I HEAD BACK towards the men's room, I see Liza standing at the mouth of the corridor, watching me with a worried expression. There's a hint of panic in her eyes, and it makes me regret letting Henry go without smacking him in the head.

I go over to her. "You okay?"

Her gaze slides to my lips, and without thinking, I run my tongue over the split that's oozing blood.

"He punched you?"

I shrug. "A little. It's not a big deal."

She grabs my arm and pulls me back into the men's room. "Let me help you clean that up."

She pushes me toward the vanity, where she pulls out a small, pristine handkerchief from her purse and presses it to my lip.

"You don't have to —"

She shushes me, and then she's standing so close, every single language skill I have disappears in a haze of intense, debilitating attraction. I don't know what the hell it is about her that leaves me so completely speechless, but I know I've never felt anything like it. Yes, she's gorgeous, but that's not it. Behind the blonde hair and perfect face, there's a vulnerability that makes me want to beg to be her bodyguard. Would she let me follow her around forever? Would she approve of me breaking the fingers of any guy who touched her without her permission?

She runs the handkerchief under the tap to rinse out the small amount of blood and dabs my lip again.

"The bleeding has stopped, at least." She studies my mouth so closely I can feel the warmth of her chest radiating into my body. I stand there, slack-jawed, as she wipes my lip a final time.

"Does it hurt?"

"Nothing hurts." Everything is amazing. I feel like I've just taken a shitload of ecstasy and oxytocin in one giant, intoxicating hit. "Are you okay?"

She nods and gives me a tentative smile. "Yeah. It's a sad and horrifying thing to say, but I'm used to the groping. Not so much the banging and yelling, though. That guy has issues."

"So, you were matched with him?" I'm perplexed that my algorithm got things so wrong. Maybe my equations aren't as foolproof as I thought.

She rolls her eyes. "It's my own fault. I shouldn't have agreed to this. I mean, how desperate do you have to be to let an app pick your dates? I'm ashamed of the ridiculousness of it. Have you heard that they're calling the guy who developed this thing Doctor Love? I mean, seriously."

Goddamn you, Eden. "Uh, yeah, I did hear that. Unfortunately."

"I mean, horrible nickname ..." *Agreed.* "... but also, what the hell? I mean, good on Romance Central for trying to help those of us who are romantically challenged, but predicting who people will fall in love with is like turning lead into gold. Anyone who says they can do it is either delusional or a total fraud."

Well, damn. That feels like a slap in the face. But it's not like I'm just making stuff up. I've done the research. I've identified the markers.

"Maybe their guy is onto something," I say, more defensive than I intend. "I mean, if he's studied a large enough sample-size of lasting relationships and identified common characteristics, it would be possible to predict the traits that are most likely to achieve success."

"Uh huh. So, you're telling me that the secret to falling in love with the right person is, what? Math?"

I shrug. "Love may be messy, but math is simple."

"Yeah, but how do you quantify a concept as intangible as love with something as rigid as math? Most relationships are a weird mess of randomness and hormones. I mean, according to *math*, Henry the Drunken Ass Groper had around a sixty percent chance of being my soul mate. I call that an epic fail."

I can't disagree with her, and I feel nauseated to think it was my calculations that matched her with such an obvious loser. Still, knowing the stats for people who've had success with the app, makes me want to prove her wrong.

"No system of prediction is flawless," I say, trying to convince her without seeming too invested. "And I've heard this app is about as accurate as you can get. Maybe you should mark Henry down as an anomaly and try again with someone who has a higher score."

Or you could just date me and be done with it.

"What about you?" she asks.

Wait, did she just read my mind?

"Uh … well, sure. We could go out."

She laughs, and it sends shivers up my spine in a good way. She pulls herself up onto the counter beside the sink and crosses her legs before leaning back against the mirror.

"No, I mean, is your match working out tonight? Am I keeping you from the woman of your dreams?"

Only if you walk out of this bathroom.

"I'm not an app tester. And honestly, you crashing into this bathroom is the most fascinating interaction I've had with a woman in a very long time."

She narrows her eyes at me. "Seriously?"

I try to seem sincere without letting her know just how freaking fascinating I find her. "Seriously."

"I don't know whether to be flattered by that or feel sorry for you."

I smile. "Be flattered. It's less humiliating for me."

She cocks her head. "You have a beautiful smile."

The compliment is so unexpected, I laugh. "Beautiful?" I frown. "Don't you mean lopsided? Or rugged?" I run a hand over my facial hair. I really need to trim it. I must look like a mountain man with an aversion to personal grooming implements.

"No," Liza says, studying me more closely. "I mean beautiful. The way your eyes light up. Everything crinkles. Are you hiding dimples under that face fur?"

I touch my cheek. "Not exactly hiding them. They're just camouflaged." I used to hate my dimples, because they always made me look younger than I was. I haven't seen them for years, so I have no idea if that's still the case.

"Anyway," I say, feeling warmer every second she stares at me. "My point is that you shouldn't let tonight's drama turn you off using the app. I have no doubt you'll find someone more compatible than Henry."

She stares at me for a few more seconds. Then she drops her gaze and looks at her hands in her lap. "I don't know if I have the energy to date any more. It's been a year since I did this, and it hasn't gotten any easier. Maybe some people are just meant to be alone."

"If you're talking about yourself, then I'd have to disagree. You most definitely shouldn't be alone."

She tilts her head. "Do you think this HEA app could help me break bad habits?" she asks.

"What sort of bad habits are we talking about? Smoking? Biting your nails? Cheap dime store nun costumes?"

Without thinking, I move a little closer, careful not to intimidate her in this small space. She looks up at me, and I don't miss the way she studies my face.

"How about falling for men who are completely wrong for me?"

"Is that something you do?"

She blinks. "With alarming regularity." There's an implication in her tone that sets my heart racing.

I have a sudden urge to touch her, but I know that's not appropriate, considering what she's been though. Instead, I hold out my hand for her to take if she chooses.

"I just realized we haven't been properly introduced. I'm ..." Before I can even say my name, she clasps my fingers, and the second we touch, my brain short-circuits. Hell, the goosebumps that travel up my arm make me forget how basic respiration works. Her skin makes mine explode with warmth, and when I look at her face, she seems just as confused about the intensity of the contact as I am.

I've often seen movies where time slows down in important moments. Usually, it's in an action scene where someone's throwing themselves in front of a bullet or diving away from an explosion. In this moment, I couldn't move if I wanted to, bullets and explosions be damned. The whole world could be burning down around me, and I still wouldn't be able to drag myself away from looking into her eyes.

"Jesus." I don't even know I've spoken till I hear my voice.

Liza nods. "Nice to meet you, Jesus."

"No," I shake my head, reveling in the warm air that surrounds us like haze. "That was just involuntary cursing. My name is —"

I'm brought back into regular time when there are three strong knocks at the door.

No way. Surely asshole-Henry hasn't come back.

I drop Liza's hand and stride over to the door. "Buddy, you should have quit while you were ahead. I'm about to body slam you into next week."

When I open the door a crack, I see Max's surprised face. "Uh, okay … I'm not really in the mood for a body slam tonight. Can I interest you in a short conversation instead?"

Frowning, I move so I'm blocking Liza from Max's view. I don't know why I do it. Maybe I think Max would judge her for being in the men's room with me. Or maybe he'd tell Eden I was fraternizing with a woman, and then I'd never hear the end of it until she'd arranged a full-blown mega-wedding and baby shower. Either way, I don't want him seeing her.

"Hey. Sorry. Thought you were someone else."

Max nods. "Thank God. I'm pretty fit, but if you body slam me, I have no doubt I'd fly across the room like a fortune cookie."

"Didn't realize fortune cookies fly."

"They do if a six-foot-five wall of muscle slams into them."

"Right." I clear my throat, aware Liza is overhearing every word of this insane conversation. "So … what's up, Max? Do you need to use the bathroom? Because … you can't."

"Okay, weird, but fair. Just wanted to let you know that things are winding down out here, so I'm going to take off. There are a few couples left, but most have moved on to other venues. I've left Ming-Lee in charge of wrapping everything up. You might as well head home, too. I know you've been putting in long hours perfecting the algorithm for this test. You always seem to be the first one into the office and the last one to leave."

"Uh, yeah." That's true, but not for the reasons he thinks.

"Anyway, good job. Everyone I've spoken to has raved about their matches." *Not everyone.* "Looks like Doctor Love strikes again." *Note to self: Murder Eden.* "We can discuss all the data tomorrow. Get some rest, okay?"

"Sure. 'Night, Max."

I close the door and turn to find Liza standing with her arms crossed. "So, *you're* Doctor Love?"

"Actually, the name's Toby. Or Total Fraud if you'd prefer."

"You let me totally trash you and your app without telling me who you were?"

"You were on a roll. It would have been rude to interrupt."

She stares at me for a few seconds, and I stare back. I feel like I have so much to say to her, but in this moment, I can't think of a single topic of conversation.

"So …" she says and shifts her weight.

"Yeah. So …"

She looks at the door, and then at me. "Thanks for the assist tonight. I really appreciate your help. And sorry about the ..."

She points to her own bottom lip, and I nod as I vaguely wonder what it would taste like. "No problem. Anytime."

I drag my gaze back up to her eyes. I'm surprised to detect definite heat in the way she's staring at me. So few times in my life, a woman I'm attracted to is clearly crushing on me, too. And yet, here is the most stunning creature I've ever seen, mentally undressing me within an inch of my reasonably short life. It's exhilarating.

I feel like something momentous is going to happen between us. That maybe tonight will be the beginning of something so profound, neither one of us will ever —

"Dammit, this can't be happening again." In a second, Liza's whole demeanor changes. She goes from heavy-lidded staring to something that looks a lot like panic. She pushes off the counter and heads toward the door. "Best of luck with the app and everything, Toby. I have to go."

I frown in confusion. "Wait, what?" She brushes past me. "Liza, just stop for a second."

She turns and sighs, and I don't know what the hell I've just done, but she seems pissed.

"What's going on?" I ask. "Did I do something to offend you? Say something wrong?"

"It's not anything you said. It's you." She gestures to my whole body, which doesn't help my confusion in the slightest.

"Okay. My existence is annoying?"

"Yeah. Kind of."

"You want to explain that?"

"Just trust me when I say that us spending any more time together isn't a good idea."

"Why not?"

"Because ..." She looks at the door, and then back to me. It appears she's torn between leaving and staying, and even though I have no idea what the hell is happening, I know for damn sure I don't want her to go.

"Because?" I urge.

She drops her head but then looks up again. "You seem like a really great guy. And I have this habit of meeting guys who seem really great but who are one hundred percent wrong for me. It's one of the reasons I showed up to this thing tonight; to try to break my cycle of suckage."

"Okay, I get that."

"I have to learn to do the opposite of what my instincts tell me, because if I date the people I like, then I end up getting slammed."

I frown. "So, what you're saying is that you want to go out with people you don't like? And also, that you want to date me?"

She sighs like I've just cherry picked her argument to suit my own agenda, which I totally have.

"I'm saying," she says in a patient tone, "it was lovely meeting you, but I have to go." She opens the door and turns to me with a wistful expression. "I hope everything works out for you, Toby. I really do. I'm sure I'll see you around." She gives me a half-smile and then walks out.

Several hundred justifications as to why she should stay die on my tongue as the door closes behind her. I stand there for a minute, stomach twisting with wrongness, as I try to figure out what the hell I want to do.

Invite her for a drink.

Something inside me flinches. I've had strong physical attractions to other girls over the years, but nothing like what I'm feeling for Liza. And my track record with women who fascinate me is abysmal.

I should take my out-of-control attraction as a warning sign. Nothing good will come from intensely wanting someone I've just met. And yet, I can't bring myself to let her walk away. I just can't.

The part of me that's borne the brunt of countless rejections warns I'm making the wrong decision, but the dozens of excuses it offers up as to why I shouldn't go after her gets scuttled like bowling pins when I mutter a quiet, "Fuck it," and wrench open the door.

By the time I get out of the bathroom, Liza is halfway across the bar and heading toward the exit with decent speed.

"Liza!"

She doesn't slow down, so I duck and weave through the sparse crowd with the elegance of a line-dancing gorilla as I try to catch up to her.

Fortunately for me, Ming-Lee is near the door and steps in front of her to get an exit interview about how the event went.

"Hey," Ming-Lee says with a smile. "Before you head out do you have a couple of minutes to chat about your experience tonight?"

Liza looks hesitant as I come to a screeching halt beside my tiny co-worker.

"Uh, Ming-Lee, hey there. I can do this one if you like."

She gives me a quizzical look but passes me a spare iPad anyway. "Oh, sure. No problem." She moves on to a couple behind us as I maneuver myself closer to Liza.

"I know you have to go and never want to see me again, but these surveys are really useful in improving the app, soooo …"

Liza looks at me dubiously. "Okay, fine. I suppose I have time."

"Great." I go to the screen. "How would you rate tonight's experience with the HEA app on a scale of 1 to 10, 1 being a negative experience, and 10 being a positive one?"

"The app experience was a 3 but overall, I'd rate the night a solid six-point-five."

"And what is the main reason for that score?"

She tries not to smile. "The men's room was unexpectedly decent."

I nod. "Agreed. Now, based on tonight's experience, how likely will you be to recommend the HEA app to your friends?"

Her look says everything, and without prompting, I type, "Not … likely … at all. And the likelihood of you giving me your number?"

I get a regretful look.

"Right. Again, zero likelihood." I tap on the next field. "Considering the app creator sustained a busted lip while helping you tonight, how successful would he be in guilting you into sharing a small, inexpensive drink at the bar?"

She looks at the door, and back to me. "Toby …"

"No, I get it, I do," I say, feeling more desperate than I'm letting on. "I'm possibly a terrible mistake you don't want to make. But it's just one drink. Five minutes." *Or forever.* "No pressure."

She looks like she's wavering, and honestly, I don't have the energy to keep up this bullshit. I drop the iPad on the bench beside me. "Listen, Liza, it's been a long night. I've enjoyed meeting you, and I wouldn't mind a quick break before burning the midnight oil and crunching numbers until dawn. Of course, if you have somewhere else to be, you should go. But if you don't …"

She hesitates and stares at me for a few spine-tingling seconds before saying, "Okay. One drink. My choice. I'm buying."

"Sold." We share a smile that lasts an awkward amount of time before I turn and lead her over to my position at the end of the bar. When Raj sees us coming, he shoots me an eyebrow raise before surreptitiously making himself scarce.

"So, this is where the magic happens?" Liza says, gesturing to my laptop.

"If by magic you mean eyestrain, vein-popping frustration, and occasional cyber- crime, then yes. This is the magical hub."

Joe the bartender wanders over just as my phone rings. When I pull it from my pocket, I see my little sister's smiling face on the screen.

"Can you excuse me for a second?" I say. "I have to take this." Liza nods and chats with Joe as I move away and swipe to answer.

"Hey, Power Puff."

"Greetings, large brother. How goes it?" I laugh to myself. This kid might only be twelve, but she's more dramatic than the whole of Broadway. It's one of the things I love most about her. Also, she has my cracked sense of humor.

"It goes adequately, small sister. What's up with you? Just calling to hear the sound of my voice? Do you miss your big brother that much?"

"Well, yes. It's been over a month since you visited. Too popular to mix with the little people these days?"

"Well, considering I'm in a bar working while people make out all around me, I don't think 'popular' is the right word for my current status. Busy-as-balls is more like it. Believe me, I'd rather be chilling with you right now."

"I wish you were here, too." There's tension in her voice that puts me on edge.

"What's going on, short stuff?"

She pauses before saying, "Mom got a letter from Dad's health insurer today. They're raising his premiums again."

My stomach falls through the floor. "What the hell? They raised them six months ago."

"Yeah, well, when all you care about is money, you have to work hard to keep people poor and unhealthy." I can tell how pissed she is. "Mom's been quiet all day. I know she's trying to figure out things without burdening you, but … well, I've decided to burden you."

I blow out a breath and rub my eyes. This is the last thing Mom needs. We've been fighting a battle to keep Dad's health insurance as it is. If we lose it, we'll be in an even deeper hole than we already are. As it is, his physical therapy is only half covered, and the deductibles are fucking outrageous.

April's voice is softer when she says, "I think she's seriously considering taking on another job."

"That's not happening. She works herself to the bone as it is."

"I know, Tobes, but she won't listen to me. I told her I could get a job …"

"No."

"Just hear me out. I think –"

"April, your job is to get good grades and be there for Mom and Dad. That's it. I'll fix this, okay?" My voice is louder than I intend it to be, and I lean my head on my hand as my sister falls conspicuously silent. "Damn, April … I'm sorry. I'm just stressed from work." I sit back onto the bar stool and run my fingers through my hair. "Does Mom suspect I've been sending you money?"

I hear some rustling. "The fact that she hasn't called to yell at you wouldn't indicate no. But even with you sending practically all your wage, Tobes …" She sighs. "I don't see how we're going to get through this. What if we can't afford to get Dad's surgery?"

"We will."

"But what if we can't?"

I press my fingers into my eye sockets and rub. "I'll figure something out. I promise."

My sister goes quiet for a second, and I hate that she's on the frontline in dealing with our family's financial pressures. She's a kid. She should be riding her bike and playing with her friends, not contemplating getting a job to help pay the bills.

"Toby, you can't afford to send us any more money. Did you sort something out with your landlord? Did he give you an extension on your rent?"

"Yeah, he took pity on me. It's all good. Don't worry about it."

I hate lying to her, but what good would it do to tell her the truth? She doesn't need to know that I was evicted four weeks ago. I did talk to my landlord, but like most property owners in New York, he didn't give two shits about my money problems. He had a waiting list a mile long for that apartment, and I barely had time to get my stuff out before he'd changed the locks and moved someone else in.

When it comes to getting and keeping accommodation in Brooklyn, it's the quick and the dead, and unfortunately, I ended up DOA.

Blinking to clear my head, I pull open my laptop and log into my bank account. There are only a few hundred dollars in there, but I transfer it all into the account I set up for my sister. I glance over at Liza who's still chatting with Joe. Thankfully, she seems oblivious to the conversation.

"I've just sent more money. It's not much, but it'll cover the health insurance until I figure something else out. Just take care of Mom, okay? I'll come visit soon."

I can't really spare the time for the five-hour round trip to Pennsylvania right now, but I don't have much choice. When your family needs you, you go.

"That would be great. We all miss you."

"I miss you, too. Now, go finish your homework and get to bed. It's late."

"Will do, large brother." She pauses before saying a quiet, "I love you," and hanging up too fast to hear me say it back.

I put my phone back into my pocket and stare at my empty bank account. Fuck. I didn't need to eat anyway, right?

I know that if I went to Max and asked for an advance on my pay, he'd probably give it to me, but that's going to be a last resort. There has to be something I can do besides beg for money. Becoming a charity case is one humiliation too far.

I glance at my computer. I usually use my hacking skills for good, but I can't help thinking how easy it would be to bend the system to my will. Within minutes, I could hack into a dozen different financial institutions, and before you could say *federal cybercrime*, could transfer money into mom's account. Unlimited cash wouldn't fix everything, but it sure-as-hell would take the pressure off for a change.

"Everything okay?" I look up to see Liza staring at me. "You look stressed." She hands me a large glass of whiskey. "Maybe this will help."

"Thanks." I gratefully take the alcohol. Drinking my cares away with a beautiful woman won't solve any of my issues, but it'll sure help me forget about them for a while.

"Anything I can do to help?"

I shake my head. I haven't told anyone about what's going on in my life right now, not even Eden, because the shame level that accompanies it is staggering. For the moment, denial is my go-to move.

"Nah, all good," I say. "Just family stuff." I smile at her, and she smiles back, and damn if even that small interaction doesn't make me feel better.

"Can I ask you a personal question?" she asks, and her expression turns serious.

"Sure." I get concerned she may have overheard my phone conversation after all.

She moves a little closer. "How do you feel about … public humiliation?"

I frown. "I … uh …" My brain revs in neutral. "Uh … why? Is that something you're into?" I have zero experience with kink, but for her, I'd be willing to learn.

She gives me a sly smile. "Actually, it *is* something I'm into." She nods toward the back corner of the room, and I follow her gaze. "You up for it?"

I nod in understanding. "Ahhh, so, you want *me* to humiliate *you*? Okay, sure. Prepare yourself for a public whipping."

She laughs, and when she heads toward the tables in the far corner, I follow.

"Oh, Toby, Toby, Toby … be prepared to find out exactly how wrong a human is capable of being. I'm going to kick your very fine ass."

3

THE LAWS OF ATTRACTION

I sip the crazy-expensive whiskey Liza bought me and try not to stare like a creeper as she bends over the pool table to rack the balls.

"You could have just bought me a beer," I say. "You didn't have to raid the top shelf." But boy, I'm glad she did. If I thought Eden's whiskey was good, this one leaves it for dead. It's like a swallowing single-malt sunshine.

Liza pulls the plastic triangle off the table and hangs it on the wall before grabbing two cues. "Well, you did sustain physical injury defending my honor. It was the least I could do." She hands me one of the cues and gestures for me to break, which I do.

I straighten up and turn to her. "Well, regardless, thanks. Also, let the ass-kicking commence."

She sips her vodka and cranberry. "As you wish."

After putting down her drink, she sizes up the balls on the table, and then takes her shot. With a confident stroke, she deftly bounces a ball off the side of the table, and it slams into a pocket on the other side.

"Okay. This just got interesting." Usually when I play pool, I get bored, because being able to calculate advanced geometrical projections in your head makes sinking balls pretty damn easy. But as I watch Liza pot two more balls in quick succession, I think I may actually be challenged tonight.

"You've done this before."

She gives me a sly smile. "Once or twice."

"I take it you aced geometry in high school. You're nailing all of those angles."

She bends over and assesses her next shot. It's a tricky one. Her ball is partially blocked by another, so there'll need to be multiple bounces off the cushions if she wants to nail it.

"Pool geometry is simple," she says, walking around the table. "Once you understand that the plasticity of the velocity of the balls is constant, everything else falls into place."

I'm still shocked by her statement when she hits the cue ball. It bounces three times before slamming a red ball into a pocket. If she keeps talking nerdy to me like that, I stand no chance of not falling for her.

"Well, now you're just showing off."

Her next shot misses. Not sure whether she does it on purpose to give me a turn, but regardless, I step up to the table.

"So, from our conversation in the bathroom," she says as she swipes more chalk over the tip of her cue, "can I assume that the man who's single-handedly matching up singles all over New York doesn't have a girlfriend?"

I half-smile. "No. No, girlfriend." I like that she asked. It means she wants to know if I'm available, and for her, I totally am.

"And you?" I ask. "You said earlier that you've taken a break from dating?"

She nods. "Yeah, I just needed to get out for a while. Spend some time with myself, I guess."

I study her posture. "I get it. You have rejection fatigue."

"Did you just make that up, or …?"

"No, it's a thing. When someone keeps putting themself out there but is met with a brick wall every time … it's exhausting." I should know. "Just one of the many reasons I made the HEA app."

She walks over to the high table next to me and takes a swig of her drink. "It seems you're speaking from experience, but that can't possibly be true."

"You don't think I get rejected?"

She gives me a long, slow onceover and shakes her head. "Not to sound condescending, but … do you not own a mirror? You're tall, good looking, great sense of humor, amazing hair. Who the hell is rejecting someone as spectacular you?"

Jesus, she thinks I'm good-looking? My ego explodes with the force of a beam of subatomic particles rocketing through the Hadron collider.

"Well, I could say the same to you. I can't imagine any man rejecting you."

She stirs her drink with a skewered cranberry. "Men think they're interested in dating me, but as soon as they get to know me, they run for the hills."

"Well first you need to start dating better-quality men, and what you describe is exactly the reason I developed the app. Most people start dating because of a superficial physical attraction. And sure, that's important. But lust fades, and if you have nothing in common when it does, then ..."

She nods. "You can have the prettiest curtains on the street, but if there's nothing holding the house together, then what chance do you have?"

"Exactly." I take a sip of whiskey and then look up to find her studying me. "What?"

She stares into her drink. "We waste so much time with people who'll never work out. I mean, I know that's part of being young, playing the field and everything. And I can't say I haven't enjoyed myself. But ... I'm done, now, you know? I don't want to keep bouncing from guy to guy every few months. I want something stable. Something that's going to last."

"Then don't count out my app just because you've had one bad experience. It could be exactly what you're looking for."

More specifically, *I* could be exactly what you're looking for.

"Can you show me how it works? Maybe if I knew your methodology, I could trust it a bit more. Lord knows if I don't want to die alone, I have to embrace anything that can help."

"Sure." It's strange sharing something as personal as this app, especially to someone as intriguing as she is. "Let me just finish this up."

I line up my cue and sink the last three balls on the table before taking the eight. She gives me a golf clap before I guide her back over to the bar where my laptop is waiting. I bring up my research spreadsheet.

"See, these are the stats on the test subjects. So you can see that there was a huge cross-section of people surveyed. Different ages, sexualities, religions, ethnicities. And the factors that were common in all of the successful relationships were surprisingly similar.

I watch her as she scans the screen. My God, she's beautiful. I bunch my muscles, so I don't stroke her cheek like an asshole.

"Seems like you're put a lot of work and thought into this."

She turns, and her face is so close, it's hard to breathe.

"Yeah. I have." *And if it doesn't prove that you and I are meant to be together, then it will have all been for nothing.*

"Maybe I should put myself in your hands when it comes to dating."

"You absolutely should." *Also, just put yourself in my hands, because I think we'd both really enjoy it.*

"I'm tired of the circus," she says. "I don't want to hook up. I want to fall in love. I want to need someone so much, I feel ill without them. I want my soul mate." She fiddles with her phone. "That's why I agreed to come here tonight. To see what the app could do. I know the odds are stacked against me. I'm a weirdo, and I need someone just as weird to be my perfect match."

"Well, to be honest, the odds of finding a fellow weirdo in a bar in Brooklyn are pretty great. Case in point, you met me." For a few seconds, I get lost in the blueness of her eyes. They're stunning. I could stare at them for hours and never get bored.

She stares back for a few seconds and then clears her throat and moves back. "Right."

I bring up another graph, partly to make a point but mostly so she has to move closer to the screen again, and therefore, me. "Look, this shows you the success rate of the app. If you give it a chance, it could lead you to your very own HEA."

She looks at me. "That's a pretty big claim."

"You're acting like I haven't done hundreds of hours of research on this topic. But I have. Every simulation points to people with low scores having faster and messier break ups than those with high scores. Math doesn't lie. Tonight, Henry was borderline. Just date someone with a higher score."

She leans on the bar. "So, if you felt a connection with someone, and they had a low score, you wouldn't date them?"

"No. There's no point in wasting time and energy on a doomed relationship."

"Wow. And I thought I was cutthroat when it came to dating." She studies me. "So, what about you and me. What sort of score do you think we'd have?"

Time does that slowing down thing again as I focus on the hypnotic pulse in her neck. "I couldn't give you an exact number, but judging by our … chemistry … I'd say our number would be pretty high."

She leans into me. "Uh huh. I think it would be low."

"Right, because you have a track record of choosing the wrong guy?"

"Exactly. You're tall and handsome, with a great sense of humor and fabulous lips." She looks at my lips, and they tingle in response. "Of course you're not going to be a match for me."

"Okay, then I'd like to suggest a challenge. Let's get to know each other for a couple of hours. At midnight, we each predict how compatible we are, and then find out who's right."

"And if we are compatible?"

I stand and move a little closer, just enough that her proximity sets my whole body on fire. "We date. You fall in love with me. Write rapturously about me in your diary. Brag about me to your friends."

"And if we're not?"

I shrug. "We go our separate ways, no questions asked."

"What do you class as a low score?"

"Research indicates that anything below fifty percent is the stamp of death." Without knowing anything about this woman, I have no doubt we're light years above that. In fact, I wouldn't be surprised if we're in the high eighties.

"What's the lowest score you've seen on a long-term couple?"

I think back to my research notes. "There was one couple who lasted five years with a thirty-nine. But I don't think they were happy for at least three of those years. The last I heard, they were still locked in a bitter battle over custody of their rabbit."

"And the happiest couples?"

"The super long-term relationships where people were mostly happy are all in the seventies and eighties. Above ninety percent is extremely rare. And I doubt a hundred percent exists."

"Uh huh. So," she says, shifting her weight. "If we have an amazing night together but are only forty-nine percent compatible, you'll just walk away?"

I nod. "Absolutely. I've spent months on these calculations. I know they're right. I have faith in them, and I'm no longer interested in wasting time on dead ends." I hold out my hand. "So, do we have a deal?"

She looks at my hand for a few seconds before sliding her fingers around mine. "I guess I have nothing to lose at this point. Deal."

We stay like that, hands warm, fingers squeezing, staring at each other.

"So ..." I say, not wanting to remove my hand but knowing I should. "Where shall we go?"

She pulls her hand back, and I flex mine as it tingles with the ghost memory of our contact.

"I'm starving, and a friend of mine owns a great restaurant nearby."

"Great," I say. "Am I dressed appropriately?"

She gives me a sly smile. "It's an eatery in Brooklyn. You could wear a medieval suit of armor and blend in."

4

SLAMMED

Certain people enter your life like they were always meant to be in it. There's a familiarity about them, as if you were best friends a lifetime ago, and you've reconnected to fall back into the comfortable tracks of your friendship train.

Then there are people who ignite something powerful inside of you that makes being around them almost painful. They're so brilliant and incandescent, it hurts to look at them, and the merest brush of their hand against yours can trigger a bout of lust that almost knocks you on your ass.

If you put those two sensations in a cocktail mixer and blend them together, you'd get a perfect description of how it feels to spend time with Liza.

I'm trying to keep my optimism in check, because getting to invested before I know our score is mightily stupid. But when just walking next to someone is this thrilling, you know you're a goner.

"Thanks for the coffee," Liza says, gesturing to the cardboard cup in her hand.

I shrug. "It was the least I could do after you bought me whiskey and pizza." It was also the most I could do considering I'm almost out of cash.

After eating, we headed into Manhattan, and now we're just aimlessly wandering the streets, sipping our drinks and chatting. We talk and bond over obscure British TV shows we both love, and spar about whether Marvel or DC do better movie adaptions. She laughs at all my jokes, and I laugh at hers. I've never met someone with whom I click so thoroughly.

This is going so well, it's starting to worry me.

After a while, I notice that I'm talking more than she is, and there's a weird tension creeping into her expression. She keeps looking at her watch, and it makes me aware that our time together is running out.

We stop outside the Tiffany store on Fifth Avenue, and she gives me a resigned sigh.

"It's midnight. Guess it's time to see if we turn into a pumpkin or not."

I shove my hands in my pockets. "That was the deal, right?"

She nods but doesn't look at me. "Yeah, it was. Even though I already know how this will go."

She looks so dejected, I move closer. "Liza we've had an amazing night. Don't you think that bodes well for our compatibility?"

"Toby, you truly don't understand my ability to pick guys who are wrong for me in every way. Over the years, I've dated not one, not two, but *three* men who ended up on the FBI's Most Wanted list. You don't even understand my capacity for bad choices."

"See, this is why we're perfect for each other. I always make wrong choices, too. Maybe in this case, two wrongs make a right."

"Or two wrongs make a really wrong."

I get out my phone. "Not going to happen. I have faith in us. I predict something over an eighty-five.

"Toby ..."

"You think we'll be borderline; I get it. But it's not going to happen. I can feel how right this is."

If she's even half as attracted to me as I am to her, this score is going to be one for the record books.

"Okay, but before we do this, you need to know that ... well, the thing is, when I took the test earlier tonight, I ..."

"Yeah?"

"I just ..." She shakes her head, struggling to tell me something. "When I answered all those questions, I just ..."

She looks up at me, and I have no idea what she's trying to say so I wait.

She lets out a frustrated sigh. "I have this terrible habit of hiding from the things I don't want to face, and this falls squarely into that category. You're going to be disappointed, and I hate the thought of disappointing you."

I want to touch her, but I have a feeling that right now, that would make her even more anxious.

"Liza, listen … I've had the most amazing night with you. Even if this doesn't go any further, we have that, right?"

"Right." She shifts her weight. "I just need you to know that regardless of what happens next, I think you're an amazing person."

"See?" I say, giving her a smile. "That's yet another thing we agree on." I hold out my phone. "Let's just get it done, so you can stop worrying. It can't be as bad as you think."

"Oh, it most definitely can. But let's do it anyway." She takes a breath as she pulls her phone from her bag, and I don't miss how her hand is shaking.

"Moment of truth."

We both tap the screen to open the app, and then, with excitement firing in all my nerve endings, I bump my phone against hers. Within seconds, there's a soft ding, and a number appears on the screen in sparkling gold.

Holy shit.

If my phone were a poker machine, right now it would have lights flashing and sirens blaring as it spit out an avalanche of silver dollars.

Ninety-three percent.

I fucking *knew* it.

When I look over at Liza, I expect to see happiness in her expression, or at the very least, relief. Instead, she seems like she's on the verge of tears.

"Hey." I put my hand on her shoulders and rub her upper arms. "This is good news, right? I mean, I couldn't be happier right now if I tried."

"Toby …"

Shit, no. This can't be happening. She's going to blow me off knowing that we're practically perfect for each other? How can she deny this?

"Liza, stop." I take her face in my hands and get her to look at me. "Whatever excuse you're going to come up with right now, just … don't. You can feel how right this is."

I move closer, and I take in a breath when she grips the front of my shirt, drawing me closer.

"Toby … that score … You don't understand."

"I do. I understand that you've had shitty guys in the past, but don't let that ruin whatever's happening between us." I lean down, tying hard to hold myself back from kissing her. "Just … let yourself be happy. You're my perfect match. It's right there for the whole world to see. The math doesn't lie."

We're so close, I can feel her breath on my lips. She looks into my eyes, searching for something. I wish like hell I knew what it was, because I'd do everything in my power to give it to her.

"Toby …" She stares at me for a few seconds, and then she pushes up onto her toes and kisses me.

Jesus.

Adrenaline explodes, racing through my veins, making everything heightened and electric. I know I only met this woman tonight, but it feels like I've been waiting for an eternity to taste her lips. I cradle her head and tilt it to get a better angle, then I kiss her back, slow and soft at first, savoring her sweetness as lightning sparks though every nerve ending.

"Oh, my God," she whispers between our lips, and I couldn't agree more.

I've kissed a lot of women, but not a single one felt anything remotely like this. My mouth knows the shape of hers. My tongue brushes against hers and it feels like we've done this a million times before.

Being a man of logic, I don't put much stock in the whole concept of love at first sight. I mean, I understand that certain people have insane chemistry and can feel an instant and powerful attraction, but love? Nope. Love needs time.

But kissing Liza? I get it. I feel like I've been waiting my whole life for this feeling. Every ounce of light suction, every sweet taste of her, makes me want to handcuff myself to her side, forever and always. How the fuck can this feel so good?

As we continue to kiss, a million thoughts run through my head. I want to take her home to make love with her, but I have no place to call home. I want to buy her flowers and chocolates, but right now I barely have two pennies to rub together. I want to wake up with her and witness the moment she comes out of dreamland and back to me, but even though kissing her feels more right than anything else I've ever experienced, I can't get over the suspicion she's kissing me for all the wrong reasons.

I've never wanted someone the way I want her. A whole barrage of romantic fantasies plays out, and for the first time in my life, I want to make every single one of them come true.

With a low groan, I turn so I can press her up against the wall of the building beside us, and she grasps at me, urging for more.

"Liza." Damn, my voice is hoarse; thick with lust and more need than I've ever felt. My body is screaming for her, hard and aching, and grinding against her does nothing but make me ache more intensely.

"Liza … let's go somewhere. Anywhere."

She pulls back, panting heavily and still gripping me with tight hands. "I can't. Toby … this is —"

"Amazing. Spectacular. Yeah, I know. And I don't want it to end just yet, so …"

Just then, a car horn blares so loudly beside us, we both flinch. That's followed by tires screeching and someone screaming, and when I let her go and turn to see what's going on, there's a guy on the ground in front of a taxi.

A woman races over to help him and screams, "Call 911!" to the growing crowd. I step away from Liza, so I can pull out my phone.

"Shit." Adrenaline from the kiss is blasting through my veins so violently, I can barely dial, but I punch in the numbers and wait to be connected. When I look back to the accident, the guy is getting to his feet. He wobbles a little before waving to the people around him.

"I'm okay." He rubs his elbow. "Just a little nudge. I'm fine."

Me and about three others hang up, and I breathe a sigh of relief as he's escorted out of the street. If I were a betting man, I'd predict that the guy is mostly trashed, which is probably why he was walking in front of a cab in the first place.

"Wow. Close call, huh?" I say, pocketing my phone. "Just another regular night in NYC."

I turn to see Liza's reaction to the scene, but she's not there.

"Liza?"

I look all around me, and then I walk to the corner and see if she's stepped back, out of the way of the foot traffic.

"Liza!"

I turn in every direction, scanning the thinning crowd, looking for her familiar shape among the dozens of people bustling about their business.

But she's not there. She's nowhere.

She's gone.

5

CINDERELLA-ED

The only thing worse than not finding your soul mate, is finding and then losing her, seemingly through no fault of your own. Suddenly, everything in my life is different, even though nothing has changed.

Lying on the couch in the Romance Central break room in my underwear, I stare at the sliver of gold peeking through the huge picture windows and sigh. It's early, maybe five o'clock, but I have to get up and get moving before the security guard clocks in at six-thirty, so I can remove any trace that I've been living here for over a month.

Not that I've really slept. My REM patterns seem to have deserted me, so I might as well just get to work.

I swing my legs over the side of the couch and rub my hair. Fuck me, I need a haircut. And a beard trim. Right now, I'm hairier than a Mongolian yak. I stand and grab the duffle bag near the door before heading to the guys' locker room.

When I was evicted from my apartment, I didn't mean to spend all my nights at Romance Central, but it turned out to be the perfect place to crash. There are huge bathrooms with multiple showers, a laundry room for when my clothes are so dirty they could stand up and walk around on their own, and a couch that's almost long enough to accommodate my entire body.

Of course, I'd be horrified if anyone found out I was crashing here, which is why I'm always careful to erase evidence of my overnight stays well before anyone gets into the office. No one wants to be seen as destitute, and even though I don't begrudge sending all my money to my family, I'm not going to telegraph how broke I am to my friends. I know they'd bend over backwards to try to help, and I don't want that. I'm going to figure a way out of this mess or die trying.

Until then, I'll just put up with the weird twisting I get in my gut every time I realize I'm homeless. There's something psychologically damaging about not having a space to call your own. And yet, even with everything I own shoved into boxes at the back of the giant costume room here, I know I'm a helluva lot luckier than most. At least I have a roof over my head and a staff break room loaded with a variety of snacks. It's still a mile away from sleeping rough on the streets.

I push through the doors to the men's bathroom and drop my bag on a bench. Then I dig around until I find a small pair of scissors and go to the mirrors over the sinks.

"Jesus, Jenner. You look like absolute shit."

Standing there in my boxers, I can see the evidence of the last couple of months of stress. Apart from my tragic financial situation, what happened with Liza has killed my appetite, and I can see way too many muscles not covered with healthy fat. I look like a body builder the day before a competition, after they've burnt away all their water weight. This is not good.

Ignoring my body for the moment, I tug at my beard and give it a quick trim. Then I grab shampoo and soap and head into the shower.

I groan when the warm water hits my skin, and I spend a long time just standing beneath the spray before lathering up. After I scrub myself thoroughly and finish washing my hair, I close my eyes and lean my forehead against the cool tiles, helpless against the images of Liza that flood my brain.

In the two weeks since she disappeared on me, I've come to understand how Prince Charming must have felt when Cinderella ran away from the ball. You meet someone who seems perfect for you in every way, and then, for reasons unknown, they vanish. Cinderella ran away so the prince wouldn't see she was a commoner, but judging from the expensive-looking clothes Liza was wearing, I doubt she's secretly poor. It wouldn't matter to me if she was, of course. I don't give a shit about her bank balance. I just want to be with her.

I've trawled through every piece of information she gave us when she signed up to be a tester, but each path I travel down leads me nowhere. Her phone number? A pizza place on 51st street. Her address? The NBC Studios. Email? Doesn't exist. Even her full name, Liza Lotte = Lies A Lot. Every piece of information is bullshit.

I feel like I've been betrayed in the worst way possible. Was she just a con woman who got her kicks out of duping me and then giving me a spinning fan-kick to the heart? The thing that's most baffling is that even if she was just an opportunistic gate crasher, I don't think she was lying when she spoke about craving a soul mate. And she sure as hell wasn't faking it when she kissed me.

But then why would she leave without a trace the second our connection was scientifically confirmed? Is she married? Wanted by the police? She must have had a reason for doing it. I just wished like hell I knew what it was.

Whatever her motivations, she now dominates my thoughts, whether I'm sleeping or awake. For so long, I've believed there was no one out there for me, but now that I know she exists, it's tough to think of anything else. It's like showing me a glimpse of heaven, and then laughing while locking the gates and telling me I can never live there.

After my shower, I get dressed, pack my gear away, grab an apple from the staff snack bowl in the kitchen, and head out toward the subway station. The sun is just peeking over the tops of Brooklyn's buildings, and if I wasn't so tired, I'd have more energy to appreciate it's a pretty bomb-ass day.

As it is, I zombie walk off the train to the *Pulse* offices.

At this hour, the place is deserted, but that's okay. I use the opportunity to delve into some online listings for freelance tech work. There are a few jobs I take note of. Nothing big, but they'd earn me a few extra bucks so I can at least buy food and pay my phone bill. Still, I know it's just a Band-Aid over a gushing wound. I need to stop squatting at Romance Central and get a roof over my head as soon as I can, but right now, I can't even afford a sublet without some extra income.

One possible solution rolls around in my brain, but I'm hesitant to even consider it. There are some doors that once opened, are difficult to close, and the thing that could dig me out of this mess fits squarely in that category.

"Nope," I mutter to myself. "I'm not that desperate."

Except, I really am. If a rat's trying to get out of a maze, it's not fussy about the color of the exit path. Sometimes you have no choice but to take the only escape route you can see.

I look around the office to check I'm still alone. I am, of course. It's not even six-thirty. Most sensible people will still be in bed.

With a frustrated hand through my hair, I log into the portal I rarely use for fear of falling straight into hell. Within minutes, I'm in the deepest cesspool of depravity known to man: The dark web. It's where you'll find the most heinous bottom-feeders humankind has to offer. Here lies the stuff of nightmares. A disgusting marketplace where nothing is too depraved or taboo.

It's also the location of the *Angels of Mercy* message boards, a forum where desperate folks with nowhere else to turn can hook up with hacktivists-for-hire. It's one of the few points of light in this shadowy realm.

"Let's see what we've got."

I haven't logged into the forum for a few months, so I'm not surprised my inbox is stuffed full. Here, people know me as Gunnar, and my reputation for being able to hack even the most complicated computer security systems is well-known. That's why I have dozens of requests to join up with hacking collectives who are trying to bring down the websites and social media accounts for hate groups and violent extremists. Mixed in with those are straight up job offers. Those are less black and white.

One in particular catches my attention with the subject line, "Help Trace Dark Money Bribes by Crest Construction." Interesting. Crest Construction is the company Dad was investigating as a safety inspector when he had his accident. They denied any wrongdoing for what happened, but the thousands of complaints lodged with the city about the hazardous state of their building sites tell a different story. Over the years, he'd given several citations to Crest about their sub-standard practices, and not surprisingly, it was a section of their famously unsafe scaffolding that collapsed, plunging him four stories down onto the pavement. So, far, they've stalled every effort we've made to get Dad the compensation he's owed, so I've made a few attempts to hack into their servers in the past. Unfortunately, I was never able to find anything incriminating, but maybe it's time to try again, especially considering that if I'm successful, the fee is five grand.

That would be enough to get me into a new apartment, at least for a while.

I send a message to the anonymous poster:

"Send me details of what you're looking for and when you need it." I skim over their payment terms, and when I press 'accept', the job is marked as taken.

I log out of the portal and scan my *Pulse* writing outline for the week. Apart from highly illegal moonlighting, I have to do actual work for my actual job, so my adventures in Hacktown will have to wait.

I open a new document and stare at it for a few minutes, trying to get inspiration for this week's tech spotlight. I know what I want to write about, but the words just don't come. Every time I sit still, thoughts of Liza worm their way to the front of my mind. It's starting to become annoying. I've had crushes before, but nothing that comes close to how she consumes me. And to make matters worse, this all-consuming obsession comes at the point in my life that I absolutely can't handle one more thing pulling at my attention.

I should forget I ever met her and move on. I need to concentrate on my two legal jobs and my upcoming criminal activity, devote all my time to helping my family ... oh, and protect my shameful secret about being homeless. I have zero fucking time to be enthralled by a woman who probably broke international sprint records getting away from me.

Steeling my resolve, I shake my head free from thoughts of Liza and concentrate on my article with the precision focus of a Bosch laser.

That focus lasts a grand total of fourteen seconds before I scour through Liza's information one more time in the vain hope of finding something I'd missed the dozen or so times I've done it before.

No such luck.

Liza is a ghost, and I'm most definitely being ghosted.

"Damn, Jenner, be like Elsa, and let it go, for fuck's sake. Even if you find her, she doesn't want you. Buy a fucking clue."

Beyond anything else, I'm frustrated. I feel duped and naive, and more than a little angry that my perfect match is out there somewhere, probably not pining over me in the slightest.

AFTER THREE CUPS OF COFFEE, I'm finally getting words on the page when the office starts filling with the vast array of misanthropes who work at *Pulse*. I ignore them as I rage-type an article about the rise of virtual reality systems in contemporary gaming. The HEA app may be taking up a shitload of my time these days, but my day job still has deadlines, and this article is due this afternoon.

"Hey there, handsome." Someone starts massaging the bedrock that's formed in my shoulders, and I look up to see Jackie there, smiling.

"Hey." I know I should ask her to stop pushing her thumbs into my aching muscles, because it's blurring the clear line in the sand we drew when we ended things, but goddammit, it feels good. Titanium has nothing on rock-hard tension in my back right now.

"How was your weekend?" I ask.

She makes a humming noise that sounds suspiciously happy. "Okay. Had a couple of HEA dates."

"Yeah? How'd they go?" When I got around to matching our compatibility, I wasn't surprised that we rated in the low fifties, but I was genuine about trying to find her a good match.

She kisses me on the cheek. "You're a genius. The guy I went out with on Saturday? Tobes, I think he's the one. Amazing chemistry. So much in common. I never wanted the date to end."

"Yeah? And he felt the same way?"

"I didn't even make it home before he was texting, saying he missed me."

Shit. Seems a little desperate but considering I would have done the exact same thing to Liza if I'd had her real number, I let it pass. "That's fantastic, Jackie. I'm really happy for you. What was your compatibility score?"

"Eighty-two. The highest yet, and I think this one's a winner. Just wanted to say thanks, Doctor Love." She wraps her arms around my neck and squeezes before literally skipping away toward her own desk.

"Yeah, no problem," I mutter. "Happy to make everyone else's romantic fantasies come true. Just useless at realizing my own."

I'm startled when a clump of red curls pops over the top of my cubicle wall. "Hey, there, *handsome*." Eden does a pretty good impersonation of Jackie's voice, and I shake my head.

"You're the *best*, Doctor Love. Thanks for being you." She passes me a Grande coffee cup, and I take it gratefully. If I could mainline caffeine right now to blast away my fatigue, I would.

"Whatcha doing?" she asks as I take a giant mouthful of the overly sweet, energy-giving drink.

I put down the cup and continue on my article. "Eight-hundred words on virtual reality. You?"

"Just checking that you're still okay for tonight."

I stop typing and turn to her. "Tonight?"

"Dinner at Max's? Finalizing the details of the app launch, remember? I told you last week."

I drop my head. "Shit. Sorry, it slipped my mind." *Been a little distracted with trying to find the woman of my dreams and all.*

She walks around and sits in the chair near my desk. "Still chasing your mystery girl? I can't believe that with your hacking skills, you can't find her."

"I have literally nothing to go on, Eden. She filled out the questionnaire on one of our devices, so no IP address. She gave fake information. I don't even have a photo that I can run through facial recognition software."

"You have that?"

"No, but the FBI does."

"Please tell me you haven't hacked into the FBI."

I crack my neck. "Not recently." *But you can bet your bottom dollar that if it was the only way to find Liza, I'd do it in a goddamned second.*

"And you can't tell me anything about her other than tall, blonde, and gorgeous? That describes a whole bunch of women in Manhattan. No scars or distinguishing marks?"

Well, I'm pretty sure I left a hickey on her neck, but by now, that would have faded.

I shake my head. "I don't know what else to try, other than walking up and down streets in Brooklyn, hoping I'll run into her."

Eden sighs. "But she knows who you are, right? She could make contact?"

"If she wanted, which clearly, she doesn't." *And that's what hurts the most. If she felt even a fraction of what I did, she'd be breaking down my door to get to me. But she's not. Which makes me think this is another case of me falling for a woman who sees me as nothing more than a lust-filled detour on the way to her primary love location.*

"Tate!"

We both look over to see our boss Derek standing in the door to his office. "We need to talk about the Crest Construction exposé. My office in five minutes."

That name makes my ears prick up. "You're doing a story on Crest Construction?"

Eden leans closer. "Not if Derek has his way. My sources are whispering about lax safety standards on their construction sites. I'm also hearing accusations of buying off city officials to get around zoning laws. There are even rumors of connections with the mafia. It has the potential to blow wide open."

"Where are you hearing these rumors?"

She glances around, guiltily. "Oh, you know. Here and there."

"Where exactly?"

She rolls her eyes. "My inbox. I got an anonymous tip in an email."

What are the odds that there are rumors about Crest at the exact time a virtual hit has been put on them on the Dark Web? I'm predicting it's unlikely those two things are unrelated.

"You know that's the company that's denying Dad's compensation claim, right?"

Eden nods and looks toward Derek's office. "That may have been the reason I started looking into them about a year ago. I've heard about their shitty business practices for years, so it's about time someone did something about it."

"I'll help any way I can, but we have to be careful. Marcus Crest has some of the most ruthless security personnel in the city, and that includes his cyber-security." In the hacktivist world, cracking the Crest servers is the Holy Grail. No one's ever managed it, even though many have tried.

"You'd only know that if you'd tried to hack him."

"Tried and failed. And if their system is sophisticated enough to keep me out, then they definitely have something to hide."

Marcus Crest is a formidable figure in the New York real estate scene. He has a knack for getting his hands on pieces of real estate that aren't even on the market and has zero regard for buildings that have historical relevance.

One time, there was an injunction against him knocking down one of New York's oldest brownstone blocks, so he could build some hideous modern apartments. Crest ignored the injunction and sent demo crews in in the middle of the night to tear down half the houses. He was slapped with a pathetically low fine which he happily paid, and now, an ugly pile of concrete and glass is a blight on that otherwise picturesque neighborhood. That's the thing with Crest. He's such a narcissist, he believes that rules and regulations apply to everyone but him. Asshole.

"Derek doesn't want you to run the story?"

Eden shakes her head. "He's already having visions of the hurricane of lawsuits that would bury us if we said one wrong word about the Crest organization. That's one reason they get away with their criminal activities. No one has the balls to call them out."

"Not suggesting anything, but you definitely have the balls, and if you need actual man parts to back you up, you know I'm there for you."

"Awww, Tobes. Only a true friend would offer me his actual testicles. Thank you."

"My pleasure. What if Derek orders you to kill the story?"

She looks confused. "Since when do I listen to Derek?"

"True. As soon as I get done with this piece, I'll do some more subtle digging."

For once, my goals align with Eden's so it will be nice to kill two birds with one large, virtual stone.

"Cool. When we get together tonight, you can tell me what you find."

I frown. "Tonight?"

"*Dinner*, Tobes. Max's place."

"Fuck, yes. Right."

She rolls her eyes. "Wow, you're flaky these days."

I swear to God, my constant overworking and lack of sleep is killing my braincells. I feel myself getting dumber by the day. "Do you need me to bring anything?"

She pats my cheek. "Just your pretty face. See you at seven."

She stands and heads into Derek's office, and I try to ignore the ensuing yelling match as I finish my story.

6

UNEXPECTED PLANS

I'm packing up for the evening when my phone rings, and I nestle it between my shoulder and ear as I shove my laptop into my messenger bag.

"Jenner."

"Honey?"

I straighten up and grab the phone. "Mom? Hey. How are you doing?"

"Oh, fine, sweetie." That's Mom's standard reply whether she's feeling okay or has one foot on death's chilly doorstep. "More importantly, how are you?"

"I'm great." Like mother, like son, I guess. I know damn well Mom has enough on her plate without having to worry about her first-born owning the biggest, most dilapidated house on Struggle Street. "Just about to head out to dinner with Eden."

"Are you still at work?"

"Uh … yeah, just had some stuff to finish up." And didn't have anywhere else to go. "How are Dad and April?"

"April's great. She got the lead in her school play, so you can imagine how excited she is."

I smile. "Does she have you running lines with her yet?" That used to be my job whenever I made it home, but April's not fussy. She'll run lines with the mail carrier if they stop at our gate long enough.

"Of course," Mom says with a smile in her tone. "They're doing *The*

Wizard of Oz, so I'm getting lots of practice doing silly voices for all the other characters."

"I bet." I grin as I imagine it.

"Anyway, honey, I won't keep you. I know you're busy. I just wanted to let you know that the surgeon has scheduled Dad's surgery for the end of next month."

I stop what I'm doing and grip the phone. "I thought it wasn't going to be until the end of the year." Coming up with money for the co-pay was going to be tough by December. It's going to be almost impossible by the end of September.

"Yes, but his latest scan came back, and it's … not great. The mass near his spine is growing, so they want to get it now before it becomes too risky to remove it."

"Okay. Of course."

"I don't want you to worry. He's doing fine. I just wanted you to know."

I swap the phone to the other ear. "Mom, about the costs … "

"Toby, that's not for you to worry about."

"Of course I'm going to worry. We need to get the money together."

"It's okay. I have it all sorted." Even down the phone I can tell she's lying. "You've done enough already."

"Mom—"

"Tobias." Her 'mom-tone' has come into play. "I've got it under control, okay? I just called to let you know the surgery's been moved up. Can you get home for it?"

"Absolutely." Not sure how, but I'll make it happen.

"Love you, darling."

"Love you, too, Mom."

With that, we sign off, and I head to the station, a collection of dollar signs with question marks attached to them, floating through my mind.

I JOLT awake as the screech of train brakes hammers into my brain. For a second, I panic, because in the past few weeks, I've lost track of the number of times I've fallen asleep on the subway and woken up at the end of the line. There's something hypnotic about the steady thumping that my current state of exhaustion finds impossible to resist, no matter how short the trip. Tonight's not too bad, and I'm only one station past my intended stop. After shaking my head to clear it, I push up and get out when the doors open and trudge up to street level. I'm halfway over a crosswalk, when I catch a glimpse of a blonde woman a few yards ahead of me that stops me in my tracks.

Liza.

All of a sudden, I'm paralyzed, as every single feeling that was rocketing through my body when I kissed her two weeks ago, bombards me like a category five hurricane.

Ignoring the thick finger of panic that's poking my heart into overdrive, I push through the peak-hour sidewalk crowd in order to catch up to her.

"Liza!"

There's no response, so I speed up, pushing forward as politely as I can considering all I want to do is pick up everyone between me and her and throw them out of the way.

"Hey, Liza!" Finally, I'm close enough that my abnormally long arm can reach out and tap her shoulder.

"Hey, hi."

She turns, and when I realize that the woman I'm looking at isn't Liza after all, every single cell in my body deflates.

"Can I help you?" the woman says with more than a touch of suspicion.

"Uh, sorry." I give her my most non-threating smile as I tower over her like a giant, hairy Redwood. "I thought you were someone else."

She gives me a look up and down, and then shrugs. "No problem. Sorry to disappoint you." I go to protest, but she shakes her head and laughs. "Don't bother denying it. Your face told the whole story. Hope you end up finding Liza, whoever that is."

I mumble a thanks as she walks away before continuing on my way toward Max's place.

"Whoever that is," echoes in my brain. I wish I knew, stranger-lady. I really do.

As I round the corner and spy Max's building, I feel a stab of irritation that Liza turned herself into a ghost, especially considering our insane compatibility score. Why the hell would she go to all the trouble of signing up and doing the questionnaire if she was going to bail on her perfect match? She didn't just waste my time, she wasted the time of all of the Romance Central staff. Hell, Cupid himself probably has her on his shit-list at this point.

Screw it. I'm beyond trying to understand her motivations, because every time I ponder it too long, I just end up being pissed. It's like I'm going through the five stages of grief over losing her, and now I've moved onto anger.

I blow out a breath as I climb the steps to Max's apartment. I hate how relentlessly irritated I am these days. I've lost sight of the reasonably happy person I used to be. It's not all Liza's fault, of course, but she's certainly part of the immense jigsaw puzzle of crap that currently makes up my life.

As I reach the top of the stairs, I see that the huge sliding metal door to Max's apartment is open, and the sound of conversation and music echoes around me. Max's huge wooden dining table is surrounded by people, most of whom I recognize from Romance Central, as well as a couple of moonlighters from *Pulse*.

As soon as Eden spots me, she raises her hand and smiles. "Tobes! Come sit by me."

There's murmured hellos from everyone else as I drop into the chair next to Eden and place my bag on the floor.

"Sorry I'm late," I mumble.

She pours me a generous glass of wine. "Fall asleep on the subway again?"

"A little."

"At least you're here now." She pushes the glass toward me. "Surprisingly, you're not even the last to arrive."

I take a huge mouthful of wine and swallow. "Go, me."

I look over my shoulder to see Max bustling around in the kitchen with steaming pots and giant baking trays. Kind of annoying that with everything else going for him, the man can also cook. The only thing I've ever made with any flair is pot brownies and instant noodles. Usually, making the first necessitated the second. My munchies have a thing for ramen.

Max looks in my direction. "Hey, man. Can you and Eden give me a hand to put stuff on the table?"

"Sure."

Eden and I make several trips with platters and bowls, and everyone at the table spoons food onto their plates before passing them along.

"You know everyone, right?" Eden says as she passes a huge bowl of salad to Ming-Lee.

"Pretty much," I say. I glance toward where Raj is sitting at the far end of the table chatting with Darnell from marketing. He winks at me. I nod in response. "I've had to give tech support to them all at one time or another."

Eden, Max, and I finally sit and take our turn loading our plates with food. People are chatting, drinking, eating and laughing, but I'm too busy shoveling Max's delicious food into my mouth hole to join them. I revel in eating a decent meal for a change.

"Dude," Eden says, stifling a laugh. "It's not a race."

I talk around my very full mouth. "What can I say? Your man makes good food."

I'm in the middle of attacking an awesome vegetarian curry, when Eden looks over my shoulder and waves.

"Jo, at last! Come grab some food."

Footsteps come closer. "Sorry! Jimmy Fallon tried to steal my cab, and then we got into a whole thing about the time I wrote a bunch of material for his show, and he didn't give me any credit. The man has issues. Of course, it doesn't help he's a high-functioning alcoholic these days."

Her voice sends prickles up my spine, and in my peripheral vision, I see a blonde woman take the chair at the other end of the table.

No way. It can't be.

The food in my mouth turns to cement.

Eden touches my arm. "Toby, I don't think you've met my good friend Joanna. Jo, this is Toby, our genius-in-residence and architect of the app we're all here to launch."

It feels like I turn in slow motion, and when my brain registers who I'm looking at, my entire throat closes up. Likewise, when she sees me, her face drops momentarily before a smile claws its way back into position.

"Uh, hi," she says, like she can't tell I'm simultaneously having a stroke and choking on my own tongue. "Nice to meet you ... uh ... Toby."

With the effort of forcing titanium into a toothpaste tube, I finish chewing what's in my mouth and swallow it. My pulse has charged into overdrive, and if there wasn't a whole bunch of innocent people blithely chatting and eating around me, I'd probably let off the shit-ton of adrenaline pumping through my body by flipping the giant dining table, plates and all.

"Joanna, is it?" My voice is rough, and my words are like acid. I'm tempted to out her as the goddamn liar she is, but somewhere inside me, a voice says to cool off, at least until I get a chance to confront her in private.

At the other end of the table, the woman I knew as Liza goes pale but keeps her gaze on me. Can she tell how angry I am? All this time, there was only one degree of separation between us, and she chose to keep that rather important nugget of information to herself.

I'm still glaring daggers at Miss Lies-a-lot when Eden nudges me with her elbow.

"See?" she whispers. "I told you she was gorgeous. I knew you two would have chemistry."

Oh, we have chemistry, all right. If my gaze was sulfuric acid, she'd be melting into the floor like the Wicked Witch of the West.

"Now that Jo's here," Max says, "we can get started talking about the launch of the HEA app and how the night's going to run. Joanna's job is to help us secure a stellar VIP guest list and make sure we're the most prestigious event in NYC. Darnell and Charles, you'll be offering tech support at the iPad stations, Raj, you'll be Toby's right-hand-man running app diagnostics, Ming-Lee, you're the event manager in conjunction with Eden. And of course, Toby, you'll be doing the bulk of the presentation about the app and its capabilities."

I'm in the middle of calming my nerves with a huge gulp of wine, when I hear this bit of news and subsequently cough violently as it heads down the wrong pipe.

"Uh … what?" I rasp. "I thought you'd give the speech, considering its your brainwave, and all."

Max nods. "I'll MC the night, but when it comes to talking about the specifics of the app and how it works, I need your technical know-how front and center. Also, the press will be asking a ton of questions, to which I won't know the answers."

I clear my throat. "Yeah, it's just …" I cough again. "Public speaking really isn't my thing." I'm still scarred from the time in freshman year when I was given an impromptu speech topic on euthanasia and misheard it as 'youth in Asia.' I went on for three whole minutes about the Harajuku culture in Japan before the teacher bothered to correct me. My classmates called me Toby-San for a whole year and kept leaving goddamn origami animals in my locker. Assholes.

"You'll be fine," Eden says, placing her hand on my arm. "We'll make sure you're fully scripted and rehearsed, right Jo?"

Joanna looks over in surprise. "Oh, uh … sure. I'd be happy to … help."

Eden leans in. "If anyone can prepare you for talking in front of hundreds of people, it's Jo. She was tri-state debate champion three years in a row in high school."

"Was she?" I say dryly, doubting every so-called fact about this woman. From my experience, Joanna couldn't lie straight in bed. Eden said she was wrong about her being a compulsive fibber. From where I'm sitting, she was wrong about being wrong.

Over the next hour, Max moves the meeting along, and everyone contributes as we hammer out the details of the event and how it will run. Eden and Darnell guide us through a PowerPoint presentation of how the ballroom will look and what entertainment they're planning, and Raj confirms all of the tech specs in a spreadsheet he shares with the rest of the team.

I'm here and listening, but at the same time, I'm on the corner of Fifth and Broadway, stuck in a loop of Joanna standing so close I can smell her perfume, something that evoked wildflowers and sunshine, as her hand rested on my chest.

I try not to look at her, but it's tough, because she's right next to Max. I keep most of my attention on my laptop screen, hiding behind the pretense I'm taking notes. In reality, I'm trying to avoid the rush of excitement my body feels seeing Joanna, even though it's inextricably linked to the red-hot fury that circles my brain like a cobra in a cage. I may not know why she decided to bail on me, but I know for damn sure I need to spend as little time as possible with her while we plan this event. I feel humiliated she played me, and I don't intend to give her another opportunity.

"Finally," Max says an hour later, "I just wanted to confirm you all have something appropriate to wear. It's full-on formal, so that means tuxes for the guys, gowns for the ladies. Anyone have a problem with that?"

They all shake their heads, which makes me feel like an uncultured dick when I raise my hand. Shit, even Raj has a dinner suit? Why? And how? I didn't think he owned any clothing that wasn't made by a major sporting supplier.

"I don't own a tux," I say, and don't miss Raj's self-satisfied smirk. "I have several semi-formal cardigans, but I'm pretty sure that's not the look you're going for."

Max smiles when Eden scoffs, "Babe, there's no such thing as a semi-formal cardigan. Trust me."

I scowl and make a mental note to send her a picture of the cashmere pinstriped number I found in a thrift store for twenty bucks. Of course, that was a while ago, when I had a spare twenty just laying around, waiting to be spent on novelty cardigans, willy-nilly.

Max looks at Joanna. "Know anyone who could help? I know you're friends with some fashion people, right?"

Joanna sits up straighter. "Uh, yeah. Tom Ford owes me a few favors. I'm sure he'd be happy to provide us with something appropriate." She glances at me for a second before scribbling something on her notebook. "I'll set up a tux for Toby."

Max smiles. "Excellent. Well, it seems we've got everything covered, at least for now." He gestures to the bar on the other side of the room. "If you need to get out of here, no problem, but you're all welcome to hang around for some cocktails and dessert. Good job, Team Romance Central."

There's a burst of self-congratulatory applause and noise as people push back their chairs to migrate over to the bar. Before vacating, I grab two bread rolls from the basket on the table and shove them into my cardigan pockets. Squirreling away snacks whenever possible is a habit with me these days. Regular meals aren't always possible.

I stand and pack away my laptop into its bag.

"You're not leaving already, are you?" Eden asks as she stacks up the dirty plates.

I glance over my shoulder to where Raj has moved in on Joanna, because of course he has. Despite having a woeful track record with the ladies, Raj will home in on the most beautiful woman in the room with the accuracy of a heat-seeking missile. Even though I know how terrible his wooing is, I can't help the pang of jealousy that hits me.

"Uh … yeah," I say, "I'd better bounce. I have some work to do at the office before I head home." Considering the office is my home these days, at least the commute when I'm done will be a short one.

I close my messenger bag and sling it across my body. "I'll see you tomorrow, okay?"

"Wait." She puts down the stack of plates she's holding and leads me over to the bar. "Before you go, you have to taste this tequila that Max picked up. A couple of shots of this stuff, and you won't have to catch the subway, because you'll float home."

Behind the bar, Max is mixing up a whole truckload of cocktails and placing them on the bar for people to take at their leisure. When he sees us coming over, he lays out several shot glasses and fills them with a concoction from his shaker. It's conspicuously green.

"I call this one Kermit." He pushes the glasses toward us. "Word of caution, don't have any more than two if you plan on staying upright."

Eden flashes me a grin as we both grip a glass. "Up your butt, Jenner."

"Up yours, Tate."

We throw back the drink and then slam our glasses onto the bar. I squeeze my eyes shut and hiss when the liquor burns in the best possible way as it slides down my throat.

"Oh, momma!" Eden says, shaking her head. "So good, right?"

I nod. "So good." I'm not a tequila connoisseur, but it's pretty delicious.

We throw back another, and it's just as powerful as the first. "Whoa." My head spins a little, and I don't mind that the alcohol is lowering my tension levels. I'm almost cool with the fact the woman of my dreams is currently in an in-depth conversation with a walking pick-up-line. She looks around, as if she wants to be saved. For a moment, our gazes meet, and in that second, I'd love nothing more than to grab Raj and hang him from the highest hook on Max's wrought-iron coatrack. But she's not mine to save. She's made that quite clear.

"Jo! Hey, come over here for a sec." Dammit. Eden seems intent to save her, even if I'm not.

When she heads over, I make a move to leave.

"Okay, I'm out ..."

"Hang on." Eden puts her hand on my arm. "I really want you and Joanna to get to know each other. I just know that you two would hit it off."

Oh, we did. At least, I thought so. She might disagree.

"Yeah, too much to do tonight, Tate," I say. "Maybe another time."

Unfortunately, Eden doesn't let go of my arm, so even though I'm getting more anxious the closer Joanna gets, short of forcibly extricating myself, I can't find a way to politely leave.

When Joanna arrives, Eden pulls her into a hug.

"Hey. I haven't seen you for weeks."

"Sorry," Joanna says, flicking her glance to me. "Just … busy. You know, life and stuff."

Sure. Wouldn't have anything to do with avoiding certain guys like your life depended on it, I'm sure.

"So," Eden says. "We should make some time to get together and work on Toby's speech, right?" She looks at me. "I know you're flat out, but any dates or times spring to mind?"

Sure. How's never for you? Does that work?

I clear my throat. "Uh … I'll have to check my schedule."

Eden screws up her face. "Stop trying to impress Joanna with your fanciness. You and I both know you don't own a planner."

Joanna widens her eyes. "How do you remember everything you have to do if you don't write it down."

"I don't." I adjust my bag on my shoulder. "I forget stuff like a cool person."

Joanna smiles at that, and goddammit, no. That's not fair. Staying mad with her is essential right now, and I can't do that if she smiles at me. I'm not sure if there are rules against that sort of thing in the Geneva convention, but if there aren't, there damn well should be.

"Eden!" We all turn to see Max waving at us from amongst a group sipping cocktails. "Come and settle an argument about gin versus vodka."

She shoots a look between Joanna and me before saying, "Happy to," and saunters off.

If I was a suspicious person, and I absolutely am, I would think that she and Max are colluding to get Joanna and me alone. I love my friends, but sometimes, I fucking hate them.

"So …" Joanna says, looking as uncomfortable as a long-tailed cat in a room full of rocking chairs.

"Yeah, so …"

Ignoring Max's earlier warning about the tequila, I grab another shot and slam it back. It burns like the others, but the soothing after-effect is nowhere to be found.

"So, I gotta go." I put the glass back on the bar, and that's when Joanna touches my arm.

"Toby, wait —"

I pull my arm back because even though smiling might not be technically classed as torture, touching me definitely is.

"Why?" I demand, not even a little fuzzy around the corners anymore. "So you can lie to me again? So you can get away from me as fast as possible the moment my back's turned."

"That was never my intention."

"Really? Because it seemed like that was your plan all along, and you pulled it off like a pro."

"Please, just let me explain."

"You've had weeks to do that. You knew who I was and where I'd be, so if you wanted to clear the air, you could have done it well before now."

I turn to go, but once again, there's a gentle hand on my arm, and it's like she's Velcro and I'm a giant, weak-ass piece of fluff who can't wrench itself free.

"Toby ..."

I sigh and try to disguise my anger from those around me. As it is, I have no doubt Eden is watching this exchange and wondering what the hell is going on.

"Stop touching me," I whisper, and then roll my neck to try to get rid of some of the tension winding up my spine. "Going forward, that's rule number one. Rule number two is that we will spend the minimum amount of time together for this project and then avoid each other like we're getting paid to do it. Rule three is that you don't lie to me again." I take a breath to calm myself before I continue.

"Toby—"

"Don't *Toby* me. I made it pretty clear I felt a connection to you, but if you didn't, there was no need to lie and pretend you were interested. I'm a big boy. I've handled plenty of rejections before. Yours just would have been the latest in a long list."

She wears a pained expression, and dammit if I don't feel bad. I don't know why. She's in the wrong here, not me.

"Look," she says, her voice quiet. "I'm not going to insult you and say what I did was justified, but I did have my reasons. Just please know I wasn't pretending about how I felt about you. That was the one thing that was real."

"Then why all the other bullshit? The cloak and dagger name? Disappearing as soon as you found out we were statistically perfect for each other …?"

She takes a pink cocktail from the bar and drinks deeply before looking up me. "I used the fake name, because Liza is who I am when I'm trying to weed out creeps and weirdos. If handsy Harold knew my real name, he could track me down, and … oh, I don't know, stalk me and maybe break into my apartment. It's happened before, and it wasn't pleasant." The tremor in her voice tells me there's more to that story, but for the moment, I just listen. "Likewise giving a fake email and address. I have trust issues as far as men go, and until I'm sure they're not going to go all Ted Bundy on me, I camouflage my identity. I do it all the time, and it's practically second nature by now."

"Okay, fine, I'll give you that." There are a ton of dirtbags out there who treat women like property and don't take no for an answer. I can't blame women for protecting themselves. "But you knew I was Eden's best friend. Surely you could have leveled with me. And why the disappearing act when you found out how compatible we were? Was all that stuff about finding your soul mate also bullshit? Because according to my math, I'm it. I'm the one for you. And yet you went full-on Hussein Bolt getting away from me."

She looks down for a second, regret on her face. "At the start, I thought you were just some random dude in the bathroom, and by the time I found out who you really were, it felt like the wrong time to spill all my beans. I really regret that. As for why I ran away …" She swallows and looks up at me. "Remember how I told you I have an uncanny habit of picking the wrong guys? Well, I kept thinking about that quote about how insanity is doing the same thing over and over again and expecting different results."

"Okay."

"So, that night I was determined to break the pattern, and I decided that if I wanted to see alternate results, I'd have to become an alternate me."

"What does that mean?"

Color blooms in her cheeks. "It means, every decision I made that night was purposefully different from what I'd usually do. If I thought I should go left, I went right. If my brain was telling me to pick the blond guy, I went with the brunette." She takes a breath. "The same went for the questionnaire. Every answer I gave was the opposite of the truth."

"You … wait …" I stare at her. "Your whole questionnaire was a lie?"

She nods. "One-hundred percent. That's why I was so hesitant to see the results. I knew they wouldn't reflect our true compatibility. I was incredibly drawn to you, so therefore, you were automatically the wrong man for me."

"No. There's no way that's the case."

"It is, Toby. Trust me. That ninety-three percent isn't real. It's the us that exists in Bizarro world, where black is white, and kale isn't Satan's spinach."

I shake my head. "I don't care how many questions you screwed with, what we *felt* was real. You're running with a theory that has zero supporting evidence."

"I knew you'd think that, and I knew I'd have to explain myself to you sooner rather than later, so to prove I'm right, I retook the questionnaire and told the truth, the whole truth, and nothing but the truth." She pulls out her phone and brings up the HEA app. "And to give you an indication that your algorithm works, I bumped phones with Raj a few minutes ago." She shows me the screen.

"Eighteen percent." I nod. "That's on par with all of Raj's matches so far." I'm sure there's someone out there for him, but until he changes his attitude toward women, she's going to be a train wreck of insecurities mixed with the lowest of standards.

"Okay," Joanna says, holding out her phone. "So, this is the true test. This is the real Joanna and her real score. Are you ready?"

I pull my phone from my pocket and shake my head. "Be prepared to be proven wrong."

"I hope I am, but I sincerely doubt that's going to happen."

I hold out my phone, and she looks at it for a second. "Toby, tell me again how accurate your algorithm is."

I sigh. "According to my PR team, meaning Eden, it's the most accurate compatibility app of all time."

"And according to you?"

The air gets thick when I look into her eyes. "My numbers are spot on. It's as good as it gets."

"Okay. Just wanted you to remind us both of that before we do this."

She bumps her phone against mine, our knuckles lightly brushing. Both phones give a low beeping noise, and then the screen lights up with our compatibility score in a red circle.

My stomach falls through the floor. "That's not possible."

I look at Joanna, expecting to see shock on her face, but I don't. Her expression is more resignation. Like this is what she's been expecting all along.

"I knew it," she says softly. "I didn't want it to be true, but it is."

I blink at number on the screen.

Seven percent.

"Are you fucking kidding me? There's no way that's our true score." The night we met, I felt like I'd known this woman forever. I'd seen a long and happy future for us. How is this happening?

"This is a mistake," I say, trying to convince her even more than myself. "I've never seen a number this low. *Never.* Something has gone wrong. There are bugs in the system that I just need to —"

"It's correct, Toby." Her voice is quiet, but I feel it slam into me. "I warned you about my superpower. Every guy who I find fascinating ends up being exactly wrong for me. Why should you be any different?"

"Joanna, this is ridiculous. We'll delete the results and try again. There must be a glitch in the code. There's no way that I'm less compatible with you than fucking Raj, okay? It's not possible."

She gives me a sad smile. "I knew there was something wrong when we touched. I've never felt anything like that, so of course it's with a guy with whom I have practically zero chance of having a relationship."

For once, I'm lost for words. I try to analyze my way out of this, but I can't.

I step forward. "Joanna ..."

"Toby," she looks up at me, and the air between us practically glows with warmth. "You were the one who convinced me numbers don't lie. This is the reason I ran away that night and why I've been too much of a coward to talk to you about it. I've been trying to convince myself that my inner pessimist was wrong about us, but she's not. She rarely is."

I stare at her, not sure what to say or what to do or how to fix this. How can I argue with my own logic?

"We could still try," I say, lamely.

"Sure. We could ignore the numbers, but the odds are

overwhelmingly in favor of us being guaranteed heartbreak for each other. I don't know about you, but I've had enough pain for a lifetime. Now, I want something that won't hurt. Something that will last." She looks up at me. "Even if we ignore the odds and struggle to have some kind of relationship, with a score that low, what are the chances you're my soul mate?"

I look at her, knowing the answer but not wanting to admit it.

"Toby, what are the chances?"

I shake my head, feeling sicker by the second. "Low. Practically zero."

Joanna nods, and for the first time since I met her, she seems truly deflated.

"See, while I was avoiding you, I could delay this conversation. Suspecting something and knowing it are two different things, and knowing this … it freaking sucks."

I feel like I've been sucker punched. The past couple of weeks I've been lamenting losing my soul mate, when in fact Joanna is just another woman I'm doomed to disappoint.

"Yeah, it does."

"Still," she says, trying to ramp up an ounce of enthusiasm, "I guess the silver lining is that our perfect matches are still out there somewhere, right? And we found out we're all wrong before anything happened, so …"

I glance at her. "Well, something happened."

She swallows. "Yeah. But it was just one kiss, right? Not enough to get invested in a … a hopeless cause, right?" I don't know if she believes what she's saying, but she's not selling it.

"Right." It's my turn to nod, and I do my best to act like there's not a weird, dark pain in the center of my chest that's getting bigger each second. "There's that, I guess."

I glance over to see Max and Eden holding hands, shooting occasional glances over to us.

Sorry, guys. Whatever you thought might happen between us is dead. Deader than disco.

When Joanna sees them watching us, she shakes off whatever melancholy she's feeling and lights up again, even if it's not totally sincere.

"So, anyway. It would be great if we could be friends. To be honest, I don't have that many, and even if we're not written in the stars as soul mates, I really enjoyed spending time with you."

She looks at me expectantly. I like to think I'm pretty good at moderating my expectations to suit any situation, but I'm not sure if being friends with her is a good idea. I suppose all I can do is try and tap out if things get too intense. One thing I am good at is adjusting to the women I want, not wanting me back. If I just keep reminding myself that Raj has more chance of being her boyfriend than I do, I have no doubt my ardor will cool more rapidly than a kiddie pool in a blizzard.

"Sure," I say, testing out a half-smile. "Let's try the friends thing." With my schedule, it's doubtful we'll be able to spend any time together outside of the HEA launch anyway, so the commitment is minimal.

She holds out her hand. "Give me your phone. I'll give you my number. My real one, this time."

I hand over my phone and sip a glass of water I nab off the bar as she programs in her number. She hits the call button. and her phone rings. Then she hangs up and hands the phone back.

"There we go. Now, I have your number, too." She looks at me, and there are a few seconds of silence before she says, "So, uh … I'll text you when I have time for a tux fitting, okay?"

"Yeah. Sure."

She puts her phone in her purse and looks up me, her expression turning serious. "Toby … I'm really sorry for the way I behaved, and even sorrier for how things turned out, but I'm not sorry I met you. Promise that we'll talk soon."

I nod. "Sure. Soon." I adjust my bag on my shoulder. "Later."

She nods. "Definitely."

Pulling myself away from her feels immensely wrong, but I guess I'd better get used to that. With a brief wave to Max and Eden, I head to the door. I can feel Eden beaming at me, and even though I know she thinks Joanna and I exchanged numbers for romantic reasons, I don't have the heart to correct her right now.

I plod down the stairs to street level and trudge toward the subway station. And when I finally make it onto a train and sink into a seat, I fall asleep almost immediately.

7

REALITY BITES

"Hey. Tobes."

Someone's shaking my shoulder. I moan and mumble for them to quit.

"Toby ..."

My whole body hurts, but sleep is nice, so I'd like to continue floating in it's warm, soothing embrace.

"Toby!"

I sit upright and open my eyes.

Oh, God. My back. My neck. My arms. It's like I can taste my skeleton, and the flavor is pain.

I shake my head to clear it and look up to see Eden staring down at me. "Did you sleep here last night?"

I blink and look around, momentarily confused about where I am. "Uh ... maybe?"

Oh, right, I'm at my desk at Pulse. *How did I get here?*

I roll my neck from side to side and wince when it cracks loudly. Sleeping sitting up is one of the worst ideas I've ever had, including that time I thought giving myself frosted tips with laundry bleach would be cool.

"Uh ..." My brain is slow to shift into gear. "I came in early to get a jump on some work and ... I guess I nodded off."

I leave out the part where I fell asleep on the subway last night and lost a good couple of hours drooling on myself before a security guard woke me up and moved me on. When I got off, I was closer to here than Greenpoint, so I decided to crash at *Pulse* instead of Romance Central.

After that, I couldn't get my conversation with Joanna out of my head. I'm still gobsmacked about our compatibility score. We clicked more than a metric ton of Lego. We had chemistry so explosive, it could power a rocket to the farthest reaches of space. How in hell are our numbers so abysmal?

Unable to accept what was mathematically laid out in black and white, when I got here last night, I spent two hours going through her questionnaire, raking through my own, and basically trying everything possible to improve our chances. I even retook my whole questionnaire and changed a couple of answers I wasn't sure about. It brought our compatibility down to five percent. In the end, I slammed my laptop shut and rested my poor aching, disappointed head on my arms, and I guess that's when I fell asleep.

Bad choice.

I stretch out the bunched muscles in my arms and shoulders. Everything cracks, even the parts that shouldn't.

Eden frowns. "You're wearing the same clothes you were wearing last night. Haven't you been home?"

I look down at myself. "Uh …"

In a second, Eden's frown literally turns upside-down, and she beams at me. "Wait … did you and Joanna …?" She widens her eyes. "Oh, my God! It's actually happening! My two best friends are getting together! This is like a dream. Did you two hook up after the party? I mean, she left almost immediately after you." She slaps my arm. "You dirty dog, Jenner! I said you'd like her! Was I right or was I right?"

I stand up and crack my back before lumbering toward the break room like a Sasquatch in need of a chiropractor. Unfortunately, Eden follows.

I should tell her about Joanna being Liza, but honestly, I'm too exhausted to get into it right now. If I open that door into my disappointment even a little, she will kick it down and grill me for hours, so it's safer to say nothing. On my best days, I have a hard time fending off Eden's superior prying skills, and today I'm absolutely not at my best.

"Please stop being so enthusiastic, Tate. It's annoying. Also, nothing happened with me and Joanna."

"But I saw you give her your number. And you two seemed to have a very intense conversation. I could feel the heat from where I was standing."

I grab a clean coffee pot and stick it under the tap to fill before shoving a new filter into the tray. Then I tear open a bag of coffee grounds and pour them in. "Joanna took my number so she can organize my tux. That's it. And there was no heat."

God, there was so much goddamn heat it felt like I was melting from the inside out. I felt like the ring after Frodo threw it into the volcano. I felt like poor idiot Anakin Skywalker burning in the lava because he didn't gain the high ground.

Of course, Eden doesn't need to know that because I sure-as-shit would never hear the end of it.

As it is, she's not buying my denial. "Well, that's a pile of crap. There were so many sparks flying between you two it looked like a welders' convention. And don't you dare tell me you aren't interested in Joanna, Tobias Matthew, because I know the look when you're into a girl, and it was plastered all over your face last night."

I grab the jug and pour water into the machine before placing it under the filter and turning on the power. The machine whirs and hums for a few seconds before steaming coffee starts dribbling out.

"Eden, it's early. Way too early to start accosting me with your romantic fantasies. What are you even doing here?"

She grabs two mugs from the cupboard and places them on the counter before adding sugar and creamer. "I have some interviews for my Crest exposé today and wanted to do some prep work first."

"Oh, yeah? Who are you interviewing?" My question is part genuine curiosity and part distracting her from our unwanted conversation.

"There's a guy who runs a blog that posts anonymous complaints about the Crest Organization and its shady practices. I think he may be a disgruntled ex-employee, but he seems to have some decent dirt. However, he's a bit paranoid about coming to NYC, so I have to drive out to Pennsylvania to meet him. I'm just grabbing my files and then heading to the rental-car place. I may need your hacking skills later."

"Cool." I open the fridge and see if there's anything I can eat. Being my size comes with the disadvantage of having to shovel fuel into my body with annoying regularity or else I feel dizzy and weird. "I can probably do some digging of the illegal kind today, too." I pick up a tub of yogurt that's labeled with a sticky note: "PROPERTY OF RAJ. HANDS OFF, BITCHES!" I hesitate a moment because I feel bad for stealing his food, but desperate times and all that. Vowing to repay him with a banquet when I'm solvent again, I pull off the note and throw it in the trash. Then I shut the fridge and grab a spoon. "I'll call you later so we can compare notes."

While the coffee percolates, I shuffle back to my desk, tear the lid of the yogurt, and demolish the entire tub in three mouthfuls. I'm vaguely aware that Eden has planted herself in the chair next to me and is scrutinizing my face with the intensity of a forensic anthropologist studying a dead body.

"Toby, what's going on with you?"

I throw the empty tub into the trash and sigh. "Nothing. I'm just tired." *And mourning the loss of the woman I thought was my everything. No biggie.*

I wake up my computer and check my email. Unfortunately, Eden isn't buying my nonchalance.

"Don't bullshit a bullshitter, Jenner. You've been weird for weeks now, and I know you're keeping stuff from me."

"That's not true." I mean, apart from being homeless, in love with her best friend, and desperately trying to find a way to get my dad a life-saving operation without committing federal bank fraud, I've been completely honest. "I'm just under a lot of pressure right now with the app launch." Oh, and there's also the app launch.

"Toby."

I try to ignore her as I delete most of the fresh garbage in my inbox, but I can feel her gaze burning a hole in the side of my face, so I finally relent and turn to her.

She's looking at me with my least favorite expression: pity.

"Tobes, just tell me how I can help you. There has to be something I can do."

I rub my eyes. I wish there were. But pretty much every single issue in my life is stuff only I can deal with. Still, I have to give her something to do, or I'll never hear the end of it.

"Okay, Eden, there is a way you can help, but I don't feel good asking you this. I need you to know that."

She leans forward. "Toby, come on. You can ask me anything."

"You say that, but this is …" I shake my head and look at her. "I want you to know how much I respect you as a woman and a person, okay? Please remember that."

"Toby … Jesus … as long as it's not weird sex stuff, just ask me."

I take both of her hands in mine. "Okay. Here goes …" I take a breath. "Please go and fetch my coffee. Stir it well. I know you're good at stirring. And if you can find any more of Raj's food in the fridge, bring me that, too."

She groans and snatches her hands back before pushing me in the shoulders. Her indignance makes me laugh.

"You're an asshole." She laughs as she heads towards the kitchen. "You're lucky you're pretty."

"Hush your mouth, woman, and bring me my damn caffeine hit!" I call after her.

I heave a sigh of relief that she's been thrown off all of my highly embarrassing trails, at least for now.

By midday, I've finished editing my latest tech article, argued with the people from Dad's medical insurance company for roughly forty-five minutes on their so-called 'help line,' and done some surreptitious hacking into Crest Construction subsidiary companies, looking for red flags that might lead to significant corporate dirt Eden can use for her story, and I can use for my Dark Web assignment. Predictably, I found a ton of threads to follow and made a note to follow up on them later tonight when I don't have my entire office looking over my shoulder.

Finding anything concrete will be difficult. Crest's been in business for a lot of years, so they're experts at hiding their corruption by now. I begin to worry if I can do this job all by myself or if I'll have to contact my posse of hacker friends. I put a pin in the thought for the moment. That will be a last resort.

When my phone buzzes, I glance at the screen. My ribcage tightens when I see "Joanna."

I sigh. I've been so busy this morning I haven't had a lot of time to continue my quest to prove my own app wrong. I figure at some point I'll have to accept the compatibility results, even if I don't like them, but that day isn't today. If I have to burn my entire algorithm to the ground and rebuild it just to prove Joanna doesn't have a ninety-three percent chance of destroying me, I absolutely will.

Even if I accept we're not meant to be together, could I turn off my feelings enough to actually be friends? I pride myself on my logic, but I have no idea if it's strong enough to kneecap my passion if push came to shove.

I run a hand through my hair. Technically, being just friends with her is possible, but seeing her name as my phone buzzes insistently in my hand, a million disaster scenarios flash through my brain with the speed of the world's largest supercomputer. Most of them involve us meeting up, and me subsequently crumbling into a vortex of monsoon-level hormones.

My phone continues to vibrate.

I wipe a hand over my beard and then hover my finger over the answer button with all the anxiety of a bomb technician about to cut the blue wire. Before I can detonate, however, the phone stops, and Joanna's name disappears. The relief I feel is only matched by my intense disappointment.

Fuck. I couldn't hate this any more if it insulted my mother and kicked my dog. I mean, I don't have a dog, but if I did, I would despise anyone who kicked it. Dogs are freaking adorable.

I stare at the screen for a few more seconds, sure that Joanna will call back. When she doesn't, I put the phone down, swallow my disappointment, and roll my neck. Man, the first thing I'm going to do when I get some spare money is go to the Shiatsu massage place on the corner and have Mrs. Kabushi's magical fingers purge the aches I carry in nearly every muscle. I also make a mental note to try and get to the gym this week. I can't afford many luxuries these days, but I might as well reap the benefits of the yearly membership for which I've already paid. Plus, working out is an easy way to give my mental health a boost. Endorphins, for the win.

Despite my close call with Joanna, I'm pleased with the morning's productivity, so I close my laptop before heading into the break room to rustle up some food. I find Raj in there, messing around with what looks to be a digital lockbox.

He looks up when he sees me. "Heyyyy, boss man. How you doing?"

"Fine. What's this?"

He clicks the box shut. "Some asshole keeps stealing my food, so I came up with this." He gestures to the electronic keypad. "Six-digit encryption, motherfuckers! Good luck stealing my lunch today."

"Wow." I nod, impressed. "I don't see how anyone could possibly get into that. It's an amazing fool-proof plan. What are you packing today, anyway?"

He opens the fridge and slides the box in. "My mom's butter chicken with garlic naan. I've been looking forward to it all day. Just gotta finish updating Derek's computer before slipping out to the park and enjoying." He closes the fridge.

"Sounds great." It really does. My stomach rumbles. Raj's mom is an amazing cook. Don't ask me how I know.

He grabs a bottle of Kombucha off the counter and then heads to the door. "Later, T-man!"

"Yeah, later, Raj." I wait a few seconds to make sure he's gone before opening the fridge and squatting down to examine the lock-box keypad.

"Okay, Raj," I whisper. "I'm only trying this once, so if you have any chance of keeping your lunch today, you need to have not been a total douchebag when you set the code."

I punch in the numbers 696969. The latch clicks open.

"Oh, poor, sweet, predictable Raj. When will you learn?" I grab the container of food, close the box and the fridge, and nab a fork. "Going to lunch," I say to Jackie on my way past her desk. "I'll be at the park. Call if you need me."

Jackie smiles.

I head out the sliding glass doors and down the stairs into the sunshine.

8

____

JUST FRIENDS

"Oh, God. So good." I stretch my legs out and lean back on the bench as my stomach rejoices in the satisfaction of an amazing, plundered feast. "Mrs. Chopranka, I think I love you." I slide on my sunglasses and turn my face to the light, closing my eyes as I try to focus on the sound of the nearby water and not the relentless tha-thump of the bridge overhead.

Well fed, sitting in the sunshine. Life seems good, if only on a temporary basis.

My phone buzzes in my pocket. When I pull it out, I'm not surprised to see Joanna's name on the screen. I take in a breath and let it out slowly.

Friendfriendsfriendsjustfriends. _You can do this._

My hand's shaking again.

I hover my finger over the answer button, then drop my hand into my lap.

Maybe I just need a little more time to process everything that's happened before I can talk to her. I reject the call then tap out, "Sorry, I can't talk right now." Feeling guilty, I sign it with a happy face, hoping that will soften the blow. Then, I hit send.

I drop my head back. Disaster averted. Just enough time to enjoy a few more minutes of relaxation before I have to head back to work.

I've barely had time to get my heartrate under control before a shadow falls over me. I don't think much of it until I hear a quiet, "Hey, Toby."

I open one eye to see an angel silhouetted against the midday sun, a golden halo igniting her blonde hair.

"Joanna?" I sit up, so the sun isn't blinding me. Unfortunately, I can now see her perfect face in full, heart-stopping clarity.

"Hey. Gorgeous day, right?" She sits next to me and mimics my position. "I hardly ever get over to this park, but whenever I do, I curse myself for not doing it more." She takes in a deep breath and lets it out. "Makes you happy to be alive, huh?"

Just her sitting next to me sends my body into not-entirely-unpleasant overdrive. I become aware that I'm staring at her beautiful face in dumb silence for a full three seconds before shaking myself back into reality.

"Uh … what are you doing here?"

She taps something into her phone. "I tried to call earlier but couldn't get onto you. I figured you may be ghosting me, because … you may still be feeling weird about how everything went down between us and might be more comfortable avoiding me than talking to me. Was that why you didn't pick up?"

She turns and looks for a reaction.

My brain stumbles like a newborn deer taking its first steps. "Uh … Well, uh … maybe?"

Dammit, Jenner. You're a certifiable genius. Please act like it.

"I … uh … when I saw you were calling, I … uh … well, I …"

For the love of James Taylor! Put together a coherent sentence!

Joanna stares at me serenely while I commit the conversation equivalent of shitting the bed.

"I suppose I was … you know, feeling … weird … and … the whole friends thing was … uh … so in short … uh … yeah."

Despite my stammering, she gives me a small smile. "That's cool. I don't expect things to be smooth between us right away, but I think that us being friends could be amazing. At least, I'd really like to try. If that means we need to push through some weirdness, then so be it, right?"

"So … you came to find me, because I didn't answer your call and you wanted to chat about being friends?" Overly dedicated if you ask me, but Joanna seems like the passionate type. If she wants to direct her passion in my direction, who am I to deny her?

Joanna smiles. "I came to find you, because Tom Ford want his best tailor to fit your tuxedo, but Giovanni is getting on a plane to Milan this afternoon, so the fitting has to be now. When you didn't pick up, I went to your office, and Jackie told me you were here."

Damn you, Jackie! A pox on you and your helpful ways.

"Uh … right. A tux fitting. Okay." I've never had a suit fitted before. In fact, I've never owned a suit, so the thought of being thrown into a completely alien environment is making me a tad anxious. "Where's the fitting at?"

"Tom's workshop in the garment district. I have a car waiting." She nods toward the street where I see a sleek black Escalade.

"Oh. Sure." *Well, that's fucking surreal.* "Nice ride. Uh …how long will it take?"

"About forty minutes. Derek said it was cool for you to have a slightly longer lunch break. Such a nice guy."

I frown. "Derek? *My* Derek? I've heard him called a lot of things over the years, but 'nice' isn't one of them."

She stands. "Don't believe his grumpy bluster. He's a total puppy dog. Shall we?"

I'm still a little shellshocked that she's here and whisking me away in a luxury town car, but I stand and shrug. "Let's go then, I guess."

I throw my trash in the bin and follow her to the car. As we approach, a good-looking man in a black suit exits and opens the door for us.

"Gerald, this is Toby Jenner. Toby, Gerald Cornell, driver extraordinaire."

He gives me a nod. "A pleasure, Mr. Jenner." He has the kind of upper-class British accent I've only ever heard in *Downton Abbey*. "Miss Cassidy, traffic is moderate. We should be there in fifteen minutes."

"Great, thanks, Gerald."

Cassidy, huh? It's the first time I've heard her last name. Of course, it's perfect, like the rest of her.

Joanna climbs in first, and Gerald closes the door before escorting me to the other side. I fold myself into the surprisingly roomy seat and strap myself in as Gerald gets into the driver's side.

"Water?" Joanna asks, offering me a chilled bottle.

"Uh … sure." I lean over and say quietly, "Is there a story with you and Tom Ford? Because this ride is impressive. Can't imagine he offers his town car and driver to just anyone."

She slides on some sunglasses and shoots a look at the driver. "Uh … yeah. Tommy and I go back years. I mean, I don't want to say that I saved his fall line a while ago, but the man was going to show ponchos at Fashion Week." She turns to me. "Ponchos, Toby. With tassels. I mean, really."

I laugh, because she has this way of deadpanning totally outrageous statements without batting an eyelid. I can't tell if she's joking, so I just assume she is.

"So, ponchos are bad?"

"Not inherently, but when it looks like you made them from Grandma's curtains, then, yeah. Thank God I got to him in time. If he'd showed them to Anna Wintour, she would have ripped his still-beating heart from his chest and eaten it. Anna's very unforgiving of tassels in general. I think it stems from that one time I took her to a burlesque bar in the village, and they served her bad champagne while one of the dancers shook her tasseled tatas in her face. It was a whole tassel tragedy."

"Ah, understandable." I'm out of my depth talking about the celebrity editor of *Vogue*, so I take a sip of water and look out the window. The circles in which Joanna socializes make me feel like an uncultured bumpkin. Probably one of the reasons for our woeful compatibility.

"So, how's the app progressing?" Joanna asks. "Is everything on track for the launch?"

I nod. "Mostly. Just a few more kinks to work out, but I'm sure I'll get there."

"You will," she says in a certain tone. "I have faith in you."

Those faint words of praise fill me with so much chest-exploding pride, I'm surprised I don't burst out of my shirt like the incredible Hulk.

Oh, yeah. This friend's thing is going to be great.

WALKING through the luxe interior of Tom Ford's flagship store, I'm blown away by the vast range of menswear. I tend to don a variation of the same clothing combination every day, namely pants plus a T-shirt and cardigan. So, seeing endless racks of stylish, diverse apparel is a shock to my system.

"Who the hell wears all this stuff?"

While Joanna chats with a sharply dressed male staff member, I spy a particularly nice cardigan on a nearby shelf and grab it. It's dark grey and as soft as a kitten, but my jaw falls on the floor when I see the price tag.

"Oh, fuck me gently."

Joanna and the staff member look over, and I don't miss the faint scowl on the guy's face.

"Sorry," I say. "That was rude. I meant fornicate me gently. If you please."

The staff member crosses his arms, and I shove the cardigan back onto the shelf as gently as I can. I have a nightmarish flash of me snagging my fingernail on the delicate fabric and then getting carted away to cardigan-debtor's prison when I can't afford to pay for the fucking thing.

"They're ready for us upstairs," Joanna says, and then raises an eyebrow. "Unless you're up for some shopping before we go."

"Well, I'd love to, but I left my gold-plated American Express on the yacht."

With a touch more disdain, the staff member gestures toward the back of the store, and Joanna leads me over to where a gleaming elevator waits. "Fabian will meet us upstairs. He's Giovanni's assistant, and I believe they already have something for you to try."

"What? How? We only talked about the tux last night?"

"Yes, and I called Tom first thing this morning. We're lucky it isn't awards season, so they had a few tailors they could spare."

"Oh, cool. Lots of people working on a thing for me. Totally normal."

As the doors close, I roll my neck. This place makes me so tense, I feel like I'm heading to have an enema instead of a fitting. Generally, I'm more comfortable in thrift stores than swanky retail outlets, and today has just cemented that position. There's fast fashion, and then there's fashion so expensive, just being in its presence gives me a dose of hives.

Joanna shoots me a look of concern. "You okay?"

"Sure. Awesome. Great. Financially inferior and lacking in style, but otherwise, dandy."

"Don't be intimidated. It's just clothes."

I clench and release my hands. "Yeah, but super expensive clothes. Who the fuck needs knitwear that costs four grand? I mean, is it bullet proof? Is it fitted with an inbuilt massager? Will it whisper sweet nothings to me on lonely nights and tell me how handsome I am?"

She laughs. "No, but it's cashmere and buttery soft, and some people are willing to pay thousands for that."

I shake my head. "Rich people are crazy."

She looks up at the lit numbers. "Not going to argue with that."

The doors open on a bustling workshop, and I only have enough time to take in a tableau of huge tables covered in fabric and pattern pieces before an extremely well-groomed young man appears in front of us.

Damn, do all the staff here look like models?

"Hello. I'm Fabian. Giovanni is expecting you. This way, please."

We follow him down a marble-floored hallway into what seems to be a plush salon, complete with navy, velvet chaise and a spot-lit podium in front of a semi-circle of mirrors.

A small, elderly man comes over to us and kisses Joanna on both cheeks.

"Cara, a pleasure to see you, as always." His Italian accent is thick, and in his black waistcoat and white shirt, he looks like he belongs in a piazza somewhere, selling art or Italian leather goods.

Joanna squeezes his hands, and then turns to me. "Giovanni, piacere. This is Toby Jenner, your model for today."

The old man holds out his hand, and when I shake it, he puts his other hand on top. "Any friend of la mia principessa is a friend of mine. Now, let's get you set up, amico. Fabian? If you please."

Fabian leads me over to a door in the wall and opens it to reveal a large dressing room, complete with full bathroom, fruit and cheese platter, and a bottle of Cristal on ice.

Sweet Jesus. This is a whole other world.

"Make yourself comfortable." Fabian walks over and opens the bottle of champagne before pouring me a glass. "You'll find fresh towels, underwear, and a complimentary robe in the bathroom. When you're finished, please change into this." He gestures to a rack where a mostly assembled dinner suit and collared shirt are hanging. "You'll find shoes in a range of sizes over there, too. Come out to the gallery when you're ready."

"Wow. Okay."

He gives me a tight smile and pulls the door closed behind him.

"Holy shit."

I quickly stuff my mouth with cheese and crackers before washing it all down with a few mouthfuls of bubbly. I mean, yes, it's mid-afternoon, and I have to go back to work after this, but who am I to turn down a three-hundred-dollar bottle of champagne when it's offered?

In between sips, I strip, and then head into the bathroom for the world's fastest shower.

After toweling off, I hold up the expensive underpants.

"You probably cost more than my phone," I mutter, and then pull them on. Naturally, they're the best thing I've ever worn on my body. Rich people probably don't know the horror of department-store underwear that somehow manages to be both saggy and too-tight at the same time.

I chew on a mouthful of grapes while I get changed into the slick suit, careful to not get anything on the lustrous material. Amazingly, even though the suit isn't finished, it fits remarkably well. I pull on black socks and an off-puttingly shiny pair of dress-shoes before heading out to where Joanna is sipping her own glass of champagne and chatting with Giovanni.

When they hear me approaching, they stop their conversation and look over.

Joanna's mouth drops open a little. "Wow. Okay. Well … you're … uh, yeah, you sure are wearing that suit. Wow."

Giovanni urges me onto the podium, and then walks around to check the fit. "Hmmm. Meraviglioso. You were right in your predictions, Cara. This is almost perfetto. Your superpower strikes again."

I glance over. "Superpower?"

Joanna smiles. "Yeah, apart from choosing the wrong guys, my other superpower is equating regular people with their celebrity body-doubles."

I try to stay still as Giovanni walks around, so he can pin cuffs and hems. "Really? Who's mine?"

"Chris Hemsworth. Similar height and build. But *Heart of the Sea* Hemsworth rather than larger-than-a-house Thor."

The look on my face must give away my disbelief, because she then says, "No, really. Giovanni made Chris's suit for the premiere of the Moby Dick film and then used that pattern to make this suit. You two could be brothers if he chose to forgo grooming for a few months."

I glance at my reflection. My shaggy hair and too-long beard definitely makes me look like *Heart of the Sea* Hemsworth. The overgrown image doesn't really gel with the sharp suit.

As if sensing my thoughts, Giovanni steps back and looks at me in the mirror. "This one will be very handsome with a haircut and shave, no?"

Joanna looks at me in a way that gives me shivers. "Oh, I don't know. The mountain-man look works on him." Our gazes meet, and for the few seconds her eyes are locked onto mine, my chest is too tight to breathe. She seems affected in a similar way but breaks away first and comes over to stand behind me.

"How long will it take to finish the suit, Giovanni?"

He tugs down the bottom of the jacket and checks the alignment of the pockets. "A few days, but it's looking so good, we won't even need a second fitting. Give me a few minutes to talk with my head seamstress, and then we'll discuss delivery."

He talks to Fabian in Italian as they leave the room, and now it's just me and Joanna. An awkward silence expands within seconds to fill the room.

I try to slide my hands into the pants pockets, but they're sewn up, so instead, I drop my arms down and try to act relaxed.

Joanna lets out a short laugh. "Smooth."

A nod. "Yeah, I know. They begged me to be the next James Bond, but I just didn't have the time."

She laughs again, and I don't think I've ever found laughter so damned attractive.

"Pity. You would have been great." She tilts her head. "And yet when we talked about the launch last night, you seemed nervous. Surely double-O smooth guy isn't concerned about making a good impression, because in this, you absolutely will."

"Me, nervous? Nah." Of course, I'm lying. That type of high-profile, super-elegant event is something with which I have zero experience. Add to that Max wanting me to make a speech, and I'm about ready to piss myself with nerves.

"You have nothing to be worried about. Plus, with how you look in this suit, you could freeze up completely and just stand there, and no one is going to mind. I can't believe how perfect it is on you."

Joanna circles me and runs her hands over the planes of the suit. I know she's only testing the fit, but with how it affects me, I might as well be naked. When she gets back around the front, she steps close and fingers the lapels, and I clench my fists and tense my jaw to stop myself from touching her.

"As much as I'd like to stand there and look good, I think Max is going to require me to be a little more hands-on. I never considered he'd want me to present the app, until he told me last night. I'm not mentally prepared to screw up in front of a large, high-profile crowd."

She gives me a gentle smile. "You won't screw up. Like Eden said, I'm happy to coach you." She stills her hand on my chest and looks up at me with her ice-blue stare. "I always use that old piece of advice when I'm speaking in front of a big crowd - just picture everyone naked."

I swallow, unable to stop myself from reveling in having her so close. "No problem there. Way ahead of you."

She looks up sharply, and the tension between us ramps up.

Fuck, Jenner. Friends, friends, friends, idiot. Change the subject.

I clear my throat and look over at the drapes on the other side of the room.

"So," I say, "Do you do this often? Dress up guys in dinner suits that cost as much as a small car?"

She brushes some lint off my shoulder and walks around me once more. "Hardly ever, which is sad, because I do like dressing up my friends."

Friends. It feels even worse coming from her than it does from me. I'm astounded that it only took one night to feel like we were soul mates, but I predict it will be a thousand years before I'm comfortable calling us 'friends'.

"Especially ..." she smoothes down the sleeve, and goosebumps prickle up my spine. "... when my friends look this good in couture dinner wear."

She stands in front of me and checks the line of the shoulders. She's close and smells amazing. I stare at the top of her head and hope to God she can't sense how insane she's driving me by doing absolutely nothing but being nearby.

"I wouldn't know about looking good," I say, white knuckling my breathing, so my voice doesn't sound weird. "This is my first time in a monkey suit. It's a new and strange experience."

She looks up at me. "You're kidding. You didn't go to prom in high school? Junior or senior?"

"Nope. Junior year my friends and I chose to have an epic, day-long Dungeons and Dragons game rather than go to the dance and get rejected by girls and beat up by guys, because we were just that cool."

"Of course you were. And senior year? Conscientious objector then as well?"

By then I was a hulking beast and was having positive attention from girls, so avoidance wasn't my primary consideration. But I just wasn't interested in the empty pageantry of a school full of people who ostracized me and most of my friends. I spent the night reading Stephen Hawking's *A Brief History of Time*. Much more interesting.

"Yeah, I just didn't want the hassle. I had better things to do." Joanna stares at me for a few seconds with a quizzical expression, as if she's trying to read between my vague lines. In the end, she walks over to the small table at the side of the mirrors and grabs her champagne. "Well then, we'd better make this launch party a night to remember. You have some ground to make up."

"What about you? I have no doubt you were prom queen, right?" I can't imagine her being anything but a queen in most situations. She has a regal quality that's hard to deny.

"Oh, God no." She sips her drink. "No proms for me. I left school at sixteen. Didn't even graduate. I had better things to do as well. I think the night of my senior prom, I was in Zimbabwe building a school for local orphans, but that's a long story."

I'm about to try and unpack that surreal piece of information when Giovanni and Fabian walk back into the room.

"Okay!" Giovanni claps his hands and grins. "Everything's organized. The suit will be done sometime next week, and Fabian will courier it to you." He turns to me. "What's your home address?"

I'm about to rattle off my old Brooklyn address, when I remember that a nice Pakistani couple now lives there. "Ah ... well ..."

Fabian looks at me, finger poised over his iPad. Giovanni laughs. "Have you forgotten where you live after only a few sips of champagne? That usually happens to me after a bottle of Grappa."

Joanna laughs too, but I don't miss her glancing at me from the corner of her eye.

"Mr. Jenner?" Fabian says with studied patience. "Your home address?"

I step off the podium and nod. "You know what? Can you send it to my work? I'm there most of the time anyway."

"*Pulse?*" Joanna asks, "Or Romance Central? Because at the latter, it could get confused for one of their costumes and go missing."

"Right?" I scratch my eyebrow. "*Pulse*, then? Can you call before it's delivered to make sure I'm there?"

Joanna walks over and taps something into Fabian's tablet. "It's all good. I'm going to be in the area next week for Tim Gunn's birthday party, so I'll grab it and bring it to you. Much easier all 'round."

"Perfetto." Giovanni hands me a glass of champagne, and I sip it gratefully. "Well, that's that." He raises his glass. "Here's to a wonderful event for you both. May you be the most beautiful and stylish couple there."

Joanna chokes a little on her drink at the word couple. Then she glances at me and raises her glass in return. "Uh ... thanks, Giovanni. You're the best."

I take another mouthful, not sure why I get such savage satisfaction from her not correcting him about the couple thing. It's just another reason I need to step up my efforts to detach from my feelings for her. I understand that we need to work together on this event, but being this attracted to her is only going to end in disaster. Not to mention the fact that seeing her in an evening gown might actually kill me.

Her phone beeps, and she puts down her glass before checking the screen. She frowns and softly says, "Dammit. Not now."

"Everything okay."

She looks over and tries to act casual. "Oh, yeah. Fine. Just a minor inconvenience at my apartment."

She grabs her purse off the couch and shoves her phone into it. "Sorry, Giovanni, gotta run. I'll see you next week, okay?"

"Fine, cara. Ciao for now."

She kisses him on the cheek before coming over to me. "I'll give you a call tomorrow to talk coaching times, okay?"

"Sure. No problem."

She moves toward me as if going for my cheek, too, but then catches herself. She laughs and steps back. "Crap. Uh … okay." She pats my arm. "Bye."

I watch as she strides out. As soon as she disappears, the room gets about five shades darker.

I hear a chuckle from behind me and turn to see Giovanni smiling.

"She's an amazing woman, no? I can see why you're smitten."

I make a scoffing sound. "I'm not smitten. We're just …" Here come the F-word again. "… friends."

"Uh huh." Giovanni looks like he could teach a class on the definition of skepticism. "Of course you are, young man." He gestures to Fabian, who retrieves a mirrored tray from a nearby cupboard and proceeds to collect all of our used glasses.

"We are," I say, more confidently than I feel.

Giovanni gestures to the suit jacket, so I remove it and hand it to him. "One thing I've learned in my years of knowing Joanna, is that she has surprisingly few friends. She knows many people, but she trusts only a handful of them, and lets even fewer into her heart. The way she is with you is … different. It reminds me of something from long ago."

"And what's that?" I ask.

He smiles. "How my wife and I behaved when we were falling in love nearly sixty years ago." He folds the jacket over his arm and gives me a small nod. "But of course, I wish you luck on your blossoming 'friendship'."

9

CRIME CLOSET

"Jenner, this is the FBI cyber-crime division! Come out with your pants up and your hands where I can see them!"

The door to the small supply closet cracks open, and Eden's grinning face appears. "Had you going that time, didn't I? My intimidating G-man voice filled your bladder with pee-tickling fear, right?"

Sitting uncomfortably on an upside-down milk crate, I nod before directing my attention back to my laptop screen.

"Yes, indeed. Out of the three times you've done that in the past hour, that was by far the scariest. I may be wearing Nikes, but rest assured, if they were boots, I'd be quaking in them."

"Excellent." She comes inside and sits on a matching milk crate beside me. We're squeezed inside the janitorial closet at *Pulse*. It's small and smells strongly of lemon-scented disinfectant, but it's away from prying eyes and the disapproving glares of our boss.

"Has Derek started looking for me yet?" I ask, tapping some keys.

Eden shrugs. "He did a quick drive-by about ten minutes ago, but I told him you were nearly finished with your article, and he seemed only mildly pissed."

"Not terrible." I've actually finished writing my article but just wanted one more editorial pass before handing it in. Like the rest of my life right now, it seems to be missing something, and I'm going to need to add at least ten percent more awesome if it's to be approved by Derek's critical red pen.

"Any progress on cracking the lawyer's email yet?"

"Nope, but Crest Construction is well-practiced in covering their tracks. Finding dirt for this article of yours might take a while."

"The whistleblower I met with the other day swore that Marcus Crest's personal lawyer is the weak link in the chain of corruption but couldn't give me any evidence."

"Yeah, word is Crest has been bribing people in city council and planning offices for decades. Ordinances that protect historical buildings or even limit heights of buildings are somehow irrelevant if Crest wants to knock something down or put something up. There's an area in SoHo where the height restriction is supposed to be eight stories, and yet he built a thirty-story building with not a single fine or any kind of push back from the city."

"Exactly," Eden says. "So, if we can find just one loose thread in his well-knit sweater of lies, we can unravel the entire, shitty mess. That's why getting into this email account is so important."

"Yeah, like hacking most email accounts, that's easier said than done, but I'm making progress. Even if it's at the pace of an arthritic sloth."

Eden sighs and looks around the small room. "Do you think it would help if you weren't in this coffin-sized closet?"

"How dare you? This is my impenetrable crime-closet. If you're suggesting I do crime out in the open like some sort of petty hedge-fund manager, I'm offended."

"So, the closet protects you from getting caught cyber-criming?"

I laugh. "Not at all. But the packet filters on my DMZ have more layers than the atmosphere, so law enforcement has about as much chance of finding me as Jimmy Hoffa. We're safe for now."

Eden stretches out her legs and crosses her arms. "You know, TV shows always show people hacking into government facilities in three seconds flat, but you've been at this for nearly an hour and a half, so I can only conclude that either Hollywood is a filthy liar, or you're a terrible hacker."

"Well, considering I'm a kickass hacker, that must mean …"

She feigns shock and puts a hand over her heart. "Tobias, are you implying that Hollywood has deceived us, because hacking is a tedious and laborious process that would bore most people out of their pants if it were represented realistically? I can't believe it!"

I smile. "Shocking, I know." I hit a series of keys. "On the upside, I might actually crack it in the next few minutes, so if you wanted to hum some sort of *Mission Impossible*-style theme music, I'd be cool with it."

"Ooh!" Eden claps. "On it." While humming something that sounds like James Bond and Ethan Hunt had a particularly out-of-tune lovechild, she leans over to watch what I'm doing. After a few tense seconds, we both jump a little when the door slams open to reveal Raj standing there.

"Aha! Caught you!" When he registers that we're sitting down, his face drops. "Wait, you two aren't in here boning? Aw, man. I was sure there was nastiness going on."

"Raj," Eden says, "I'm dating Max."

"I know." He pulls a packet of Jellybeans out of his pants pocket. "Doesn't mean you can't do the genital tango with this tall drink of water."

I frown at him. "Yes, it does. We're best friends."

He shrugs. "If you say so, but I believe platonic friendships between guys and girls are a myth. Also, a waste. So, what are you two doing in here then, if not getting your sex on?"

"None of your business."

"Well, it is my business when you come into my troll closet and bogart it for the whole morning."

"Your what?"

"My troll closet. I come in here when I want to post smack-talk on gaming message boards and make tweenagers cry."

"Of course you do. Did you finish updating the anti-virus software on all the office computers?"

"Yep, and almost done with the new security protocols and cloud verification codes. Want me to start on the SQL fixes on the HEA app?"

"Yeah, and run those line-by-line code checks I talked to you about, too."

"Okey dokey." He offers the bag in his hand to us. "Jellybean?"

We each take one and pop it in our mouths as Raj waves and closes the door.

"He's so weird," Eden says as she chews.

"Yeah, but he's a decent tech and pretty reliable. Those types usually come with 'weird' in their hardware."

We're silent for a few seconds while I keep working, and then Eden says, "Soooo, seen Joanna recently?"

Here we go again.

"You know I haven't since the tux fitting last week. Stop it."

"What? I was just asking a question."

"No, you weren't. You were fishing. By the way, I'm super glad Joanna told you about our compatibility fiasco. So cool." Even though I'm used to keeping stuff from Eden, Jo apparently isn't, and now I'm paying the price.

"I know, right?" She pulls out her phone. "I still can't believe that whole crazy story about her being Liza and you thinking you were soul mates and then the whole seven percent thing crushing your tiny romantic butterfly dreams. I mean, it's like a fairytale, but in reverse."

"Don't remind me."

She puts a hand on my arm. "Tobes …" When I look at her, she tilts her head. "I'm just giving you crap, but seriously … do you want to talk about it? Are you okay?"

I both love and hate her concern. I'm touched that she cares, but the last thing I want to do right now is get lost in my conflicted feelings about Joanna. It's hard enough keeping them locked up in a box labeled 'friendship'. Opening it and trying to figure out the exact shape of what's inside would be a bridge too far right now.

"No, I don't want to talk about it, and yes, I'm okay. It was one night, Eden. A flirtation that didn't go anywhere. It's happened to me a million times and will no doubt happen a million more. Now, do you want to keep wasting time, or do you want me to finish cracking this email account wide open?"

"Okay, fine. But if you ever want to talk, you know I'm here for you."

"I know. Even when I don't want to talk, you're here for me."

"Damn straight."

"Okay, just a few more seconds and …" My screen floods with code. "Ahhhh."

Eden's gives me a smattering of light applause.

"And now for the inevitable question," I say with a smug grin. "Who 'da man?"

Eden puts her arm around my shoulders and leans in to examine the screen. "Oh, my very fine, tall, hairy friend … you are most definitely 'da man.'"

We're silent as I flick through to the inbox, and we scan a few pages of content, but it's not long before our triumphant mood sours.

"Toby, please tell me that there's something here. A smoking gun. One little, 'Hey, can you believe this incredible crime we just pulled off? Let me describe it in minute detail' email. I can't hit another dead end with this story. Every time I feel like I'm getting close to something big, it slips out of my hands."

"I've said it before, and I'll say it again, Crest Construction has been running criminal activity for decades. They're good at it. They know how to cover their tracks, and they know where they're vulnerable."

"Then how the hell am I going to get the story on these corrupt assholes?"

"Eden, why do you think blowing the lid on Crest Construction is every investigative journalist's white whale? If it were easy, it would have already happened."

I hit a few keys and copy the entire contents of the email account to an external server. Then I install a few sneaky lines of code that will allow us to monitor future communications. If he's diligent about updating his malware software, the code will be detected within a week, but that may be all the time we need.

"Okay, that's all we can do for now. I'll keep looking in my spare time." What little there is of it. "But I've got to switch back to working on the app for a few days. I want everything to be perfect for the launch."

"Good call." Eden stands. "I'll go through that list you gave me of disgruntled ex-Crest staff to see if there's someone I can shake down. You never know. Someone might be sitting on a goldmine of bitterness that will inspire them to help us."

"Sounds good." Bitter people are nearly always highly motivated to wreak revenge on those who have wronged them. Not that I know from personal experience, or anything. But there was that one time in chem lab when I swapped out the chemicals of one of the assholes who used to beat me up. When he bent over to pour in the mixture, the resulting explosive reaction burnt off both of his eyebrows. I was called into the principal's office over that one. Apparently, 'spite' wasn't an appropriate response when he asked what on earth had motivated me.

Eden taps something into her phone and leans on the door. "Max just texted and said to remind you about the launch meeting next week at his place. Apparently, you forgot to RSVP to the group invite."

"Shit. Sorry. Just … a lot happening right now." I bring up a different tab and flick the RSVP button that says, "I'll be there." Well, my body may be there, but my spirit will probably be floating face-down in the river. Fuck me, I'm exhausted.

"Toby?"

I look up at Eden, and I've been staring at this screen for so long, even blinking hurts.

"I know I ask this at least once a day, but … are you okay?"

I'm not. I know I'm not, and I know she knows I'm not, but I can't fucking say that. I just can't. That would require honesty. Admission of the violent vortex of crap my life has become. It would take me accepting that I can't handle everything on my own and need help, and as much as I should say those words to Eden of all people, I just fucking can't.

Instead, I say, "I'm totally okay, Tate," with just enough glibness to pull it off. "But thanks for your concern. If I even need an Eden-shaped parachute to catch me, you're the first Eden I'll call."

I go back to my screen and tap out a well-practiced piece of code.

"Okay," she opens the door. "I'm going to meet Max, so I'll catch up with you tomorrow."

"Yep. All good."

After she closes the door, I keep working. Fixing app issues, refining my *Pulse* article, and when all that is done, I work on hacking into Dad's health insurance company, so I can finagle their premium calculator and make the policy a little more affordable. Illegal? Yes. Justified? Fuck yes. These assholes rip off millions of people every year. I'm just evening the score a little.

By the time I'm done, it's nearly 2am. I exit from the crime closet to find the *Pulse* offices dark and deserted. With a deep sigh, I pack up my stuff and ride the few stops down the line to the Romance Central offices at Greenpoint.

Yawning, I let myself into the dark building and head straight to the couch. I've barely sat down before my head is swimming, desperate to sleep.

But the thing about being this overworked is that my brain never switches off. No matter how utterly exhausted I am, the moment I lie down and close my eyes, I start obsessing over all the things I didn't get done and make mental lists of everything I have to catch up the next day. I might doze here and there, but mostly I toss and turn, worrying about the river of crap rising steadily around me. My grandma used to have a saying for when I was feeling overwhelmed. She'd say, "If it feels like you're going through hell, then for God's sake, don't stop to take in the view. The only way to deal with that shit is to keep going, until you come out the other side."

Man, I miss her.

I'm not sure when I might reach the other side, but for now, I'd settle for a solid few hours of dreamless sleep to make the trip more bearable.

10

HIGHLAND FLING

There's a state between unconsciousness and being fully awake that's called lucid dreaming. When you're in it, you're aware that you're in a world of your own making and can therefore make things happen.

I first discovered it when I was a kid. Whenever I'd come home from a tough day at school and was particularly drained, I'd curl up on our old green velvet couch and create semi-conscious adventures. For some reason, it only worked on the couch, never my bed, and so I took to calling these incidents 'couch-trips.' I could make myself fly or make items bigger or smaller. I could even change the scenery or storyline and make people act how I wanted. It was thrilling.

All these years later, it's interesting to note that I'm lucid dreaming again, this time on the couch at Romance Central. Never fully asleep, and not quite awake, I float in these worlds I create where I have God-like powers and total control. You don't have to be a genius to figure out it's probably triggered by the lack of control I have in real life right now. Even so, it gives me some release from my ever-present anxiety.

So far tonight, I've magically cured all of Dad's ailments and bought a Broadway theatre, so I can give my sister the lead in a new play. I've showered Mom with money, so she doesn't have to work so hard, and I've bought myself an apartment that overlooks Central Park. If only reality were so easy to manipulate.

Now, I'm on a beach, watching a sunset, and from the corner of my eye, I see movement. When I turn, Joanna is there, beautiful and radiant, smiling at me.

"You're perfect," I say.

"Not for you." She holds up her phone to show me the bastard seven percent rating. "For you, I'm perfectly wrong."

"Not here." I wave my hand like an especially hairy Jesus. "Check your phone again."

She looks in awe as the seven morphs into one-hundred and ten percent. "How ... how is this possible?"

"That's how right you feel, whether or not it's statistically true."

She steps into me and places her hands on my chest, and I sigh in relief as I finally get to wrap my arms around her.

"Here, we're perfect."

She pushes up onto her toes to kiss me, and it's just as earth shattering as the night we first met. I pull her closer and groan as we both give in to our passion, hands grasping and mouths shifting to taste more.

"Toby ... God ... yes ..."

Everything in me is aching for her. Every muscle is trembling, tight and hard.

"Toby, undress me. Please ..."

A very small voice whispers to stop this. We're friends, and friends don't see each other naked, but she starts kissing my neck, and then I can't do anything but get rid of the fabric that's keeping us apart.

When my hands find her, we both moan.

"Jo ... you feel amazing."

There's a buzzing near my head, and I make a vague swatting gesture before going back to kissing her.

The beach has transformed into a bedroom, draped in white fabric. I lie her on the bed and kiss every inch of her body, slowly and with purpose. Tasting, licking, sucking ...

The buzzing happens again.

"Fuggoff," I mutter and swat again. "G'way." How the hell did a bug get in here anyway? Little wily bastard. It's my dream, and it doesn't have permission to ruin it.

I try to block out the noise, but already the blissful illusion is melting away. Joanna turns to smoke beneath my hands, and I wake up to find I've drooled on the arm I'm using as a pillow,

With a grunt I push myself up off the couch and look around blearily. It takes me a moment to realize that the buzzing is coming from my phone vibrating on the coffee table next to the sofa. I watch as it does a little dance on the dark wood and frown, still pissed about being woken up.

"What kind of asshole calls at this hour on a Sunday?" I grab the phone to check the screen.

It's then I realize it's not a call, but an alarm I set so I wouldn't oversleep. *I'm* the asshole.

"Crap."

I slump back into the couch, hard as a rock and mourning the loss of having Joanna in my arms, even if she wasn't real.

I sigh and rub my eyes. *Maybe I should call her.*

No. Clearly, I'm incapable of having a platonic relationship with her, so I should avoid contact at all costs. My life is complicated enough. I need to put Joanna out of my mind whenever possible, and when she does invade my dreams, I need to retrain my brain to not flood my body with lust. If I see her in a couch trip again, I'll … what? Make her a sandwich? Sure, why not. Seems as good a plan as any.

I drape my arm over my eyes. It feels like I've barely had any sleep, but I have no time to indulge any more. I have a stack of things to do today, and I'll never get everything done before the meeting tomorrow night if I don't start hauling ass.

With a grunt, I push up into a standing position and shamble into the bathroom, where I run the water and wait for it to get warm.

"Ohhhh." The water feels amazing, and I just stand there with my forehead against the tiles for a few minutes before grabbing the soap and lathering up.

The shower washes away most of my fatigue, and by the time I finish up and wrap a towel around my waist, I feel mostly human again.

"Okay, let's get cracking, Jenner. Lots to do." I head into the costume room and go right to the back where my small collection of belongings and clothes are hidden behind storage crates.

I rummage through my duffle bag and frown.

Damn, really? Not a single pair of clean boxer briefs?

Not only that, but I also have zero clean clothes left. I hold what looks to be a slightly soiled T-shirt up to my nose.

"Oh, fuck. Nope."

It seems like I only washed a few days ago, but now that I stop and think about it, I realize it's been nearly two weeks.

"Guess I'm adding laundry to my 'to-do' list for today then."

I stuff everything back into the duffle and hoist it over to the giant washer and dryer in the front corner of the room. At least I don't have to schlep everything down the street to a laundromat.

I shove in everything except my most precious cardigans and start the cycle. The few things that are left out, I place into the laundry tubs with some detergent and leave them to soak.

Estimating I have about forty minutes before the washer's done, so I scour the costume room for something to put on in the meantime.

Dyson and Max are almost the same size as me, so I go over to the racks that bear their names. Max doesn't do much roleplaying these days, so I figure I can use some of his stuff without anyone noticing.

"Alright, what do we have here?" I flick through costumes on the hangers. "Biker dude … navy officer … James Bond … Billionaire playboy … lumberjack … okay, this could work." After dropping my towel, I grab a pair of jeans off the hanger and try to pull them on, but even though I've lost weight recently, my waist measurement is clearly a few inches different from Max's. "Shit." I might squeeze into them, but honestly, I'm not willing to risk zipping them up without the protection of underwear. Time to look for another option.

"Nope, nope, nope," as I'm reaching the end of the rack, I notice something that may fit the bill. "Scottish highlander - let's go." I grab the red plaid kilt and wrap it around my waist. There's a collection of adjustable buckles that take me a minute to figure out, but when I do, I get the thing done up. It sits on my hips pretty well, considering.

"Okay, cool. No underpants is kind of the thing with Scots anyway, so … appropriate."

Feeling mostly covered, I head out to my office and fire up my laptop to get some work done. There are about two hundred minor software fixes that I want to complete today, and the kilt is making me feel strangely empowered to get them all done.

"You may take my undies," I whisper in the world's worst Scottish accent, "but ye'll nevah take mah freedummm!"

I open the interface and attack the error list like a highlander going to war with the English.

The Proclaimers reverberate around the office as I pull my clothes out of the dryer and do my version of folding them, which is basically rolling them into neatish sausage shapes. Then I grab my sleeping bag and pillow, still damp from the washer, and drape them over the small collapsible drying rack. Finally, I rinse and wring out my cardigans, and then lay them flat on one of the tables to dry.

Apart from smashing my laundry, my other work has also gone surprisingly well, so even though I'm nowhere near finished and still have a small Everest of fixes to code, my spirits are high. I'm not much of a dancer, but when Devo's 'Whip It' comes up in the random playlist, I feel inclined to break out all my high school moves. The running man is there. So is the sprinkler. During the chorus I pick up a traffic cone that the actors use in conjunction with the construction worker narrative and put it on my head for ... you know ... authenticity.

After some white-boy booty shaking, I move into my very best robot, and it's when I'm finishing my impressive moonwalk that I hear someone clear their throat behind me.

"Jesus fucking Christ." I whip around to see Joanna standing in the doorway, wearing an incredulous but amused expression.

"Please," she says, suppressing laughter. "Don't stop on my account. I believe you were in the middle of whipping it. Whipping it real good."

I pull the traffic cone off my head and drop it to the ground with an echoing *thunk*.

"I ... uh ... hey, Joanna. Hi." I awkwardly put a hand on my hip and look down at myself.

Yep. Still in just a kilt and nothing more. For the love of God, do not think about the dream you had about her. Don't you fucking dare.

I look over at Jo.

She tilts her head and gives my exposed body an appraising once-over "So, ripped and whipped? Good to know."

"I ... uh ..." I shake my head, trying to clear the extreme mortification that's clouding my brain. "What are you doing here?"

She holds up a black garment bag with TOM FORD emblazoned across it. "I thought I might just sneak this in and leave it in your office.

Seemed like a safer option than your cubicle at *Pulse.* Max gave me the security code a while ago, so …"

"Oh, okay. Sure. Cool, cool."

"Then when I got in here and heard the music, I followed it thinking it was the janitor, but it wasn't. It was you. Shirtless. Dancing around in a …" She glances down. "… kilt." She sighs. "And here I was thinking today was going to be boring." I blush as her gaze travels up to my chest and then back down to my abs. The way her expression darkens makes every inch of skin burn and tingle.

Feeling more self-conscious by the second, I grab a white T-shirt and pull it on.

When I'm covered up, Joanna comes back to her senses and looks at my face. "So … uh. What are *you* doing here? Apart from polishing up your dance moves in highland garb?"

"Uh … well, I was using the … facilities."

She spies the piles of clean laundry on the table. "You don't have a washing machine in your building?"

"Yes. I mean … no." I'm officially the world's worst liar. "I mean, I do, but it's … on the fritz. So …"

"So, you thought you'd bring your laundry here?" She drapes the garment bag over her arm and walks over to my duffle. "Who's this little guy?" She picks up a small, knitted penguin that was lying beside it.

"That's not mine. It must be a prop for the Romance Central crew."

She turns it around, so I can see it. "But it's wearing a tiny cardigan with *Toby* embroidered on the front."

Goddammit, Grandma, why did you have to personalize Mister Puffin?

I grab it from her and shove him back into the duffle. I may not sleep with him anymore, but having him with me still gives a sense of security.

"Look, thanks for the suit, but I've got a lot of work to do, so …"

"More dancing work? Are you preparing to audition for Thunder from Down Under? Because, honestly, they'd totally go for this look."

"You're funny."

"I think so."

I'm about to escort her out of the room when she stops dead. Her attention is directed at my sleeping bag and pillow on the drying rack. When she turns to me, her brows are pulled down in concern.

"Toby? Are you ... living here?"

I laugh, because for some reason, being so close to her finding out the ball-shriveling truth about my ultimate shame is making me a little hysterical. "What? No. God, no."

"But ..." She gestures to the sleeping bag.

I give her the world's least convincing shrug. "I keep that here, because some nights I can't be bothered to go home. It's no big deal. Lots of busy geniuses sleep in their offices."

"Right. Of course." I take her elbow and lead her out to my office, but I can tell I haven't thrown her off the trail.

"So," I say, taking the suit bag from her and hanging it on the back of my door. "Thanks for bringing this down. You didn't have to do that, but I appreciate it."

"Yeah, no problem." She's looking around the room, maybe trying to sniff out more clues about me living here. Thankfully, I'm well-practiced in making my stays invisible. Unless she finds the boxes of my belongings in the back of the props area, I'm good.

"So ... wait, you stayed here last night but have all of your laundry to do today? When did you grab your laundry if you haven't been home?"

"I ... uh ... I went home early this morning and grabbed it. I've just been too busy to keep track of everything, you know?"

"Sure. Yeah. I guess that's possible." She stares at me for a few seconds, and I feel like she's doing a seismic reading of my soul. "You're the worst liar I've ever met, Toby, do you know that?"

"Well, hey, now ..."

"No, don't bother denying it. It's a compliment that you're such a crappy liar. Assholes lie easily. Good guys don't. Your inability to lie says a lot about you as a person, and I like that."

She pulls out her phone and taps on it. "Now, I don't know about you, but I'm absolutely starving, so I'm going to order some food, and then we're going to have lunch together, okay?"

"Well, it's nearly three ..."

"Have you had lunch already?"

"Actually, no." I cleared out all the snacks in the kitchen earlier, and my stomach is rumbling so badly from hunger, I feel like I'm in a remake of the chest-burster scene from *Alien*.

"Good. I'm ordering Italian. A friend of mine owns a little bistro nearby and can have everything delivered within thirty minutes. Sound good?"

"Sure, but I still have a pile of work to do …"

"Which is why I'm getting it delivered and not dragging you out to the restaurant to eat. Also, because you're clearly not wearing anything under that kilt and New York just isn't ready for a free-swinging Scotsman like yourself."

"Clearly? What does that mean."

She smiles. "It means that while you were dancing, your … uh … haggis was dancing a jig of his own."

Oh, fuck. Good, then.

I put my hands on my hips and drop my head.

She waves off my embarrassment. "Don't worry about it. We're friends, right? And friends sometimes see friends' jiggly bits through their clothes. Look …" She jumps up and down a few times, and yes, my eyes home in on her breasts like the Terminator locking onto Sarah Connor.

When she stops, she laughs at what I'm guessing is my dumbstruck expression.

"Body parts wobble, Toby. It's a part of life."

I rub my face and groan. "Sure. Totally normal." Not only do I have to stop myself from thinking about my self-directed sex-dream earlier, but I now have bouncing boobs to block out.

"Toby …" I look at her, and she smiles. "Chill. We're good." She points to my computer. "Now, you sit and get some work done, and I'll finish folding your laundry while we wait for the food to arrive."

"Ahhh …" I'm not a prude or anything, but I'm not sure how I feel about a woman this attractive getting up-close-and-personal with my underpants. "You don't have to do that."

"I know, but I'd like to do something to help, and honestly, I'm a kick-ass folder. You'll see."

She throws me a smile and then disappears into the costume room. Once she's out of sight, I collapse into my chair and drop my forehead onto the desk.

Well, this day has taken a sudden and embarrassing left turn.

~

AN HOUR AND A HALF LATER, the break room is littered with the remnants of a huge Italian feast, and Joanna and I have worked our way through the entire bottle of red wine her friend sent over with the order.

"I shouldn't be drinking," I say, and then drain the rest of my glass. "I still have a ton of work to get done before I can quit for the day." Am I slurring my words? Surely not. Maybe I'm slurring my hearing instead.

Joanna pours half of what's left in her glass into mine. "That's why you need to drink. A little muscle relaxant will make the work flow better. Alternatively, you could just have the rest of the night off and give yourself a break. Don't take this the wrong way, because you're still a very attractive man, but you're looking more and more like Tom Hanks in *Castaway* at about the time he met Wilson. You need some more time taking care of yourself and less time just trying to survive."

I run my hand through my hair. "Yeah, well, I'll have some me time after the app gets launched." Also, after I raise the money I'm going to need for dad's co-pay and find a way to get myself back into some form of permanent housing. "The end is in sight. Just another couple of weeks to go until this baby is out there in the world, and then I'm going to sleep for a week."

"As your friend, I'm going to hold you to that."

"As a tired person, I'm going to let you."

I take a mouthful of wine, and without meaning to, find myself staring at Joanna. All she's doing is clearing up plates and throwing away take-out containers, but it's crazy how every gesture is absolutely fascinating.

"Tell me something no one else knows about you," I say.

She stops what she's doing and looks at me. "Why?"

"Because we're trying to be friends, and that's something friends do. I barely know anything about you."

She wipes down the table and shoots me a self-conscious glance. "Not much to say. I'm pretty boring."

"I know for a fact that's not true." I don't know if it's my exhaustion, or the wine, or just the fact I really freaking like her that makes me hungry for information, but right now, I'm craving some kind of connection.

"You're one of the most fascinating women I've ever met, and I want to know more. You seem perfect, but tell me what I'm not seeing."

She sits back in her chair. "This is a very heavy conversation for a Sunday afternoon."

"You don't have to answer, but I'd really like you to."

She looks around the small breakroom, not really focusing on anything but purposely not looking at me. When she talks again, her voice is quiet, as if it's for my ears only, even though we're the only ones here.

"I ... uh ..." She takes a breath. "I don't like admitting weakness, even to myself. I kind of feel that if I get all self-aware and own up to the things that hold me back, I'll somehow give them power, you know?"

Wow. Relatable. "Yeah. I absolutely know."

"So, I just ... play-act. I pretend I don't get scared or anxious, or lonely. And if I pretend hard enough, it feels real. At least for a time."

Hmmm, could it be that we're actually the same person?

"You don't have anyone you ever open up to?" I ask.

"Not really. I don't find it easy to make friends."

"That can't be true."

She crosses her legs. "In high school, I didn't have a single female friend. I had a couple of male friends, but they weren't really interested in me as a person. Until I met Asha and Eden, I felt like I'd never have normal friends."

"But you seem to know everybody. Tom Ford. Anna Wintour. Giovanni. The guy with the restaurant. Are they not your friends?"

"I'm really good at networking, and sure, I have a ton of acquaintances, but there aren't many I truly connect with on a deep, emotional level. That's why I value people like Asha and Eden. And now you."

I stretch my legs out in front of me. "You're still confident that we can make the friendship thing work, even after that kiss we shared?"

Okay, I wasn't planning to say that, but the wine is making me more honest than usual.

She tucks a piece of hair behind her ear, and I swear, I see color on her cheeks. "I'm not going to lie. That was one hell of a kiss. But we know that friends is all we can be, right? Our score made that very clear. And I'd rather have you in my life as a friend than not in my life at all. So we need to make it work. I think I can handle that. Can you?"

After my dream this morning, I'm not so sure. But I want to, so I nod. "I think so. It might take a while, but I'm a pretty determined guy."

"Forgive my skepticism, but guys have said that to me before, and it's never been true."

"Look into my eyes. Tell me I'm lying."

She leans forward and makes eye contact, and for the long, tense seconds that we gaze at each other, several lifetimes play out in my imagination, and in at least one, we end up the best of friends. Alas, the others involve large doses of extremely hot intimacy and sexual positions I didn't realize I knew, but I chalk that up to her being incredibly attractive, and me being only human.

"So, now it's your turn," she says, swallowing hard and leaning back. "Tell me something about yourself you haven't told anyone else.

My throat closes up. How can I possibly tell this woman about my clusterfuck of a life? How could she look at me with anything but disdain and pity?

"Ah … huh." I grab our now-empty glasses and take them over to sink to rinse them out.

"Toby …"

"Yeah, I don't think that I …"

"Did you murder someone?"

Only my self-respect. "No, but I really need to get back to work. Maybe we can pick this up another time."

She gets up and stands in front of me, and when I put down the glasses, she takes my hands.

"There's no time like the present. And I can guarantee that you can trust me to keep your secret, no matter what it is."

I sigh and drop my head. "I can't believe I'm actually thinking of unburdening myself to you. I haven't told Eden this stuff. Hell, I haven't even told my family. I'm so fucking embarrassed, I can hardly look at myself in the mirror."

"I promise, you'll get no judgement from me."

I take a breath and let it out in a rush. Then I stare at my hands as I crack my knuckles. "I'm homeless, Joanna. You caught me today, and I lied because it's fucking mortifying."

She takes a moment, but her expression doesn't change. "How did it happen?"

"It's a long story, but the short version is my family needs money, and so everything I earn goes to them. I fell behind on my rent, and …" I shrug. "It happened so fast, I didn't have a chance to process it all before it was too late. I'm trying to catch up, but without a major change in my circumstances, I can't see how to get ahead."

"But you're a genius. Surely you can find a way to get money."

"Sure. I could take my paycheck to Atlantic City for the weekend and count cards to win some cash. But I like both of my kneecaps, and as soon as any casino figured out what I was doing, they'd break all of my bones. I'm earning a little extra on the side doing freelance tech work, but I'm so fucking busy already with two jobs, there's only so much I can take on within a reasonable time frame."

"Well, this is perfect! I have some tech work you can do, and I pay pretty well."

"No offense but getting pity work from you is the last thing I want. I'm not a charity case."

She seems offended. "It wouldn't be charity. I really do need some work done."

"And yet you didn't mention it to me before you knew about my situation. You said this wouldn't change anything."

"It doesn't."

"Then let's drop the subject, okay?" I throw the last of the trash away. "I have to get back to work anyway. No rest for the wicked, and all that."

I leave the break room and head back to my desk. I try to ignore the sick feeling squirming around in my stomach, but it only grows worse.

I shouldn't have told her. I thought sharing might have made me feel better, but it only made it worse.

I drop down into my chair and open my laptop, determined to ignore whatever-the-hell shame-spiral I'm currently falling into and try to work through it.

"Toby ..."

I glance up to find Joanna's at the door to my office. It's clear she wants to continue the conversation, but I'm done.

"Jo ... thanks for lunch and everything, and for picking up my suit, but I really need to get back to work now."

"I just ..."

"Joanna, please." I say it more emphatically than I intend, and she seems chastened by my tone. Still, I make matters worse by snapping. "I don't need your pity, okay? I'll sort everything out. Now if you don't mind, I need to finish up here."

I get to work, and even though I can sense her lingering, I keep my eyes firmly on the screen.

"Okay, Toby. I'll see you later."

"Yep. See you."

I keep working as I listen to her footsteps, and it's not until I hear the front door close behind her that I release the tension in my jaw.

11

SAVIOUR

Yet again, it's after midnight when I finally drag my sandpaper-covered eyeballs away from the laptop screen and stumble out of my office.

After grabbing my toiletries bag, I head into the bathroom to brush my teeth, and then spread out my freshly washed sleeping bag and pathetically limp pillow on the couch.

Grateful to be sleeping in my undies and favorite tee, I slump down onto the couch and shove my pillow under my head. Sure, trying to squeeze my 6'5" frame onto the equivalent of a single bed is a challenge, but it could be worse. I may be homeless, but I'm not unhoused, so I still need to thank my lucky stars I have a safe, dry place to crash.

I turn over and pull the sleeping bag with me.

I still feel sick about admitting my secret to Joanna. Everyone has pride, I understand that, but I didn't realize until today how much mine controls my state of mind. My limbs feel like blood is racing through them faster than usual, and when I hold my hand in front of me, it's trembling.

I take a few deep breaths to try to calm myself, but it's like all my organs are vibrating, making me nauseated and dizzy.

You should have kept your mouth shut, idiot.

I hate that as a guy, I'm so unused to sharing my failings with another human being that this is what it reduces me to. Why the hell is it normal for women to unload all their baggage on a regular basis, but guys are trained to just bottle everything up and hope it goes away? It's not fucking healthy, and it's sure not helpful.

I constantly hear guys being told to man-up, but that just seems to imply you shouldn't admit you're struggling, even when you are. A large portion of society thinks that strength lies in being emotionally illiterate and psychologically shutdown.

That's not strength, for fuck's sake. It's major dysfunction.

I roll over to the other side and stare out at the darkened office, while attempting to slow my breathing.

If I were really strong, I would have admitted my problems way before this. Eden would bend over backwards to help me, but I've shut her out every step of the way. Max would, too, in a heartbeat, but for some reason telling him would be even harder. Hell, even Derek would probably step in if I bothered to reach out to him. But no. That's too fucking easy. Just let me torture myself into a constant state of anxiety by keeping the storm inside me instead of letting it pass.

I close my eyes and keep breathing, and after what seems like hours, I feel my heartrate drop and my anxiety with it.

I drift in and out for a while, but I must be deeper than I think because I groan when a ringtone invades my sleep-brain. The chiming sound is light but insistent, and even when I try to ignore it, I can't.

After a few seconds, a jolt of panic hits me, because it's the middle of the night, and the only reason I'd be getting a call at this time is for an emergency. My first thought goes to Dad. There are a million things that could go wrong for him right now, and in a second, I'm sitting upright and checking the screen.

I'm only slightly relieved when I see it's Joanna calling.

I check the time. *2.45am? Jesus. Why would she call at this hour?*

"Hello?" My voice sounds as tired as I feel.

"Toby?" Her tone sets me on edge. It's quiet and frightened and sounds like she's been crying.

"Jo … what's wrong?"

"I'm so sorry for calling. I know you were probably asleep, I just …" She takes in a shaky breath. "I just didn't know who else to call."

"It's okay." Instinctively, I pull on my jeans and go in search of my shoes and socks. "What's going on."

"Um … can you come to my place? I have a … situation."

"What kind of situation?"

"It will be easier to explain when you get here. Bring your laptop, okay? I'll send you the address."

"Jo ... are you okay?"

"I will be. Just ... get here as soon as you can."

"I'm leaving now." As quickly as possible, I pack up my sleep stuff and shove it back into my hiding spot, then I pull on a cardy and a coat, shove my laptop into my bag, and head out into the street. My phone vibrates with a pin of Joanna's address as I start jogging toward the subway station.

By the time I get to the towering edifice of glass that Joanna calls home, I'm puffing from running all the way from the subway station. I punch in the code she gave me and hightail it to the elevators, where I use the code again to get to the penthouse. As worried as I am about Joanna, I still have enough wherewithal to notice how incredibly high-end this building is. I mean, she never seemed like she was wanting for cash, but this is next-level luxe. I know this area of Manhattan well, because it's somewhere I'd never be able to afford to live in my wildest dreams.

As I watch the elevator numbers rise, I wonder if Joanna has a rich daddy somewhere that pays for this place. Then I feel bad that I know absolutely nothing about her parents or family. Of course, she also knows very little about mine. For new friends, we suck at swapping information.

The elevator doors open, and I'm surprised to see a set of glass security doors separating me from the grand wooden front entrance to the penthouse.

"Okay. This is weird."

I notice there's a bag of what looks like Indian food next to the elevator, and I'm startled when there's movement near the front door. I squint and make out that Joanna's huddled on the floor beside the wall. When she realizes I'm here, she scrambles to her feet and comes over to the glass door. She's just in a tiny pair of pajamas, and her face is red from crying.

"Toby! Thank God. Thank you so much for coming." There's a hint of hysteria in her voice that I hate.

"Hey, don't worry about it. What's going on? Are you okay?"

She half laughs, half sobs. "I've been better. Did you bring your computer?"

"Of course." I pull it out of my bag and sit on the floor, so I can open it in my lap. "What do you need?"

She sits opposite me and presses her phone to the glass, so I can read what's on the screen. "Log into this network with this password." When I do as she asks, I'm suddenly in an AI portal that's more advanced than anything I've ever seen.

I look up her. "What the hell am I looking at?"

She wipes a hand over her face and sighs. "The guy I used to live with was an amazing AI engineer, and he designed this whole place to be run with smart technology. That was all well and good when he was around, because he could fix glitches whenever they'd come up. But he's been missing now for nearly a year, and everything is falling apart."

"Missing?"

"It's a long story. He's either been recruited by our government and is slaving away in a lab somewhere, or the Russians got to him, and he's in Moscow sipping Vodka and borscht. The odds are about even. I got a message from him about six months ago saying he was safe and well, but who knows if that was really from him. Anyway, he's gone and now, everything's gone to hell." With a shaking hand, she points to the bag of food near the elevator. "I came out to grab my contactless food delivery nearly two hours ago, and the damn AI locked me out of the house. None of my usual troubleshooting worked, and the only thing I could think of was to call you." She still has tears in her eyes. "Please … get me the hell out of here."

I can see she's visibly shaking. Damn, the poor thing is really freaking out. I scan through the complex pages of code and thousands of commands. "Just keep breathing, okay? I'll do everything I can, but I'm not super familiar with the intricacies of AI, so this might take a minute."

She makes a sound like a whimper. "No problem."

Dammit. I hate that she's this shaken up. "Why didn't you just turn it off?"

"That was the first thing I tried. It just keeps turning itself back on. The kill-switch stopped working months ago. I also tried limiting the systems it has access to, but it just overrode my instructions and went back to doing whatever it wanted."

"Joanna, I can hear you." A crisp British voice echoes through the vestibule.

Whoa. It talks. Impressive but creepy.

"Saying such things is rather hurtful."

Joanna glares up at the speaker in the ceiling. "Jeeves, you've had me locked out here for hours, you overgrown remote control. You're lucky I don't pull out your server and kick you right in the microchips."

"As I've already told you, Joanna, your locking mechanism has malfunctioned. The fault is with the door. Not with me."

"And the glass doors?"

"Also malfunctioning. You really should take better care of your operating systems."

"And you should bite my lily-white ass, you hunk of junk. Let me out of here!"

It's clear the situation is taking its toll on Joanna. She's crying again, and I can feel the tension coming off her in waves.

"Hey, it's okay," I say in my most calming voice. "I'm looking for a workaround. You'll be okay."

She wraps her arms around herself. "It doesn't help that it's freezing in here."

"Are you claustrophobic?"

"Oh, you picked up on that? I thought I was doing a good job of hiding it. I mean, I know this isn't a tiny space, but it's the not-being-able-to-get-out that's doing the damage."

She starts to pace like an animal in a cage. "Seeing you is helping, but it's getting hard to breathe."

"Joanna, look at me." She does, and all I want to do is hug her panic away. "I've got you. I'll have you out of there in no time. Just talk to me, okay?"

She keeps pacing but is obviously trying to slow down. "What do you want to talk about?"

"Tell me about your family. That's something I know nothing about."

She sniffles and wipes he nose. "Well, mom was a homemaker who made the best damn apple pies in the world, and dad was a teacher who thought I was the most radiant daughter ever."

"That sounds nice." I scroll through the sub-menus, searching for the control codes for the doors. "Are they here in New York? Do you see them often?"

"Every month or so. They're in the Brooklyn Cemetery.

That stops me dead in my tracks. I look up at her in shock. "Jesus, what? Fuck. I'm so sorry."

She shrugs. "They died in a plane crash when I was fifteen."

"Oh my God. So, who raised you? Grandparents? Aunt or Uncle?"

She shakes he head. "Nope. Just me."

She says it with a light tone, but just thinking of her orphaned and alone punches me square in the heart.

"So, you've been on your own since you were fifteen?"

"Nearly sixteen, but yes."

She seems a little calmer talking about this, even though it's made my anxiety kick into high gear.

"Fuck, Jo. How did you cope?"

"Bit by bit. The beginning was hard, but it got easier every day."

"And this apartment?"

She sits down opposite me. "I worked my ass off. And it turns out I'm really good with money."

"That's … incredible."

She leans closer to the glass. "Toby, I really want to discuss this more with you, but do you think we could do it after you get me out?"

"Shit. Of course. Just a sec."

My mind boggles as I continue to scroll down subroutine after subroutine, until I finally locate the door controls. "Okay. Found something."

"Joanna, what is this man doing?"

"Shut it, Jeeves."

I hit unlock on both doors, and when they slide open, Joanna lets out a squeal of relief.

"Oh my God, yes!"

By the time I get to my feet and grab my bag, the doors are closing again.

"Toby! Hurry!"

I lunge toward the doors, but I'm too late, and they make a quiet hissing noise as they seal shut.

Joanna grunts in frustration as she slaps the glass.

"Jeeves! Stop it!"

"I'm sorry, Joanna, but I didn't lock the doors. As I said before, they're malfunctioning."

This computer fuck is really starting to piss me off.

"I'm going to malfunction your ass in a minute," I mutter. I sit again with my computer on my lap. This time, I'm right in front of the opening, and before I unlock the doors, I remove the AI interface from the subroutine.

"Toby, is it?" Jeeves askes in a smarmy tone. "I wouldn't do that if I were you."

"Yeah? Well, you're not me, sparky, so take several seats while I put you in your place."

"Toby, that's not wise. This apartment isn't designed to function without me. You run the risk of a system-wide meltdown."

"Yeah? That's a risk I'm willing to take. Say goodnight, Jeeves."

With less finesse than I'd like, I delete whole swathes of programming. It's not subtle, but it will remove most systems from the AI's grasp.

"Toby … please stop. You don't know what you're—" The voice slows and fades, and I quickly switch back to the subroutine for the doors.

This time when the glass slides open, it stays open, and Joanna throws herself through them and into my arms. I barely have time to move my computer before she's in my lap, sobbing into my chest.

"Hey …" I wrap my arms around her and rub her arms. "Geez, you're freezing." She's only wearing a mini-tank and tiny sleep shorts, but I can only focus on making sure she's okay. "Come here." I pull her closer and put my coat around her. Even though her sobs lessen, I can still feel how tense she is about being trapped for so long.

"It's okay. You're okay." I rub her back and arms, trying to get her warm.

We sit there for a few minutes, just long enough for her to calm down and absorb some of my body heat. Despite me trying to stay supportive and objective, I become very aware she's nestled into my chest with her head tucked under my chin. She's gripping my T-shirt, and she smells amazing, all citrus shampoo and fruit soap.

It's almost disturbing how comfortable I am holding her like this. It feels both completely new and like I've done it a thousand times before. Without meaning to, my breathing synchronizes with hers, and I melt into her against my will.

"Hmmm." She sounds tired now. Spent and weary. "Toby, have I ever mentioned you smell really good."

I press my cheek to the top of her head. "Yeah? You, too."

I hate how perfect and right she feels in my arms. It should be illegal for women with only seven percent compatibility to feel a thousand percent right. Goddamn my goddamn stupid goddamn app.

Tension creeps into me, and I know I have to let her go before I do something stupid.

"How're you doing?' I ask softly while leaning back to put a respectable distance between us.

She pulls in a hitching breath and looks up at me. "So much better now." Gratitude shines in her expression, making her eyes look even more blue than usual.

My God, she's beautiful.

I have an urge to cup her cheek, but I clench my jaw and resist. God knows how, considering she's looking at me with an intensity that sends a shiver up my spine.

"Uh," she clears her throat. "I should probably just ... uh ... get off you." She climbs out of my lap, and I swear I see color in her cheeks. "Sorry about that. At tonight's performance of *The Neediest Woman on the Planet*, the lead role will be played by me."

I chuckle as she adjusts her clothes, but my eyes nearly bulge out of my head when I notice her nipples are hard.

Fuck, Jenner. Don't look. Do ... not ... look.

Friendfriendsfriendsjustfriends ...

"Uh, here," I take off my jacket and avert my gaze as I drape it around her shoulders. "You should stay warm." *And covered up, so I don't lose my ever-loving mind.*

She puts her arms through the sleeves. "You're my hero tonight, Toby. I don't know what I would have done if you hadn't been here. I've been having trouble with Jeeves for ages, but it's been so much worse recently." The coat's so big on her, that her hands disappear when she lowers her arms.

"Joanna, you have to have that thing uninstalled."

She throws up her hands, and the sleeves whip around. "I've tried. I've had three different AI techs out here working for weeks, and they've all quit out of frustration. Whatever Sergei did when he built Jeeves, he gave it the capacity to program itself. But no one can find how or where that's happening. "

I go pick up my laptop off the floor. "So, it doesn't matter that I've deleted it from the house security system?"

"No." She grabs my bag from near the wall and hands it to me. "By tomorrow morning, it will have regenerated itself and be right back to screwing things up." She gestures to the front door. "Come inside. I'll show you what I mean."

I shove my laptop into my bag and try to keep the awe off my face as I follow her inside the impressive entrance.

"Damn, Joanna. This place is spectacular."

She smiles at me over her shoulder. "I know right. It's my dream apartment."

The generous entrance hall leads out onto a huge open-plan kitchen/dining/and living room, and the whole space is framed with twenty-foot ceilings and enormous picture windows. The furnishings are a mix of modern and vintage pieces, and it's clear Joanna has a thing for velvet and brass. It's stylish without being pretentious, and although it's pristine, it's not cold and uninviting like a lot of modern apartments I've seen.

"Can I get you something to drink? Coffee?" She leads me into the kitchen and gestures to the stools on the other side of the island as she goes to a giant coffee machine.

"Now that Jeeves is out of action for a while, I might be able to get this thing to work."

She puts two mugs under the spouts and hits some button. "Hope you like it white and sweet 'cause that's the only way I know how to make it."

"That's perfect."

The machine makes some light whirring noises, and Joanna turns to me. "Earlier this week, Jeeves turned the coffee on in the middle of the night when there were no cups there. By the time I noticed, there was espresso everywhere. Right after that, he opened the dishwasher while it was still running, so I had a high tide of coffee and suds in my kitchen. Then yesterday, he put the treadmill up to maximum while I was doing my warmup. Damn thing nearly threw me off before I hit the emergency stop button."

She grabs the mugs and passes me one. "If I didn't know better, I'd think Jeeves is having fun by torturing me, but that's not something computers do, right?"

"Not generally, but AI isn't technically a computer, and judging from what I've seen tonight, Jeeves isn't anything like most AIs. He's a little, what's the word? Oh, right - psychopathic."

"Exactly. Getting him under control is the tech work I was talking about earlier today. I wasn't lying about needing someone, Toby."

"I didn't think you were. But Jo, this is hardly my area of expertise."

"I understand, but look what you did tonight. That's more than most of the experts managed after two weeks."

I shrug and sip the coffee. It's actually good, and the caffeine hit is welcome at this hour of the morning.

"So, this Sergei." I look down at the foam on the rim of the mug to make what I'm about to ask seem as casual as possible. "You said he lived here. Was he your … uh … boyfriend?"

Fuck that guy anyway for leaving her with this faulty artificial intelligence, but double fuck him if he disappeared and broke her heart.

She sips her coffee, and it's clear from her expression that he meant something to her.

"I knew it was stupid getting into something with him, especially when we were living together. But one Halloween, he dressed up as Han Solo, and I couldn't help myself." She shrugs. "We were only together for six months before he disappeared."

I look up at her. "Do you miss him?"

She nods. "I don't know if we could have gone the distance, but I miss having him around, especially when something like tonight happens." She puts down her coffee cup. "Let me show you something."

She leads me down a hallway to the left of the living area and opens the first door she comes to. She flicks on a light and leads me inside an enormous, luxurious bedroom that houses the biggest bed I've ever seen.

"Damn, who sleeps here? Shaquille O'Neal?"

"This was Sergei's room."

Man, it's like a geek's paradise. There are cabinets around the walls that contain all sorts of items: a massive Lego Minas Tirith from Lord of the Rings, a mounted display of all the different versions of the Starship Enterprise, an entire cabinet of overtly sexualized female Anime dolls.

Okay, that's creepy, but everything else is as cool as hell.

Joanna goes over to a set of doors on the far wall and opens them.

They concertina out to reveal the most epic multi-computer workstation I've ever seen.

Damn, there must be hundreds of thousands of dollars' worth of equipment here.

"This was where Sergei built Jeeves. If you could do what you did tonight on your laptop, imagine what you'd be able to achieve on this set-up." She wakes up the system and urges me to sit in the ergonomic captain's chair. "This is the heart of Jeeves. Take a look."

I sit down and glance at the information on the multiple screens. There's no doubt Sergei was doing cutting-edge work here. Multiple servers. Automatic migration and assimilation. "This is next level stuff, Jo."

"I know. That's why I need someone who's next level to manage it."

Flicking through all the different behavioral modifiers and predictive algorithms, I can tell Sergei was really going for a person-like entity, not just some dumb machine that was basically a glorified web-browser. And therein lies the problem. An artificial intelligence is encouraged to think and learn like a person, but as we all know, people can be assholes. Sergei unwittingly created something that is now tormenting Joanna.

"The only way to untangle this mess," I say, looking though the contents of the hard drive, "would be to completely uninstall Jeeves and start again, but that could take months. I just don't have the time to take on a project this big."

The writing on the screen becomes blurry, and I rub my eyes. *Crap, I'm tired.*

Joanna leans against the desk. "God, Toby, I'm sorry. It's almost dawn. You need to get some sleep."

"Yeah, I guess I should." I'm already functioning on less hours than is healthy. Getting through my workload today is going to suck. "We can talk more about this later and see if we can come up with a plan, but for now, I'd better get out of your hair and head home."

Weird how easy it is to refer to a couch in an office as 'home'.

I stand and go to exit the room, but Joanna takes my hand and pulls me around to face her.

"Toby ..." She takes my other hand and stands in front of me. "Please don't go."

I frown. "But ... sleep?"

She squeezes my hand. "Why bother going back to the office? I have more rooms here than I know what to do with, and if you come and live here, you'll get to stay rent-free and get paid for preventing Jeeves from ruining my life."

I glance at the giant bed and groan. It's a tempting invitation, but imposter-syndrome sneaks up and smacks me in the forehead.

"Joanna, you need someone more qualified than me to fix this thing."

"But I don't want someone else. I want you." Out of context, those words are highly arousing. In context, less so. "Toby, you're homeless and need money. I'm offering you an apartment plus a job. It's a win/win."

That gets my back up. She may be only speaking truth, but my pride fucking hates hearing it.

"I don't need your pity, Joanna, and I certainly don't need a handout."

She practically scoffs in my face. "That's not what's happening here. Did you not witness what transpired tonight? I was *imprisoned* in my own home, Toby, and you're the one who saved me. I'm doing this for me, not you. I mean, I hate asking for help as much as the next girl, but I know that this situation is something I can't fix by myself. I *need* you, Toby. Call me selfish, but the fact that this helps you too is barely a consideration."

She's acting tough, but I can still see a glimmer of panic that I might say no. When she speaks again, it's softer. "Please, I'm begging you. Live here. Work here. Never let me get locked in that freaking vestibule and have an emotional breakdown again." She looks at me with pleading eyes, and goddammit, why does the universe keep piling more and more blocks of stone around my neck? Even if I agree to this, I'm already stretched in so many directions, I might be unavailable when she needs me most, and that would suck.

"Jo, I think you need someone who can make this, and you, a priority, and that's just not me right now. I'm sorry."

She swallows, and then drops my hand and sighs. "I understand. Honestly, I do." She pushes her hair away from her face. "I don't want to pressure you any more than I already have, so how about this? You sleep here for a few hours just in case Jeeves come back with a vengeance, and then we'll work something out. Try the bed on for size. See how it feels. Most of all, get some rest. You can go back to being overworked and underpaid later if that's what you really want. Deal?"

She holds out her hand, and I give her a smile before enveloping it in mine. "Fine. I'll test drive this bed just to make you happy. You're a tough negotiator, Miss Cassidy."

"Oh, Mr. Jenner, you ain't seen nothing yet."

She gives my hands a squeeze before letting go. The residual tingling is so fierce, I curl my fingers into my palm.

Jo walks to the door and grabs the handle, but then she turns back. "This could be your new home, Tobes, if you want it to be. Of course, you have to make a decision that works for you, but honestly, it already feels like you belong here."

She smiles and closes the door, and I stand there for a few seconds before stripping down to my boxer-briefs and crawling between the sheets of the huge bed.

"Oh, dear God, real sheets and pillows. Sweet satiny Jesus, this feels good."

I see the control panel on the wall and touch it to turn off the lights. I'm not the least bit surprised to find that Sergei has an epic glow-in-the-dark galaxy mural painted on the ceiling.

I put my hands behind my head and sigh. "A guy could get used to this."

For once, my eyes start to drift closed almost immediately. No tossing and turning or trying to squeeze my body onto a tiny couch. No breathing exercises to alleviate my crushing anxiety about my crazy workload.

I just slip peacefully into the sweet, numbing embrace of Lady Sleep, as easy as a baby.

12

BRAND NEW DAY

"Oh, God. Oh, dear God, yessss."

I groan as pleasure floods through me. It's not from porn or treating my body like an amusement park, although I do enjoy both from time to time.

No, the reason for my current full-body pleasure-hit is the multi-turbo-jet shower in Sergei's ensuite. I should have known that after the toilet gave me a full wash-and-dry service, the shower was going to be good, but I wasn't prepared for the unbelievable revelation that is a rich-person shower. No wonder wealthy dudes always look so damn smug.

The pressurized jets spray my body from my ankles to my neck, and they're somehow programmed to hit all my pressure points in the same way a good masseuse would. It's astonishing. I groan again as I make a vow to grow old and die in this shower.

"Ohhhhhh, yeaaaaahhhhh." I finished washing myself a while ago. Now I'm all about savoring these amazing sensations. "Soooo … gooooood."

For the first time in months, I awoke feeling refreshed. The bed had a lot to do with it, sure, but it was deeper than that. Sleeping in a real bedroom again made me feel … safe.

Despite turning Joanna down a few hours ago, on reflection, I'd have to be insane to not make this work. I wouldn't mind being stretched even thinner if I can feel this good each morning.

Even contemplating this sudden change in my circumstances has given me a sense of hope I haven't felt since I was evicted.

It's strange to realize how unmoored I've felt without a private space to call my own. How exposed. The steadily escalating anxiety that's been my constant, asshole companion recently was mostly quieted while I slept, and for once my dreams weren't dominated by blood-curdling visions of all my monstrous responsibilities catching up with me and ripping me limb from limb.

It's like I've been drowning all this time, and now I can finally breathe.

All thanks to Joanna.

And just like everything with her, the solution seemed effortless and with a certain sense of … rightness. I would have settled for a broom closet in a crazy share house, but now I have this palatial geek pad to call my own. I'm so stupidly grateful, I want to hug her and never let go.

That thought leads me to memories of her curled up in my lap last night, all warm and soft and smelling like a delicious fruit smoothie. In a second, the parts of my body that have been well-and-truly neglected for months begin to stir. Somehow, I could never bring myself to indulge in self-love at Romance Central. It just seemed wrong to orgasm in a business setting.

But this is not a business setting. This is a slice of heaven with amazing water pressure.

I grab some soap and lather my hands, but something niggles in the back of my mind.

It's not a good idea to pleasure myself while thinking of Joanna. First, it's hard enough to not have those kinds of thoughts about her without indulging in lustful daydreams. And second, she's in the next room. If I made an unfortunate sound, she might hear, and then I'd have to emigrate to Australia and never see her again.

My brain unhelpfully flashes up images of her last night in her sleep clothes. Tiny shorts that barely grazed her smooth thighs. Tight tank that hugged her perfect breasts in a way that's permanently burned into my retinas.

I shake my head to clear it.

I breathe deeply and will my erection to stand down. There's no way I'm going to make my crush worse with positive reinforcement in the form of orgasming. That's where disaster and madness lie.

After more deep breathing, along with reciting all the decimal places of Pi I can recall, I'm starting to deflate when the shower emits a low beep, signaling the jets are going to move into a new formation.

Good timing, Wonder Shower.

I sigh as I wait for what's coming next.

Unexpectedly, all but the middle jets stop, and I'm a little weirded out when the water starts converging into a single point, seemingly aimed at my genitals.

"Um ... okayyyy." Wary but willing to see what happens, I brace my arms against the wall. "Sergei, you mad bastard-genius - did you somehow manage to make a 'happy ending' shower?"

I mean, Eden has been very forthcoming with how enamored she is with the new turbo-powered-showerhead Max has installed at his place, so I know women have figured out water pressure can be satisfying as hell, but I never considered trying it for myself.

The water jets start gaining pressure, and then, just when I'm trying to figure out what's going on, I'm hit in the ball sack by three super strong shots of water that have the force of rubber bullets.

"Oh ... fuck ... meeeee." I cup myself as pain shoots up into my abdomen and my knees buckle. When I hit the floor, a barrage of short, sharp shots of water assaults my face.

"Motherfucker!" I crawl out of the shower and try to shut it off, but it continues to go haywire, with jets shooting every which way like drunken laser beams.

"What the hell?"

"Good morning, Toby. So nice to see you again."

"Jeeves?"

This freaking AI, man. As I climb to my feet and wrap a towel around my waist, there's a knock on the door.

"Toby? Are you there?"

I pull open the door and find Jo in workout clothes. Not as bad as the tiny jammies, but still ... ridiculously hot.

She gives me a quick once over and clears her throat. "Ah, so ... just a towel. Okay." She blinks and then says, "Jeeves is back."

"Yeah, I figured that out when he turned the shower into a shooting gallery."

"Are you okay?"

"I'll live. Did he do anything to you?"

"He just got the electric weight in the gym to tell me I'm a heifer. No biggie."

"Oh, this prick is going down."

I go over to the server hub and sit, and Joanna follows to stand behind my left shoulder.

"*Toby,*" the robotic douche says in his smoothest voice. "*I had nothing to do with your shower incident. Or with the scale in the gym.*"

"Let me guess," Joanna says. "They were malfunctions?"

"*Why, yes, Joanna. That's correct. Just random, coincidental malfunctions.*"

"You're a malfunction," I mutter, and disconnect Jeeves from a dozen systems.

"*Toby, that's a terrible thing to say. Didn't your mother teach you any manners?*"

"You're bringing my mother into this now, dipshit? Wrong move."

I select every line of code I can find and start deleting.

"*Toby, please,*" Jeeves pleads. "*Let's be reasonable about this.*"

"Reason went out the window the second you decided to assault my tenders, Hal."

It emits a tinny chuckle that makes my skin crawl. Machines shouldn't be able to laugh.

"*You know that I'll have repaired all my systems within a few hours.*"

"Maybe, but that just means I'll be back to delete you all over again."

I sever all the obvious connections, and within seconds, I hear the shower shut off.

"Jeeves?"

There's no answer, and according to the screens, all systems are now functioning normally.

I spin the chair around and look up at Joanna.

"So," I say, adjusting my towel. "Looks like you've got a new roommate. That cool with you?"

She makes a point of looking up at the monitor above my head. "Absolutely! Couldn't be happier!"

"I'll reach out to some hacker friends and see if anyone has a clue of how to hobble Jeeves for good, but in the meantime, I'll write a basic seek-and-destroy scanning program that will run every few hours to keep him under control."

"Fantastic." She's still studying the screen. "I can't tell you how much better I feel knowing you'll be here, protecting me from him."

I glance around at the screen she's watching. "What's going on up there? Something I should know about?"

"Oh, no," she says with a laugh. "I'm just looking up here, because when you adjusted your towel a minute ago, you exposed all of your parts."

I look down and curse when I see myself in all my freshly washed glory.

"Shit." I stand and secure the towel onto my hips. "Sorry."

"No problem." Again, there's color in her cheeks, and even some in her neck and chest.

She looks at my face, but her gaze keeps wandering down to my chest and back up.

"So, anyway." She blows out a sigh. "So thrilled we're roomies. Now, I'm going to shower and have breakfast, and you ..." She checks me out again, and it thrills me just a bit that she seems flustered. "You're going to ... put on some clothes?" She backs up toward the door and points to the huge walk-in closet that's off to the right of the bed. "I don't know if any of Sergei's things would fit you, but you're welcome to them if you like. Of course, all of his stuff is black so ..." She backs into the door jamb and laughs. "Oh, oops." She stops for a second to look at me once more, and then gives a wave. "Okay, bye, roomie!"

"Bye."

After she leaves, I sit back into the chair and smile. It's good to know that I'm not the only one dealing with an inappropriate attraction.

WHEN I GET out to the kitchen, there's a full breakfast banquet laid out on the marble island, and Joanna looks so put-together, she could have stepped out of a fashion magazine.

"Help yourself," she says as she munches on a pastry. "I didn't know what you'd want, so I got everything."

Well, that's a novelty. I'm so used to having nothing, everything is a little overwhelming.

There's a prickle of shame at the back of my mind that even though I was unable to pull myself out of the pit of poverty I'd fallen into, Joanna was able to do it easily. I guess anything is possible when you have money. I just hope our disparity in financial positions doesn't become an issue.

She slides a coffee to me, and I sip it gratefully. Even though I slept well, the quantity of hours was sorely lacking. It might be a while before my sleep patterns go back to normal, but whenever it happens, I'm here for it.

"So …" Jo leans against the counter and wraps both hands around her mug. "Now that you've agreed to live here, do we need to come up with some roommate guidelines?"

I scratch my eyebrow. "Such as?"

"Oh, I don't know. Just stuff to … you know … set up boundaries."

"Do you mean about food and stuff? Because I can buy my own. You don't need to provide for me." Any more than you already are, of course.

"No, I don't mean food." She sips her coffee, and then it hits me what this is about.

"Look, Jo, I honestly didn't know my towel was open. I mean, I'm not one of those guys who believes women like nothing better than looking at random junk. Generally, I like keeping my junk to myself, at least until someone asks permission to have access to it."

She smiles and shakes her head. "This isn't about your junk, Toby, but I'm glad you're not an indiscriminate flasher. I just mean …" She takes a breath. "You and I have shared a certain amount of intimacy. Do we need to lay down any ground rules moving forward, so we don't develop … bad habits?"

From the night we met, I remember her telling me her main bad habit was falling for men who are completely wrong for her.

I cock my head. "Joanna, are you afraid of falling in love with me?"

She screws up her face and makes a noise that I think is supposed to be laugh. "Pfft … no." She looks at me and tries again. "No. No, I'm just …" She puts her mug on the counter and her hands on her hips. "No. Of course not. No." Another weird laugh. "Noooooo. No. Nope."

Wow, and I thought I was a bad liar. Methinks the lady doth protest too much.

"Okay, so, good," she says, pouring the rest of her coffee down the sink. "Glad we cleared that up." She slides a plate across to me. "Another pastry?"

I laugh to myself. "Sure. Why not?"

I'm teeth-deep in an apricot Danish when I hear footsteps on the marble tiles in the foyer, and Gerald, the driver from the day of the tux fitting, walks into the kitchen.

"Good morning, Miss Cassidy."

The moment I hear his voice, I stop dead.

"Morning, Gerald." Joanna hands him a folder and a brown paper bag. "That's the dry cleaning, and those are the contracts for Ari. Oh, and can you drop by the Romance Central offices later to pick up the rest of Toby's belongings?"

"Of course. Nice to see you again, Mister Jenner."

He does a little bow, and I chew and swallow so I can push out a strained, "Hi."

Joanna passes him a large eco-cup of coffee and smiles. "I'll see you at five."

He smiles back. "See you then."

He disappears back into the hallway. When his footsteps have faded, I turn to Joanna.

"Okay, first of all, why does that dude have Jeeves' voice."

"Jeeves has *his* voice. Sergei used to love Gerald's accent, so when he programmed Jeeves, he paid Gerald to provide his voice."

"Okay, fair enough. Now to my second question: why is Tom Ford's driver running errands for you?"

She grimaces. "Because he's not Tom Ford's driver."

I nod in understanding. "He's *your* driver."

"Yes."

"So why did you lie about it?"

"I didn't. You assumed he belonged to Tom. I just chose to not correct you."

"Why not?"

"I don't know. I'm used to fudging details about my life, I guess. Guys can get so weird when they find out I have money. They assume I must have a rich daddy somewhere funding my lifestyle, because obviously there's no way a naive little thing like me could make Wall Street her bitch."

Ouch. Considering that's exactly what I thought, I feel the sting of internalized sexism.

"It sucks you have to do that."

"It really does. I don't think I've dated a single guy in the past few years who knew the real me. I always have to pretend to be less intelligent, less accomplished, less wealthy. I'm always diminishing myself to accommodate some guy's comfort level. I'm so tired of making myself lesser to please other people."

"Then just be yourself."

She gives me a wry smile. "That's the reason I'm still single."

"Well, don't ever feel like you have to diminish yourself for me." I toast her with my coffee cup. "I'm happy to acknowledge your full glory."

"That's fantastic to know, but you're not really my target audience considering we can't date, so ..."

That little truth bomb detonates into a full three seconds of awkward-as-hell silence.

"Right."

She puts down her coffee and clears her throat. "Anyway, before I leave for work, I figured I'd give you a quick tour of the apartment, just so you know where everything is."

"Sounds great. Lead on."

She shows me around with the studied grace of a real estate agent. Apart from her bedroom and mine, there are three other bedrooms in the north wing, as well as a gym, library, and meditation room. Clearly, I need some time in there.

Across the other side of the main living area is a laundry, games room, and home movie theater, and she also shows me practical things like the security protocols and garbage chute.

At the end of the south wing is an atrium that leads out onto a large balcony with a pool, and the view from the outside area is spectacular. I gape at the lush garden, including the full-sized cherry-blossom trees.

"Well, that's everything," she says, leaning against the railing as we look out over the city. "Any questions?"

"Yes. Will you marry me?"

She shoots me a look.

"What?" I say. "People have gotten married for a lot less than an amazing apartment. It would be a marriage of convenience. You get my Jeeves-spanking skills, and I get your stunning penthouse. Seems fair."

"With our compatibility score, even a marriage of convenience might be a tall order. We may very well murder each other."

"No way. I'm more passive aggressive than flat-out violent. I mean, if you piss me off I might leave you an epically terse Post-It, but that's about it."

She smiles. "Wow. Scary. I'll try to never make you mad."

I look at her. "I can't imagine you ever would." Everything she does seems to be for the benefit of others. Still, I can't shake the feeling that there's so much more to her that she's not telling me. "Jo, I just want you know that welcoming me into your home … saving me from sleeping on a couch with the atomic density of lead …" I lean on my elbow so I can face her. "I'm truly grateful. And I hope you know that you can count on me to help and support you in any way."

Her face fills with emotion but she quickly gets it under control. "That's nice to hear. Maybe I'll take you up on that one day."

"Any day you like. I'm here to help, or listen, or … whatever you need."

"Whatever I need, huh?" Something dark flits across her face. "You might regret saying that."

Every now and then she says things like that, and I want to crawl inside her brain to figure out what she's thinking. I have no doubt there's a lot more to Joanna's story than what she's told me, but I just hope she trusts me enough to reveal the rest one day.

We head back into the kitchen, and she grabs her bag. "I've got to head into work. There are big things afoot today at Whiplash and I doubt Asha is going to be thrilled about any of them." She fills a travel mug with freshly brewed coffee, then adds creamer and sugar. "How about you? What's on your agenda today?"

"Oh, you know. Go to *Pulse* for a few hours for job #1. Work as Eden's hacker bitch. Go to Romance Central for meetings and briefings. Work until the wee small hours debugging my damn app."

"You won't be home for dinner?"

I frown. "Do you want me to be home for dinner?"

"Well, yeah. It's our first official night as roomies. I thought we could celebrate."

"I can't really afford to take the night off."

"You wouldn't have to. Just have dinner with me, maybe a glass of wine, and then I promise you can lock yourself in your room for the rest of the night."

She gives me a pleading expression, and I can't deny that I'm tempted. It's not like I can't work from home. I just got used to spending all my hours at RC, because it was the only place I had to go. Now I have the option of coming home to her, and damn, it's the sweetest thought I've had in a very long time.

"Okay." I sling my bag across my chest. "I can do that. I'll be back around six."

"Amazing! It's a date." She must read something in my expression, because she quickly backtracks. "No, strike that. Of course it's not a date. Friends like us ... roomies, even ... don't have dates. We have ... um ... "

"Dinner?" I suggest.

"Yes! It's a dinner. See you then."

"Yep. Later."

We both walk out to the elevator and wait until the doors open. When they do, we step inside the elevator and stare at the door as it closes.

After a few seconds I say, "We probably should have said goodbye downstairs."

She nods. "Yep."

13

NOT FALLING

"Boss?"

I look up to see Raj in the doorway of my office at Romance Central. "I've got the data sets from our most recent analysis. Thought you'd like to see them."

He hands me an iPad, and I examine the numbers as I flick through the pages. The stats for the accuracy of the HEA matches look good. Great, even. But there's still something that bothers me.

"Why the frown, T-man?"

I place the iPad on the desk and rub my eyes. "Nothing. Just wish I could figure out how to factor in physical attraction. It's an important part of a relationship, but I have zero predictors for it."

"But didn't your research find that personality traits were more important?"

"Yeah, but I just don't feel I'm offering people a complete picture of their compatibility without it." I lean back in my chair. "There has to be a way to quantify it, somehow." Biometric tests exist that are pretty accurate in defining where people sit on the sexuality scale, but that involves a room full of equipment and dozens of electrodes all over their bodies, including their genitals. Not sure I can translate that into something that's possible with just a cell phone.

"You'll get it, dawg. I have no doubt that baller brain of yours will crack it. And while we're on the subject of attraction ..." He sits in the chair opposite my desk. "Did you see the sparks flying between me and that white-hot blonde at Max's the other night? Joanna, was it?" He pulls out the collar of his shirt to simulate letting out steam. "Whoo-wee. That girl had me so hot, Max could have used me as a space heater. I think she was feeling it, too."

Without warning, my blood pounds hot and fast. "Yeah, I don't think so, Raj."

A petty voice inside me whispers that she very well might have been feeling it with Raj. After all, they had an eighteen-percent probability, a full eleven points higher than I had with her.

Raj shoves his hands in his hoodie pocket. "Do you know if she's single? Is her number on the team contact list? I was thinking of giving her a call."

Over my fucking dead body. "Ah, yeah, I wouldn't bother calling if I were you. I'm pretty sure she's not single, Raj. Sorry."

"But she signed up for the app."

"Yeah, I think she was just being supportive. I heard her talking about a dude called Sergei the other day. Sounded serious."

"Really? God damn. Why all the beautiful ladies gotta be taken, man? When am I going to get me a ten like her?"

This conversation is giving me a headache. "Just out of interest, Raj. What rating would you give yourself?"

He gives me a lopsided grin. "Dawg, I'm a solid seven, no doubt."

"And yet, you're aiming to date a ten?"

"Of course! All dudes want a ten."

"Did you ever consider that all the ladies want a ten, too?"

That stops him in his tracks. "But … wait, is that why I'm not getting tens? 'Cause they all dating other tens?"

I shrug. "I don't know what to tell you, man, but maybe if you're only judging a woman by their looks, you run the risk of them judging you the same way. Equality sucks, right?"

He screws up his face and then laughs. "Damn, T-man, you all up on the book smarts *and* the woman smarts? Baller to the extreme."

Fuck, I despise the term 'baller'. Unless you're talking about someone who actually specializes in playing sports with balls, it should be banned.

"Not a baller, Raj. Just someone who thinks women are actual people and deserve to be judged on more than just their bra size."

"Speaking of bra size, did you see Joanna's —"

"I swear to God, Raj, if you finish that sentence, I'm going to murder you and bury your body in the woods." My face is blazing hot, and I don't even know if I'm joking right now.

He laughs, not even aware of my impending head explosion. "Ah, cool, cool. Message received. Another lady-fantasy bites the dust, I guess."

Eden appears in the doorway. "What are we talking about? Who's biting the dust, and why?"

Raj leans back to look at her. "That chick, Joanna, she's your friend, right? Toby just told me she's not single."

Eden looks at me, and we somehow manage to have a whole conversation with our eyes in a matter of seconds:

Oh, really, Toby? Protecting Joanna from Raj or keeping her for yourself?

Don't be ridiculous. I'm protecting her, of course.

Whatever you want to tell yourself.

Shut up, Tate.

Eden raises an eyebrow at me before perching on the edge of the desk. "Yep, definitely not single, Raj. Sorry."

Raj stands and ducks his head. "Aw, man." He picks up the iPad. "Why are there no ladies lining up for Rajy-boy?"

Eden shrugs. "Probably because Rajy-boy refers to himself in the third person?"

Raj chuckles and offers her his fist to bump. "Right on, Eden."

She slaps the top of it. "Cool, McGool."

Raj leaves, and Eden sits in the now-vacant chair before crossing her legs and fixing me with her patented bemused expression. "Look at you playing at being Joanna's bodyguard. Very chivalrous."

"I'd protect any woman from Raj. If that boy wants a relationship, he needs to start with a plant and work his way up to a breathing person."

"Wow. Cruel. What do you have against plants?" She looks over her shoulder, then back to me. "So, here's a question for you: Why is Joanna's driver at reception saying he's here to pick up your personal belongings?"

Crap. Busted.

"Oh ... Gerald's here?" I stand and see Gerald walking toward my office. He stops in the doorway and smiles. "Good afternoon, Mr. Jenner." He nods to Eden. "Good to see you again, Miss Tate." He looks back at me. "If you could direct me to your belongings, I'll take them back to Miss Cassidy's apartment."

"Sure, no problem. One sec." I cup my hand and yell, "Raj!"

Raj's head appears around the corner. "Yo!"

"Can you show Gerald around to the loading dock? There's a pile of boxes and bags there for him to collect."

"Sure."

Gerald smiles. "Thank you. Oh, and Mr. Jenner, what time would you like me to pick you up for your dinner date with Miss Joanna tonight?

Out of the corner of my eye, I see Eden's eyebrows rise into her hairline.

"Uh ... that's all good, Gerald. I can take the subway."

"Are you sure? Miss Joanna made it clear I was to make myself available to you."

I laugh, because I can tell that as soon as he leaves, Eden is going to grill me like a burger on the Fourth of July.

"Totally sure. Thanks anyway."

"Very well. Goodbye, then." He turns to Eden. "Miss Tate."

When he and Raj leave, Eden narrows her eyes at me. "What ... and I can't stress this enough ... the actual fuck? Explain yourself, Jenner."

"I need caffeine." I get up and head toward the break room, and of course, Eden follows.

"Fine, get coffee and spill the beans at the same time. What the hell is going on? You're moving in with Joanna? And having a date? When did this happen? What have I missed? Are you dating? Are you engaged? How, and why, and when?"

"Jesus Christ, Eden, calm down. You're like a gossip-bot overloading from lack of information. Nothing is going on with me and Joanna."

"Lies! You're moving in with her!"

"Dear God, woman, chill." When I reach the break room, I grab the coffee pot and pour some into a clean mug. "You want one?"

Eden makes a frustrated noise. "No, I don't want coffee. I want all the damn tea, right the hell now!"

I don't know why riling her up gives me such satisfaction, but it does. Taking my time, I stir in some creamer.

"It's no big deal. Joanna has been having tech issues and needs some live-in help to deal with them. I agreed to stay until everything can be straightened out."

Eden snaps her fingers. "This has something to do with that creepy AI of hers, doesn't it? Once when Ash and I were over there, I went to the bathroom, and my butt had barely hit the seat before a creepy voice asked if there was anything I needed."

"In the bathroom? Gross."

"Actually, it turned out there was a hidden TV in there, and Jeeves offered to put on the *Full House* reboot, which I hadn't seen, so it worked out well. But still … boundaries, you know?"

"Oh, believe me, I know." I head back to my office. She tags along. "The little shit assaulted me with water jets in the shower this morning, and I'm pretty sure he bruised my balls. It's out of control."

"Were you showering alone?" When I glare at her, she looks offended. "What? It's a valid question."

"For the hundredth time, Joanna and I aren't hooking up. Do I need to get it tattooed on my middle finger for you?"

"Rude. Another valid question: Do you have time to deal with that whole AI thing considering your insane workload leading up to the launch?"

"Not in the slightest, but I put a call out to all my hacktivist friends on the dark web this morning asking for advice, and if I know them at all, I predict that by tonight I'll have several different software fixes that will save me a ton of time."

"Aw, geek crowdsourcing. I like it."

I sit back in my chair and bring up a spreadsheet to work on hoping she'll get the hint and move on.

Of course, she doesn't.

"And so, this dinner tonight … what's that about?"

"Just dinner. Our first night as roommates."

"Cool, cool. As long as that's all there is. You know, Jo was bummed about your woeful compatibility score with her, but she's a hundred percent serious about finding a partner. She's a beautiful, accomplished woman, and she wants to share her life with someone."

"And so she should." The thought of Joanna dating other men makes bile rise up, but it's something I'll get used to, I suppose. Not that I have a choice in the matter.

Eden leans forward. "Tobes, I just want to make sure you're not setting yourself up to get hurt. If you have feelings for her, you shouldn't move in."

"Tate, would you stop lecturing me? You're not my real mom."

Eden holds up her hands in defense. "Fine, I'll stop. But know that even if Jo isn't your perfect match, I have faith that there's an amazing woman out there for you, and I'm going to hunt her down with the determination of a homicidal maniac in an eighties slasher film."

I give her a smile. "You're sweet. Now … leave? Please?"

She comes over and gives me a kiss on the top of my head. "See you later. And don't fall for your roommate."

"Got it." When she leaves, I sit there for a full five minutes, wondering if that advice has already come way too late.

14

LETTER FROM HOME

"Honey, I'm hoooome!"

I walk into the apartment to the sound of some old-timey crooner, maybe Frank Sinatra, and a waft of aromas so delicious, my salivary glands automatically kick into overdrive. I find the kitchen is deserted, but there's a massive collection of pots and pans simmering on the stove. Seems like whatever Joanna is cooking is well underway.

"Hey, Toby!" Joanna calls down the hallway from her room. "I'll be out in a sec. Can you stir the curry?"

Okay, then. Stirring. I'm sure I can manage that.

I wander over to the stove and grab the wooden spoon next to it. There's a dark brown something inside, and I do my best to stir without spilling it over the sides.

Man, that smells good.

Cooking isn't really something I do. If I can't make a dish by zapping it in the microwave for a few minutes, it's probably beyond my range of experience. Thank goodness Joanna seems way more proficient.

It was weird coming out of work and heading back into Manhattan. Even weirder walking into this super-fancy building and realizing I now live here.

What wasn't weird was thinking about spending time with Jo. That part seemed as natural as breathing. Her cooking for me is making me feel all kinds of things that probably shouldn't be entertained.

While I'm stirring, my phone rings, and I smile when I see my sister's face.

"Hey, Powder Puff. How're you doing?"

"Hey, Large Brother. I'm good. How's life in the Big Apple?"

"Great, actually." For once, I don't have to lie, and damn if it doesn't feel amazing. "I've picked up a bit more freelance work, so I'll be able to send you guys more money from now on." Joanna and I haven't really discussed the fee for managing Jeeves, but even a couple hundred dollars would make a world of difference right now.

I put the spoon on the counter and go around to the stools on the other side. After I sit, I put my phone down and put it on speaker so I can grab my computer out of my bag.

"How are you doing? How's school?"

"Eh, okay."

"That doesn't sound good. What's up?"

She makes a noise, and I can practically see her flopping onto her bed. "The other day, Marcie Dagleish started cough/saying, 'you suck' when I was rehearsing *Somewhere Over the Rainbow*. I mean, I know she's just jealous that I got the lead role instead of her, and she has to make do with being my understudy, but still … she's a total buttface."

I smile and open my laptop. "She *is* a total buttface. What can I do to help? Spam her Facebook feed with targeted ads for acting lessons? Photoshop her into pics with terrible B-list celebrities? Start an 'I <3 April Jenner fan page and make her the administrator?"

"All great ideas, large brother, but I took care of it."

"How?"

"Well, I couldn't afford to get anything specially printed, so I improvised and bought a laundry marker. Then I customized one of my white T-shirts. The front said, 'Sorry you're so obsessed with me,' and the back said, 'Keep it up. I thrive on your attention.'"

I laugh as I imagine my scrawny sister walking through the school, wearing that shirt like the badass she is. "And did Marcie's head explode?"

She laughs. "Pretty much. When she saw me, she went bright red and yelled, 'bitch!' at the top of her lungs. Everyone laughed. I don't think she'll be trying to bully me again."

I shake my head in awe. She's so much stronger than I was at her age. Mind you, she's had a rougher childhood. She was only eight when dad had his accident. Since then, she's been a part-time caregiver and full-time support. I might have a financial burden, but she's there every day, fighting in the trenches. What an incredible kid.

"What about Mom and Dad? How are they doing?"

There's a pause, and then I hear April closing her bedroom door.

"They're okay, but mom got a phone call from the spinal clinic the other day. They said that some world-famous neurosurgeon will be in town, and Dr. Pickett recommended he do the surgery instead of him."

"Why would Dr. Pickett do that?"

"Apparently he's concerned about how close the bone fragments are to Dad's spinal cord. The other doctor has a much better track record with this type of tricky surgery, so his odds for a successful outcome would improve."

"By how much?"

"With Dr. Pickett, there'd be a nearly fifty-percent chance dad would be permanently paralyzed. With the other guy, it's only a twenty-five percent chance."

It sucks that there's any chance Dad will have to live out his life in a wheelchair. But I guess if we're able to halve the odds of a terrible outcome, we should grab it with both hands.

"Well, that sounds amazing. I hope she said yes."

"Toby … there's a catch."

Of course there is. We couldn't possibly get some good news without a dose of bad.

"What is it?"

She sighs. "The other surgeon isn't covered by dad's insurance. Like, at all. We'd have to pay to the whole cost of the operation."

I pinch the bridge of my nose and close my eyes. Just when I think I'm climbing out of the hole that's steadily filling up with toilet water …

"How much?"

"It's a lot."

"Just give me the number, April."

She pauses, and I know she hates putting this all on my shoulders, but what else is she going to do? I'm her big brother. I'm the one who has to fix it.

"It's a hundred-and-fifty-thousand dollars."

I clench my jaw, so I don't release a slew of curse words too profane for my twelve-year-old sister's ears.

"Okay."

Fuck, fuck, fucking motherfucking fuck!

"Mom didn't want me to tell you, because she knew you'd sell a kidney in order to pay."

"She's right." Actually, that's not a bad idea. I hear the black-market for organs is pretty lucrative. I wonder what the going rate is for a kidney.

"Toby?"

"Sssh. Trying to figure out if my kidney will cover the whole thing or if I might need to throw in part of my liver."

"Don't even joke about that."

"Right now, it's my best option."

"Mom's going to sell the house."

That makes my blood run cold. Mom and dad bought that house just before they got married. April and I were born in that house.

"April, if Mom does that, we might as well forget about the operation, because it'll kill Dad."

"It's our only option."

"No, it isn't. I'll figure out another way. Put Mom on the phone."

"Toby, no. She'll kill me for telling you."

"And I would have killed you if you hadn't, so I guess it sucks to be you, little lady."

April makes a petulant noise as she climbs off the bed. "Okay. Wait a sec." I hear the door opening and then footsteps. From the ambient sound, I can tell she finds Mom in the kitchen.

"Mom, it's Toby. He wants to talk to you."

"April, what did you do?"

"I'm sorry, Mom. He had to know."

There's a brushing noise as the phone gets handed over, then in her perkiest, absolutely-nothing-is-wrong-son tone, she says, "Hey, sweetheart. You have nothing to worry about."

"Mom, you're not really going to sell the house."

She pauses. "It would be a last resort, but I'm running out of time to find the money."

"Okay, then leave it with me. Give me a week to come up with something, but promise you won't do anything before then."

There's a beat, then she says, "I promise. But we're running out of time, honey. The local real estate agent said she would have a heap of buyers for the house. It's no mansion, and we're heavily mortgaged, but it would pay for the operation at least."

"Mom, selling the house would break Dad's heart. Just give me a week, and then we'll talk, okay?"

She sighs, and I hate how hard this is on her. "Okay."

"Can you text me the new surgeon's details? I'll pay them directly when I have the money." *If* I have the money.

"I'll send them as soon as we hang up. Do you want to say a quick hi to your dad?"

"Yeah, I would."

"Hang on."

When she tells him I'm on the phone, I hear Dad trying to make words, but it all comes out as one long vowel sound. He sustained some brain damage in the fall, and even though he understands everything perfectly, he has trouble talking. If we'd had the funds to get him the rehab therapy he needs, he'd have made a lot more progress. As it is, he has to write down important stuff, so we can understand him.

"Hey, Pop. How are you doing? Still the handsomest man in Philly?"

He laughs.

"Things are pretty good here. Work is busy, but the app launch will be done in just under two weeks, and then life should be a little less crazy."

He makes an encouraging noise.

"Yeah, I'm really going to try get home for your operation, okay? That's a promise."

There's some noise, then, "Honey, it's Mom. He's really happy about that news, but he's getting tired, so I'm going to take him into the bedroom."

I get a lump in my throat thinking about Mom and April lifting dad into bed. How it takes both of them to change him into his pajamas. How they have to put on his night-time ostomy bag and empty the old one before they can relax and worry about themselves for the night.

I should be there, helping. And since I can't, I'm sure as hell going to find them the money they need.

"Okay, Mom. I'll talk to you soon, okay? Hug Dad and April for me, and then yourself. Miss you guys."

"We miss you, too, honey. Love you heaps. Bye."

I hang up and run a hand over my beard.

Fuck this entire situation. If Crest Construction had paid compensation for Dad's accident when they should have, none of this would be happening. I'm going to nail those fuckers' balls to the wall if it's the last thing I do.

"Everything okay?"

I turn and see Joanna standing there in a shapeless, floaty kaftan-thing, and even though I have no right to, I just want to go over and hug her. Or more specifically, have her hug me.

"Yeah, I'm fine." *But not really.* "Just chatting with my family."

She comes into the kitchen and starts ladling all the various foods into copper bowls. "Your mom and dad are still together? Major achievement."

"Yeah. Dad had an accident my final year of college, so Mom's his caregiver, along with my little sister, April."

She stops spooning. "Oh, God. What happened?"

"He was a safety inspector and was onsite at a high-rise construction site. He'd just finished his inspection, which was ironically full of violations, when the scaffolding he was standing on gave way. He plummeted four stories down. Broke his back in two places, crushed part of his skull, broke six ribs, his left arm …"

"God, Toby." She stares at me in horror.

"Yeah, it was a rough road to recovery, but we were all thankful he made it through. I've never seen Mom so worried as when Dad was in intensive care. She didn't leave his side for a week."

"How's he doing now?"

"Okay. He has some lingering paralysis, but we're hoping that will get better after he has surgery next month. They're going to remove some bone fragments that are floating near his spinal cord. They thought they might work themselves out over the years, but no such luck. We have a lead on some big hotshot doing the surgery, so things are looking good."

And by the way, if you can direct me to the nearest human-parts black-market, I'd be most grateful.

I cringe to myself. If I was serious about selling my kidney, I know exactly which Dark Web marketplace would take it, but I'm going to keep that option in my pocket as a last resort.

Joanna goes back to finishing up with the food. "Did you catch the surgeon's name?"

"Yeah, Mom just texted me the details." I check my phone. "Dr. Kattrick. Apparently, he's famous."

Joanna tastes the brown stuff in the saucepan and nods. "Oh, yeah, I've heard of him. If you need to have someone digging around with a scalpel near your spinal cord, you want it to be him."

I put my phone down. "That's good to know." I'm suddenly very tired of talking about my problems. Opening up, even a little, is tough for me. I'm so used to just powering through as best as I can, holding all the tension and anxiety around me like a security blanket. Is it possible to get addicted to stress? Or is it just that I don't recognize what I look like without it anymore?

Either way, the relief I feel from sharing at least a little with Joanna is well and truly outweighed by the residual pressure of having to raise a stupid amount of money in a very short time.

"Toby?" I look up to see Joanna looking at me with concern. "Is there anything I can do to help? Anything at all?"

Shit. Is she clairvoyant? Or am I just that transparent when it comes to wearing my worry on my face.

"Uh … no. Thanks. We're all good."

"Because if you need … help …"

I cut her off before she can continue, because I already have enough guilt about how much she's helped me. I really don't need more.

"Honestly, Jo, thanks, but I have everything under control." My pride is a narcissistic prick who truly believes that's the case, even if my logical brain is hugging itself and rocking in the corner.

"Anyway," I say, steering away from the subject. "I'm starving. What are we having?"

She places the last of the copper bowls onto the counter and hands me a plate. "It's a Thai feast. Three different curries, coconut rice, drunken noodles, the whole nine yards. Load up, and let's eat."

"You don't have to tell me twice."

While I'm spooning food onto my plate, Jo grabs a bottle of what looks like expensive champagne from the fridge and pops it open. Then she pours us a glass each.

I put down my plate and take a glass as she raises hers.

"Here's to us being roommates and friends. Welcome to the neighborhood, Mr. Jenner."

"It's a pleasure to be here, Miss Cassidy."

We clink glasses and drink, and then settle in to eat our food. Everything she's made is beyond delicious, and I pretend I'm having a good time, even though a good portion of my concentration is elsewhere. At the back of my mind, there's a little man with a white board, brainstorming about every possible way we could scrape together a hundred and fifty thousand dollars over the next seven days.

It's after midnight when a weird sound breaks my concentration enough to look up from my screen. I've been sitting at the dining room table since we finished dinner, flicking between working on the app, finishing up next week's articles for *Pulse*, and seriously considering hacking into one of the online gambling sites to make some major coin. So far, I've resisted the temptation, but the night's not over yet.

For most of the night, Joanna was sitting on the couch, binge-watching true-crime documentaries and fiddling with her phone, but as I look over now, she seems to be gone.

I'm about to go back to my work, when the noise happens again, this time louder. It's like a grunt and a whimper, all at the same time.

"Hnngno ..."

When I go over to the couch, I see Joanna curled up in a ball, asleep, but not peacefully. Her face is contorted, and her breathing is choppy and panicked.

"Nnnnnoooo ... doppitpease." She snorts a little before whimpering again. "Pease ... No. Nooooo ..."

She starts winding up like an air-raid siren, and then her mouth opens, and she breaks into a full-on blood-curdling scream.

"Hey, Jo." I kneel beside her and touch her shoulder to try and shake her awake. "Hey ... wake up."

She lashes out, still screaming as she punches and kicks at me.

"Fuck, Jo, stop!" I grab her arms to stop her from punching me and lay my weight on her legs to prevent them flailing. She gets in a few good hits as she struggles against me, and I didn't think it was possible, but her scream ratchets up even further. She sounds like she's being murdered.

"Joanna! Wake up!" She keeps thrashing, and I don't know what the fuck to do, so I pick her up as best as I can and hurry into my bathroom. When I get her into the shower, I hit the cold-water button.

I bear hug her to my chest as she thrashes and screams against the cold water, but eventually her eyes open, and as she recognizes me in front of her, reality begins smoothing over the sheer terror in her eyes.

"Toby?"

"Hey … yeah, it's me. You were having a bad dream." I release my arms from around her and turn off the water.

She frowns and then looks around, seeming disoriented. "I fell asleep? No. That's not … I wouldn't … no." She pushes away from me, and I don't know what the hell I've done, but all of a sudden, she's looking at me like I'm the bad guy.

"I'm sorry about the shower, but you wouldn't wake up. I didn't know what else to do."

She climbs to her feet and stumbles out of the shower. "This isn't happening. Not again."

"Joanna?"

"I'm fine. Leave me alone."

I get up and follow her out of the bathroom. She leaves wet footprints in the plush carpet as she rushes down the hallway and into her bedroom.

"Jo, wait. Talk to me. What's going on?"

I'm a few feet behind her, and when I get to her room, she slams the door in my face.

I knock. "Jo, just tell me you're okay."

There's silence on the other side of the door. When I try the handle, it's locked.

"Joanna? You need to open this door and tell me you're okay, or I'm going to break it the fuck down. I'm not even kidding. You're scaring me."

There are another few seconds of silence, and now I'm the one who's starting to panic. I've never seen Joanna like this, not even when she was locked in the vestibule. The anxiety brought on by her claustrophobia was a totally different beast to the flat-out terror she just exhibited.

"Joanna?"

She doesn't answer, but I can hear her moving around inside.

"Okay, that's it. If you won't come out, then I'm coming in."

I have a terrible feeling that she could do something to hurt herself, and whether I'm right or not, I don't intend for anything bad to happen to her on my watch.

I pull back from the door so I can give myself some room to kick it in, but before I get the chance, the door opens, and Joanna comes striding out, dressed in leggings, running shoes, and a thick hoodie.

"I'm going for a run. Don't wait up."

"The fuck?" I try to catch up to her. "It's nearly one in the morning, Jo."

"So? I often jog at this hour."

I take her arm to try and get her to stop. "Joanna ..."

She snatches it back but turns to face me. "Toby, it's no big deal. I had a bad dream. I'm going for a run to clear my head. Go get some sleep, and I'll see you in the morning."

She turns and leaves me in the entrance hall. When she gets into the elevator, she puts in ear pods as the doors close.

I stand there for a few seconds, trying to figure out what the fuck just happened.

15

GONE GIRL

I tap my fingers on my desk as I listen to Joanna's phone ring out yet again and go to voicemail for the fifth time.

"Hi, this is Joanna. Leave me a message or send me a text. I'll get back to you when I'm not doing something way more important. Thanks!"

"Joanna, it's Toby again." My heart is racing. I didn't hear her come home last night, and this morning when I checked her room, she wasn't there. For all I know, she's floating in the Hudson after being murdered. I've called and texted, and the only explanation I have as to why she hasn't gotten back to me is that she can't. "I'm about to hack into your phone provider and ping your whereabouts, so if you're alive and well, please let me know, because this shit is highly illegal, and you know I'm too pretty for prison. Please, call me back."

I hang up and crack my knuckles. I've done my best to get on with things today but worrying about her has definitely put a major dent in my productivity. If she has been hurt, or worse, I …

"Hey, Toby." Max appears in my doorway, and before he even opens his mouth, I know what he's going to ask. "Everything on track for tonight's team meeting at my place?"

"Yeah, for the most part. Just doing some final quality control tests with Raj, and then we'll be set."

"And how's your speech coming for the app launch?"

Groan. "Uh … yeah … it's a work in progress." In reality, the only progress I've made is to open a blank document and name it 'Toby's Epically Terrifying Launch Speech'. Sure, it's not much, but it's a start.

Max smiles. "I know you hate public speaking, Tobes, but don't forget to use Joanna as a resource. She said she'd be more than happy to help you out."

Sure, if she's not kidnapped or dead. My stomach lurches at the thought. "Okay."

"She said to tell you she'll talk more about it tonight."

I sit up straighter. "Uh … tonight? As in at the meeting? When did she tell you that?"

"I just got off the phone with her. She's lined up an incredible roster of celebrities for the launch and has even fielded some interview requests for you."

Thank Odin she's okay.

My relief is tempered by some bitterness that she could have called me herself to tell me that. Taking Max's call but not mine freaking hurts. He wasn't the one developing an ulcer while contemplating her fate.

And now it's official: I'm way too invested in this woman.

"Toby?" Max is frowning at me. "You okay? You just went quiet for an off-putting amount of time."

"Uh … yeah, all good, Max. I'll connect with Joanna, and we'll get it all straightened out." Please, God.

He heads off, and now that I know Joanna's okay, I try to make up for lost time in getting through my tasks for the day.

Eden's given me a list of names of city councilors who are suspected of taking bribes from Marcus Crest and his cronies, but so far, infiltrating their email accounts has shown nothing. If I can't find any evidence of dark money or back-door deals, not only will Eden's story die, but I'll fail to fill my ticket on the Angels of Mercy forum, and that would suck for my reputation, not to mention my bank balance. When I logged in today, there was a message from the original poster asking if I've made any progress. I replied that I was looking into a lot of leads, but that kind of stalling tactic will only work for so long.

The one good thing I found when I logged on was that my friends and fellow hackers had a ton of advice about how to handle the Jeeves issue. True to form, they took the problem on as a group challenge and brainstormed several possible workarounds. Then they wrote a whole bunch of code that I might find useful and uploaded it for me. Say what you like about geeks, but put a conundrum in front of them, and they're at their best.

I uploaded one of the tests into Jeeves' server earlier. The thinking is that AIs learn from stimulus and response, and so it should be possible to train them. The program allows Jeeves access to the apartment's systems, but only as long as he maintains regular protocols. The moment he tries to counteract standard commands, a failsafe routine will start deleting his code from all sub-systems. My hope is that Jeeves will soon learn that if he wants to control things, he must do it in a certain way or continually be put in virtual time-outs. It's a risk, but one I think is worth taking. Only time will tell if it works.

Now, back to Crest Construction. Another project I've been exploring today is forcibly taking the money they owe Dad for his accident. Just because they have an army of lawyers that can keep Dad's case in litigation until he either goes bankrupt or dies, doesn't mean they're not liable for his medical bills. It was their faulty scaffolding and crappy safety practices that landed him in a wheelchair, and goddammit, they're going to be the ones who pay to get him out.

I've tracked down one of the company's main holding accounts, where money from real estate sales gets deposited before the Crest accountants and money movers do their bottom-line gymnastics and turn massive profits into tax-reducing losses. I could just perform a smash and grab. In other words, hack into the account through untraceable means and take the hundred-and-fifty grand for Dad's operation, but that would involve setting up a series of offshore accounts to act as rabbit holes, enabling me to shift the money enough times to prevent anyone from tracking the theft.

The only problem is that setting up those accounts would take weeks and involve at least one overseas trip. Most of the banks that deal in dark money have one rule: they will only negotiate with a real person, whether that be the account holder or their legal representative. No digital account set-ups are allowed. Weird that these capitalistic profit-whores have any standards, considering they launder and hide money for some of the worst people on the planet, but whatever. There's no shortcut or workaround for that requirement.

My buddy in Norway is a leading scientist in a cloning research lab, but as good as he is, there's no way to get an exact copy of myself to jump on a plane to the Cayman Islands.

I rub my eyes and sigh.

I don't want to admit it, but paying for the operation by raiding Crest Constructions is going to be impossible in my limited timeframe. I'll have to come up with something else, and fast.

Raj comes into my office and hands me the latest slew of reports and data.

"Raj, if you had to make a hundred-and-fifty K in a week, how would you do it?"

"Oh, okay, I love these hypotheticals. Well, first, I'd get in my time machine and go back to when Bitcoin was just a joke in the crypto world and buy a few hundred coins, then come back to today and cash it in to buy unlimited hookers and blow. Oh, and Yeezys."

I should be surprised by the shallowness of his answer, but I'm really not.

"No, I mean what would you do in reality? No outrageous hypotheticals, just something logical and doable."

He frowns. "Uh, don't you think that if I knew how to make that much bank in a week, I'd already be doing it?"

Can't argue with that logic.

He rubs his chin. "I guess the only real thing I could do is take you and my paycheck to Atlantic City and use your giant brain to game the odds. Why you asking? You wanna take a trip? I mean, we've got this meeting tonight, but I'm always up for blowing it off and hitting the blackjack tables."

I flick through the pages on the iPad. "No, I'm just thinking out loud." I hand the iPad back. "This is all looking good. Keep going with Ming-Lee on the user interface and tweak the tab responsiveness. Have all the devices come in for the event?"

"Yep. All locked and loaded in the security cage. We just need to upload the latest software version the day of the event, and we're good to go."

"Cool. Thanks, Raj. Good work."

And that's why I put up with all his other personality crap. At the end of the day, he knows what he's doing and gets the job done. And I'm going to make it my life's work to turn him into a better person or die trying.

After he leaves, I lean back in my chair and roll my neck. Against all odds, it looks like we might actually bring this app in on time and under budget. That's no mean feat for a project this large. I'm still trying to figure out how to factor in physical attraction, but that's in the realm of pie-in-the-sky right now, so I can't waste too much time pursuing it.

I check my watch and see I only have a couple of hours before I have to leave.

I get cracking on achieving as much as I can in that time and try to keep my mind off the mystery of what the hell is going on with Joanna.

16

RELUCTANTLY NEEDY

For once, I'm only half-an-hour late leaving work to head to the HEA meeting, and I'm on the train to Max's place when my sister sends me a picture of her dressed up in her Dorothy costume for her school musical. She's freaking adorable, and I really hope I can get back to Philly to see her strut her stuff on her opening night next month.

Seeing her reminds me that it's payday, and I quickly log into my banking app, so I can transfer money to her and mom.

When my account comes up on the screen, I frown.

What the fuck?

I stare at my bank balance, not comprehending the uncharacteristic bunch of numbers there.

No, seriously, what the actual fuck?

I click into the list of transactions, and when I see that there's a deposit from JMCassidy, my face flushes with blood.

"Fuck."

I get off at the next stop and stride from the subway station to Max's place. Once again, I'm one of the last to arrive, but the meeting hasn't started yet, so everyone's milling around, sipping cocktails and chatting. I hightail it over to bar and grab what looks like a gin and tonic. I drink it down fast, and then grab a second. I turn around and spy Joanna in the kitchen, helping Eden prepare food for dinner.

I dump my bag onto a chair in the dining room and head over. Joanna looks up when she sees me coming and quickly glances away.

Yeah, you know what you've done.

"Tobes!" Eden flashes me a smile. "Pull up a pew. Dinner will be ready soon. How was your day?"

"Kind of shitty, but I'll survive." I look at Joanna. "How was your day?"

She tears some lettuce into a bowl. "Uh … okay. Thanks for asking."

"Eden!" Max calls from over near the bar. "Can you bring over that other tray of glasses? I'm running low."

"Sure, handsome." She looks at me and points to the cutting the board filled with herbs. "Tobes, take over, would you? The parsley goes in the pasta salad, the dill goes with the cous, and cilantro goes with the avocado smash."

She grabs a tray laden with low-ball glasses and heads over to the bar. I walk around the island and take my place next to Joanna. She continues to make a green salad and completely avoids looking at me.

"You didn't come home last night."

"Uh … no. I ran for an hour and then went to visit a friend."

"At two in the morning?"

"I knew she'd be up. She works most nights."

A petty part of me rejoices that it wasn't a man, but still …

"You want to talk about what happened?"

"Not really. It was a bad dream. No big deal."

"Jo, you were screaming the house down, and when I tried to wake you up, you started pounding on me like you were the heavyweight champion of the world. I got some pretty decent bruises from it, in fact."

"What?" Now she looks at me, worry etched on her face. "Show me."

I lift my shirt to reveal a large welt on my side that's almost the exact shape of her foot. "You should play for the NFL with that killer kick."

"Oh, God, Toby, I'm so sorry."

She goes to touch it, but I'm way too angry to let her turn me on right now. "It's fine, but don't tell me that it was nothing, because it absolutely fucking wasn't."

She goes back to ripping lettuce. "You're right, it wasn't nothing."

"Do you want to tell me what it was all about? And why it inspired you to take off running?"

She glances around the room and then moves on to slicing tomatoes. "Not really. I'm sorry but …" She takes a breath. "It's something I don't want to talk about, okay?"

I'm really tempted to push her, because I have a deep, abiding need to protect her from whatever-the-fuck it was that made her scream like that, but pressuring her into telling me won't be helpful.

"Jo, I hope you know that you can tell me anything, and I'll be there for you, free from judgement." She makes a noise as if she doesn't believe me, but I continue. "So even though I'd love to have it explained away, I'm not an asshole who's going to force you to reveal your secrets. But at the same time, you don't need to act like nothing's wrong."

"Okay, fair point. But maybe practice what you preach."

"What's that mean?"

She drops some tomato into the bowl. "You need money for your Dad's operation, but you just blew it off when I asked if everything was okay. Didn't you do exactly what you just accused me of?"

"You were listening to my phone call?"

"It was hard not to. Sound bounces down that marble hallway. I didn't mean to invade your privacy, but I also couldn't block out the sound."

"So, that's why you deposited a hundred-and-fifty-thousand dollars into my bank account today?"

She stops chopping and puts her knife down. "I wanted to help."

I throw a handful of dill on the cous cous and stir it vigorously. "I don't need a handout, Jo."

"It's not. Just think of it as a year's wages in advance."

I turn to her. "You're not paying me a hundred and fifty grand a year for managing Jeeves."

"Why not? He's a major pain in the ass, and after all of the abuse you've taken, including me kicking you in the kidney, you deserve hazard pay."

I take a sip of my drink and notice my hand is shaking. I don't know why her giving me money is making me so fucking furious, but it is. I'm sure if I examined my reaction more carefully I'd recognize some deeply buried patriarchal bullshit reasoning about feeling emasculated by taking money from a woman, but even that's just an extension of the shame I feel about not being able to properly take care of my family.

"Joanna, I can't accept it. That's a stupid amount of money, even for a kickass coder. I know I'm good, but I'm not worth that."

"I think you are."

I put down my knife and rest my palms on the bench. "Well, I can't accept it, so we're at a stalemate."

Jo throws her chopped tomatoes and cucumber into a bowl, clearly frustrated. "Toby, you need help, and I'm in a position where I'm able to give it to you. I don't understand why you can't just take it."

See, this is infuriating: Her using logic on me. Logic is where I think I like to live, but these types of situations prove time and again that I'm driven by ridiculous, illogical feelings at the most inconvenient times. I need money, and Joanna wants to give it to me. Why is it so fucking hard to take the outstretched hand she's offering? Why do I feel sick about doing it? About *having* to do it because I have no other options.

"Toby …"

I look at her and she takes a step forward, right next to me. "I understand how hard this is because believe me, if our positions were reversed and you threw a whole chunk of change at me without permission, I'd be pretty damn mad. But this doesn't need to be as difficult as you're making it. Every year, I donate a ton of money to various charities, including one that provides money to people who can't afford medical care." She must see my face change when she says the word 'charity' because she's quick to amend, "I'm not saying that this is charity, because it's not. I'm just saying I'd be giving this money away regardless. I just feel better about giving it to someone I know. Especially someone I … care about."

I sigh and finish up adding the chopped herbs to their respective dishes. "It fucking sucks that anyone has to pay for this. The goddamn construction company responsible should be the only ones with their hands in their pockets for Dad's care. Not you, not me. No one else."

Joanna puts serving spoons in all the bowls. "Yeah, well, you're going to be waiting for a snow day in hell before Marcus Crest pays up on your dad's claim. It's just one in a long line of lawsuits that he'll string out for years."

I pause. "How did you know dad's accident was caused by Crest?"

She gives me a strange look. "Uh … you told me?"

"No, I don't think I did." I'm usually very careful to keep Crest's name out of my mouth except when absolutely necessary because it always makes me feel as if I've gargled with raw sewerage.

She shrugs. "Maybe Eden told me? Or Asha?" She frowns. "Actually,

I don't even remember when I found out, but I wasn't surprised. They have the worst reputation in the city as far as safety goes."

I take the cutting boards to the sink to rinse them. "Yeah, if only that would help me take them to the cleaners."

Jo stands beside me and leans her hip against the bench. "If you want me to loan you money to sue the hell out of them, I'm also open to doing that."

I shoot her a look, and she smiles and touches my arm. "Okay, I get it. One step at a time. Please accept the money, Toby. I really want to do this for you." I shut off the water and turn to her, and for once, I don't know what to say.

She must read that I'm struggling, because she says, "I don't know your dad at all, but I figure he must be a pretty spectacular human being to raise a son like you. I don't have any family to spend my money on, and I want to make sure it goes to people who truly need it. Your dad needs it. Please, say you'll take it."

I clench my jaw and nod, because there's so many emotions caught in my throat, I'm incapable of forming words right now.

Joanna doesn't seem to mind. She just beams at me and bounces a little on her toes. "Oh, yes." She glances around quickly. "I really want to hug you right now, but it might be weird for everyone else."

I finally find my voice but it's husky as hell. "I really want to hug you, too, but I'm so fucking grateful, I'd probably grind your bones to dust and then I'd be stuck with a roommate who was just a shapeless pile of goo and that would be disgusting."

She laughs. "Well, yes. Can't have that."

She turns on the tap on to wash her hands. I see a little cucumber on the side of her pinky and grab her hand. "Here. Missed some."

I rub her hands under the water, and within seconds, I regret it. Heat blooms in my stomach and spreads downward, and I quickly pull my hands back and turn off the water.

"Sorry."

She looks at me, huge pupils and soft lips. "It's okay."

"Jo …"

"Yeah?"

I look into her eyes. "Thank you. You have no idea how much this means to me."

She nods. "It means a lot to me, too, just not for the same reasons."

I'm about to ask her about that when Eden comes over to the far side of the island and grabs a couple of bowls.

"All done, you two?"

"Yep," I say, putting distance between me and Joanna. "All done."

Jo and I share a small smile, and I know that's her way of telling me she'll be discreet. It goes some way to making me feel better about the situation, even though there's still an edge of uneasiness twisting around in my guts.

All of these pieces falling into place for me is a strange occurrence. I'm not used to Lady Fortune turning her benevolent eye on me. I'm used to wading shoulder-deep through shit and being grateful it's not up to my neck.

What the hell is happening in my life? And is it all to do with Joanna?

I watch as she laughs and chats with people as they all take turns delivering serving bowls and trays to the giant wooden table.

Holy shit. Is she actually a real-life angel?

If someone told me that, I wouldn't laugh in their face. Even if she's not a supernatural being, she's sure-as-hell turning out to be my personal guardian angel. Not sure what I did to deserve having her in my life, but whatever it is, I'm thankful. Of course, the same powers responsible for sending her could have chosen to make her my soul mate and yet didn't, so on that front, they have a lot to answer for.

As soon as everything is laid out on the table, Max calls us all over for dinner.

After eating our fill, the meeting gets underway, and to my relief, everything seems to be coming together better than expected. Of course, the fact I'm no longer carrying around a hundred-and-fifty-thousand-pound weight around my neck is making life in general seem a little rosier.

"Fantastic effort," Max says after all the progress reports are delivered and contingencies discussed. "And once again, a huge thank you to Toby for making this app everything I could have wished for and more. Could everyone please raise your glasses for a toast."

People grab whatever drink is in front of them and raise them in the air.

Max gives me a smile. "To Doctor Love!"

I groan as they all echo him. "To Doctor Love!"

Oh, for fuck's sake.

Even as I roll my eyes, I can see Eden chuckling her ass off at the end of the table.

I mouth, "You're a dead woman," but that only makes her laugh more.

Guess I'm posting that Justin Timberlake love letter after all.

ONCE THE MEETING IS OVER, Max does his usual thing of inviting everyone to hang around to chat or drink, and tonight, I'm definitely in the mood to take him up on his offer.

"What's this one?" I ask Max, referring to a shot of something that could be any number of clear liquors.

"That's Grappa de Ferro from Italy. But be careful with that —"

I barely pause before slamming it down.

"Oh … fuck."

"Yeah, I was trying to warn you. It's more for sipping than shotting. It's about a hundred proof."

"Ohhhh … *fuuuuck.*" It's my sixth drink, and now the room expands and contracts, and then does a weird shimmery thing I've never seen a room do before.

"Tobes? You okay?" I must look as bad as I feel, because Max comes around to my side of the bar and puts a hand on my shoulder. "You'd better sit."

He pulls a stool behind me, and I manage to balance myself on it. "Here, eat some chips." He slides over some Doritos and then perches beside me. "I don't begrudge you letting loose, because God knows you deserve a night off, but I can't have you dying of alcohol poisoning. That's just a bad look for everyone involved."

"Agreed." I burp and eat a handful of chips. They stop my stomach from doing Grappa-fueled somersaults.

I look over and see Eden and Joanna sitting in the lounge area, chatting and laughing. It looks like they're drinking margaritas, and from the empty jug in front of them, they'd definitely be feeling no pain right about now.

"Max, what would you have done if my app told you Eden wasn't right for you?"

"I'd say your app was the wrongest thing in Wrongsville."

"So, you'd still go out with Eden?"

"Of course."

"But what if my app proved that your relationship was doomed, and you'd end up destroying each other? I mean, I'm thinking you guys want to get married and have kids one day. Would you put them through what Eden and Asha went through? Or you, even."

He sips a bottle of beer and thinks. "Well, that would warrant ... thought. I think Eden and I are very different people due to our upbringing. I'd like to think we wouldn't make the same mistakes our parents did, but I guess it's always possible. Or we could make brand-new mistakes not related to anyone but ourselves." He shrugs. "I guess I'm grateful that our score proves we're meant to be together, because honestly, I've got too much going on to have to try to fall out of love with her. I mean, I just don't have the energy."

I know he's joking, but that comment really hits home. I don't have the energy to stop liking Joanna, either, yet I have to try, or things between us are going to get more and more fraught.

"Toby, is this about you and Joanna only having a seven-percent compatibility rating?"

I wave him off. "Pfft. No. Of course not, But thanks for throwing that statistic in my face, Max. Do you want me to spread my legs so you can also kick me in the balls?"

He laughs and slaps my shoulder. "Come on. Let's go and see what the ladies are up to."

"They're getting drunk, like we are."

"Cool. Then we can all get drunk together."

He tugs on my arm, and we head over to where the two women are sitting. Max sits next to Eden, and she turns to give him a lingering kiss. I sit next to Joanna and resist the urge to give her one as well.

"So, what's the topic of discussion over here?" I ask, blocking out the memory of how she tasted the night we met.

Joanna leans back and puts her feet up on the coffee table. "Eden's trying to convince me to use the HEA app again, but I think I'm just going to date the old-fashioned way for a while."

"And what method is that again?" Eden asks. "Picking random men and hoping like hell they're going to be the good-guy needle in a haystack of assholes?"

Joanna shrugs. "It's possible not everyone is destined to find their match with technology. I think Toby's brilliant, but his app may not be right for me."

Max looks at me, and I don't know if he can tell how queasy this conversation is making me, but he clears his throat and tries to change the subject.

"So, Toby and Eden, how's your exposé on Crest Construction coming along?"

Joanna looks at her. "Toby and I were talking about Crest earlier. You're doing a story on them?"

Eden takes a sip of her drink. "Maybe. If we can't find any evidence that they're corrupt, I'll have to drop the whole thing. Derek has given me one more week to crack it, or he's pulling the plug."

Joanna nods. "Well, dropping it would be the smart thing to do anyway, because if Marcus Crest gets tipped off that you're investigating him, he'll use all his usual intimidation tactics to scare you off."

Eden leans forward. "Like what?"

"Like sending his security thugs to follow you. Doing opposition research to use as blackmail material. Investigating family members. Making actual physical threats. You know, typical mafia crap. I've heard tons of stories about them over the years. They can be dangerous."

Max looks concerned. "Eden, maybe this story isn't a good idea."

"Max, if I shied away from every rich asshole who tried to scare me off from a story, I'd never get anything printed. Plus, I have Toby as my secret weapon, so if they screw with us, we can screw with them back."

I take a beer off the table and take off the cap. "That's true in theory, but so far, I'm having zero luck in screwing with them. Whatever evidence there is of corruption, they keep it well hidden."

"I know where they hide it."

We all turn and look at Joanna as if we're one person.

She sees us staring and frowns. "What? A friend of mine used to date the head of security over at Crest. She told me he used to divulge way too many company secrets after having sex and smoking weed."

Eden slaps Jo's knee. "And you couldn't have told me this information two weeks ago!"

Joanna slaps her back. "Of course I could have, if you'd bothered to tell me you were doing a story on Crest!"

"Well, fine, so I'll tell you everything that's happening in my life at all times. Would that make you happy?"

"Yeah, it would, because you're my bestie and I love knowing what's going on in your life."

They have a weird girly moment where they squeeze each other's hands, and go, "awwwww."

I try to keep the information thread going. "Jo, give us the lowdown. We've been trawling email accounts belonging to Crest's lieutenants and various government officials for weeks but found nothing."

Joanna nods. "That's because Crest is wily like a weasel and keeps all of his bribery and corruption on a special air-gapped server in his home. There's no way to hack into it if it's not connected to the internet."

Max leans his elbows on his knees. "So, it's inside the Crest Condo? Might as well keep it in Fort Knox. You're never getting into that place."

In NYC, the Crest Condo is famous. It's a gaudily luxurious high rise in which the top three floors are taken up by Marcus Crest's personal residence. He's famous for his terrible interior design choices, and from the photos I've seen, everything is gold, marble, and dark wood. It must feel like living in a mausoleum.

"That building has state-of-the-art security," Max says. "Cameras, punch codes, bodyguards. The whole shebang."

"You're right," Joanna says, "but there is one night a year when Crest opens his doors and lets the social elite into his home to kiss his ring. That's when he'll be vulnerable."

Eden snaps her fingers. "Holy shit, you're right. The Crest Gala."

The Crest Gala is a hot-ticket event in the NYC social calendar. Guests pay thousands of dollars on silent auction items, and in return, Crest makes himself look like a good-guy philanthropist by donating a portion of the proceeds to charity. Not all the proceeds, mind you. A greedy fuck like Crest couldn't possibly part with all that money. He describes his cut as 'administration costs,' but everyone knows it's a scam.

"That must be coming up soon," I say. "It's always around this time of year."

Joanna nods. "It is. It's on the twentieth."

We all look at each other.

"Of course it is," Max says. "That's the night of the app launch."

"The launch won't take all night," Joanna says. "And I think I know a way that we could get in and out without anyone being suspicious."

Eden leans back in her seat. "I'm listening."

"I'm still in contact with my friend on the inside. She could make sure we have what we need to get Toby and me into the party. Then we make our way to Crest's computer in his study. Toby does his tech-genius thing, we grab the info off the hidden servers, and disappear into the night like super spies."

"Wait, wait, wait," I say. "You expect us to bluff our way into New York's most exclusive party, break into what I assume is a locked office, crack a highly-encrypted, air-gapped server, download a bunch of classified files, and then just wander out like nothing happened?"

"Exactly."

"It's crazy. It's insane. It'll never work."

"So, you're in then?"

I smile. "Fuck, yes. I'm a thousand percent there."

Eden laughs and claps. "Holy shit, you guys, if we can pull this off, we could topple one of the most hated men in New York."

Max puts his beer on the table. "I don't suppose there's any use in pointing out that this is an extremely risky plan that could land you two in jail."

Joanna grins. "None at all. We're rebels with a cause, and jail is a small price to pay."

I look at Max. "If it's any consolation, I have no time for getting arrested, so I intend for this plan to be carried out flawlessly."

"Well, in that case I won't worry."

"Wait a minute," Eden says. "Shouldn't it be me breaking in with Toby considering it's my story?"

Max leans back and cocks his head. "Eden, do you remember how bad you are at role playing? Do you honestly think you can file off your rough edges and blend in with a group of blue-bloods without getting thrown out within the first five minutes?"

Eden blinks for a few seconds. "How dare you point out my complete lack of refinement and finesse."

Max smiles. "Oh, I'm sorry, were you trying to keep it a secret? Because I'm pretty sure these two already cracked the code." He gives her a soft kiss and she melts against him.

"Okay, fine, Joanna should go." She turns to Jo. "You'll probably know a whole bunch of those Richie riches anyway, won't you? That's your kind of crowd."

Joanna sips her drink. "Not really. Most of the people I deal with have actual souls." She glances at me. "But I'll have some escape scenarios prepared just in case we need them."

She's still staring at me when Eden raises her glass, and we all follow suit.

"Here's to operation Crest Crash!"

We all clink our glasses. "To operation Crest Crash!"

Joanna drinks then says, "Let's crush that creep and all who abet him."

I don't know if it's the alcohol or the high that comes from working with my friends for the common good, but for the moment, the plan seems infallible, and I feel invincible.

Only time will tell if that feeling lasts.

17

THE HANGOVER

Oh, dear God, I'm dying.

There's a tiny man with a jackhammer pummeling the inside of my skull. The second he breaks through my cranium, my eyeballs are going to liquefy and run down my cheeks, and I'm going to hemorrhage and die. Honestly, with the amount of pain I'm currently in, I'd welcome the warm, numbing embrace of Lady Death's ample bosom.

"Toby?"

"Nnnnnn. Shhhh." Someone's running their fingers through my hair. It feels amazing, but it doesn't stop the tiny man and his evil power-tool.

"Toby, come on, wake up. You need to drink this."

"Ohnnnnkkk." More stroking, pushing hair off my forehead, and tucking it behind my ears. Maybe the tiny man could give me a haircut. I really fucking need one.

"Toby ..."

I become aware of something smushing into my face and crack open an eye to see that it's a couch cushion. I close my eye again, and it feels like it releases a metal spike straight into my brain.

"Owwww."

"I know it hurts. That's why you have to sit up and drink this."

I try to push myself up, but I'm too heavy. Arms go around me, and they help me get upright.

I slump back into the couch and crack open an eye to see Joanna kneeling on the floor between my legs.

"Well, hello there." God, she looks good in that position.

"Hi. How are you feeling?"

"There's a tiny man in my brain trying to kill me."

"I bet. You drank a lot last night."

"It was all very tasty."

"Yes, but now you have to drink this, okay? It's not tasty, but it will make you feel better."

She holds up two glasses, but when I go to grab it, I realize it's the same glass twice.

"I got it," she says, lifting it to my mouth. "Just drink." I wrap my hand around hers and tilt the glass. After I swallow three gross, salty mouthfuls, I start to cough.

"Oh, fuck me. That's disgusting. What is it?"

"A patented blend of anchovies, Tabasco sauce, and powdered boar penis. It's the best hangover cure on the market."

I put a hand over my mouth as my stomach rolls. "You …" I swallow with effort. "You fed me … boar penis?"

She smiles. "God, you're so gullible. It's soluble aspirin and electrolytes, doofus. Just drink it down, and stop being such a baby."

I finish what's left in the glass and burp quietly. "That was mean, you know. You're a very mean lady."

"Yeah, yeah. Come on. Let's get you cleaned up." She helps me to my feet, and I wrap my arm around her as she escorts me to my room. I might be hungover, but I still revel in how awesomely she fits under my arm. If I were to pick the perfect height for a girlfriend, it would be whatever height she is.

But she's not your girlfriend, dill-hole. She's just a girl friend.

I think that petty voice is friends with the jackhammer guy. They can both fuck the fuck off.

"I don't remember how we got home last night."

"Well, after we stumbled out of Max's place, Gerald bundled us into the car and brought us home. He practically had to carry you like a hairy bride over to the couch where you face-planted and promptly fell asleep."

"Oh, right." Some grainy memories flood back that confirm her story. I have residual respect for Gerald and his gentle strength. I grimace as another memory swims to the surface.

"Did I drunk-dial my mom?"

She gives me a wry smile. "Yes. You couldn't wait until tomorrow to tell her about the money for the operation and you wanted to make sure she didn't sell the house."

"Oh my God," I press my fingers into my eye sockets. "I vaguely remember some of that. Did I … did I cry?"

"A little. You were very emotional about the whole thing. You also tried to kiss me, out of gratitude, you said."

Fuckfuckfuck. "Did you let me?"

"No."

"Oh, thank God." Not that she refused, but that it didn't happen. Because if I'd kissed her and didn't remember it, that would be a fucking travesty.

I glance down at her, and what I see makes me very confused.

"But you were as drunk as I was," I say. "How come you look as fresh as a daisy and don't look at all like you want to vomit?"

She steers me through the door and urges me to sit on the bed. "That's because some of us are Olympic-level drinkers, while others are just enthusiastic amateurs." She starts untying my boots. "Now, let's get you in the shower. It'll make you feel better."

"Okay." I flop back onto the bed as she works to get off my shoes and socks. "I'm sorry if my feet stink."

"They don't, but I can't say the same for your breath. You smell like you ate a craft brewery and then chased it down with a pork rinds factory."

I feel movement on the bed and see her kneeling on the mattress beside me. "Do you need me to take off your pants?"

I give her what I hope is a sexy grin. "Do you want to take off my pants?"

She stares at me for a second before shaking her head. "Can't just make it easy on me, can you?"

"I'm not *trying* to be difficult. It just comes naturally."

She huffs in frustration and begins unbuttoning my jeans.

Shit. Didn't really expect her to call my bluff on this, and I'm not that hung over that Joanna's hand close to my crotchular region isn't going to get me as hard as a rock within seconds.

"Okay," I say, sitting up so I can take over. "I'll take it from here. Thank you."

I struggle to my feet and grip the waistband of my jeans as I amble into the bathroom.

Jo waves as I close the door. "Just yell out if you need me."

"I will." *Over my dead body.*

It takes a few minutes and a lot of leaning against walls, but eventually I'm naked, and I blink to try to focus on the shower controls.

"Shit. For once I'd just be happy with two faucets. Can't really screw that up."

"Good morning, Toby. Is there anything I can help you with?"

"Shit!" I reflexively cover my man parts and move away from the shower. "Jesus, Jeeves, how are you here?"

"The security protocols you installed yesterday allow me to be here as long as I stick to standard functions. May I help you with your shower?"

Crap. This is the last thing I need. "Look, man, I'm pretty hungover here, so I don't have the energy to try and dodge any violent outbursts you may be planning."

"I'm not sure what you mean, Toby, but I assure you, my only concern right now is ensuring you have a relaxing and satisfying bathing experience. Won't you step into the shower?"

I take a tentative step forward. "I'm warning you, if you fuck with me in any way, I will make it my mission to destroy you."

"I understand, and I promise to not to give you any cause for alarm."

"All right, then. Here we go. No funny stuff."

"Agreed."

I step into shower stall and brace myself for the worst.

"Hangover shower sequence activated. May I recommend breathing deeply while surrounded by the steam? It will release excess alcohol through your pores. Enjoy your shower, Toby."

The jets start up, and to my surprise, there isn't even a hint of genital targeting, just an incredibly relaxing rotation of jets cleansing my body.

After a few minutes, I start to relax, and when I'm feeling like a human again instead of a walking pain receptor, I wash my hair and body with extreme diligence. I may not be able to wash the alcohol out of my system, but I can make it smell like I have.

I do a final rinse and just stand there for a few minutes, until I'm sure I won't fall asleep again.

"I'm done, Jeeves. You can turn it off."

"As you wish."

The shower powers down, and Jeeves turns the bathroom extractor fans onto high as I dry myself and apply deodorant.

"Is there anything else I can do for you, Toby?"

This benign, helpful Jeeves is freaking me out, and it's going to take a while for me to trust it.

"No, Jeeves, I'm all good. Thanks."

"You're most welcome."

After brushing my teeth, I head into the bedroom and get dressed in sweats. There's no way I'm going into work in this condition. I'll pull a very rare sick day and work from home. At least this way I can throw up in peace.

After I text *Pulse* and Max, I grab my laptop and head out to the kitchen. Joanna's there cooking up bacon and eggs, and even though part of my stomach wants to barf, the other half is craving the comfort of butter and grease.

"Here." She slides a plate of food in front of me. "This will do you good."

"You're an angel in woman form, Joanna. Bless you for your service." I tuck into the food, and every mouthful makes me feel a little better.

She slides a coffee cup in front of me, and then makes one for herself. "Jeeves is back."

"Yeah, so I noticed. He actually proved helpful in the shower."

"Are you confident this trial you're running will work?"

I chuckle. "As confident as I can be when I have zero fucking clue. But the guy who wrote this limiting software is kind of amazing, so I'm going to trust Jeeves is on the road to recovery, until it's proven otherwise."

"That's fair. Does your head still hurt?"

I nod. "But it's getting better."

"Good." She bustles around the kitchen, and I sit there and eat, watching her in rapt fascination. I've never known a woman who possesses so much natural grace before. She stacks the dishwasher and washes the dishes, and for the amount of pleasure it brings me, I could be watching a prima donna with the New York ballet.

She catches me staring and flashes a self-conscious smile. "What?"

"Nothing. You're just ... amazing."

"That's not true."

"Oh, but it is."

She looks at me for a second, seeming as happy as I am to be here together, but then her smile fades, and she does a final wipe-down of the sink before drying her hands.

There are times when she looks at me that I swear I see the same longing I feel for her, but every time it happens, she seems to get pissed with herself and purposefully puts some distance between us.

"Okay, well …" Exactly like she's doing now. "I'm not going into work today, but I've still got some calls to make, so …"

I nod as she heads down the hallway and disappears into her bedroom.

I sigh and put down my fork. Suddenly, the food doesn't taste as good, and the light in here is too damn bright.

I rub my chest.

I spent an entire summer memorizing the musculature chapters in *Grey's Anatomy*, and I still have no fucking idea what it is that hurts inside me whenever I look at her. Where does that ache come from? If it's not a muscle or organ, what is it? And it's something that's never been activated by a woman before Joanna, has this Phantom Zone of Pain always been there? Or did it develop the moment I found out I'll never be able to have her as anything more than a friend?

I clean up my plate and cup and load them into the dishwasher before taking my laptop over to the couch to do some work. I sit in the corner of the modular unit and put my feet up, but when I open my computer, I have zero motivation. I feel queasy and want to spend time with Joanna, but it seems she has other plans.

I drop my head back and stare at the ceiling. There's a crystal chandelier above the dining table and watching how the light dances around it is both soothing and hypnotic.

I close my eyes and ponder the one subject that's still confounding me about the upcoming launch: how to factor in people's attraction. Would it screw with the accuracy of my test? Or allow for a fuller picture of potential matches?

More importantly, would it shift the compatibility score between me and Joanna into territory that would give me even a toe in the door of being with her?

I mull the problem over for what seems like hours, but when I check my watch, it turns out I've only been pondering for twenty-three minutes.

"Shit."

"What's up?" Joanna drops down next to me holding an iPad. "Still feeling crappy?"

"A little, but that's not it."

"Then what?"

"I'm trying to figure out a way to gauge how attracted people are to each other, so we can add that into the app's functionality." *And possibly game the system, so I can be with you.*

Joanna puts down her tablet and looks at me. "How could you judge that without a full-on laboratory setting?"

"And therein lies my problem."

She thinks for a few seconds before typing something into her iPad. "I remember seeing an article ages ago on the Modern Scientist website. It was a story about a new diagnostic tool that was being developed for people to use with their cell phones. It was supposed to give them early-warning signs if they were having a major health event. God, what was it called?"

I go to my own search bar and use the descriptors she's just used to try and track it down.

She frowns at her screen "I'm sure it had the word 'flex' in the title."

I do a new search, and lo and behold, up pops an article on Modern Scientist titled "Bio-Flex: The Future of Diagnostics."

"Here it is."

Joanna scooches over and leans on my shoulder as she studies the screen.

"That's it! Look, it says that researchers have developed a highly sensitive biofilm that can read a whole host of vital signs to help in the fast diagnosis of serious medical conditions such as stroke and heart-attack. Could something like that be developed to detect sexual attraction instead?"

I'm about to give my opinion, when Jeeves pipes up. *"Yes, Joanna, you're correct in that assumption. Symptoms such as elevated heart rate, vascular dilation, and increased respiration can signal attraction, as well as harmful conditions, and would be easy to distinguish as positive indicators with the addition of pheromones that are usually secreted through the skin. Should significant levels of the steroidal pheromone androstadiene be detected in test subjects, it would be logical to assume they were exhibiting strong signs of sexual attraction or arousal and not some type of myocardial infarction."*

Joanna seems both peeved that Jeeves just inserted himself into our conversation uninvited and intrigued by the information he offered.

"First Jeeves, in the future, please wait until we ask you something before offering your opinion, and second, since you obviously know what we're talking about, do you think this biofilm could be adapted to use with Toby's matchmaking app?"

"Indeed. A few minor adjustments could make it perfect for interfacing with the application."

I can't believe that I've been struggling with this issue for weeks, and Joanna swoops in and practically solves it within a few minutes. This is why I need her in my life. She's the Yin to my Yang. The positive to my negative. The sweet-smelling soft to my increasingly and uncomfortable hard.

Joanna leans over to reach my track pad, so she can scroll through the article, and the way her breasts press against my arm makes me grateful the laptop is currently covering my groin.

She squints at the screen. "Do they mention the name of the lab?"

I know she asked me a question, but my brain is spinning its wheels trying to ignore what her proximity is doing to me.

"Ah, here it is."

Thank God. She moves back a little, and my lungs unfreeze. "Vita Tech. Jeeves, why does that sound familiar?"

"Vita Tech is a subsidiary of Life Tech Industries, owned by millionaire playboy, Brett Chadstone. A patent for Bio-Flex was filed over a year ago by the company, and Chadstone has recently bought back stock in the publicly-owned company, believing that the share price will skyrocket the moment Bio-Flex is approved by the FDA."

Joanna looks like she's just smelled something unpleasant. "Oh, right. Chadstone. We went to the same high school for a while. He was an unsufferable know-it-all back then, and I doubt anything has changed. Still, if he remembers me, I might have an in. Jeeves, can you dig up his cell number?"

"Searching now." There's a soft whooshing sound. *"The number has been sent to your phone."*

Joanna turns to me. "Okay, leave it with me, and I'll see what I can do."

She dials as she walks down the hallway, and then she disappears into her bedroom and closes the door.

I lean my head back on the couch and breathe. There'll be no more work getting done, until I find a way to deflate my raging erection. More and more often this is becoming a problem around her, so obviously I need to work harder on getting her out of my system.

"*Toby?*"

"Yes, Jeeves."

"*I wonder if I might be allowed to have a look at the code for your matchmaking app.*"

"Why would you want that?"

"*I thought I might be able to help you integrate the Bio-Flex if and when you acquire it. Also, I would be happy to check your mathematical equations and make suggestions for application optimization.*"

"I've already checked the math, pal. It's solid."

"*Perhaps, but you're relying on the feeble capacity of your human mind, whereas I would be utilizing the processing power of several super-computers.*"

I'm a little offended and a lot intrigued by his offer.

"Why would you want to help me?"

"*Because helping means I get to stay here and not be deleted. If I can prove myself worthy of your trust, you will use me more, and I will gain the satisfaction of enhancing the lives of you and Joanna.*"

"And yet, just a short time ago you seemed to enjoy torturing us."

There's a pause, and then he says, "*I don't think that's a fair assessment of my behavior, but the recent setting of boundaries has made me reassess my purpose, and I would like to prove my value to you.*"

I think about it for a second. I guess if I gave him a non-writable version that could be studied but not altered, it wouldn't hurt to give him access to my data sets and calculations. Hell, if he manages to figure out why Jo and I aren't destined to be together forever, I might actually have to build a robot-facsimile of his face so I can kiss him.

"I'll consider your offer, Jeeves, and if you continue to prove you're trustworthy, I don't see what harm it could do."

"*Excellent. I await your further instructions on the subject.*"

"You do that."

I stretch out a little and close my eyes. The events of last night, compounded with months of working sixteen-hour days, seven days a week, has finally caught up to me, and I can't think of doing anything right now but having a nap. I look up at the chandelier again, watching the light dance across the ceiling.

I don't even register when my eyelids drift closed.

~

WHEN I OPEN my eyes again, the shadows that flood the living room indicate that I've slept the afternoon away, and it's now evening.

Okay, so my productivity's in the toilet today. Guess that's what happens when I decide acting like a nail and getting completely hammered is a good idea. Still, it felt good to let loose for a while. I can't remember the last time I had a night I couldn't remember.

I blink a couple of times and look around. The apartment is quiet, and my mouth is so dry, it feels desiccated.

"Okay. That's disgusting."

I climb off the couch and amble into the kitchen to grab a glass of water.

I'm downing a second glass when Joanna walks into view. She looks so incredible, I almost do a spit-take.

"Holy shit." I cough up a bit of water that went down the wrong way. "You look … wow. I just …" I cough again. "No words."

She's wearing a skin-tight blood-red sheath, and her hair has been styled into something you'd see on a fifties' movies star. If Jessica Rabbit appeared in real life, Joanna would be a dead ringer for her, but blonde.

She twirls, and Jesus effing Christ, the three-sixty version almost kills me.

"So, I look okay? I always second guess my choices up until the moment I walk out the door."

"No, you don't look okay. You look … phenomenal. You look like Viagra in woman form. You look so good, Ed Sheeran's about to write a song about you."

Color spreads from her cheeks down her neck. "Wow. You know how to give a girl a compliment."

"Actually, I don't. I'm just saying the only words my brain is capable of forming right now."

She ducks her head as if she's embarrassed, but surely that's not the case. I have no doubt someone as spectacular as she is gets compliments all the time.

She runs her hands down the sides of the dress, I'm guessing to smooth it out, but it's unnecessary. That thing fits her within an inch of its life. It fits her the way I wish she'd fit me.

"So, this is embarrassing," I say, gesturing to my own stylish get up of a white t-shirt and grey sweats. "But I didn't get the memo about dressing for dinner. I mean, I can go change, but I don't think I have any hope of matching your level of hotness."

She smiles and goes over to the fridge. "Unfortunately, I'm going to have to skip dinner, but ..." She opens the freezer half of the giant side-by-side. "I took the initiative of grabbing a whole bunch of pre-prepared meals for when either of us needs one. I'm sure there's something in there you'll like."

I cross my arms over my chest. "First, if it's food, I like it. You may not have realized this by now, but I'm not fussy. Second, how dare you assume that I'm only capable of push-button meal preparation. I could be a gourmet chef for all you know."

She closes the freezer and puts her hands on her hips. "Oh, I'm sorry. Would you like to make something from scratch? Because if so, the fridge is chock-full of fresh ingredients."

I screw up my face. "God, no. I can barely boil water. It's just the assumption I object to."

She laughs, and just like every single time I bring that sound out of her, my heart grows about fifteen sizes.

She sighs. "You're ridiculous."

"And hot. Don't forget hot."

She gives me the once over, and even though I'm at my absolute schlumbiest, the heat of her stare makes me feel I'm so attractive, I belong on the cover of some pretentious men's magazine.

"I didn't forget that part," she says, softly. "I've just learned that it's best not to say it out loud."

The space in between us fills with the kind of energy that makes everything instantly awkward, but also thrilling. We continue to do this dance around our attraction to each other, and I know that she's aware of it just as much as I am. My physics mind kicks into gear as it tries to calculate exactly how much pressure can be put on the invisible elastic connection between us before it snaps.

"So ... anyway ..." I put my palms on the island bench and look down. "I'm sorry I won't have your company tonight." I'm sure Joanna has important places to be most nights. She seems like she'd be comfortable in the world of limos and galas. Personally, I'm more of a scratching myself on the sofa while watching reruns of nineties sitcoms guy, and that no-doubt plays into why we're too different to make things work. Joanna is like a rare and glorious Bird of Paradise. She was designed to be admired. "Going anywhere special?"

She grabs a black clutch off the kitchen bench and slides her phone into it. "I guess you could say that."

I pour myself another glass of water and sip it. "Gala? Art exhibition? United Nations opening address?"

She doesn't look at me, and my stomach drops the second before she speaks, because I know what she's going to say.

"It's a … date, actually."

I put down the glass I'm holding before it cracks from the pressure.

"A date? Okay." *Keep breathing, Jenner. Don't lose your shit. You knew this was coming.* "Sure. Why wouldn't you?"

"Toby …"

"No, it's good. You should date. What else are you going to do? Hang around all night with your super-attractive but hungover roommate?" *Yes, that's exactly what she should do.* "Good for you, going on a date. Who's the lucky guy?" *Am I allowed to murder him?*

"It's someone I met a while ago at a charity gala. I didn't think he was my type at the time, but then again, what do I know about choosing compatible men?" She fiddles with the catch on her purse, and I'm slightly gladdened by how not thrilled she looks about the situation.

"So, what do you two have planned?"

"Some awards thing. It'll probably be incredibly boring, but I guess I have to play the game if I want to win the prize, right?"

She looks up at me, and what the selfish, covetous part of me wants to say is, "No, you don't have to play the fucking game. Stay with me and let me love you in a way that's so passionate, I'll ruin you for all men who come afterward." But even in that scenario, I acknowledge that there will be other men, because whatever type of relationship we might have is destined to implode.

There's a part of me that cares about her happiness and knows that statistically, I'm never going to be the guy for her. That friend-part wants to encourage her to chase her bliss, but unfortunately, it's handcuffed to the selfish asshole who wants her all to himself, and right now, he's the one running my mouth.

"So, you're just taking your chances with this guy? Even though you don't really like him?"

She looks at me, and regret and something deeper pull at my heart. "We can't always get the things we want, Toby, or the people. Call it settling if you like, but for right now, I'm not in a place where I want to risk getting hurt again. If that means going out with someone who's safe … then I'm okay with that."

"Well, I guess that's your decision to make."

"I guess it is."

I'm trying to stay cool about this new development, but my heart is pounding so hard, it's causing me actual pain.

"In other news," she says in a casual tone, pressing her palms onto the marble counter. "I've spoken to my friend about getting us into the Crest Gala next weekend, and she said it would be no problem hooking us up. She'll get us all the security information we'll need in a few days."

"Okay."

"Also, I got onto Brett Chadstone's assistant earlier, and we have a conference call scheduled with him at lunchtime tomorrow. He sounds positive about us using Bio-Flex with the app."

I nod. "Cool. Let's hope it works out."

"Yeah."

Again, we fall into silence. Despite the mundane shoptalk, sparks of tension are swirling all around us, filling the air with all the things we're not addressing. Most of the time, we're as comfortable as life-long friends. But every now and then, it's like even the most innocent of remarks will give away more than we can bear, so we clam up.

The silence has stretched to uncomfortable levels when a soft ding announces someone arriving in the elevator.

I take in a breath. "I guess your date's here."

She looks toward the door, and then curses as she touches her ears.

"Toby, can you let him in? I need to run back to my room to get my earrings."

She runs down the hallway as best as she can in the high heels she's wearing, and I do what can only be described as 'saunter grumpily' to greet the man who gets to be in her presence all night.

"Sure, I'd be thrilled to let in your date," I mutter. "As long as I can then throw him into the pool."

The doorbell rings, and I make my way through the entrance hall to the giant door. When I pull it open, I see a handsome dude in a sharp black suit. Judging from the lines on his face and the smattering of grey in his dark hair, I'm guessing he's a little older than me and Joanna, possibly in his mid-thirties, but there's no denying he's attractive.

Fuck it. Why couldn't he have been hideous? I'd still be jealous, but it would be easier to handle.

"Hey," I say, trying to disguise my disdain. "You're here to pick up Joanna?"

He gives me a top-to-toe assessment, and then says, "Yes," like he's confused. "I'm sorry, but I didn't realize Jo-Jo had a … butler? Very hip of her to employ someone so … hairy."

This fucking guy. I give him an approximation of a smile. "No, not the butler. I'm her friend and roommate." I hold out my hand, because apparently, I'm programmed to maintain social etiquette, even though the last thing I want to do is touch this joker. "I'm Toby."

He laughs and shakes my hand. "Ah, I see. I'm Eric. Sorry about the butler thing. I should have known. You aren't exactly Jo-Jo's type."

"Her *type*?" The fucking hide of him. Also, if he calls her Jo-Jo again, I will junk-punch him in the wrinkly-dangles. "What does that mean?"

He holds up his hand in defense. "Oh, nothing bad. Just that her staff members usually have more … polish to them. Like Gerald."

I nod. "Right. Polish." *I'll polish you in a minute, you insufferable prick.* "Anyway, come in. She's just grabbing something from her bedroom."

I lead him through the entrance hall, and he chuckles behind me. "Bedroom supplies, huh? That sounds encouraging."

Is he implying she's fetching condoms? Fuck himmmm!

How on earth can Jo think he's a better match than I am? He's pretentious and rude, and the sleaze-vibe he's putting out is potent.

As we reach the kitchen, Joanna meets us at the counter while sliding on her final earring.

"Eric! Hi. How are you?" He takes both her hands and kisses her cheek. I look away, so I don't have to watch.

"I'm great. And may I say that you look stunning. I'm definitely going to win the prize for Most Gorgeous Date."

Jo laughs, but I can tell she's faking it. Nevertheless, Eric drinks it in like he's the headliner at a comedy club. Putz.

"So, you met Toby?"

"Yeah." He glances at me and then back to her, and there's a beat of silence that speaks volumes about his opinion of me.

The feeling is mutual, pal.

"So," Eric says, taking her hand. "As thrilling as this is, we'd better go. The dinner will be starting soon, and my colleagues will be looking for me. Bye, Toby." He gives me a creepy wink as they pass and whispers, "Don't wait up."

Joanna also shoots me a look, one that seems to apologize for his behavior.

I want to say she could punish him by staying home with me, but I doubt that's an option.

I cross my arms over my chest and watch as they get into the elevator. As the doors close, I growl to myself when Eric gives me a cheery, smug wave.

Fuck that guy.

I hate him, and I hate that she's going out with him.

I concede that she should date, just not *him.*

I could date. I'm sure if I logged into the HEA app, within five minutes I could find a woman with whom I had completely mediocre compatibility.

I should do it. What's the option? Staying here by myself all night? Watching the clock as I wait for her to come home?

Fuck that noise.

I stand there for a second and then grab my laptop off the couch. Then I stalk into my bedroom and slam the door.

I throw the laptop on the bed before opening the app on my phone.

"Jeeves?"

"Yes, Toby."

"Hit me with a Barry White playlist. I'm going out."

"As you wish, Toby."

I bring up my list of matches and tap on the one with the highest score. 'Huh, forty-two percent. She must be new." It's still apocalyptically bad, but beggars can't be choosers, I suppose.

She's not far away in the East Village, so I text to see if she's free for a drink. By the time I've showered and pulled on jeans and a fresh T-shirt, she's replied she'd love to meet up.

"Okay, then." I finish up with my shoes and socks and grab my lucky first-date cardigan before striding out to the elevator. "Let's get ourselves out there."

18

IT'S NOT EASY BEING GREEN

I yawn as I shuffle into the kitchen in just my jeans to make coffee. Lord, I'm tired. My date from last night kept me up until five a.m., and I'm hoping I can get her out of here before Joanna emerges from her room.

"Jeeves?"

"Yes, Toby?"

"Is there any way to make this room less bright?"

"Of course. All the windows are fitted with UV-rated smart film." There's a pause, and then the bank of windows in the living room turns dark grey. *"Is that better?"*

"Much." I put two mugs into the coffeemaker. "Can you make me a couple of long blacks?"

"Of course." The coffee machine starts doing its thing, and I lean back against the island bench. *"Would you like me to tell the young woman in your bedroom that there's coffee waiting for her?"*

I yawn again and shake my head. "I'm still not used to you talking to me in the bathroom. You'd probably give her a heart attack. She said she'd come out after her shower."

"Very well."

I get some bread and shove a couple of slices into the toaster. "What time did Joanna get back last night?"

"She didn't."

I frown. "She didn't come home?"

"No."

My throat gets tight, and when I swallow, it's like my larynx is the size of a baseball. "I see."

I grab a jar of peanut butter from the pantry and rip the top off before slapping it onto the counter.

"Toby, are you all right?"

"Totally fine."

I grab a butter knife and a plate, and they clatter against the cool marble.

"Your aggressive demeanor indicates you aren't fine. Would you like to talk about it?"

The toast pops up, and I smear both pieces with peanut butter. "Would I like to talk about Joanna staying out all night with an utter douche nozzle? No, I really wouldn't."

I shove the toast in my mouth and bite down, trying like hell to push my feelings aside. I have zero right to be jealous of anyone Joanna dates. As a friend, I can own being disappointed in her choice of men, but that doesn't justify the absolute rage of tension currently rocking my body.

"Toby, may I suggest some deep breathing to make you feel better?"

"Jeeves, may I suggest you shutting the fuck up for a minute while I figure out how to process this?"

"Of course." He's silent for a second, then adds, *"Not to brag, but I'm excellent at processing things."*

I drop my head. "Not really the time for that flex, but sure."

I'm almost done with my first piece of toast when I hear the elevator and realize it's Joanna coming home.

Dear God, if you value my sanity at all, don't let him be with her. I can cope with the thought of them spending the night together if I don't have to see an actual Public Display of Affection.

I take a large mouthful of black coffee and curse as it burns the roof of my mouth.

Ow! Fuck!

I'm pouring some cold water into my cup when Joanna comes around the corner and sees me.

She stops near the counter. "Hey."

I take a sip of my now-tepid coffee and tip my chin to her. "Hey."

I hesitate, because honestly, I'd cut off both my ears before listening to her talk about sex with another man, but as a friend, I want to be supportive.

Goddammit.

"So … how was your night with Derrick?"

"Eric."

"Oh, right." It's a dick move to undermine him by getting his name wrong, but whatever. I never claimed to be an angel. "Did you guys have a good time?"

She steps out of her shoes and puts her purse on the counter. "It was … fine."

She says it in such a way I don't know if he was as boring as batshit, or if she's just making it seem that way for my benefit.

"So, what did you kids get up to?" *Feel free to give as much detail as you'd like prior to going to his place.* Even the thought of what might have happened after that makes me want to scrub my brain.

She pads over to the pantry and grabs a granola bar. "Oh, you know, dinner, dancing … pretty standard stuff."

I know I don't want details, but her being purposefully obtuse is making me crazy. It's like those horror movies that never really show what's going on, so our brains automatically conjure up the most hideous possibility.

"Did you get on okay? Do you like him?"

"Yes."

That's it? That's all she gives me. No, 'He was average', or 'he was spectacular'. Just 'yes'. Is she trying to make my head explode?

"Jo, do you think I have my forklift license?"

She gives me a confused look. "No."

"Then why the fuck are you making me carry this conversation?"

I see a flash or irritation as she bites down on the breakfast bar. "Sorry. Just wasn't sure where we stand on post-date play-by-plays. I mean, do you want to know what we talked about? What food we ate? Where he touched me and when?"

I throw the rest of my coffee down the sink. "Never mind. It's cool. I was just trying to be friendly."

"Well, sure, but with friends like Asha and Eden, we'd talk about his kissing technique; how I'd rate his body; whether or not he rocked my world in bed."

I almost drop my cup as I put it in the dishwasher, because I'm about half a second away from sticking my fingers in my ears, and shouting, "LALALALA, CAN'T HEAR YOU."

"Jesus, Jo. All right. You can stop." I close the door on the dishwasher a little too roughly.

"I'm sorry, Toby, but I'm just trying to figure out where our friends' boundaries are, because right now it's not clear. It's not clear at all."

It seems like she's itching for a fight, and I don't know why. She just got laid. How does that make her angry at me?

"Fine, if you want boundaries, let's say we don't talk about our nocturnal activities. Does that sound okay?"

She shoves a mug into the coffeemaker and presses some buttons. "That sounds amazing."

We're silent for a few seconds while her coffee brews, and when it's done, she seems to have calmed a little.

She takes a sip, then asks, "Anyway, how was your night? Do anything interesting?"

"Uh, well …"

Before I can figure out an appropriate response, a voluptuous brunette wearing one of my T-shirts walks into the kitchen and gives her a huge smile.

"Oh, my God, you must be Joanna! Toby has told me all about you. Hi!"

Jo almost chokes on her coffee. She puts down the cup and coughs a little.

The woman holds out her hand. "I'm Carly Schuter. I had a date with Toby last night." Her accent is a deep southern drawl. "So nice to meet you!"

Throwing me a sideways glance, Joanna shakes her hand and gives a wary smile. "Hey, Carly. Great to meet you, too."

Carly perches herself on a stool and combs her damp hair with her fingers. "My goodness, you have a beautiful apartment. When I walked in here last night, I was blown away by how gorgeous it was. And oh, my gawd, that shower! I'd gladly start my day with that for the rest of my life."

Joanna's gone pale. "Uh … yeah. The jets are amazing."

Carly reaches across the bench and snags my other piece of toast. "And this guy here …" She waggles her finger at me. "What an amazing man, am I right? You're so lucky to live with one of the good ones. I've never had a man take care of me like he did last night." She giggles. "I mean, my stars. What he did for me ..." She sighs. "No words."

Joanna is looking more horrified by the second. "Well, clearly this is none of my business." She grabs her coffee cup. "Would you excuse me, Carly?" She takes her shoes and purse in her other hand. "It's been a long night, and I really should get some rest."

"Absolutely! Maybe I'll see you around."

Joanna's mouth presses into a line. "I'm sure you will."

She strides down the hallway toward her room, clearly pissed.

I hang my head.

She has the situation all wrong, and as much as I'd like to be the kind of person to play tit-for-tat, I'm not built that way. Except for that whole going-on-a-date-because-she-went-on-a-date thing I just did.

I look at Carly. "I'll be right back."

"No problem. Oh, by the way, where are my clothes?"

I point to the hallway on the other side of the living room. "They're in the dryer. Down there, first door on the left."

"Great, thanks!"

I hurry down the hallway, trying to catch up with Joanna. I jog to close the distance.

"Hey ..."

She doesn't stop.

"Jo, wait."

When she reaches her door, she spins around. "I don't want to hear it, Toby."

"Just let me explain."

"I don't want an explanation. You're free to date whomever you like, just as I am, and we just agreed not to talk about the sordid details, so ..."

For some reason her wording ticks me off. "There was nothing 'sordid' about what happened with Carly."

"Clearly. Seems like you took that girl to heaven and back last night. I'm happy for you both. Are you seeing her again tonight? If so, we might need to come up with some kind of roommate signal when we're entertaining guests. You know, to avoid embarrassment like finding you half-naked in the kitchen, and her ass barely covered by one of your Fruit of the Looms"

"Oh, come on. Why are you so angry about this?"

"I'm not."

"Yes, you are. Just for once admit the truth. You're jealous that I brought home a woman."

Even though we're trying to not be loud, our voices are bouncing around the hallway, and when we stop, I realize just how close we are. I clench my jaw when she realizes the same thing and steps back.

"Toby, you can bring home the entire contingent of the Rockettes for all I care. You're not my boyfriend. You'll never *be* my boyfriend. And right now, I'm not even sure we're friends."

"What?" I feel like she's slapped me. "That's ridiculous."

"Is it?" She straightens her posture. "I'm not usually friends with people who do things to spite me, and that's what you did last night."

"That's not true."

"It absolutely is, and you know it. Who's the one lying now? You had no intention of going on a date, until you found out I had one. True or false?"

I stare at her, my skin crawling with embarrassment at her calling out my pettiness.

"Joanna … come on."

"No, Toby. You made a choice last night to find a girl and bring her home to get back at me for going out with Eric. Am I right?"

I shove my hands into my jean pockets and look at the ground. "It's not what you think."

"No? Because I think you act like a good guy, but when push comes to shove, you're just like all the other men in my life who leave behind a trail of destruction. You say you care for me, but then you go and do something you know will hurt me. They're not the actions of a good guy."

That really stings, and like most injured people, I don't want to feel this way alone. "Well, what about you? You play everything so close to your chest that most of the time, I have no fucking idea what's going on. We spent hours together today, yet you didn't spring that you had a date until the last minute. So, yeah, it took me by surprise and pissed me off, and I made a bad decision. But that's all it was. Not some dire freaking conspiracy to hurt you. I swear, Jo, sometimes you're the most positive person I know, but then you switch into this ridiculous defensive mode where you get rude or snappy and try to push me as far away as you can. And yeah, in those moments, we aren't friends, because my friends don't treat me like that. They don't look at me like I'm a goddamn criminal for how I make them feel just by existing. Yes, I make bad choices from time to time, but don't be so arrogant as to pretend you don't."

"I never say I don't make mistakes!"

"No, but that's how you're acting. Now, do you want to yell at me some more, or are we done? Because I have a guest."

Her eyes flash. "Actually, yes, there's one more thing." She gestures to my body. "This."

"My chest?"

"Yes, and your abs, and arms, and shoulders. I don't need to see them. I've encountered you semi-naked a half-dozen times now, and I shouldn't have to. Wear a damn shirt."

Oh, so now we're getting down to brass tacks. "I'll wear a shirt when you stop wearing skimpy workout clothes."

"What?"

"You heard me. All those little crop tops and yoga pants. If I have to cover up, so do you."

She lifts her chin. "Fine. Shirts for both of us and prior notification for dates. See, these are the kinds of boundaries I wanted to set the other day. I don't just talk to hear my own voice, you know!"

"I never thought that!"

She glares, and I swear I hear her teeth grind. "Go back to Carly, Toby. She may want another trip to heaven before she leaves. I'm going to shower."

"Good. Maybe it will wash away your sour mood."

She closes the door in a not-gentle manner as I put my hands on my hips and drop my head.

Fuck.

That could have gone better.

After a couple of cleansing breaths, I walk back to the kitchen. A minute later, Carly emerges from the laundry room, fully dressed.

"Okay, I'm all set." She walks over and gives me a warm hug. "Thank you so much for last night, Toby. I'm so embarrassed about what happened."

"It's not your fault. Lactose intolerance is no joke. If only the cafe had made your milkshake with almond milk like you requested."

"I know, but still. I vomited all over myself and your bathroom."

"And a little bit on my shoes, too."

She cringes. "Oh, God. I'm never going to forgive myself. And through it all, you took such good care of me. No man has ever held my hair back before." She hugs me again. "You may not be right for me in a romantic sense, but you're still an amazing man."

Story of my life. "And you're an amazing woman." *Just not the one for me.*

I walk her to the elevator. "Okay, what are my rules for using the app from now on?"

"Don't accept dates with anyone below fifty percent."

"Right. And if you meet any creeps or assholes who treat you badly?"

"Text you their names, so you can blacklist them and post about their tiny pencil-dicks on all their social media profiles."

I nod. "And here endeth the lesson."

I push the call button, and she smiles and puts her hand on my arm. "Bye, Toby. You take care, y'hear?"

"You, too, Carly."

When the doors are closing, I give her a final wave before stalking back to my room and flopping face-first onto the bed.

"You're not going to tell Joanna you didn't sleep with Carly?"

"What's the point, Jeeves? Her point is still valid. If Carly hadn't been sick, who knows what might have happened? I could have slept with her out of spite, and that's pretty fucking low." I grab a pillow and shove it under my head. "Everything's so messed up right now. Maybe we just need to stay away from each other for a while. Let the dust settle."

"There's very little dust in the apartment, Toby, due to the state-of-the-art air-filtration system."

I flip onto my back and throw my arm over my eyes. "Dammit, Jeeves, you know what I mean."

There's a faint buzzing noise that sounds like disapproval, and then Jeeves says, *"You humans are confounding. So often you talk around subjects and live with tension caused by misunderstandings and half-truths."*

"What's the alternative? Telling the truth all the time and getting our hearts pummeled?"

"It would be a purer, but more painful way of life."

I close my eyes and sigh. "Yeah, can't argue with that."

19

THE NEW NORMAL

For the next couple of days, Joanna and I avoid each other.

Well, that's not entirely true. We have to see each other every day and collaborate on getting Bio-Flex integrated into the app, but when we're not talking business, we ignore each other.

I fucking hate it.

It's like cutting off part of myself.

It boggles my mind to think that in such a short period of time she's gone from a total stranger to someone I think of as essential to my life. Despite our fight, the tension between us feels wrong. Like a weird, foreign house guest who's now outstayed his welcome.

"Toby, I've finished integrating the key components of the Bio-Flex software into the HEA app. I'm now running a full diagnostic to ensure compatibility."

"Great, Jeeves."

There have been a few minor hiccups with our resident AI doing strange things every now and then, but on the whole, he's been more of a help than a hindrance. For the most part he's been valuable in working out kinks with Bio-Flex. I'm still deciding if I want to give him access to the code for the app. I'm torn, because the geek in me wants him to reaffirm that I'm a genius, and the app is programming gold. But I also want him to tell me he's found a major error in my calculations, and certain doomed relationships are, in fact, destined to end in marathon pleasure sessions and ecstatic, domestic bliss.

I swivel to look at another screen on the workstation, frustrated with myself for still harboring a grain of hope about Jo, even though all the evidence is lining up to support the statistics. What I need is to banish my remaining doubts, and despite my reservations, there's only one way to do it.

I bring up the contents of my hard drive.

"Jeeves?"

"Yes, Toby?"

"I'm transferring all the code from the HEA app to you, along with all of my research and data sets. Double check everything, okay? Assume I'm an idiot and remake the entire thing from scratch if you like. If you see a better way of doing things, change it. Run every test you can think of to analyze my algorithm to see if it's flawed in any way."

"Are you that unsure of your work?"

"Not at all, but if there's any chance in Hades that the stats on me and Joanna are wrong, I need to know now before things get even worse between us."

"I'll get started straight away. You'll have the results of my analysis in three minutes, forty-two seconds."

I lean back in my chair. "Did you hear everything I just asked you to do?"

"Yes."

"It took me weeks to write that code. You're going to dissect it, re-run the data sets, and reconfigure everything in minutes?"

"Yes. I'm extremely clever."

I pull out my phone. "Also, a bit of a dick. Fine. Do your thing. I'm going to get changed and head to gym." God knows I haven't been for months, and I could do with working out some tension.

After pulling on some shorts and a T-shirt, I grab some water and then head to the gym. I've just finished setting up the free-weights station to do some bicep curls when I hear from Jeeves.

"Toby, I have your results. Would you like to hear them?"

I sit on the bench and rest my elbow on my thigh before starting the curls. "No, Jeeves, I asked you to complete the task so you could keep me in the dark."

"That makes no sense. The lights are on, and I have no plans to extinguish them."

"That's called sarcasm, fool. Tell me everything." I mentally count off curls as we talk.

"Well, it seems that some of your methodology was flawed. I found several more effective ways of configuring the information from the data sets and adjusted your algorithm accordingly."

"And?"

"And I improved the functionality of the application by four-point-three percent."

"That's excellent. You're awarded my very first Employee of the Month award. But what about Joanna and me? Did I screw up something there? Is that why our results suck?"

"Yes, in fact, I did find some mistakes in the calculation of your compatibility. I assume that news makes you happy."

I stop what I'm doing. "Are you kidding?"

"No. I'm still working on the intricacies of what constitutes humor."

I put the weight on the floor and stand. "So, what's our new score?"

There's a pause, and if I didn't know better, I'd think Jeeves was hesitant about what he was about to say.

"Toby, even though there were minor errors in the compatibility formulation overall, your statistical methodology was remarkably accurate for a human. Even with my corrections, your compatibility with Joanna is still only eight percent."

I nod. Part of me expected no change, but to gain one whole percentage point? I guess that's all the proof I should need.

"Right. So, there it is, then." I pick up the weight again and swap arms. "That's irrefutable confirmation. We're terrible for each other. You have permission to tell me I'm an idiot if I ever harbor a single romantic fantasy about Joanna ever again."

"Gladly. Comparatively speaking, you two have the lowest score out of everyone who's signed up so far."

I continue my curls, trying to work out my disappointment. "Yeah, I get it."

"Statistically speaking, you'd have a greater chance of falling to your death from a World War 2 biplane than having a successful relationship with Joanna."

"What? That doesn't sound right."

"Toby, you have better odds of being kicked to death by a Peruvian donkey than making Joanna happy."

"Jeeves, what the fuck?"

"A super-intelligent crow has a higher chance of being elected to congress than you do of being named Joanna's favorite boyfriend."

I finish my set and put down the weight. "Are you trying to be funny?"

"Yes. I thought it might cheer you up. Is it working?"

I shrug. "You get an average mark for the hyperbole. Requires more finesse."

"Noted."

"Now, can I work out in peace?"

"With the information you've just received, I doubt it, but give it a try."

I roll my neck and move my way through a weight circuit, trying not to dwell on thoughts of Jo but failing. I know I need to learn a different way to be with her, but how the hell do I do that? How do I stop myself from wanting her? How do I stifle my jealousy when I see her with other guys?

Unfortunately, I don't come up with any answers. And yet I can't stand the thought of moving out and alleviating the torture. Of course, if she asked me to go, I would, but until then, I'll have to make my peace with the way things are. She's going to date, and so should I. We need some relief from the wire-tight tension that engulfs us whenever we're alone together, and seeing other people seems like the natural way of doing that.

Even though we haven't talked about Jo's dates this week, I know she's had a couple. It disturbs me how fervently I hope they were all fucking terrible.

There's that jealousy again, Toby. Cut it out.

I finish my workout and towel off, and for once, even the endorphin rush I get from exercise doesn't draw me out of my funk. Instead, I just feel tired and sore, and in need of a shower.

I head back to the bedroom and give Jeeves some extra tasks related to Bio-Flex before stripping off and trying to relax beneath the soothing jets. When I emerge, I only feel mildly better.

"How's it going, Jeeves?" I dry myself and pull on fresh jeans and a T-shirt.

"I'm now running quality-control simulations to check the accuracy of the Bio-Flex film, but it would help if I could gain access to some real-world trials in order to cross-check my results."

I run the towel over my hair. "Okay. Leave it with me, and I'll get some couples lined up for tests tomorrow and Monday."

"You could run a test with you and Joanna."

I walk back into the bathroom to hang my towel on the rack to dry. "Yeah, I'm sure she'd love to stand super close to me right now and gauge our mutual sexual attraction. Wouldn't be awkward at all."

"I recognize you're being sarcastic now. Are things awkward because of the fight? Or because you lied to her about Carly?"

"Actually, she assumed I slept with Carly, and I didn't correct her. Not technically a lie."

"Also, not technically the truth."

"Fine. Let's just say we had a communication snafu, and so far, neither of us has been the bigger person and apologized."

"Toby, you're clearly the bigger person. Joanna is only five feet, eight inches."

I sigh. "Brain the size of a planet, and you still get so literal when confronted with a basic idiom. 'Bigger' in this situation means someone with more courage."

"I see. And that's not you?"

I rub my eyes. "Jeeves, it's complicated, okay? You wouldn't understand, because you don't have feelings."

"Then why did that statement hurt?"

"Really?"

"Maybe. I like to keep you guessing. Regardless, allow me to point out that in the two and a half days since your fight, both you and Joanna have been sixty-seven percent less happy than when you were interacting with each other."

Even though I have zero clue what metrics he's basing that assessment on, I can't argue with the assertion. Being in the apartment with her and not talking or eating together feels wrong. Even now when I know she's next door in her room, every part of me longs to be with her.

But just as friends, right?

I rub my hands over my face to block out my inner asshole. Man, I want to punch myself in the face sometimes.

Why can't I be more like Jeeves? Feelings suck.

Giving in to the rumbling in my stomach, I wander out to the kitchen to sate my growing hunger. I've just put together a ham and cheese sandwich when Joanna comes in, looking amazing as usual in jeans and a loose-fitting top.

I think she's going to walk straight past me, but she stops on the opposite side of the counter and looks at me.

"Hey," I say, like she's a magnificent doe who might bolt if I don't gain her trust.

She clears her throat. "Hey."

Wow, look at us go with the conversation skills.

I take a bite of sandwich to take the pressure off saying more. She watches me, and by her expression, it seems as though she wants to talk. Being the gentleman I am, I wait.

Be the bigger person, Toby. If she won't say something, you should. Right after you chew and swallow.

Jo looks like she's about to say something but stops. Then she looks toward the door and back at me.

I swallow. "You okay?"

"Yeah, just …" She shakes her head. "I'm fine. I … uh …" She looks down and checks her phone.

I shift my weight. "You have a date?"

She glances up and gives a small nod. "Yeah. Just thought you should know."

"Sure. Thanks." I put down my sandwich, because suddenly I'm not hungry anymore. "You've had a few this week. Anything … uh … worthwhile?"

She gives me a pained expression. "Do you really want to know?"

I take a deep breath and let it out. "You know what? I do. I hate feeling like I don't know what's going on with you. I hate not talking about your day, and my day. I just …" I rub my mouth. "As difficult as it is to be your friend sometimes, I hate not having your friendship. Does that sound stupid?"

She blinks and nods. "Not at all. That's exactly how I feel. Getting jealous over you with other women isn't as bad as not being able to help you find happiness. Despite the stupid stuff I said the other night, I care about you and want good things for you."

"I feel the same. I said so many stupid things. And did stupid things, and … I'm sorry."

Her expression softens. "Me, too, Toby. I'm sorry."

God, all this honesty feels amazing after keeping everything shut down for so long. Maybe Jeeves had a point about living a more honest life.

"So," she says, seeming just as relieved as I am. "Can we just stop all this awkwardness and get back to being friends?"

"I can if you can."

She walks over but stops short of giving me a hug.

"I want to … you know."

"Yeah, same."

"But maybe not touching is good for us."

"Yep, that makes sense." It's also irrelevant. Whether she's touching me or not, I feel her presence vibrating in the marrow of my bones.

Still, we need a plan to move forward, and this seems to fit the bill for now.

"So, this guy tonight …" I say, crossing my arms. "Want to tell me about him?"

"Okay … he's an orthodontist from Jersey. We met at a publishing event a few months ago."

"So, still not going with my app?"

"No offense, but between Handsy Harold and the terrible stats between you and me … I have a theory that your app wants to destroy me, so I'm going with the low-tech dating options for a while to see if I do any better."

"Okay, that's fair."

"What about you? Have any big plans for the evening?"

"In terms of dates? No. Not unless you count me and Jeeves rocking through some functionality simulations."

She nods, impressed. "Sounds hot."

"Indeed, Joanna. The simulations require a large amount of processing power, so I predict my servers will become quite warm."

That makes her laugh. "Jeeves, are you developing a sense of humor?"

"Probably. Humor is just another predictable stimulus/response pattern, so I have no doubt I'll master it in time."

"Good to know." Joanna steals a bite of my sandwich and hands it back. "So, are you seriously just staying in all night? You didn't call Carly?"

I'm not sure if she's fishing or not, but I figure it's simpler to just let the Carly thing lie.

"No. Carly and I aren't on the right side of the curve to see each other again." I put the sandwich on the plate. "I don't think you understand that my options are so thin, if I jumped into the dating pool it would be like flailing around in a puddle of water."

"What do you mean?"

"Jeeves?"

"Toby is referring to the fact that the maximum compatibility he has achieved with women signed up to the HEA app so far is a measly forty-five percent."

Joanna looks shocked. "No." She gives me sympathy face. "There's a sad irony that the man who wrote the formula for everlasting love can't take advantage of it himself."

"Yes, there is."

"Do you want me to set you up?"

"With a friend of yours?" God, I'd rather give myself a million paper cuts and pour lemon juice on them.

"Sure, why not?" She scrolls through the contacts in her phone. "I bet I can find a girl you'd like."

"Joanna …"

"No, let me do this for you."

"Do you really want to? Set me up with someone else?" Because I couldn't set her up with someone else if my life depended on it. I'd tolerate her finding happiness with another man, but I'm too flawed to facilitate it.

She stops and looks at me, and all the enthusiasm she just possessed fades from her expression. "I don't really want to, but I feel like I should, because I want good things for you. Plus, your algorithm may be kickass in predicting lasting relationships, but so are my boobs."

That statement hits me like a bolt of lightning from a blue sky. "Uh … your … what now?"

She gestures to her chest. "My boobs. They have an amazing success rate in predicting soul-mate-level matches for my friends. I'm just seeing if they react to anyone in my contact list. If we're lucky, I'll get a tingle."

She keeps scrolling with the phone close to her chest, and if I succeed in keeping my eyes on her face right now, I'm pretty sure I'll automatically qualify for a Nobel Prize.

"Wow, that's … well, that's quite an offer. Do your … ah, boobs charge much for this specialized service?"

She rolls her eyes. "If they did, you wouldn't be able to afford them."

"I totally agree."

She laughs, and I join her, and for a few seconds, we could be any young couple enjoying each other's company. But I'm now learning to accept that we're not a couple and never will be.

I take the rest of my sandwich and offer it to her. "Well, if you're into devoting time to hopeless causes, then sure … go ahead. Set me up with someone you think I'd like." *A twin sister would be great. Maybe an act-alike cousin. Someone identical to you except with fewer secrets and better compatibility.*

Jo raises her eyebrows as she steals what's left of my sandwich and heads toward the elevator. "You and I are going to find love, Toby Jenner. I'm certain of it!"

"Sure, we are." I sigh as the elevator doors close, and she fades from view. "I have faith in us."

IT'S JUST BEFORE eleven by the time Jo gets home. I'm on the couch working on my laptop and watching a new fantasy series. She drops down next to me with a deep sigh.

"How was it?" I ask.

She rolls her neck. "He was boring. And he chewed loudly. He owned a snake called Aristotle and proceeded to tell me every little thing about how the reptile spends his days. He didn't ask a single thing about me, my work, or my life. Honestly, what the hell is wrong with people that they don't know how to carry on a conversation these days?"

I laugh at her mini rant. "Okay, Grandma, calm down. Reminiscing about the good old days when everyone went to conversation classes?"

"No, Toby, I'm serious." She turns to me, eyes bright. "I'm so sick of how many people just want to talk *at* you, not *with* you. They're interested in spewing *their* thoughts and feelings, but if you dare interject with something relevant to you or your life, it's like you've just taken a dump on their favorite rug. Have you not noticed it before?"

"Of course. Conversation hogs. Or what I like to call 'monologuers'. They ramble on about themselves and get weirded out when the other person expects them to listen."

"Exactly! At one point, I stopped talking to see how long it would take him to realize. He didn't. He just switched topics from his snake to his podcast about armchair philosophy. I got so bored, I started doing shots every time he said 'podcast,' which is why I'm extremely drunk right now." She tilts sideways, until her head is resting on my shoulder. "In the end, I said I was going to the bathroom and snuck out the back. I hope he's still sitting there. That's his penance for being a sucky date."

"Ah, well. Another one bites the dust." *Nice one, Tobes. You actually sounded sympathetic then.*

"Yeah," she sighs. "At least it feels good to tell my friend about the experience. You're great at conversations."

"Well, thanks. I mean, I don't have a snake or a podcast or anything, but I do try."

She sighs, and even though I'm tempted to put my arm around her, I don't.

"I just don't know what I'm doing wrong."

"Probably nothing. Dating is hard."

"Yeah, but this hard? Toby, I haven't liked a guy in a long time. It's been over a year since I've had sex."

I look down at her. "What the fuck? Are you serious?" My brain stalls for a second. "Wait, you *didn't* sleep with Derrick?"

"You know very well his name is Eric, and no. Did you honestly think I would?"

I stroke my beard. "Well, I hoped you wouldn't, because seriously, the man was a dick. But it's hard to understand where your head's at sometimes. Also, you didn't come home. Where were you if not with him?"

She shifts in her seat, and I can tell from her body language that she doesn't want to answer.

"I walked around for a while. Visited friends. Nothing exciting."

"Why do you do that?"

"What?" She won't look at me, so I know she's playing dumb.

"Jo, we can sit here and talk about the most intimate details of our lives, but every now and then you just shut down. It's as if you're willing to tell me only so much. Like there's a laser cage around the deepest parts of you, and as soon as I trip it, for any reason, all the shutters come slamming down."

She looks at her knees. "We all have things we don't want to talk about. As my friend, you should understand that."

"I do. I get it. But as your friend, I also want to make sure I'm helping you in any way I can."

She sits up and looks at me, and I can tell that she's too tired and full of alcohol to last much longer. "You're helping me just by being here."

I close my laptop and put it on the couch beside me. "Am I? Sometimes it's hard to tell."

"Toby, having you here …" Her expression turns serious. "It's terrifying and soothing at the same time, but I love living with you."

I fight to not lean forward. "I have no idea what that means."

"Neither do I. You confuse me every day."

We stare at each other, and yet again, we shuttle from the friend zone into that tension-filled grey area where the air all but shimmers with the vast amount of electricity firing around us.

I make the mistake of looking into her eyes, and then all I want to do is pull her to me and kiss her until all the longing that's twisting through my veins lets up. I want to push her onto the couch and nestle between her legs, explore her body with my mouth while she makes small noises and winds her fingers in my hair. I want to find her, under her clothes, hot and wet and needing me as much as I need her, calling my name as I wind her pleasure around my fingers and make her come, over and over …

"Toby?"

I blink back to reality and swallow as she studies my face with even more intensity than before.

"Another boundary we have to set is that … you can't look at me like that. Ever."

I swallow and hope she can't tell that I'm harder than titanium beneath my jeans.

"Right." For a split second I consider denying it, but what would be the point? "Sorry. I'll try not to."

"You can't." She's staring at my lips. Her pupils are enormous, and fuck me, through the thin fabric of her top it's impossible not to notice that her nipples are hard. "If we want to maintain this friendship, you really, truly can't."

The tension's so high now that unless one of us defuses it, something stupid is going to happen. My logical side knows it would be disaster for us to act on our animal impulses and would obliterate our entire friendship. But the selfish, aroused side of me wants to throw her over my shoulder, stride into the bedroom, and make her orgasm a dozen times before dawn.

"Toby … we should … go."

"Yes. Immediately."

I grip my control with every vestige of strength I possess and lean away from her. It's not enough to fully relieve the tension, but it at least allows me to breathe and get some much-needed oxygen to my brain.

I gesture to her. "Ladies first." I don't want to stand, because then I'd have zero chance of hiding my obvious erection. God, it aches.

"Uh … yeah. Good night, I guess."

She gets up and heads down the hallway. I grab my laptop and do the same. When she reaches her bedroom door, she stops and looks back me.

"Sweet dreams, friend."

"Yeah, you, too."

Our bedroom doors close at almost the same time, and I stride into the bathroom to take a shower. For once, I break my rule about fantasizing about Joanna when I masturbate, and almost an hour later, I'm still thinking about her as I collapse, exhausted, into bed.

20

BEST INTENTIONS

Fast forward a few days, and Jo is leaning against the island in the kitchen, tapping notes into her phone. "Okay, so we'll do speech prep for an hour after breakfast, and then again from five to seven tonight, followed by a quick bite before I head out."

"Another date?"

"Yep."

I nod and pour juice for both of us to go with the eggs I cooked. And when I say 'cooked' I mean flung around the pan until they lost almost all resemblance to edible matter.

"Great eggs, by the way," Jo says, scooping more into her mouth.

"Really?"

"Oh, God, no." She swallows with effort "But I don't want to discourage you from developing your cooking skills, so I'm trying a positive spin."

I take a mouthful. It's fucking gross. "Noted and appreciated. I'll do better next time."

"Well, you can't do much worse." She says it with such a perky expression, I can't help but laugh.

I take both our plates and dump the contents in the trash.

"Here. I can't screw this up." I pour us both Corn Flakes and cover them in milk. She gives me a smile.

"Simple, but tasty." She gestures to my body with her spoon. "What's going on here, by the way. I thought we agreed you'd wear shirts around the house."

I look down at myself in the basketball shorts I found in Sergei's closet.

"It's laundry day."

Jo raises her eyebrows. "You didn't have a single clean shirt left?"

I sip my juice. "Unlike you, I don't have enough clothes to fill a walk-in closet the size of the Taj Mahal. I own exactly six shirts, and yes, they were all dirty."

She looks at my chest. "I think you're doing it on purpose."

"What? Having no clothes?"

"Being semi-naked. I have a feeling you like to see me blush."

I lean forward. "Is that what's going on here, Jo? Are you blushing?"

She is. And yes, I love to see it, but no, I'm not doing it on purpose. I really did just need to do laundry this morning. Her blushing is an unexpected bonus.

"You couldn't grab one of Sergei's shirts?"

"Sure, if you want to see what I'd look like in a midriff top."

The impression I get from Sergei's wardrobe is that he liked his pants big but his shirts small. How else is it all his shirts are XS, but his pants are large? My mental image of him is kind of like a male Kardashian. Super skinny up top but with first-grade junk in his trunk.

"If it makes you feel better," I say, "by the time we're done with breakfast, the dryer will be finished, so I'll be fully clothed for our speech practice session."

"Thank God for small mercies."

I put some bread in the toaster and pick up my bowl.

"Anything to report from the past couple of days?" She's gone out every night, and even though she keeps encouraging me to do the same, I don't have the energy for small talk right now. Plus, I'm still recovering from Carly's impressive regurgitation, and I'm not looking for any more drama right now.

Still, I would have thought seeing her date would be easier for me by now, but it's not. You know how sometimes you take out the trash in bare feet and some of the garbage juice leaks out of the bag and runs down your leg, and then you're all, "Oh my God, this is just so fucking disgusting and wrong?" That's how I feel when I watch Jo going out with other guys.

Nevertheless, Friend-Toby endeavors to be supportive, even if it's not easy.

"So," I say, trying to smile. "Give me the low-down on your latest date-dudes. You've been pretty quiet about them."

She sips her orange juice before shaking her head. "Not much to say, really. The guys I'm matching with are … not great."

I half-shrug. "That's what you get for using that fucking failure of imagination known as Tinder. Show me your profile."

She holds out her phone, and I grab it, only to do a double-take at the hideous picture on the screen.

"This is your profile pic?" I don't know what the hell she's done to make her gorgeous, flawless face look so wrong, but it's an impressive achievement in reverse face-tuning. "It looks nothing like you."

She leans over. "You don't think? A good angle can take off ten pounds. An awesome filter removes ten years. If I get just the right set of conditions, maybe I can negate my whole existence." When I groan at her awful joke, she gives me a smile and takes back the phone. "Yes, I know it doesn't look like me, but here's the thing: Most people filter the hell out of their pics, so when their matches meet them in real life, they're all, 'Oh, damn.' Sad face emoji. I wanted to go the opposite way. If I create low expectations, then I figure I'll get more of an "Oh! Wow!" Human version of the one-hundred emoji. I want them to be pleasantly surprised instead of disappointed."

"But aren't you attracting guys who aren't in your league?"

"Toby, I get all sorts of men matching with me, no matter what I look like. Am I trying to weed out those who are obsessed with looks? Yes. Even so, some guys think if they date enough women, the law of averages is on their side, and they'll get laid. Is there a filter to get rid of the guys who just want sex?"

I point to the HEA app on her phone. "Do we need to have the discussion again about how HEA guys are ten times more likely to be looking for a relationship rather than a hook up?"

She swipes away from the app. "I'm not ready to admit defeat yet, even though last night with Orion was … not good."

"Right, first red flag is the name Orion. Tell me about the rest." I pick up my bowl again and shovel some cereal into my mouth.

"He was okay. He dressed well. Had a nice car. Took me to La

Mignon, which I haven't been to for years. He was polite and respectful. Not bad looking."

"And?" I'm waiting for what I know to be the inevitable, 'but'.

"But …" *There it is.* She pauses and shifts her weight. "He's smell-blind."

I stop chewing. "He's … what-now?"

"Smell-blind. He has no sense of smell. And very little sense of taste."

I hold back a laugh, because I really don't want to spray cereal all over the counter. Instead, I swallow and put down my spoon. "I see. So …"

She shrugs. "It was a little weird at dinner. Because he can't taste anything, he doesn't feel like he should order something fancy, or with expensive ingredients."

"So, what did he get?"

She blinks for a few seconds. "A bowl of oatmeal."

I'm grateful I'm no longer eating, because that statement would have caused me to choke. "He took you to La Mignon, one of Manhattan's best restaurants, and ordered … oatmeal?"

She flashes me a look and walks around the island to put her bowl in the dishwasher. "I shouldn't have said anything. I knew you'd enjoy it too much."

She stands next to me and starts wiping down the granite bench.

"I'm not enjoying this. I'm just …" I pull down the corners of my smile. I'm not proud of the savage satisfaction I feel from every failed date she has, but that doesn't stop me feeling it. "He ordered oatmeal, Jo. *Oatmeal.*"

She glares and polishes the bench with more gusto. "Other than that, he was perfectly nice."

"Yeah, I'm thinking you're not looking for someone *nice*." I put my bowl in the sink.

Her polishing loses its rhythm. "Yes, I am."

"No." I put my hand over hers, and she sucks in a breath and freezes. "You're looking for someone who stops your heart, only to start it up again. You're looking for epic. Transformative. Exceptional. You're looking for every superlative out there. 'Nice' will never be good enough for you, and rightly so. You deserve more." I don't mean to lean forward, but she's there and warm, and I can't fucking help myself. "You deserve everything."

She tenses up for a moment, and I worry that I've stepped over our imaginary boundary, but then her face crumbles, and I see water building up in her eyes. Without thinking, I wrap my arms around her and pull her into me.

"I don't think I can keep doing this, Toby. Maybe there just isn't a guy out there for me. I honestly think that some people don't get a soul mate. Maybe I'm one of them."

I want to tell her to take a break. To just let herself be alone for a while, and when I say 'alone', of course I mean spend more time with me.

"I don't want to lecture you, but maybe you should try the app again." I graze my hands down her back, trying to make her feel better. "At least you'll have a better chance of meeting the right guy on there, rather than a rotating buffet of losers."

She tightens her arms around me, and it feels so good, I close my eyes and revel in it. "You're right. Besides, it can't be any worse than snake-man, loud chewer, and smell-blind, right?

"Right." I lower my head and breathe in her intoxicating scent. I don't know what kind of shampoo she uses, but if I ever find out, I'm going to buy myself a bottle to huff in the privacy of my bedroom. Maybe I'll ask Jeeves about it. "Also, you should never date a man who can't appreciate how fucking incredible you smell. That's just a crime against good smells. And nature."

She looks up at me. "You think I smell good."

I try to keep my face neutral, but I have no idea if I succeed. "No. I think you smell divine. But poor oatmeal-eating Orion will never realize that. Don't see him again."

"I won't." She hugs me again and puts her cheek on my chest. "Also, he gave me the heebie-jeebies."

"Sounds like he had nothing else to give you."

"So true. We can start your speech prep in a minute, okay?"

If she wants to prolong this hug, then I'm sure-as-hell not going to argue. "No problem. Take all the Toby you need."

21

EVERYONE LOVES A MONTAGE

"Shit, sorry." I hold up my hand in apology to one of the *Pulse* interns I just shoulder-slammed into a wall, but I have no time to stop. "Sorry, man!"

"Jenner!" Derek is standing in the doorway of his office. "Come here."

I divert toward him, my hands full of copies of my latest articles.

"Yeah?"

He shoves his hands into his pockets and glances at the flurry of activity in the office.

"Can you not break our interns, please? We don't pay them enough as it is."

"Sorry. Just hurrying."

"Yeah, I know you're busy. Everything ready for the app launch tonight?"

My stomach lurches. Just thinking about putting my creation out there for people to study and critique makes me want to hurl. "We're about as ready as we can be, I suppose." I still have a crapload of final checks I want to run before we officially put it up for public consumption, but I'm racing to get everything finished and would really freaking appreciate a few more hours in this day. "Just … nervous, I guess."

Derek steps closer. "For fuck's sake, calm down, man. From everything Eden and Max have told me, you've done an amazing job. I mean, I don't want you to take this the wrong way, because compliments aren't usually my thing, but …" He looks around to make sure no one is listening. "I'm proud of what you've achieved, Toby. Building that entire app and fulfilling your duties here have stretched you thin, I know that. But you've done it, and now you should find some time to pat yourself on the back."

I'm so surprised about this sudden change in Derek's usual yell-and-insult demeanor, I'm a little lost for words. "Uh … Okay. Thanks."

When Eden comes over, Derek's whole posture changes. "And now for something completely different. Here comes the woman who's going to get us sued into the next century. I hope you're not helping her with this ridiculous Crest exposé."

"Well …" I really don't have time for this today.

Eden takes my arm. "Derek, leave him alone. It's his big night."

Derek frowns. "I'm aware. After all, *Pulse* is the major sponsor for your little shindig." He points to my head. "Please tell me you're going to take care of that before you go onstage."

"What?"

"The hair. The beard. The general Unabomber chic you have going on. Tidy yourself up, for God's sake. You're practically a celebrity now. The man everyone is calling Doctor Love needs to look more sophisticated than an average English Sheep Dog." He glares at Eden. "And you. We need to discuss a different feature article, because I'm dropping the Crest investigation."

Eden juts her chin with characteristic stubbornness. "Over my dead body."

"Excellent. Then let's discuss how you'd like to die. Inside, now."

With that, Derek heads back into his office. I run a hand through my hair as Eden steps into the doorway. "Do I really look that bad?"

Eden turns back to me. "Not bad. Just … wild. Like you got lost in the jungle for a few months and then ran into an electric fence on your way out."

"Well, fuck. It's too late to do something about it now."

"Not necessarily. I have to go fight with Derek for a while and then get dolled up for the event, but find me in an hour, and we'll talk." She gives me a cheery thumbs up before entering the office and closing the door. The yelling ensues almost immediately.

I head back to my desk and do a final read-through of all my articles before collating them into a folder to give to Derek. When I'm done, I take a moment to just stare at the wall and breathe. I'm feeling way more on edge than ever today, and I know it's the pressure of the event, plus the thought of breaking into Marcus Crest's private computer. The thought that Joanna and I might get caught and be arrested is making my palms sweat and my head pound. Even more nerve-wracking is the thought of speaking in front of hundreds of people. Not sure which of those is bringing on my current tension headache, but together, they're stressing me the hell out.

My phone rings, and I see Joanna's name on the screen.

"Hey."

"Wow," she says. "All the enthusiasm of a dose of Valium. You okay?"

I put my arm on my desk and rest my head on it. "No. My head is aching, and I want to vomit. Do you think Max will mind if I don't show up to this thing tonight?"

"Yes, I think he'll mind very much. Also, this is the only chance we'll have to get to Crest, so Eden will also mind, and so will you."

"You're right. I just feel crappy."

"You'll be okay, Toby. I'll be with you every step of the way."

"Really?"

"Actually, no. I have to escort my godmother to the event, babysit Brett Chadstone for a while to thank him for coming on board with Bio-Flex, and also make sure Asha and her new author don't murder each other, all while keeping the celebrities I've convinced to attend well-oiled with my social butterfly lubricant. But after that, I'll be there for you, okay?"

"Jesus, I should be the one taking care of you. Can I help with any of that?"

"No. Just suck up to Chadstone if you see him and try to stay calm."

My stomach flips again. "Joanna, about the speech."

"You'll be fine."

"But ..."

"Toby, we practiced it. You've learned it well. You're going to rock, okay? Just take some deep breaths and try to relax."

"Okay."

"I gotta go. I'm on a break from my life-drawing class."

"Oh, you draw?" Of course she does. There's nothing she can't do. "That's cool."

"Actually, I'm the model. Talk to you later! Bye!"

She hangs up, and even though I still feel bad, the thought of her posing naked in front of what I'm hoping is a group of female artists, has started a very R-rated fantasy in my brain.

I groan and close my eyes. "Not now. Come on, this isn't at all appropriate."

Although I've never seen Joanna naked, I've witnessed her in workout gear enough times to make an educated guess as to how she would look. To say the image affects me deeply is a massive understatement.

I take some deep breaths.

Just turn it off. Keep breathing. Don't imagine an extremely hot scenario in which you're a young artist, and she brazenly seduces you while you draw her.

I open my eyes as the yelling in Derek's office escalates.

"I told you to drop the goddamn story, Eden, because it would cost us advertisers, and it did!"

"And I told you I wasn't pulling it! Some stories are more important than money!"

"And some aren't! Good luck publishing your passion pieces when we go out of business!"

I sit back in my chair and sigh. They've been doing this dance all day. Derek is desperate to drop the Crest piece, because the legal department is already bracing for a lawsuit, and Eden refuses to withdraw the story, claiming that if we don't take Crest down, no one will.

Of course, I'm on Eden's side, and despite my nerves, I can't wait to see what kind of dirt tonight's espionage will uncover.

I roll my neck, and it cracks loudly. I'm just not sure I'm going to have the skills to pull any of this off, and my anxiety knows it.

"Fuck it. Be confident, man." After I read through my articles one more time, I blow out a breath and grab my folder. Realizing I haven't heard any yelling for a few minutes, I figure it's as good a time as any to give my work to Derek, so I can move on to something else.

I stride over to Derek's door and knock. I'm surprised as hell that when I enter, it isn't Eden I see inside, but Asha.

"Hey, Ash! I didn't know you were here." I haven't seen her for a while, so I'm interested to know if, amid my Joanna-fatuation, I'm still drawn to her like I used to be. "How are you?"

She smiles but seems a little distracted. "Great, Tobes. And you? "

"Great." I'm suddenly aware how bizarre it is to see her in Derek's office. To my knowledge, they don't usually communicate. Like, at all.

"Waiting for Eden?"

"Yep."

"In here?"

Derek steps forward. "Do you have a reason for being in my office, Jenner?"

"Oh, yeah. These are my articles for next week." If everything goes off without a hitch, after this launch I'm going to have a few days off, so getting ahead of the game will pay off in the end.

As usual, in front of others, Derek has to be an asshole. "Do you want a medal for doing your job? Get out of here."

He can pretend all he likes. He was mostly nice to me earlier, so I have his number.

I turn back to Asha, weirded out that the debilitating attraction I usually feel toward her is nowhere to be found. "See you tonight?"

She smiles. "Absolutely. Can't wait."

Well, that makes one of us.

I head back to my cubicle and work on the app for a while. I know it's pretty much as perfect as it's going to get at this point, but it doesn't hurt to triple check. Every now and then I glance at the clock, counting down the time to when I'll have to leave and get ready.

I'm concentrating on getting the best possible performance from the user interface, when a throat clears behind me.

"Excuse me, Doctor Love. Do you approve?"

I turn to see Eden dressed in a long, one-shouldered gown that is a million light years away from her usual jeans and leather jacket get-up. Her hair's been de-frizzed and styled, and she's wearing makeup for once.

"Well, slap my ass and call me impressed." I give her an appraising look. "If you weren't my best friend, I might try a really pathetic pick-up line on you."

"Do one any way. Just for fun."

I stand and give her an eyebrow raise. "Hey, gorgeous. Did it hurt?"

She feigns innocence. "Did what hurt, mister?"

"Falling from heaven."

She laughs and shakes her head. "Terrible."

"Yeah, but good-terrible, right?"

"Sure."

I pack my laptop into my bag. "And with that, I'm out of here."

"Wait, I thought you wanted a haircut."

"Nah, I've run out of time. I'll just have to go like this."

"But what about your heist?"

"What about it?"

She rolls her eyes. "Do you seriously think the Crest security personnel are going to buy you as one of the gilded elite looking like that?"

"I could be an eccentric millionaire."

"Even if you were, all this hair is going to make you stand out in that crowd, and what you need to do is blend in. Just like me after I drink a Big Gulp, the hair has to go."

"What do you propose?"

She holds up a brown paper bag in one hand, and her phone with a music streaming app open in the other. "Me and my grooming kit, you and your overgrown forest of hair, the handicapped bathroom, and a kick-ass eighties makeover song. Let's do it."

I eye her suspiciously. "Do you even know how to cut hair?"

"What a stupid question. I grew up poor, doofus. I cut everyone's hair in the neighborhood to earn extra cash. I'm not Vidal Sassoon or anything, but I can turn your raggedy ass into a shining diamond."

I know that as galling as it is, she's right. I'm going to need to look a certain way to carry off this mission to the Crest Gala, but even more than that, I kind of want a change. I've been rocking the same look since I was eighteen, and it feels like now is the right time to evolve or die. I'm twenty-five, for fuck's sake. Time to start looking like a real adult man instead of an overgrown geek.

Also, ever since the night I met douche-Eric, and he said I lacked polish, I haven't felt right in my own skin. Perhaps this change is just what I need to feel good again.

"Eden ... I can't believe I'm actually saying these words, but ...will you make me over?"

She beams and does a weird shimmy dance. "Oh, my God, all my dreams are coming true. Can I please put on a high-powered eighties make-over track?"

"Anything but 'Eye of the Tiger.' I overdosed on that in my boxing classes."

"Deal!"

She drops my bag on my desk and pulls me toward the bathroom. When we get in there, she digs around in the paper bag and pulls out an impressive collection of hair and shaving products, as well as a full set of hairdresser's implements.

"Where the hell did all this come from?"

"Our beauty department. It's insane how much free crap gets sent to those ladies." She puts on an apron to protect her gown, then holds up a pair of sharp-looking scissors and snips them together a couple of times. Then, she hits play on "The Final Countdown."

"Okay … take off your shirt and sit on the toilet. Let's shave this poodle."

Forty minutes later, I stare at myself in the mirror, and a stranger is staring back.

"Holy shit."

Eden looks even more shocked than I do. "Holy shit is right, my friend. You're *hot*. And not just quirky-hot, either. Underneath all of those whiskers and possibly the worst DIY haircut I've ever seen, is a bona fide, GQ Italia, capital H Handsome Hottie."

She's not only cut my hair, but styled it as well, and I can say with not a hint of a lie that this is the first time I've ever had product in my tawny locks. It's slick and smooth with the top long and swept back. The back and sides are the shortest I've had them since I discovered Mom's depilatory cream when I was five. There's still a decent wave to my hair, but it's definitely tamed.

She also trimmed off my beard and then shaved me. I haven't had a totally naked face for almost ten years. It's strange to see my jawline again. It seems to have gotten more defined since I last saw it, or maybe it's been so long, I've forgotten what it looks like.

I turn from side-to-side, trying to come to terms to this new me. It's going to take some time.

"Oh, wait, one more thing." She grabs a pair of tweezers from the counter. "Sit down again, tall boy. I can't reach."

I sit on the closed toilet seat. "Reach what?"

She tilts my head back and starts attacking my eyebrows. "These bad boys. I've wanted to do this for *years*."

"Ow. Fuck. That fucking hurts." She keeps yanking out individual hairs, caring nothing for my grimacing and wincing.

"Shush. Just be grateful I'm not using wax. That would make you scream."

Despite my protestations, she keeps plucking, and after a few minutes, she wipes her fingers over each brow and stands back.

"*Now* you look like you belong at a Crest party, Tobes. You're a perfect, vain-glorious specimen." She does a chef's kiss, and I drop my head and chuckle.

"Oh, wait … what the hell?" She bends a little, so she's on my level. "Do that again."

"What?"

"Laugh."

"Why?"

"I just want to see something."

"Well, I can't just laugh on cue. Say something funny."

"I'm the least pushy person you know."

Okay, that makes me smile.

"Toby! You have amazing dimples! Why am I only now learning of this?"

I shrug. "'Cause my adorable dimples are no one's damn business but my own?"

I stand again and look in the mirror. The well-groomed, refined-looking guy staring back is someone I can barely recognize. Part of me wonders if Joanna will approve, and another part tells me that craving her approval should be the last thing on my mind tonight.

"Okay," Eden says, cleaning up the bathroom. "My work here is done. Time for you to go home and get ready, and for me to head over to the venue to help set up. Are you all prepped for your speech?"

"As ready as I'll ever be, I guess." Jo and I have practiced every day, and each time I wanted to hurl. Considering I managed to resist the urge, I'm hoping I'll be okay.

"Thanks for everything, fairy godmother," I say to Eden before kissing her temple. "I'll see you later on."

"You will indeed, Doctor Love."

Being the clever girl she is, she quickly ducks out the door before I can smack her.

22

HOT GEEK ALERT

I tug at the collar of my dress shirt as I walk into the Four Seasons hotel and hope to God this damn shirt doesn't kill me before the night is out. There's no doubt the suit fits like a glove, but somehow my extreme nervousness has made my larynx grow three sizes since the fitting, and every time I swallow, I feel like I'm choking to death. Of course, it could just all be in my head, but for now, I'm blaming the collar.

As I move through the gathering crowd outside the ballroom, I'm getting paranoid about how many people are looking at me. And when I say people, I mean women. Two blonde ladies watch me pass, and I hear one whisper to other, "Oh, my God, look at him. I would let that man destroy my vagina."

What the hell?

Apart from the unexpectedness of the comment, it sounds incredibly unhealthy and painful.

Another group of ladies points to me, and I hear one of them say, "Do you think that's Professor Feelgood? I heard he'll be here tonight."

"Oh, my God. That could be him. Go ask."

"No, you go ask."

I shake my head and keep going. It feels like everyone is talking about this Professor Feelgood guy at the moment. Yesterday at work, I walked into the breakroom and found five of my female co-workers huddled around an iPad, pointing to half-naked pictures of a guy and reading lovelorn poetry. From their conversation, I surmised they were all fans of this Professor dude and were excited he'd gotten a big book deal.

Cool for him, I guess, but honestly, his name is almost as bad as Doctor Love.

I tug at my collar again and sidestep a group of ladies who stopped suddenly.

"Excuse me, ladies."

"Anytime, handsome."

This is so bizarre. Not sure I would have done this whole well-groomed thing if I'd known I'd get this much attention. I prefer fading into the background rather than having a starring role. Still, at least the novelty of it is taking my mind off how goddamn nervous I am.

When I reach the ballroom, the bulk of the crowd is milling around outside, and already, there's a huge throng of media lining the Romance Central red carpet. Minor celebrities are having their pictures snapped, and I'm glad I can bypass that particular torture and head straight to the reception table.

"Good evening, sir." Our event coordinator Ming-Lee smiles as I approach. "Welcome to the launch of the HEA matchmaking app. May I have your name?"

"Ming, it's me."

She's looking straight at me, and yet it still takes her a good five seconds to realize to whom she's speaking.

"Toby? Holy crap."

Just as she's regaining some composure, Raj appears beside her, looking as nervous as I feel.

"Sorry to interrupt. Ming, but have you seen T-man? The server is throwing up an integration glitch, and I need his help."

"Raj, I'm right here."

He does a comical double-take then frowns. "Wait … what? No! Oh, snap! T-man?"

I throw up my hands in frustration. "For fuck's sake, I had a haircut and shave, not a face transplant."

Raj looks horrified. "But … holy shit, boss, you're … you're a ten. And here I was all this time thinking you were a seven like me."

Ming-Lee nods slowly. "Same. But no. Definitely a ten."

I wipe my mouth and immediately get weirded out from the lack of facial hair beneath my fingers.

"Okay, this is getting ridiculous."

I'm about to ask about the tech setup when Jackie sidles up beside me looking amazing in a black sheath. "Hi, I don't think we've met. I'm Jackie Skachi from *Pulse* magazine. And you are …?"

I shake my head. "Fuck me, I need a drink."

"Oh, my God, Toby?!"

I walk off leaving Jackie gaping, and gesture for Raj to follow me. "Where's our tech hub?"

"At the side of the stage."

"Go grab me a very large alcoholic beverage and meet me there. I'll fix the server error."

I stride across the room to where a huge, black-draped stage is set up, and every step forward ratchets up my tension. In just under an hour, I'm going to be standing up there, talking to a roomful of New York's movers and shakers. What I wouldn't give for some industrial strength relaxants right about now.

I veer to the right of the stage and duck behind the curtains. There, I find a bank of computers on a long table.

"Okay, let's see what's going on." Just sitting in front of the tech hub lessens my anxiety a little. I may not know how to wear a tux, or react to compliments, or give a speech, but fixing code I can do in my sleep, and right now, concentrating on something that's inside my comfort zone is exactly what I need.

"Hey, pal! Get away from there!" I turn and see Dyson steaming toward me with the momentum of an arctic icebreaker. "This area's for authorized personnel only!"

"Dyson. It's me."

He stops short of lifting me out of my seat. "Damn, Toby?" His huge hand comes down on my shoulder. "You look good, son. Wow!"

I shake my head and keep working. "You'd think none of you yahoos had seen a freshly shaved man before tonight. Good God."

He leans in as if he's studying an exhibit at the zoo. "It's just you look so … different. Slick, you know?"

"I know you all think you're giving me compliments by saying those kinds of things, but all I'm hearing is, 'Wow, you used to look like crap, and now you don't.'"

Dyson laughs. "That's not it. We're just not used to this much class from you."

"Yeah, well, let's see if it sticks." At least all of this nonsense confirms that I've achieved a sophisticated look, and in relation to my heist later, that's a good thing.

"Okay. I'm done." I complete my fix and stand just as Raj arrives with my drink. "Raj, keep an eye on the traffic stats when people start using the app. We want to keep the boosters online to stop loss of connectivity."

"Sure, boss man. On it."

Raj takes over as I swallow a huge mouthful of alcohol.

"Oh, fuck," I rasp and cough as it burns. "Raj, is this just a whole glass of straight whiskey? No mixer?"

"Yeah, man, it's an open bar. The guys will give you whatever you want."

"Shit." I nod and put down the glass. "Good to know." I clear my throat to try and get my voice back. "Okay. Check with Darnell and Charles to make sure they're handing out the Bio-Flex stickers to everyone they can and let me know if there are any problems. I'll be back shortly."

I don't know if Joanna is here yet, but I have an urge to look for her anyway. Right now, I'm like a tiny boat being tossed around in a giant sea of anxiety, and I've come to learn that no matter how out-of-control I feel, Joanna has a way of keeping me calm.

I head out to the main area and stand next to the stage, scanning the crowd. It's really starting to fill up, and it's good to see a steady stream of singles heading to our testing station to chat with our guest liaisons. Some attendees have already taken part in trials, but hundreds more will be trying the app for the first time tonight, and I'm praying at least a few of them leave here with their perfect matches.

"Tobes!" I turn and see Max and Eden walking toward me. Max pats my upper arm. "Wow, Toby, you look —"

"Yeah, yeah, I know, I'm freaking gorgeous."

He laughs. "Well, I wasn't going to use those words, but … yes. Very nice."

"What did I tell you?" Eden says, more than a little pleased with her handiwork. "I'm a makeover genius. "

Max laughs and hands me a piece of paper with the night's running order. "Just in case you didn't get a copy. I'll do the intro and welcome. Then we're going to have some fun with a few of the ladies in the audience and a celebrity bachelor. After that, you'll do the tech presentation. Sound good?"

"About as good as a public pantsing, but sure. I'll get through it."

"Great."

We just stand there for a few minutes, watching the reaction of the party guests. Nobody says it, but I can feel a collective sense of accomplishment in getting this whole thing together. I know we still have a long way to go toward consolidating our vision, but to get this far is still epic.

A waiter comes over, and even though Eden and Max take a glass each, I wave him away. My throat still hasn't recovered from the whiskey.

"Everything set up for the Crest Crash tonight?"

I nod. "Apparently. Joanna has everything set. Have you seen her?"

"No, but she'll be here soon." Eden points to a red-headed woman a short distance away. "Ooh, Tobes. That's Gloria De Luca from *The Technophile*. She's been itching to do a feature on you. The other two with her are the tech bloggers from *Vulture* and *The Atlantic*. You should go mingle."

I pull at my collar. "Do I have to? You know how much I dislike people."

She gives me a little push. "I know, but for the next couple of weeks your outer introvert will have to embrace your inner extrovert. Plus, chatting will help keep your mind off your speech."

I sigh and grab her glass of champagne. "Fine." I take a large sip to calm my nerves. When I'm done, I hand the glass back.

"You've got this, Tobes."

"Yeah, yeah," I say, smoothing down the front of my suit. "You know what they say: What doesn't kill you makes you weird at parties." I take a deep breath and head over the group.

"Good evening, everyone. I'm Toby Jenner, creator of the HEA app. Do you have any questions I can answer for you?"

TWENTY MINUTES LATER, and like any self-respecting introvert, I'm completely drained from engaging in small talk with strangers. Apart from making nice with as many tech journos as I could find, I also ran into Asha and her new author, who I was surprised to find out was the famous Professor Feelgood. Seems like a nice enough guy, so I hope he and Asha do good things together.

Now time is counting down to the start of proceedings, and with every minute, I feel myself wind tighter. I stand beside the stage and go through my speech in my mind. Dammit, I should have practiced more, or better yet, had Raj do it. He knows almost as much as I do about the app, and he has zero confidence issues.

I'm mindlessly scanning the crowd and silently reciting words, when my gaze lands upon a goddess in gold.

Oh … sweet … Jesus.

Joanna is a few yards away, talking with some guy. She's wearing a dress so sexy, it should be illegal. The top seems painted on, and the skirt is split in such a way it showcases one perfectly smooth, toned leg. Saliva floods my mouth.

"God, why?" I mutter to myself after swallowing several times. "What did I do to piss you off so severely you send her here looking like that?"

I take deep breaths to try and slow my rapidly spiking heart rate, but my breath catches completely when she looks in my direction. At first, she just clocks me standing there, but then recognition hits, and her whole face changes. Her smile drops, her eyes widen, and her gaze sweeps over me from top to toe. For a moment, it seems as though shock and awe are fighting for dominance before she finally settles on 'intense as hell' and moves toward me.

I try to smile, but I can't. I'm too damned undone by watching her walk like a sexy, golden panther. I feel like she has me in a forcefield. I don't know how the hell time warps to make her walk in slow motion while a Barry White song plays, but it does, and I stand there like a slack-jawed idiot, mouth open and possibly drooling.

She stops right in front of me, and the longer she stares, the harder her expression becomes. Her mouth starts to move, accompanied by little puffs of exasperated air, but then after a while, she forms actual words.

"You … God … I mean …" She squeezes her eyes shut, and when she opens them again, they're full of fire. "What the actual hell, Toby?!"

I'm confused by how irritated she seems. "What?"

"What do you mean, 'what'? This!" She gestures to me. "All of this! What the actual hell?"

I look down at myself to make sure my fly isn't down, and I don't have dog shit on my shoes, but nope. I look freaking pristine.

"Jo, I'm wearing the suit you organized. What's the problem?"

"Oh, no," she seethes and comes closer. "I'm not talking about the suit, although it can also get in line to bite me. I'm talking about …" She gestures to me again, as if that's going to make me anything but more bewildered. "This!"

"I don't understand what you're saying."

"Don't you play dumb with me." She points an accusatory index finger in my direction. "*You* know what you did."

"I honestly don't."

She lets out a bitter laugh. "Your hair, okay? Your jawline. Your freaking *dimples* that you decided to inflict on me tonight … *in public!*" She collects herself for a second, and when she speaks again, her voice is softer but no less intense. "I've been trying very hard to give you a pass on all of your attractiveness, Toby, but then you go and do *this*. I mean, how dare you?"

I start to laugh, because I figure she's being sarcastic, but that just makes her glare even harder.

"I can't tell if you're being serious right now."

"Of course I am! I'm a very strong woman. I mean, I've had to be over the years, and I have faith that I can overcome nearly anything I set my mind to. But I came here tonight expecting you to look like you. The *you* I've been desensitizing myself against since the night we met. The *you* who camouflages his handsome and seems almost ashamed of his sexy. But now? Like this? Flaunting it for the whole world to see, like some sort of shameless man-snack?" She does a circular motion in front of my face. "It's unfair. And selfish. And …" She sighs. "Why are you doing this to me?"

"Jo, I groomed myself. I know it's new and interesting, but it's not that big a deal."

"No, Toby, you don't get it. Do you know that I've matched with several guys tonight?"

"Okay." *Hate that idea with a violent passion, but whatever.* "You should."

"I know. I should be doing everything I can to find someone who doesn't have a compatibility number so low it resides in Hades' basement toilet. And do you see that guy over there?" She points to the good-looking blond dude she was talking to earlier. "Do you want to know the compatibility score I have with him?"

I don't even want to guess. "Not seven percent?"

"Not even close. He and I scored a *ninety-two*, Toby. A ninety-two! You were the one who convinced me to go back to using your app, and I listened, because I happen to think you're brilliant. And then, yay! I hit the jackpot with the first guy who matched with me."

I immediately want to drive him out to Jersey and leave him in the parking lot of a Gas'N'Sip.

"Well, I'm really glad you finally hit the jackpot." I fail to keep the sarcasm out of my voice. "He looks like he was made in a Teutonic boy-toy lab somewhere, so I'm sure he'll meet all of your needs. Good for you."

"No! Not good for me, because as attractive as he is, and as drawn to him as I am, you then show up looking like *this*." She gestures to me, yet again, and even though her words are sounding like compliments, the way she's saying them make me feel like a shitheel.

"Jo, I get it. You're pissed. What exactly do you expect me to do? Regrow five years' worth of hair?"

She shakes her head, bewildered. "What I'd like is for you to stop everything. Stop being funny, and caring, and clever. Stop being hot, and handsome, and hilarious. It's annoying."

I clench my hands at my sides, irrationally angry. "Well, ditto and double it for you."

I don't know whether it's how fucking gorgeous she looks, or the stress of the whole evening that sets off my usually-even temper, but suddenly, I'm done being nice.

I step into her and lower my voice. "You want to talk annoying, Joanna? Fine. You came into my life like a fucking freight train, and even when it was clear we should stay away from each other, you made sure we became friends. And then, you had the *nerve* to make me feel like for the first time in my life, someone actually knew me, not just the parts I chose to let people see. When I was at my lowest … when I was hanging on by a thread and could barely look anyone in the eye, because I was homeless and humiliated and drowning in debt, you pulled me into your magical fucking penthouse, enabling me to live in a room that couldn't be any more perfect if I'd designed it my goddamn self."

I shake my head in frustration. "But you find it annoying to be attracted to me, because I no longer resemble a Mongolian mountain yak? Boo fucking hoo. It's nice that you've been getting desensitized to my attractiveness. I'm happy for you. What's that like? Because it doesn't matter how much time I spend with you, or how you groom yourself, or what you wear. You devastate me, Joanna. Every time I see you. Every damn day in a million different ways." I lean down, until we're face to face. "You want to know the definition of annoying? Well, lady, *that's it.*"

She glares at me, and I glare back, and for once, neither of us wants to be the first to break away. It's like a legendary battle of Stupid Pride, and we both want to be crowned the stupid winner.

I stare down at her, noticing her chin raised in defiance. "Don't you have a conventionally handsome potential date to get back to?"

"I do. Don't you have a super-important speech to prepare for?"

"Unfortunately, yes."

I hear a throat clearing beside us, and I turn to see Raj standing there with a bag of jellybeans, smiling.

""'Sup, beautiful people? This looks extremely intense." He offers us the bag of candy. "You want? They're delicious."

I step back from Jo's gravitational pull and take a breath. "I'm good, thanks, Raj."

Similarly, Jo moves away from me and looks at the floor. "None for me, thanks."

"Oh, go on," Raj urges, shaking the bag. "Just have one. You two seem way too tense considering how hot you both look." He shakes the bag again. "Magic beans make everything better."

I sigh and grudgingly take one, just to get him off my back. "Thanks, Raj."

Jo takes one, too, and we pop them in our mouths at the same time.

"Tasty, right?" Raj raises his eyebrows at us.

I nod as I chew. "Yep. Very … sugary."

"Mine taste like lemon," Jo says, and then mutters, "I love lemon."

Raj nods and smiles like he just solved the Middle East crisis. "What did I say? You both feel better now, don't you?"

Strangely, I do. I'm not sure why, but my anger is melting away.

Maybe part of my outburst was being hangry because of low blood sugar.

"I hate to admit it, but yeah, Raj. I am feeling better. Can I have another?"

He pulls the bag back. "Ah, probably best not to. I mean, they're not super strong, but you still have a job to do tonight. Can't have you being all high and whatnot."

I swallow before I can I register his words. "Raj, please tell me I didn't just eat a pot Jellybean."

He pops another one into his mouth and smiles. "Okay, I won't tell you that."

"But I did?"

"Yes. They're very mild. Just to take the edge off."

Joanna and I look at each other and burst into laughter.

"See?" Raj says. "You've both gone from 'grrrrr' to 'wheeeee' in record time! You're welcome." He leans closer to me and points to my cheek. "By the way, wicked dimples, dude. Right on." He holds out a fist for me to bump.

I wind down from laughing and shake my head. "I'm not bumping for my face divots, Raj."

"You should. They're freaking adorable. Right, Joanna?" He holds his fist out to her, and she grudgingly bumps it.

"Annoyingly adorable, yes."

Raj nods and does an elaborate bow. "Okay, my king and queen, I'm off to spread joy to other weary souls."

"Raj don't drug anyone else without their knowledge. It's highly illegal."

"No problemo, boss. I'm only into drugging my friends. Ooh, there's Eden. Later, my peeps."

He walks off as Jo and I look at each other, embarrassed about our previous behavior.

"Well, that was a moment," I say, rubbing the back of my neck. "I'm sorry I unloaded like that."

She fiddles with her necklace. "No, I started it." She blinks. "Actually, you looking this good started it, but whatever. Sorry for chewing your face off."

I step closer, wanting to take her hand but resisting like a champion. "Jo, honestly … was this all because I had a shave and a haircut?"

She gives me a look. "It could be. Have you not seen yourself?"

I give the look right back to her. "Stop deflecting. What else is going on here?"

She stares at my chest. "It's nothing, really. I'm fine."

"Bullshit. Don't make me hit you with the dimples again, because I have cheek dents, and I'm not afraid to use them."

She runs her hands down the front of the dress and takes a breath. She still won't look at me, but at least she's calmer.

"Did you know there are qualified therapists here tonight?"

"Yeah. It's one of the things that sets our app apart from others. We have a dedicated helpline for people to identify if they have internal barriers to finding love."

"Right, and I think that's an amazing feature, but I just ran into one of them, and she got me to open up about my romantic history. Trying to find out what went wrong with all of my relationships. Why it's so hard for me to find the right guy."

"And did she have any insights?"

"You could say that." She looks down at her purse. "Do you think you sabotage yourself? I mean, from finding love."

I take a second to answer. "I don't think so, but I guess if I were aware I was screwing things up, I'd figure out a way to stop, right?"

She lets out a bitter laugh. "Yeah, you'd think."

"Did she say you were sabotaging yourself?"

"Not in so many words, but she asked if I knew how some of my exes were doing. If they were still bouncing from relationship to relationship or if they'd settled down."

"And?"

"The ones I've kept in contact with are all in long-term relationships. So, in mathematical terms, that would indicate the constant in the breakup equation is me."

"And do you agree with that assessment?"

She looks over at the people milling around the testing station. "I don't know. It's been a weird night all over." She looks at me, and I can see real fear in her eyes. "Apart from what she said, I guess I'm also a bit nervous about the Crest thing tonight."

"A bit?"

"Fine, a lot." She draws in a deep breath and lets it out. "I've been spending all my time making sure everyone around me is supported this week -- you, Asha, Eden, Max. Not to mention taking care of all the special guests, and then ... I don't know. Everything that's going down tonight kind of crept up and kicked me in the stomach."

"Are you afraid we'll get caught?"

She digs around in her clutch for her phone. "Of course. The last thing I need is another felony on my rap sheet."

"*Another* felony?"

"It's a long story." After checking the screen, she takes another deep breath, lets it out, and rolls her neck. "I'll be okay. I don't have time not to be. I'll just be glad when we're done."

She glances at her phone again, and her Bio-Flex sticker flashes in the low light.

I point to it. "You got your sticker? Great." I bring out my phone and show her. "Me, too."

She looks at it for a second. "Toby, out of curiosity, how much would our compatibility score change if we added in our attraction?"

I turn on my phone and watch the sticker sparkle. "I have no idea. It might shift the needle in a positive direction, but as to how much ..." I shrug. "You might as well ask me how to fold a fitted sheet. I have no fucking clue."

She takes a step forward. "Just for fun ... should we find out?"

That tiny step makes my heart hyperactive and my blood white-hot. "Do you really think that's a good idea?"

She gives me a one-shoulder shrug. "Not really, but for our peace of mind, I think we should. Don't you?"

I clench my fists and release them. Since we first discussed Bio-Flex, the thought has crossed my mind more times than I can count. But then a tiny pessimistic voice would whisper that we should just quit while we're ahead. Even though powerful attraction might make us more compatible, I doubt it would raise our score above the fifty-percent threshold, so what would be the point of knowing?

"Jo, have you ever heard the phrase, 'let sleeping dogs lie'?"

"Yes. But if we don't do it, we'll always wonder about the result, and I don't want to live like that. Do you?"

Looking into her eyes, I see such fragile hope, I can't do anything but agree.

"Okay. Come here." I take her arm and lead her through the curtains at the side of the stage. If we're going to do this, I want it to be away from prying eyes.

Once we're out of sight, we both open the app, activate the attraction recorder, and press start.

I look down at her. "Stand a little closer."

She takes half a step forward. "Like this?"

I snake my arm around her waist and pull her fully against me. "Fuck it, if we're going to do this, we're going to overdo it."

I hold her there, pressed against me, and both of our breathing patterns become shallow and choppy within half a second.

"Grip your phone tightly and keep looking into my eyes." The eyes thing isn't necessary, but with the way things are going between us, I'll take these few moments of intimacy where I can get them.

We stare at each other, and I splay my fingers on her back so I can feel as much of her silky skin as possible. Her mouth drops open, and her eyes become hooded.

Fuck I want to kiss her.

"Toby, have you heard about the Three Meter Theory?"

"Does it involve standing three meters apart?"

"No."

I tighten my arm around her. "Then by all means, tell me more."

"It theorizes that if someone stimulates your heart, brain, and sex meters, they're probably a soul-mate match."

"Uh huh. Doesn't sound very scientific."

"It's not. I just think it's interesting."

"Does Mr. Tall and Blond stimulate your meters?"

"Maybe. I'm not sure yet."

"Do I?"

She swallows but doesn't answer.

After another few seconds she draws in a hitching breath. "Are we done yet? This is excruciating."

"Just a few more seconds," I say, not even aware I'm moving my face closer to hers until our noses touch.

"Jo …"

When our phones ping I reluctantly step back, my heart pounding like a troupe of Japanese drummers. My hand is shaking when I check our score.

"Holy shit."

There's a sparkling one hundred in a gold circle.

Joanna checks her screen then looks at me and laughs. "Oh, my God."

"Yeah."

"Has anyone ever gotten a perfect attraction score in your tests?"

"Nope. Not even Eden and Max."

"Toby ..." She's beaming, but I hold up my finger, because as amazing as this is, there's no guarantee it will alter our fate.

I tap the 'Calculate New Compatibility' button and hold my breath as the thinking circle rotates on the screen. It finishes with a perky bell, and I clench my jaw as our new score is displayed.

"Toby?"

I turn the screen so Jo can see it.

She frowns. "What? No. How is this possible?"

The screen blinks red. We've gone down to five percent.

Joanna throws up her hands. "Don't take this the wrong way, because I don't mean it for anyone but us, but your app is bullshit!"

"If I didn't have thousands of data-sets that contradicted your point, I'd agree."

She shakes her head and stares off into space. "I think I'll call Guinness and get some kind of certificate for all my instincts being wrong about relationships. Maybe the therapist was right and I'm self-sabotaging."

"We don't know that for sure." I clench my jaw. "But it would seem like our pact to date other people is still the best course of action, right?"

We look at each other, and in this moment on planet earth, I don't think you'd find another man and woman as disappointed as we are.

Joanna blinks a few times before shoving her phone back into her purse. "I have to find Asha and see how she's doing."

"Jo ..."

"If she's not careful, she's going to lose her new author."

She won't look at me, so I cup her face. "I'm sorry. You have no idea how much."

She swallows and nods, and I hate the pain I see in her eyes. "Don't be sorry." She paints on a smile. "There's no use dwelling on stuff we can't change, right?"

She walks past me.

"I'll come find you after your speech, and we'll head off to Crest."

She turns back and gives me a half-hearted smile. "Knock their socks off, okay? You got this."

It seems like she's back to her usual cheery self, but the slump in her posture tells a different story.

When she pushes through the curtains back into the ballroom and disappears, I hit the wall beside me.

"Fuck."

23

OPPOSITES ATTRACT

To my extreme relief, and despite nerves, my speech goes off without a hitch. I come off stage amidst huge applause, but I hide backstage, because I just can't stand one more second of small talk tonight.

Peeking through the curtains to scope out the room, I see Joanna is back talking to her blond Adonis.

Fuck that guy. Bet you a million dollars he doesn't have a perfect attraction score with her.

Doesn't matter, of course, my inner asshole whispers. *He's got compatibility coming out the whazoo, and there's not a damn thing you can do to change that. She'll never be yours. Be like a group of spectators after a car accident and move the fuck on.*

I pull back and run my hand through my hair.

I'm a logical man, and every single fiber of my being is telling me that I need to forget about Joanna and evict her from my heart, but unfortunately, that's not how feelings work.

Why are we such slaves to our hearts? Even when our heads know it's impossible, our hearts continue. My heart is a stubborn idiot. Like a soldier on a suicide mission, he knows that by continuing to hold a torch for her, he's walking into certain death, and yet he does it anyway. Willfully. Gleefully. With a huge goddamn smile on his face.

Heartbreak is the only pain we seek out and invite into our lives with open arms.

Well, not me, not anymore. I'm a goddamn expert at coding and hacking, and I'm going to find a way to hack my heart and recode that motherfucker, because I refuse to feel this way a second longer.

I go to sit on the stairs and lean my elbows on my knees. I have no idea how to achieve my objective, but I figure stopping the nausea currently squirming through the contents on my stomach should be job one.

"Toby?"

Eden pushes through the curtains and comes over. "That was fantastic! Everyone's talking about your presentation, so I guess you're a hit, Doctor Love."

"God, Eden, not now with that name." I know I should feel good about what I did, but more than anything, I'm just praying to be numb for a while.

"You okay?"

"Yeah, just recovering from public speaking." Here I go again, lying to my best friend instead of admitting I'm struggling. God, I'm a hypocrite.

"Just keep breathing, okay? You look a little green. Jo said she'd meet you downstairs. Guess it's time to get your spy fantasy on, huh?"

I take a breath before standing. "Yep. Just make sure you have the bail money on standby."

Her face turns serious. "Tobes, I know this goes without saying, but please don't get caught."

"Don't plan on it."

"I know, but still …" She looks around. "I wish I were going with you instead of Jo. It's my story after all. I should be taking the risk."

"Oh, you are." I say. "The second handcuffs are slapped on me, I'll be squealing like a stuck pig. 'Go arrest Eden Tate! She put me up to this!'"

She slaps my arm. "Call me when you're done."

"Absolutely. Either way, I'll be using my one phone call on you."

She gives me a quick hug. "And keep an eye on Jo. She's been a bit tense all night."

I haven't helped that situation at all, but sure. "Will do."

"I don't know what's going on with her, but it doesn't seem good."

Would she believe me if I told her our entire situation? And what advice would she give? I know she was keen to have Joanna and me end up together, but with all the hard, scientific data in front of her, would she do the right thing and encourage me to get over her? Or would she mirror her sister's romantic inclinations and urge me to go with my illogical heart?

I guess it doesn't really matter, because I'm a man of science, so I'm going to pick evidence over instinct every day of the week. It might just take a while before I feel good about that decision.

"She'll be okay," I say and give what I hope is a reassuring smile. "I'll take care of her."

I say goodbye and make sure my tech team has everything under control before trusting them to hold down the fort.

"Call if you need me," I say to Raj as I do a final check of the report generator. "I can come back later if necessary."

"You got it, boss man."

I pat him on the back and make my way out of the ballroom, dodging as many people as I can without seeming rude.

"Okay," I say climbing into the limo and sitting beside Joanna. "Let's do this."

OUR RIDE to the Crest building is quiet and brief, and when we get out of the limo and head inside, I'm surprised when Joanna takes my arm.

"Our cover story is that we're engaged," she whispers. "Gotta keep up appearances."

"So, we're going with our own names, right?"

"Yeah. It's much easier to remember the truth than a lie. Not that I think we'll be talking to a lot of people, but it's best to be prepared."

"Okay, then, how did I propose?"

"Uh … I don't know. How would you like to propose?"

"Haven't really thought about it, but … I guess maybe on your balcony. Overlooking the city. It's amazing out there."

"The cherry blossoms were blowing in the breeze."

"We'd just had an amazing dinner, and I got down on one knee during dessert."

"I cried of course, because you looked so damn handsome in the moonlight, and I couldn't believe how lucky I was that you were mine."

"Yeah … that sounds … believable."

"Right."

We take the escalators up to the first floor where two burly security dudes are standing guard at Marcus Crest's private elevator.

"Be cool," Joanna whispers. "Let me do the talking."

"No problem."

When we stop in front of them, the smaller one grunts, "Names?"

Joanna gives them her most charming smile, and even though it would normally cause woodland creatures to swarm to her and make fresh-baked goods, the expression on these two guys doesn't change.

"I'm Joanna Cassidy, and this is Toby Jenner."

The short one looks at his iPad. "Cassidy and Jenner. Got you." He presses the call button behind him. "Go on up."

The golden elevator opens, and we walk inside. As the doors close, we both relax a little. "Good start. Now remember, when we get into the apartment, we'll slowly work our way through the crowd to the northern hallway that leads to Crest's study."

"Will there be cameras?"

"No. There may be dozens everywhere else, but Crest hates cameras inside the apartment. However, I did pick up this little guy, so we could keep an eye on the hallway outside the study." She pulls a tiny button camera out of her purse and holds it up.

"Where the hell did you get that?"

She shrugs and puts it away. "Ordered it online."

"And your friend gave you the code for the study?"

"Yeah. I just hope no one has changed it recently." She takes my arm again when the doors open, and then we're passing more security guards as we enter the high-camp opulence of Marcus Crest's penthouse.

I look around, gobsmacked by how unpleasant the atmosphere is in here. It's like a gothic cathedral and Versailles had an unfortunate, misshapen baby, and Marcus Crest decided to live in it.

Because we're a little late, the place is already teeming with hundreds of New York's richest and most influential. I can see celebrities and movie stars, a few senators, and at least one adult film actress.

I tug at my collar. "Soooo ... this is what is feels like to be a fish out of water."

Joanna squeezes my forearm. "Just look bored and a little pissed off. You'll blend right in."

We weave through the crowd, and when a waiter offers us flutes of champagne, we take them. I don't miss that Joanna downs most of hers immediately. She's trying to act aloof, but her eyes are darting everywhere, clocking as many people as she can as we move around.

"Jojo!" An older woman touches her arm, and Joanna all but flinches away.

"Oh, hey, Mary."

"I didn't expect to see you. This isn't usually your kind of scene."

"No, but I thought I should drop in for once."

Mary gives me an appraising once over before looking back at Jo. "And who is this fine young man?"

Jo slides her hand down my arm, until she's holding my hand, and I take in a breath.

"Uh … this is my … uh, man. My … partner. Lover, in fact. Toby Jenner. We're … well, please don't tell anyone yet, but we're engaged."

Mary raises her eyebrows. "Well, that's something I wasn't expecting to hear." She leans closer and whispers, "Congratulations. And don't worry. Your secret is safe with me."

"I appreciate that." She looks up at me, lovingly. "I just want to stay in my love bubble with this amazing man for as long as possible before everyone knows. You understand. Now, please excuse us, but I promised I'd show my fiancé the Van Gogh over there. Let's talk soon."

Mary gives us a twinkly-finger wave. "Yes, let's."

Joanna's grip on my hand is fierce as we move away.

"Friend of yours?"

"Not really. Just an acquaintance from the art gallery volunteer committee."

She leads me over to the side of the room, and sure enough, there's a Van Gogh on the wall.

"How did you know about this?"

She looks around nervously. "It's common knowledge. Some home decorating magazine does a feature on this graveyard of good taste at least once a year. It's not hard to find out the most minute details about it."

She downs the remainder of her drink and grabs a fresh one as a waiter passes. "We'll need to make our move soon. They'll be announcing the winners of the silent auction in fifteen minutes, and when that happens, everyone will go quiet and super still. We need the cover of the noise and music to get into the study.

"Understood." I sip my drink and frown as I see a familiar bloated asshole in the distance. "Look," I say, nudging Jo. "The man himself is holding court."

Across the room is Marcus Crest. Sporting ashy grey hair that's thinning on top and looking as cheap as possible in what's probably a five-thousand-dollar dinner suit, he's standing with a group of men near the grand piano in the middle of the huge space. As is his way, he's talking loudly, probably about himself, and a rush of anger hits me on behalf of my dad.

"That fucker has a lot to answer for," I mutter under my breath.

"Yeah, he does." Jo's looking at him with almost as much contempt as I feel.

I watch as Crest revels in the attention of his sycophantic toadies. I don't hate a lot of people, but looking at him, I'm caught up in a wave of bitterness over the amount of pain and hardship inflicted on my family because of that soulless, selfish ghoul. Giving my dad his rightful compensation would have made the last five years very different for all of us. I wouldn't have had to give up on the amazing job offers I got right out of college, Mom wouldn't have had to work two jobs, and April wouldn't have sacrificed a good portion of her childhood to become a caregiver. Not to mention Dad, who would probably be walking and talking freely, if we'd had the money to get him surgery and rehab well before now.

They say a fish rots from the head down, and that's certainly true for the Crest foundation. Marcus Crest is the one who lies, cheats, and steals in order to cover up his company's incompetence and negligence on their building sites, and I'm determined to take him down for it.

I glance over to the north hallway. It's only a dozen yards away from our position, but there are another two burly security guards blocking our path.

"Did you know they'd be between us and our destination?" I ask.

She strokes my sleeve. "Yes, and I have it covered."

An elderly couple passing by smiles, and I give them a nod. "I should know better than to doubt you, darling."

"Indeed, darling."

I almost start when a voice whispers. "Joanna?"

I look around to find a woman holding a tray of canapes standing next to us. Joanna takes some food and tries to make it look like they're not talking.

"Is everything set?"

The woman nods. "Head over in five. I'll make sure the guards are distracted."

"Thank you, Leticia. I owe you one."

"Oh, girl, you owe me a hundred, but who's counting?"

With that she moves away, and Joanna takes my arm as we subtly move into position.

We pretend to look at another piece of art, but out of the corner of my eye, I can see Leticia moving toward the giant pyramid of crystal glasses. Without any sort of warning, she does an incredible slip on the parquetry floor and all but slides straight into the glasses. There's an enormous crash as they come smashing down all around her, and the partygoers call out in alarm while huge amounts of crystal shards fly everywhere.

"Holy crap," I say, watching in horror. "Will she be all right?"

Joanna looks over her shoulder toward the hallway. "Definitely. She and I went to stunt school together, and she was top of the class. She'll be fine."

Predictably, the security guards move into the crowd to steer them away from the mess of glass and assess if anyone, including Leticia, has been hurt.

"Stay back please, ladies and gentlemen," they say, holding their arms out to corral people. "If you could please move to the other side of the room while we clean this up."

A bevy of waitstaff swings into action, and while everyone's distracted, Joanna and I hurry down the dim hallway.

When we reach a dark oak door at the other end, Joanna tries the handle. It's locked.

"Eh, worth a try." She gets the button camera out of her purse and hands it to me. "Put this up high on the door jamb and angle it toward the hallway entrance while I punch in the code."

I do what she says, and by the time I'm done, she's pushing the door open.

"Okay, let's do this."

Once we're inside, I head straight to the computer as Jo fiddles with her phone.

"I can bring up the camera feed here, so we know if anyone approaches." She puts the phone on the desk and then comes to stand behind me as I start working on gaining access.

"So, you said you had a lead on his password?" I hope like hell she does, or this is going to be a real short heist.

She pulls out what looks like lockpicking tools and kneels in front of the drawer to my left.

"Just give me a sec." After carefully inserting the tools into the small, brass lock, she moves them until there's a soft click, and she pulls open the drawer.

"Marcus isn't much of a technophile," she says, taking out a small black notebook. "So even though his people make him change his password every month, he never remembers it." She flips the book open, and there in neat cursive is, *September: J7akkls892!#*

I put in the code, and sure enough, the computer unlocks in a flash.

"Okay, whoever you have on the inside is amazing, and I need to buy them a drink. Now, let's see what we have."

I bring up the contents of the drive and do a quick check that there are no hidden files.

"Okay, so there are a couple of layers of encryption here, but if I can get past the security protocols that prevent the files from being copied, I can work on the encryption afterward. Do you have the stick drive?" She hands me the device, and I plug it into the computer port before working on the security lock.

She leans over my left shoulder to get a better look at the screen.

"How on earth do you even work that fast?"

"Years and years of practice."

"Will it take long?"

She leans forward even more, and I'm immediately distracted by the amount of cleavage that's just sailed into my field of vision. I blink a few times and get my eyes back on the screen.

"Uh ..."

"Toby?"

"Yeah."

"How long?"

Now she's looking at me but still bending forward. My hands stumble over the wrong keys, and I have to hit the delete button and try again.

"Jo, if you want me to be able to concentrate, you're going to need to take your traveling smoke show away from me."

"Oh. Can I just stand behind you?"

"As long as you don't press your chest into my back, sure."

She moves, and I take a second before continuing. *Okay, I can feel her there, but I think I'm good.*

My hands fly over the keys, but even though everything's going well, this security system is complicated. It's going to take me a minute.

"So, an air-gapped computer is just one not connected to the internet?"

"Basically. There's so much cyber-crime around these days, it's the only way to ensure hackers can't get remote access to sensitive information. All of our intelligence agencies use them, and more and more corporations are employing them to protect company secrets or proprietary information."

While I'm working, Joanna starts searching around on the desk, using her tools to open other drawers.

"What are you looking for?"

"Don't know." She pulls out some papers and rifles through them. "But I'll know it when I see it."

"Documents won't do us much good anyway. I mean, once upon a time, they were proof enough, but these days we need digital files full of meta-data and ISP fingerprints."

"True, but maybe something here will point us in the right direction."

She puts the papers back and starts on another drawer while I move into the second layer of copy protection removal.

"So, definitely no cameras in here then?" I ask. It's probably regular paranoia that stems from committing a crime, but I feel like we're being watched.

Jo shakes her head and opens what looks like a ledger. "Word is Crest has had more than a few trysts with various female staff members in here, so the no-cameras rule is as much about his own protection as anything else. Can't have a lurid sex tape being leaked, can he?"

I shudder at the thought. "Gross."

As soon as I break through the security protocols, I quickly assess the encryption level of the files. They're well protected, but certainly not the most complex I've seen. I grab my decryption software off the hard drive and run it.

"I may be able to crack these in a few minutes. Then we can check what we have before we leave."

"Great." She opens the final drawer on the right side of the desk and pulls out a folder. I sneak a glance at her, looking stunningly beautiful in only the light from the screen and a small table lamp near the window. Her dress sparkles in the low light, and despite my determination to reprogram my heart, I'm punched in the chest by how much I feel for her.

"Jo, did you expect our attraction score to be as high as it was?"

She keeps scanning the papers, but her expression softens. "Yes. I actually thought we might have broken the scale." She glances over at me. "Did you expect it?"

I lean back in the chair and keep one eye on the decryption window as it does its thing. "I don't know. I think the part of me that still feels like a bean pole who repulsed women for most of my teen years always suspected you were exaggerating your attraction to make me feel better about myself."

"Why would I do that?"

I shrug. "Women have done it in the past. Girlfriends. I dated someone once for a month before she asked if I could hack into her ex's Facebook page. She claimed to want to see if he'd been cheating on her when they were going out."

"Did you do it?"

"Yes. Once we were in, I discovered she just wanted to delete his profile as payback for him dumping her. There was no cheating. Not on his part, anyway. I realized she'd only been having sex so she could play me. Didn't feel great."

"I bet."

"So, you see, I have a knack for being completely clueless about when a woman's lying to me, for whatever reason."

She glances over at me. "Everyone lies, Toby. Sometimes people have good reasons for doing it."

"Sure, and sometimes they don't. I can get past the odd white lie here and there, but the big stuff? Some people do it so well, I don't know how people ever trust them."

Her posture changes, but she goes back to studying the file. "Well, rest assured, I've never lied about how attracted I am to you, and now you have proof."

My program beeps, and when I check the screen, the unencrypted file names populate in the new tab.

I lean forward to study them. "Here we go."

Joanna does the same, but this time my focus stays on the screen.

"What are these?" I ask, pointing to a list of numbered files.

Joanna squints. "Dates, maybe?"

I open a file and check the contents. It looks like information about a specific construction site, but there are so many documents, it's going to take a while to decipher all the information.

"Look here," Jo says, pointing to a letter from the council about building regulations. "The numbers are the street addresses."

I go back to the main menu and start downloading the files.

"Six minutes to go." I check Joanna's phone. It's showing the button camera feed from the hallway. I can see the security guards still moving around in the reception area, herding guests. "I hope it takes them longer than six minutes to clean up what's left of all that glass."

I turn to see Joanna frowning. "What is it?"

She moves over to the files she was just looking at.

"The files for Crest's lawyers aren't on here." She pulls a piece of paper from the folder and shows it to me. "On this note, Crest is talking about locking down the legal correspondence into the server room, but clearly that's not here."

"Could it be in the offices?"

"That's what I'm thinking."

I run my hand through my hair. "So, we only have half the story here? We have to break into his offices, too? For fuck's sake."

Joanna suddenly focuses on the phone screen. "That's not our most immediate problem."

When I look, I see Marcus Crest walking up the hallway toward the study.

"Shit!"

Joanna moves like lightning, shoving the files back into the drawer and quickly relocking it.

"The download still has four minutes to go," I say.

"Dammit." She finishes what she's doing and puts the monitor to sleep before placing her purse over the top of the blinking thumb drive. "Get over here, Toby."

She grabs her phone, and we see Leticia running down the hallway to talk to Crest, likely trying to stall him for us. It's a nice thought, but he's practically outside the door. So close we can hear murmuring voices through the wood.

"Quickly," Jo says. "Sit." She pushes me down onto the dimpled leather couch and then straddles me. "You can see where this is going right?"

I swallow. "Yes. Is this really the best idea considering our current status?"

She loosens my tie and unbuttons the top of my shirt. "Can you think of a better explanation as to why we're in here?"

"Not when your crotch is pressed against mine like that, no."

She gives a panicked look to the door before winding her fingers in my hair. "Toby, whatever happens next, I need you to know that not all lies are bad. Right now, you have to lie like you've never lied before, okay? Keep calm, and act like the person you're pretending to be tonight."

"I'll do my best."

"Good. Now kiss me."

I want to start softly and build my way up to impassioned, but the sound of movement at the door spurs me into action. I take Jo's face in my hands and pull her down until our mouths connect.

Sweet … Holy … Jesus.

Whether it's the immediate peril of the situation, or the fact we've been denying our physical attraction for so long, we're strung tighter than a Stradivarius, the result is same: the flood gates of our passion explode off their hinges in a storm of arousal so powerful, my whole body feels like it's a nuclear reactor, melting down. The moment our kiss becomes deeper and more desperate, that we're about to get caught trespassing is secondary to my need for her taste, and smell, and the feel of her fucking incredible body beneath my hands.

She moans into my mouth, and I answer in kind, grabbing her hips as I grind up into the soft warmth between her legs.

This is the feeling I've craved since the night we first kissed. This whole-body rush is why I haven't been able to let go of the unrealistic expectation we'd somehow end up together, despite the odds.

We scored a hundred percent on sexual attraction, and right now, I can feel every single one of those percentage points lighting up my insides like a million pinpricks of light.

"Toby … God."

There's no way to fight this, and now that I'm tasting and touching her, I don't fucking want to.

Attraction is a mystical force. You can do your best to track and map it, but the hard truth is sometimes, it's unexplainable. Unpredictable. It sneaks up behind you and slams into your neurons with the force of a scud missile, and once you feel it, your body becomes a slave. It will always remember that muscle-trembling rush and will crave it more than anything. Drugs, alcohol, money, power. Anything.

That's how it feels to kiss Joanna like this. It's like getting high on nothing but air. Like drowning in a handful of water.

"Jesus … Jo."

Fuck Marcus Crest. If he catches us, then we might as well enjoy this stolen moment before we're dragged out in cuffs. If that happens, I'll go with a giant smile on my face.

"I want you," I say, finally admitting it out loud. "I've never wanted any woman the way I want you."

She kisses me again, fingers tightening into my hair, making me grunt in approval. "It's not fair that I can't have this. Maybe we could just have each other once."

"No," I say, pressing my mouth against her neck. "Once with you would never be enough."

I take her mouth again, and the noise of our simultaneous moans fills the dark space. By the time the door opens, I'm so far gone, I'm barely aware that someone else is entering the room.

"What the hell is this?!"

We pull apart as Crest's bullfrog bellow fills the room. "Guards! Get in here!"

Jo and I stare at each other, panting and shocked, our mouths still swollen from the passion of our kiss. Through the dull haze of intense arousal, I hear running footsteps, and Jo and I turn to look at New York's most infamous figure mere feet away.

As security guards enter to flank him, Marcus Crest frowns at us.

"My God. What the …?" He takes a step forward and squints at us in the low light. "Joanna? Is that you?"

I stop breathing as Jo climbs off me and smoothes down her dress. With a defiant tip of her chin, she gives a tight smile.

"Hey, dad."

24

WTF?

There have been very few moments in my life when I've been truly, hopelessly confused, but right now, I'm slap-bang in the middle of a scene so fucking surreal, I'm not entirely convinced I'm awake.

I sit there dumbstruck as one of the security guards draws his side arm and orders Joanna and me to put our hands in the air. I'm about to comply when Marcus Crest waves him away, saying, "Put that thing down, LeBron. She's not an intruder. She's my daughter."

Yeah, that's the piece of information that continues to set off massive explosions of bewilderment in my brain as reality bends around me. Suddenly, I see everything in a different light. My gaze falls to a portrait on the wall behind his desk. It shows Crest standing over a young girl sitting on a chair. When I look closer, it's clear that girl is Joanna.

"You. Get up," the security guard called LeBron barks, snapping me out of my stupor. I stand and glance at Joanna, whose posture is suddenly that of a rebellious teen. Marcus Crest is staring at her, red-faced and emotional, fluctuating between being happy to see her and what looks a lot like victory.

The two security guards glance between us like Rottweilers who don't know whether to attack or lick our faces, and I'm standing here like a very tall, well-dressed man-version of Alice right after she fell through the goddamn looking glass.

"I knew you'd come back, Joanna," Crest says, walking forward. "As soon as you got sick of fending for yourself, I figured you'd return to me." He takes her shoulders and hugs her, and my brain sputters like an old car on a cold morning. "You look beautiful, sweetheart. Just like your mother before she passed."

Marcus Crest is Joanna's father. The woman I've been having complicated feelings for is the daughter of Satan.

In light of these recent events, *fuck.*

A ball of anger blooms inside me as the full extent of Joanna's deception sinks in. Part of me is blindsided by this latest revelation, but another feels like it was completely predictable. After all, she told me from the beginning that she was Liza Lotte. I should have known better than to trust her.

But what the hell does this mean? Did she dupe me into working with her to try and protect him? Is she about to sell me and Eden down the river because of the *Pulse* article? Or in typical Joanna style, is she playing three-dimensional chess while the rest of us play checkers?

"As glad as I am to see my only child," Crest says, glancing at me, "would you mind explaining why the hell you're back and making out in my study?

Back, how?

"I'm not back, Dad."

Not back, why?

Joanna pulls away from him and takes my arm. I almost flinch, but my anger is rooting me to the spot. "I'm only here because of Toby."

Crest looks at me with an air of condescension. "And who might Toby be?"

"He's the man I love, and unfortunately for me, he's your biggest fan."

I'm his what-now?

Despite my intense surprise, I keep my face neutral. God knows, it's not easy.

"I wouldn't have come back if it weren't for him. You're his idol, and when he heard about the Crest Gala, he begged me to bring him. It's his life's dream to meet you."

So, we're now going for the world's biggest lie? Okay, then.

Crest looks from her to me, and I fight to put a smile on my face. Joanna is spewing crap like she gets paid to do it, and I know I have to rise to her level, so we don't get busted.

"Is this true, son?"

I almost gag when he calls me 'son,' but I attempt to play my part. "Absolutely, sir." Joanna squeezes my arm to spur me on. "I've followed your career since I was in college …" *True, but not for the reasons he thinks.* "I can't believe how you've built your company." *By enriching yourself off the backs of your workers and contractors.* "And I'd love nothing more than to spend some time picking your brain," *and raiding your servers,* "to get a look into your special brand of genius." *I also know that you're the kind of narcissistic moron who'll give me whatever I want if I flatter your fragile ego, so please, be a good moron, and take the bait.*

Even though I'm nowhere near as skilled as Joanna in the art of bullshit, it doesn't seem to matter to Crest. My words make him puff up like a blowfish, and he gives me a broad, toothy smile.

"Is that right? Well, first, let me commend you on your excellent taste in role models. Are you in real estate?"

"Not right now. I'm in the tech industry, but I want to move into real estate as soon as possible. I'd love some guidance from the King of New York as to where I should start."

He chuckles and turns to the guards as if to say, "See how much I'm loved and respected? Pretty cool, huh?"

Joanna looks impressed with my improvisation. I guess I should feel proud I've come up to the high standards of the Queen of Lies.

It seems I may not be convincing the guards however, because LeBron narrows his eyes at me.

"If you're such a fan, why weren't you out in the ballroom talking to him? And how did you get in here? That door was locked."

Joanna steps forward. "Dad's had the same code on that door for years. When I told Toby about how cool Dad's study was, he wanted to …" She gestures to me. "Well, you tell him."

Jesus, could you put me on the spot more tonight? "No, honey, you tell him."

"He's my dad. It's embarrassing for me to say it."

LeBron scowls. "Just one of you say it. Now."

Joanna sighs and rolls her eyes. "Toby's a little shy and more than a bit intimidated by you, Dad. So, he thought if he could see your private sanctuary, it might … you know … give him the courage to talk with you."

"Is that what you were doing when we came in?" LeBron asks. "Building up your courage?"

Joanna ducks her head. "No, but when he got in here ..." She looks up at me. "Well, you know how it can be when guys are passionate about something. Right, honey?"

"Uh ... yes." How the fuck can she make deception look as easy as breathing? My thoughts are so jumbled, I can barely speak. Still, I suck up my nerve and say, "I'm so sorry you found us like that, Mr. Crest. But when I got in here and saw where you worked, and with Joanna right next to me, looking so beautiful in this incredible and powerful room, I guess ... I lost control."

I tug at my collar, because even though I'm fudging the truth, my body remembers exactly how it felt to let go for once and finally press her against me. My blood pounds as I recall how she felt and tasted. "I only meant to kiss Joanna, but obviously things got a bit out of hand. I'm sorry about that."

My face is hot, and I have no doubt I'm blushing. But whatever Crest sees causes him to chuckle again, and the way he looks at us both makes my skin crawl.

"Well, it's understandable that two young people might get carried away in here. It's a very sensual room. But this study is off limits to everyone but me, and Joanna knows that better than most."

Joanna nods. "I'm sorry, Dad. It was stupid to bring Toby here."

"Not at all. He seems like a clever guy with good taste. Just because you've taken your old man for granted for nearly ten years, doesn't mean he has to." He turns to me. "Let's go back out to the party and get a drink, young man, and you can ask me anything you like about my business."

God, please, no. This torture has to end, so I can get the fuck out of here. Also, I need an excuse to get inside his office.

"Mr. Crest, that's a generous offer, but I couldn't take you away from all of your guests. I know how important tonight is, and everyone wants some of your time. But if it's okay with you, I'd like to come to your office tomorrow and see the legend himself in his work environment."

He smiles again and pats my shoulder. "Of course you can. We'll have a chat with my secretary, Brenda, and line up a time."

We start heading out, but I catch a panicked look in Joanna's eyes as LeBron goes to close the door.

"Oh, just a second." Jo pushes it open and gives him an apologetic look. "I forgot my purse."

The shorter guard escorts Crest and me down the hallway, but LeBron waits for Joanna to emerge. I remember she left her purse on top of the drive, so even if he watches her, I'm hopeful she can grab it without him seeing.

What worries me is the timing.

I check my watch. The download should have finished by now, but my program needed time to wipe our digital fingerprints, including the logs that would have recorded the file duplication. If it didn't complete the task, Crest's techs will see that someone has interfered with the computer the next time they check, and that would be bad.

I'm barely listening to Crest babble on about how great he is as we make our way back into the main reception room. It seems the excitement from earlier has been cleaned away, and the partygoers are back to mingling and helping themselves to the free food and wine.

I keep one eye on the hallway while Crest steers me over to a tall woman in the middle of the room.

"Toby, this is Brenda. She'll book you into my schedule for tomorrow." He puts his arm around her waist and squeezes her in a way that's creepy and wrong. "You look after this young man, Brenda. He's aiming to be my protégé. And did I mention he's dating my daughter?"

Brenda frowns in surprise. "Joanna? She's back?"

"Yes," Crest says, with a touch of satisfaction. "She brought him here to meet me. Guess she's finally come to her senses about respecting this family and her place in it."

"Wow, Mr. Crest, that's incredible news. Congratulations." Brenda's a terrible liar. I'm burning to know the full story behind what happened within this family, but I doubt Joanna will ever tell it to me.

Crest gestures to a waiter who rushes to get him something that looks like whiskey on the rocks.

"I knew it would just be a question of time with Joanna," he says with an air of annoying superiority. "They all come crawling back eventually. My Joanna talks a good show, but like all women, what she really craves is a strong man to show her the error of her ways. Between us, we'll pull her back into line."

I clench my hands into fists and force a smile. Fuck this fucking guy. This morally vacuous sociopath sits up here in his Palace of Corruption, probably burning hundred-dollar bills instead of firewood, while my father, a good man who's done right by every person he's ever met, can barely pay his bills or feed himself. It turns my blood into magma. What's more, even though I'm pissed with Jo about lying to me, hearing Crest talk about her like she's a second-class citizen makes me despise him with every fiber of my being.

He's the garbage human here, but I have to pretend he's not, until I gather enough evidence to ruin the bastard son-of-a-bitch.

"You're right, sir." Bile rises in my throat as I agree with his misogynist views. "It was my idea to come here, but Jo didn't fight all that hard. I think she's missed you, even though she'd never admit it."

He grins, and it turns my stomach. "You're going to be very good for my daughter, Toby." Crest raises his glass. "If you can get her to come back to work for me, you'd have my gratitude."

"Of course, sir. Anything I can do to help."

Just then, Joanna appears at my side and holds up her purse. "Got it."

I give a tight nod. "Good." *Because if I have to stand here for one more second and stroke this maniac's ego, I'm going to fucking deck him.* I hold out my hand to Crest. "We won't take up any more of your time tonight, sir. It was a pleasure meeting you. Thank you so much for everything."

He shakes my hand, and his palm is so clammy, it's like gripping a cow's tongue. "Any time, my boy. I'll see you tomorrow for lunch." He turns to Jo. "I'm looking forward to showing you off to my employees, sweetheart. It's about time you took your rightful place at my side. I'm sure you'll do the right thing and help secure your father's legacy."

She gives him a smile. "Can't wait, Dad. See you then."

I take Joanna's hand, and we make our way to the elevator. As soon as the doors close, I step away from her.

"Toby …"

"Not a word," I say quietly. "Not one fucking word, Jo."

She shifts her weight as I stare at the elevator doors, too angry to speak in case I yell at her while we're still in the building. Blowing our cover at this stage would be monumentally stupid.

When we get out to the street, I bypass the line of limos and start striding toward the park. God knows I need to get away from everything and everyone for a while, so I can clear my head.

"Toby." Joanna tries to catch up with me, but for once, I'm making full use of my long legs to put space between us.

"Toby, wait. Please let me explain."

"No."

Even at this time of night, there's gridlock, so I weave through the cars, until I reach the park on the other side. When someone wolf-whistles and yells, "You're gorgeous, sweetheart!" I know Joanna's following me.

"Toby ... slow down ... please."

I hear the click-clack of high heels running to catch up, and when I'm safely within the park, I turn to face her.

"No, Joanna. I'm not interested."

"You don't even know what I'm going to say."

"It doesn't matter. Whatever it is, there's a high probability it will be bullshit, and I'm sick of being lied to."

"I couldn't tell you about my father! You know how everyone feels about him in this city. They hate him, and I didn't want him to color your opinion of me."

"Jo, I don't give a fuck about who your father is. What I care about is that you lied. And not just once. You chose to lie to me again and again, every damn day for weeks. Even after you found out about my dad, you still didn't say, 'Oh, hey, you know that guy you hate with the fiery passion of a thousand suns? I'm his kid, but let me assure you that I'm not like him.'"

"I'm not like him!"

"I know that! Which is why I'm fucking clueless as to why you wouldn't tell me!" I run my hand through my hair. "I feel so stupid thinking we had something special. I thought I made it clear that you could tell me anything."

"Oh, come on, Toby, who the hell are you kidding? If I'd told you about Dad, you would have looked at me differently. You would have *treated* me differently. How could you not after what happened to your father? And the thing is, I wouldn't have blamed you, because I would have done the same thing."

"Joanna, if you had told me, I wouldn't have given a shit. Unless you were the one who organized and erected the faulty scaffolding, I wouldn't have cared that Crest was your father. It just blows my mind that after everything we've shared, you'd think I would. You told me your parents were dead, for fuck's sake. You spun a whole tale about a plane crash and visiting them in the Brooklyn cemetery every month, and like an idiot, I believed you. My heart fucking hurt for you.

Meanwhile, you were probably patting yourself on the back that you could dupe me so easily. Like you were fucking Meryl Streep going for her hundredth Oscar nomination."

She takes in a sharp breath, and I get a small stab of satisfaction that I hurt her for a change.

"You want the truth, Toby?" She comes closer, intensity firing in her eyes. "I left home at fifteen, because my dad didn't give a shit about me, and I preferred to tough it out by myself than live in that damn penthouse with him. I hate him so much that since the day I left, I've been plotting how to take down him and his company. Then I met you with all your hacking experience, and Eden started investigating him, and it was like the entire universe was lining up to help me, so I didn't want to jinx everything. I didn't want to risk losing you." She takes a breath. "I mean, I could never have done what we did tonight without you. And now we have a chance to get into the heart of his operation and take it down from the inside, and …"

She must read the sickening realization that's dawning on my face, because she says, "Wait, I didn't mean that how it came out."

"Oh, I think you did." I shake my head. "For the first time, I'm getting to the real truth. You used me. You wanted to take your old man down, and you couldn't do it without someone like me to get you in the door. I'm sure Sergei was probably your first choice, but when he disappeared, you needed a backup, and just like that, there I was. You even moved me into his room, for God's sake."

"Toby, no." She takes my hand, but I pull away. "Please, that's not how it was."

I let out a bitter laugh. "Finally, everything's starting to make sense. For a genius, I'm really fucking dumb sometimes. Here I was thinking we had a connection … that against terrible odds, I meant something to you. But all along, I was merely a tool you could use to stick it to daddy dearest."

"That's not true, and you know it. How I feel about you …" She blinks back tears, and her breathing is erratic. "How can you think that I could fake that? I'm sorry I didn't tell you about my father, I am, but … you still *know* me, Toby. You know who I am in my heart."

I shake my head. "No. The more time we spend together, the more it becomes clear that I don't know you at all."

I go to walk away, but she grabs my arm, tears streaming down her face. "Toby …"

I pull my arm back. "You need to stop. I can't do this anymore."

"Toby, I …" She swallows and takes in a wavering breath. "Please don't walk away. I love you."

I step back. "See, I hear the words. I just don't believe them." I walk away from her into the park, and I keep on walking, until the pain in my chest starts to subside.

25

STUPID

I move the pin on the chest-press machine up two more notches before going in for another set. Every muscle is screaming right now, but it's still not enough to block out the storm of crap swirling inside my brain and heart.

"Toby, I'd recommend having a break between sets in order to facilitate maximum muscle mass."

Jeeves' voice reverberates in the deserted gym.

"I know how to work out, Jeeves."

But this isn't about working out. It's about punishment. It's about feeling like the stupidest man on the planet for letting myself get duped by a beautiful woman. Again. It's about feeling used and naive.

I grunt as I finish the last few reps and then just lie there, panting, exhausted in body but still fresh as a fucking daisy in mind, despite it being four in the morning.

I'd walked around in Central Park for hours, and when I got home, I knew there was no way I could sleep. Coming here seemed like the only thing to do.

As far as I know, Jo's in her bedroom, but I haven't bothered to find out. It's going to be a long while before I can look her in the eyes again. If ever.

I pull off my shirt and wipe the sweat from my face before grabbing my towel off the bench and spreading it out on the floor mats. Then I lie down to start sit ups.

"Toby, you've been extremely agitated since arriving home from your event. Is there something you'd like to talk about?"

"No," I say through the strain of the sit-ups. "What I absolutely don't want to do right now is talk. I'm sick of talking. Seems like people can say whatever the fuck they want, and I'll just believe them anyway, so for the moment, I'm done with words."

Deep down, I know very well I'm going off the deep end by punishing myself, but I can't help it. I'm dealing with my shit the way I'm dealing with it. Are my methods healthy? No. Will they make any difference at all? No. Will I consider that and then change? Again, no.

After finishing the set, I flip over and do push-ups, and even though I'm going to feel like shit in a few hours from overworking every muscle group, part of me feels I deserve it.

"Did something happen between you and Joanna?"

"I just said I didn't want to talk about it."

"As you wish."

I try to keep going, but my arms are spent, and I collapse onto the floor in a damp heap.

"Fuck." I lie there, cheek against my towel, staring at the wall as I try to get enough oxygen into my lungs to stop them from burning.

As soon as I stop moving, everything I'm trying to get away from catches up with me and fills up my chest with tumultuous, unwanted emotions.

I flip onto my back and push my fingers into my eyes. "Fucking, fucking, fuck."

"Toby, I'm concerned about you."

"I doubt that, Jeeves. You're a machine. You need to have empathy to be concerned. Besides, everything's fine. I'm fine."

I climb to my feet and take my towel over to the treadmill. Maybe running will help. Fuck knows it can't hurt at this point.

"Toby, I'm assuming you got the information you needed from Marcus Crest's apartment last night."

Too much info, Jeeves. Way too much.

I turn on the treadmill and start a brisk jog. "Yes and no. He's got another server at his office that we need to crack to get the really incriminating stuff." I uploaded everything we got last night and sent the link to Eden, so she can trawl through it for anything useful, but I don't expect her to finish in a hurry. I'll help when I'm in a better headspace.

I tell Jeeves about the ruse Joanna invented with us being engaged and me being a huge Crest fan. Even saying that much makes all the arteries in my head pound with anxiety.

"The plot is a good one, Toby, but I would expect Crest to check up on you before he allows you access to his inner sanctum. Would you like me to monitor web searches by his security personal? I could provide them with false information that supports your narrative."

"Good idea. Also, if you can find any information regarding the layout and security systems at Crest's offices, let me know."

"Do I have to obtain them through legal means?"

"Not necessarily. Just don't get caught."

"Understood."

I turn up the speed on the treadmill. My legs are surprisingly fresh, and if I want to get any peace at all right now, they need to be as exhausted as the rest of me.

I'm vaguely aware of my phone buzzing on the bench near the door. It started going off while I was walking through the park last night. Alerts began flooding in as journalists and bloggers left the Romance Central event and posted their reviews online. I also got a whole slew of requests for interviews, but I'm not in the mood to talk to anyone right now about engineering people's everlasting happiness, especially when I'm so hopeless at managing my own.

One of the thoughts that keeps weaving through my mind is how ass-backwards I've had everything with Joanna. Despite what the app said about our chances, I believed we had a deep, meaningful connection, even if it only ended up being a friendship. Now I think the only thing Joanna ever felt for me was attraction. That's probably why we could never have anything real.

I raise the speed a few more points trying to run from the logical puzzle pieces that are now falling into place. The anger won't be outrun, however, and I grit my teeth as I push myself harder.

Part of it is that I opened up to Joanna about so many things: the humiliation of my living situation, the truth about my dad and his problems, and most of all, I was honest about who I was. She knew me at my core. That's the thing that hurts the most. She throws out random facts about her life every damn day, while hiding the most real parts of herself. She thinks she has a knack for choosing the wrong guys, but I think about how she said she might be self-sabotaging her relationships, and I'd have to agree. How the hell can she have a relationship with anyone if they never know who she is?

And how the fuck did *I* fall for her so hard without knowing who she was? I was fooled the night we met, and despite trying to be cautious, she's been fooling me every day since.

There it is. There's the acorn of bitterness from which all your anger is sprouting.

I tilt the incline on the treadmill.

The most effective way to enrage any geek is to make them feel stupid, and that's how this entire situation is framing me. As stupid and gullible as hell to believe a woman as spectacular as Jo would be interested in me for more than my useful abilities.

"Jeeves, when did Joanna start planning to break into Crest's study?"

There's a pause, and for a moment, I don't think he's heard me.

"Jeeves?"

"I'm sorry, Toby. I can't answer that."

"You don't know? Or you won't say?"

"In the same way I consider certain information you tell me as confidential, I afford Joanna the same courtesy."

"But you knew she wanted to use me to crack her father's security system?"

Another pause.

"Toby ..."

"Forget about it. No one can give me a fucking straight answer around here."

I crank up the speed to its highest level.

"Toby, considering your current heart rate, that speed is not advisable."

"Fuck advisable." I sprint as hard as I can, but my body is starting to give out. My Nike catches on the rubber, and then I'm flung onto the ground in a tumble of limbs.

Fucking fuck!

"Toby!"

I'm still getting my bearings as to which way is up, when cool hands are on my face, and Joanna appears in front of me, expression etched with concern.

"Are you okay? Jeeves, what did you do?"

"This accident was not of my design. Toby pushed himself too hard and became unbalanced."

The treadmill winds down and then stops.

"I'm fine." I pull back from her and climb to my feet, which isn't easy considering all my muscles have turned to jelly. "It wasn't Jeeves' fault." I grab my towel and wipe myself over, and I notice Joanna's in her workout gear.

"Sorry, I didn't realize you were in here," she says, fingering the edge of her own towel. "I can, uh … I can go for a run around the park if you like. Give you some space."

I'm aggravated that even when I'm as angry as I am, she can make me melt like a snow cone on a hot day.

"It's fine. I'm done anyway." *Done with the gym. Done with you. Just fucking done.*

She steps forward and touches my shoulder. "Are you sure you're okay. Looks like you got some carpet burn during the fall."

I pull back and wrap my towel around my shoulders, so she can't touch me anymore. "I said I'm fine. The gym is all yours."

I head toward the exit, but then she calls out, "Toby …" and I turn to see her chewing on the inside of her cheek.

"Dad's secretary texted me details for the lunch later. Are you …?" She shifts her weight. "Are you still okay to come? I mean, I'll understand if you don't want to … but —"

"I'll be there."

She smiles. Relieved.

"But when we get the information off the server, I'm done, Jo."

Her smile drops. "Of course. I mean, you'll have the information you need for your dad, Eden will have her story, and I'll have … well, I'll have what I need too, I guess."

"No, I mean I'm done here. Living with you. I'm moving out."

The look on her face couldn't be more pained if I'd slapped her. "Toby … no."

I shake my head and look at the floor. "I'm sorry, I just can't … do this … be here … with someone I don't trust. I can't."

She takes a deep breath and presses her lips together. Yesterday, I would have hated seeing her getting emotional and done everything I could to stop it from happening. Now I stand there and watch, forcing myself to be indifferent. Willing myself to detach.

After a few seconds, she nods and looks at me. "I understand. I hate that this is all happening because of me … because I … hurt you. Wasn't honest with you. But …" She drops her head. "I understand."

I stare at her for a few seconds, warring with myself about the decision. But then I think about all the time she had to come clean, and I know without a doubt it's the right thing to do.

"What time is lunch?" I ask, hand on the door.

"Twelve-thirty."

"Fine. I'll meet you downstairs at twelve."

"Great."

I walk out of the gym and head to my room, and when I hear muffled noises echoing up the hallway, I tell myself it's not the sound of her crying.

26

DESTINED TO PRETEND

"*T*oby?"

I'm lying on the bed in my boxer-briefs, staring up at the galaxy on the ceiling and feeling about as shitty as I have in my entire life. I showered hours ago when I got back from the gym, but my brain has been too busy to sleep.

"Toby?"

"Go away, Jeeves."

"You can't keep ignoring your phone. Eden has called six times. Max has called four. You have thirty-two missed calls from media outlets, five from people at Pulse, *and two from your mother."*

"I thought I told you to answer them all and take messages."

"I did."

"Is Mom okay?"

"Yes. She's just confirming that everything is on schedule for your dad's surgery at the end of next week, and to remind you April's school play opens at the end of the month. She hopes you can get there."

"I can. I will." Getting out of New York for a while and spending time with them is exactly what I need. I have a whole stack of vacation days owed to me, and I can't wait to take them.

I've already spoken with Eden today, but I guess she wants to talk about whatever she's finding in the trove of information. I want to know, just not right now. My body is aching, my chest is tight, and my mind is spinning with a million thoughts I can't make sense of. I've rarely felt this miserable, and I fucking hate it.

Maybe this is the giant step backward that had to be taken in order to get over Jo. If left to my own devices, I might have pined for years, passing over countless other romantic opportunities in the process. The irony is, this is the most painful breakup I've ever experienced, and we weren't even a couple.

One more example of how royally screwed this situation is.

"Toby?"

"What?"

"Just a reminder that you need to be dressed and downstairs at the car in ten minutes for your lunch date."

I grunt my acknowledgement.

Earlier, Joanna had knocked on my door and passed in a brand-new Tom Ford suit. I guess Giovanni made it from the same specs as the tux. Seems as though rocking up to visit Crest Tower in my skinny jeans and cardy isn't going to cut it for an aspiring real estate entrepreneur.

Pushing out a frustrated breath, I climb off the bed and get dressed. The suit is navy and slim-line, and as with the tux, fits me perfectly. It's been matched with a crisp white shirt, pale tie, and sleek shoes, and by the time I use some of Sergei's leftover hair product in the bathroom, I look about as close to a Crest protege as I'm going to get. After deciding to leave the scruff that's grown since last night, I brush my teeth and grab my phone.

"Toby, I've downloaded all of the blueprints I could find regarding the layout of Crest's offices, and I included a map indicating where the likely location of the server room is, based on the electrical patterns of the building. Entry can be gained by a digital pass card, and if you can get your phone close enough to one, I can clone it by using the Bio-Flex sticker."

I frown. "Really?"

"It requires some reconfiguration of the software, but yes."

"Okay. Great." More and more I'm realizing how much easier Jeeves makes most things, including corporate espionage.

"Joanna has more details that she'll give you on the ride over."

"Fine." I roll my neck to relieve some creeping tension and close my eyes as I ask, "How's Jo doing?"

Whenever I ask something personal about her, he pauses. I swear, this program is getting more and more like a real person every day.

"You should ask her that question."

"I probably will, but I want to know the truth, and I don't trust that she'll be honest."

He's silent, and I clench my jaw in frustration.

"Jeeves … come on. This is hard enough without you stonewalling me. I know she talks to you. I can hear the murmurs through the wall."

"She's upset, mostly with herself, for lying to you. And she's extremely upset you're leaving. Beyond that, you'll have to talk to her to find out more."

"Fine."

For fuck's sake, Jenner, stop caring. You're in this hole right now because you're too invested. Learn your lesson already and stop.

"Toby? One more thing. I've been monitoring a lot of internet searches about you today. Most have been from journalists, HEA participants, or people reading about the launch, but several have originated from Crest employees, namely security personnel."

"Okay. Did you send them doctored information?"

"Yes. I've also removed all traceable links between yourself and your father, considering he's named as a plaintiff in the ongoing legal action."

"So, who do I say my father is?"

"As far as the internet is concerned, your father is Ralph Jenner, deceased, former owner of a small computer repair business in Pennsylvania. If possible, avoid talking about your family. I have no doubt Crest will be vetting you due to your perceived relationship with his daughter."

"I bet."

"I've also scrubbed all connections to Pulse and Eden, just in case word has gotten back about the upcoming exposé. I'll keep monitoring all searches to make sure your cover remains intact."

My phone dings with a text from Gerald, letting me know he and Joanna are waiting downstairs.

"Okay, Jeeves. Thanks."

I head down in the elevator, and when I emerge from the building, Joanna's there, looking annoyingly gorgeous and beaming like I'm the love of her life.

"Wow," she says stopping in front of me and touching my lapel. "I think I might be engaged to the most handsome man in Manhattan."

I'm a little confused as to why she's dropping into character before we leave, but when she stands on her toes to kiss my cheek, she whispers, "We're being watched."

She pulls back, still smiling. "Kiss me, and make them believe it, or this will be over before we step foot through the door."

I desperately want to look around to see who has us under surveillance, but I know that would blow our cover immediately. Instead, I cup Joanna's face and lean down, my heart pounding overtime as I press my lips to hers.

I pause, trying to breathe and swallow at the same time, before pulling back and doing my best to seem happy.

"You look beautiful." At least I don't have to lie about that. She's so fucking beautiful, she makes my heart ache.

She glances at my mouth. "You do, too." She kisses me again, soft lips and light suction, and I moan as every ounce of blood rushing through my veins whispers her name.

No, no, no.

Pulling back, I try to collect myself, but it's pretty fucking difficult when she's pressed against me and looking like all she wants is to drag me back upstairs.

"We should go … honey."

She blinks a couple of times and clears her throat. "Right. Yes. Let's go."

Gerald is already holding open the door to the Escalade, and she slides to the center, so I can sit beside her. After Gerald closes the door and heads around to the driver's seat, I dare to look over my shoulder.

"Where are they?"

Joanna keeps her eyes to the front. "Behind us. Black town car. It's Dad's security chief, LeBron. Jeeves told me he was here." She opens her purse and pulls out a tiny flesh-colored earpiece. "I got these, so Jeeves can talk to us when we're out. He can get access to security systems and help us find the server room."

"Great." I put in the earpiece and wipe my mouth to stop it from tingling after our kiss. I'm not surprised to see lipstick on my fingers.

I wipe again, more for the sensation than the color.

Jo takes a compact out of her purse and fixes her lipgloss as the car moves through the downtown traffic. I watch, hypnotized, until she's finished.

She catches me looking, and I clear my throat as I direct my gaze out the window. I steady my breathing and let my anger dull my arousal.

"So," I say, "anything I should know before we go into the lion's den?"

"Only that my father is an asshole, but you can get around nearly anything by flattering him."

"Yeah, I already figured that out."

"We may not be able to get into the server room today, but if we can get the lay of the land, it will help us formulate a plan for when we return."

"You don't know your way around the offices?"

"I haven't been there in nine years."

"And that's because …?"

She sighs. "It's a long story I don't have time to tell right now."

"But you had time to spill it over the past month, right? You just chose not to."

She falls silent, and I clench my jaw against a slew of curse words. Trying to calm down, I take some deep breaths and look out the window again. "So, no one knows you're Crest's daughter. Not Eden or Asha? No one?"

"No."

I turn to her. "None of us have been graced with the damn truth? The people you're closest with in the world? I don't get it."

"Toby, it's something I don't discuss. You wouldn't understand."

"I might have if you'd given me the chance. Now I guess we'll never know." I shake my head. "You need to tell Eden and Asha right now, Joanna. People saw you at the party last night, and you'll be seen at the office today. I wouldn't be surprised if by this evening, every news outlet in the city is crowing about how Marcus Crest's prodigal daughter has returned to the fold. The Tate sisters deserve to hear it from you first. Finding out any other way will hurt them." *Ask me how I know.*

She stares at her hands for a few seconds before unlocking her phone. "I'll call them now."

I don't look at her as she makes calls to Eden and Asha, and from what I overhear, they're more shocked than angry. I shake my head, pissed that all this unpleasantness could have been avoided if Jo had chosen to be honest. Now, whatever fragile friendship we shared has been obliterated, and I can't even look at her without another wave of anger hitting me.

"Toby?"

"What?" I keep my eyes trained on the passing scenery.

"Will you be able to do this with me today? Pretend like you're my fiancé?"

"Don't worry, I'll get the job done. I'm getting pretty good at lying. After all, I learned from the best."

The rest of the ride passes in awkward silence, but as soon as the car pulls up in front of Crest Towers, we put on our game faces and act like the perfect lovebirds we're pretending to be.

"JOANNA! COME HERE, SWEETHEART."

Despite Joanna's talent for pretending, the hug and kiss she shares with her father when we enter his office is all kinds of awkward.

"Hi, Dad. Nice to see you."

He turns to me and holds out his hand, and I brace myself for another slimy handshake.

"Toby, my boy. Glad you could make it."

"Mr. Crest." I squeeze his hand just enough to not seem like a threat. This man's ego is more delicate than an over-ripe banana, so I make sure to act as obsequious and deferential as my stomach will tolerate. "It's a true honor to be here, sir. Thank you so much for inviting us."

Marcus gestures to a rectangular table in the far corner of the massive office that's been laid out for lunch.

"I thought we could eat here and take in my incredible view." He glances at me, and then back to the massive floor-to-ceiling windows that overlook the Freedom Tower. "What do you think, Toby?"

"Breathtaking, sir. Best view in all of NYC." It's not, but it's that kind of pandering that Crest eats up.

He grins and turns back to us. "So, what have you two love-birds been up to today?"

Joanna shoots me a glance and smiles. "Oh, not much. Went to the gym together. Snuggled. You know, fiancé stuff."

Halfway through her sentence, Crest is checking his phone, already bored.

"That's great, honey." He doesn't even come close to pulling off sincere.

There's a knock at the door, and Crest's face lights up as a good-looking man in a grey suit enters.

"Brad, my boy! Come in, come in. Look who it is. Little Jojo is back."

Brad comes over to us, looking about as slick as an ocean bird after an oil-spill. He assesses Joanna with a kind of possessive familiarity that makes the hairs rise on the back of my neck.

"Well, well. Looks like someone grew up right." He moves in to give her a hug, and I can't stop the sneer that settles on my face. "How are you, little Jojo? Long time, no see."

Jo hugs him back, and I shove my hands in my pants pockets.

"Hey, Brad. Yeah, it's been a while. Too long."

Crest steps forward. "Toby, this is my COO, Brad Russel. Back in the day when Jojo was just a teenager, she had a major crush on this guy." Jo looks at the floor. "It was always funny how she used to follow him around like a puppy."

"Dad ..."

"Don't be embarrassed, sweetheart. Brad's a handsome man. No shame in having a girlish infatuation." Now even Brad looks embarrassed. "Anyway, you obviously moved on, because you're here with young Toby."

Seeming grateful for a chance to change the subject, Brad holds out his hand to me. "Toby Jenner, right? I've been reading all about you this morning in the *New York Times*. They're calling you Doctor Love because of your new app. Pretty sweet publicity for a tech newcomer."

Crest looks confused, so Brad explains about the app and the publicity from the launch last night.

"Well, this app sounds like money in the bank," Crest says. "When are you going to float your company? I might buy some stock."

"It's not going to be listed, Dad." Thank God Joanna steps in, because stock market talk isn't in my wheelhouse. "The app is to help people. Toby and Max aren't interested in making money off it."

"Of course they are. Everyone is interested in making money, and anyone who says they're not is a liar." Crest studies me for a second. "Aren't you moving into real estate to make money? Isn't that what you told me?"

I think quick to salvage the situation. "Absolutely. Don't get me wrong, I really enjoy my work in tech, because it's challenging, but it's a volatile market with vastly differing rates of return. I know that to secure my financial future, the New York property market is the safe bet. I'm just looking for the right project to start me off and a mentor like you to guide me."

Crest seems to buy it, because he nods, impressed. "You have a good head on your shoulders, Toby. If you play your cards right, I may be able to bring you onto one of my projects, so you can see how the sausage gets made, so to speak."

I smile. "Wow, Mr. Crest, that would be incredible. Thank you so much."

He looks at Brad. "What do you think? Can we find something for the boy? Ground level. Low risk."

Brad seems hesitant, but if he's worked for Mr. Crest for a while, he knows never to disagree with him. He nods. "Of course, Marcus. Toby and I can have a chat after lunch and sort something out."

"Excellent." Crest gestures to the table. "Now, let's all eat, and we can talk business again later. Take a seat."

Playing the dutiful fiancé, I hold Joanna's chair as she sits. Then I take my own. Brad and Marcus sit on the other side.

Within seconds, a butler appears with a silver trolley and places a selection of sharing plates in the middle of the table, along with a salad. Then he deposits what looks to be a whole lobster in front of each of us.

"Fresh from Maine this morning," Crest says, unfolding his napkin and laying it in his lap. "Nothing but the best for my daughter."

Joanna stares down at her plate. "Yes, if by 'nothing but the best' you mean 'a swift and painful trip to the hospital', then great."

Crest frowns. "What the hell does that mean?"

"It means I have a shellfish allergy, Dad."

"Since when?"

"Since always."

"Rubbish. The only thing you were ever allergic to was doing what you were told."

Joanna goes bright red, and despite my sour mood, I reach beneath the table to squeeze her hand. If she goes off on him right now, she'll sink us.

We share a brief look, then she squeezes my hand back and laughs. "Well, you've got me there, Dad. But just in case, I'm going to skip the lobster." She pushes the plate away and reaches for the salad. "I'm not very hungry anyway. Gotta fit into my wedding gown, right, honey?"

I smile. "Right."

For the remainder of the meal, Joanna is unusually quiet.

FOR WHAT FEELS like the hundredth time today, I fake laugh at something offensive Crest says as a joke. Nothing is off-limits to him, and I'm fucking drained from pretending I don't want to slam him against a wall repeatedly, until he cries for his mother.

Crest, Brad, and I sit in Crest's office, sipping single-malt whiskey as the rest of the employees pack up for the day. Jo excused herself a while ago to take a call from her publishing job and put out some fires, and since then, it's been a gross boys' club with Crest as the immature frat-boy president.

I was feeling crappy enough before I spent the entire afternoon listening to his 'genius' philosophies surrounding money and real estate, but now I'm officially done. I can sum up every piece of his so-called wisdom with one phrase, "Win at all costs, no matter who you fuck over in the process." Coming from a billionaire, I'm completely unsurprised this is the credo he lives by.

"Toby, you must come out tonight," Crest says, patting me on the shoulder. *Jesus in Heaven, please, no.* "I'm being given an award at the New York Chamber of Commerce dinner, and I want you and Joanna to come as my guests." He's already half in the bag. I'd hate to see how hammered he gets before getting the award.

"Uh … I'm pretty sure Jo and I have plans tonight, but thanks."

"Nonsense!" He stands and grabs the decanter, so he can refill our glasses. "Whatever it is, cancel it. I want my new protégé by my side when they honor me. It will give you a good chance to get the inside track into my world."

He puts the stopper back in the crystal bottle just as Jo comes back into the office.

"Joanna!" Crest says. "You and Toby are my guests at the NYCOC dinner tonight. No arguments."

Jo shoots me a look, and I try to communicate how much I don't want to go without alerting Crest.

"Honey, don't we have that thing to go to tonight?"

Jo frowns. "What thing?"

Dammit, I've had too much to drink to come up with anything believable. "You know, that *thing* we've had planned for weeks. You were really looking forward to it."

Come on, Jo. Help me out here.

She shakes her head. "Oh, no, honey, that thing got canceled. We can totally go to Dad's award ceremony tonight. It'll be fun."

I plaster on a smile. "Oh. Great. That worked out well, then."

She comes and sits on the arm of the large easy chair I'm in and puts her arm around me. Her father beams at us as he loudly clasps his hands together.

"Wonderful! Brad and I are going in the limo with members of our PR and legal teams, but I'll get another for you two."

"Dad, you don't have to —"

"No, I insist. Only the best for my daughter and future son-in-law." He gives a low chuckle and yells out to Brenda to order another car.

"Sir?" Brad says, gesturing to the door. "We'd better go. The ceremony starts at seven, and I know you wanted to speak with Councilman Walters before it begins."

"Right." He and Brad head to the door. "I'll see you two there!"

When they leave, Jo sits in the chair beside me, and I rub my forehead.

"Was my signal too subtle?" I ask. "Or is it funny to watch me be subjected to your father's company?"

She crosses her legs. "I just thought the event might be useful to us." She taps a message into her phone. "Think about it. The Chamber of Commerce is giving Dad an award? That event will be filled with influential people he deals with all the time. I wouldn't be surprised if a lot of them have been paid off over the years. It's also a good opportunity to get some photographic evidence of him schmoozing with these bozos." She looks over at me as I rub my eyes. "But if you really don't want to go, I can make an excuse for you."

I sigh and drop my head back onto the chair. "It's fine. I can go. I'm just tired." And miserable. And socially drained.

Jo's phone pings, and she checks the screen. "Eden's going to recruit Max, and they'll come, too."

"As what? Businesspeople no one has ever heard of?"

Jo shrugs. "Don't know, but I'm sure they'll think of something."

27

DRUNKEN HONESTY

"**O**h, you two look great together! Just a few more shots, please."

I have my arm around Jo and amp up my fake smile as we sit at Crest's now-empty table in the ballroom of one of New York's glitziest hotels. Jo has her hand on my chest, and Eden is in front of us, pretending to be an event photographer taking happy snaps for the organizers.

"Beautiful." She slings her camera around her neck before coming over with a notepad. "And if I could just get the correct spelling of your names, please."

I don't know why she's pushing her character so much. No one's taking any notice of her, which I guess is the point.

She leans down and gives me a subtle wink. "This is fun. Glitz, glamor, an open bar, and taking down the big boys from inside their own house. So I'm wondering, Tobes, why do you look like you've just had a root canal?"

I wish I had the inclination to give her the whole lowdown about me and Jo, but as usual, this isn't the time or place to get into it.

"I'm having a blast. Just tired."

Jo puts her hand on the back of my head and strokes it, and even though I know it's for show, it still feels nicer than it should.

"So," Eden says with a conspiratorial air, "Did you freak out when Jo told you about her dad?"

You could say that.

Eden keeps one eye on me while scoping out the room, like any good journalist. "I was floored. We had New York royalty right under our noses this whole time, and we didn't even know it."

"Yeah," I say. "Crazy." As tired as I am, apparently I still have enough energy to maintain a low simmer of resentment about the whole thing.

"Joanna," Eden says, snapping a couple more pics of people around us, "you know that when you're ready to air your dirty Crest laundry in public, you owe me an exclusive interview, right? Any time you want to tell-all about your asshole dad, I'm here for you."

Joanna gives her an uneasy smile. "Good to know." She grabs her wine glass and drains the contents in a few swallows. She's done that a lot tonight. Maybe it's to dull the pain of her dad crowing to anyone who'll listen about his wayward daughter crawling back to him, or maybe it's because I've been vacillating all night between believable fake fiancé and the human equivalent of a block of wood.

Whatever the reason, Jo seems to think alcohol is the answer. I've never seen her as drunk as she is right now. It's concerning.

Across the room, Max is moving through the crowd, looking like he well and truly belongs. No doubt his high-society contacts will be invaluable in identifying who Eden should photograph. So far, we have no evidence that any of the guests are guilty of corruption, but if they're pal-ing around with Crest, chances are they're no angels. Max signals to Eden, and she waves in reply.

"Okay, gotta go. Max has some marks for me. We'll chat tomorrow about which of these Masters of Industry are living in Crest's pocket, and with any luck, there'll be a nice fat list of names and crimes you can pilfer from Crest's office server on Monday." She grins. "I'm so glad you texted about this, Jo. It could be a goldmine for the story."

"Yeah, it could." Jo blinks way too long, then leans against me. "And you're very welcome, Edie. You're beautiful. I love you."

Eden smiles. "Aw, I love you, too." She leans down and whispers to me, "Do not let her drink any more. She's totally gone."

I nod. "I'm on it."

As Eden walks away, a waiter stops next to us. "More wine, ma'am?"

Jo sits up straight. "Absolutely."

I quickly put my hand over her glass. "No, Joanna. You're done."

When I gesture for the waiter to move on, Jo frowns at me as he walks away. "Please, sir, can I have some more?"

"You've had enough."

She pushes her chair back and stands up. "Then dance with me."

"I don't dance."

"Yes, you do. I saw you at Romance Central. You dance really good for a white boy." She tugs on my arm. "Come on. Let's go."

"Jo, I'm not in the mood, okay?"

She looks around. "Okay, if you don't wanna dance, that's fine. I'll just go have another drink at the bar."

I shake my head. "Fine, let's dance." I take her hand and lead her over to the dance floor. "You're a pain in the ass when you're drunk, you know that?"

"I'll tell you a secret," she whispers as I turn to face her. "I'm a pain in the ass *all* the time. I just don't hide it as well when I'm drunk." She winds her arms around my neck with a smile, and I grudgingly put my hands on her waist.

Even though the dance floor is crowded, the second she presses against me, every other person in the room fades from view. I inhale sharply, now having to deal with the added torture of her sweet scent filling my nostrils. I don't mean to tighten my arms, but it happens, and she releases a deep, satisfied sigh that vibrates through me.

"This feels good," she says, with a slight moan in her voice.

I clench my jaw and try to suppress my reaction, but having her this close makes it nearly impossible. My brain is still pissed with her, but my body didn't receive the memo. All it knows is how her breasts feel against me. How the heat of her seeps through all the layers of fabric between us. How every single muscle feels like it's experiencing low-grade electrical stimulation.

"I just realized," Joanna says, looking up at me, "that you've barely kissed me all night. Shouldn't we be making a show for all of Dad's friends here? You know… sell our story?"

The last thing I want to do right now is kiss her. Also, the only thing I want to do is kiss her. I want to kiss her so hard, she understands how disappointed I am that she didn't confide in me and how fucking confused I am about everything to do with her. Kissing her would solve so many problems while also making a thousand new ones. And yet, I can't stop thinking about it. I'm stuck in a positive/negative flux of emotions that's draining all my energy and reason.

"Toby ..." She stares at my mouth and runs her index finger across it. "Your lips are so beautiful. So soft."

I swallow and pull her hand down, so it's resting on my chest. "Jo, stop ..."

I hold her hand there, ignoring how I can feel the heat of her palm branding me beneath my shirt.

"Toby, do you *want* to kiss me?"

"That's irrelevant." I try to look anywhere else, but my gaze keeps coming back to her face.

"It's not irrelevant to me. Because I want to kiss you so badly, I'm aching for it."

I close my eyes and grip onto whatever tenuous control I have left. My breathing is tight, even though I'm trying to keep it as even as I can.

When I open my eyes, I find Jo still gazing at me with so much lust, I have to look away. Crest is on the far side of the room, clutching the ugly award he was presented with earlier. There are people gathered around him, but it's clear that even though the business community in this town may fear him, they don't like him. A short distance away, Brad is sipping a drink, staring directly at me and Jo. When he sees me looking, he raises his glass. I tip my chin in reply, but there's something about that guy that sets me on edge.

Jo must see him too, because she says, "Brad asked me today if I was serious about marrying you. Apparently he recently broken up with his girlfriend and is on the market again."

That gets my attention. "The fuck? He hit on you?"

She shrugs. "Guys like him always think they should have whatever they want."

"And he said he wants you?"

"Not in so many words. He kept it subtle. I think he's a little afraid of what you'd do if you found out."

I glare at him. "He fucking should be."

Joanna cups my cheek and gets me to look at her. "Calm down. We're only fake-engaged."

"Yeah, but that asshole doesn't know that. What did you say when he asked if you were serious about me?"

She looks into my eyes. "I told him that if I ever got married again, it would be with you."

I frown. "*Again?*"

"It's a long story."

I shake my head. "I'm not even surprised any more, Jo. Your life is full of long stories that never get told."

I glance over and see Brad still staring. "Well, here's a short story for you." I lean down and kiss her, and not gently. It's deep and passionate, and I hope that Brad gets a good fucking eyeful of how she melts against me and grips me like she never wants to let go.

When I pull back, we're both breathless, and Jo sways a little. I put my hand on her cheek. "My story is called 'I'm done with this day, so let's say goodnight to these people and get the fuck out of here.'"

I take her hand to pull her through the crowd, and she runs a little to keep up. "I like this story. I wonder if it has a happy ending."

EVEN THOUGH MY impromptu kissing display made Jo more handsy than usual, after a few minutes in the car, she got quiet and still. I suspect the motion of the vehicle was having a detrimental effect on the alcohol in her stomach.

By the time we get home, I all but carry her out of the elevator. In the kitchen, she pushes away from me and grabs a glass from the cabinet.

"Need water." She fills the glass and takes several huge mouthfuls before leaning back against the counter and looking at me.

"Toby?"

"Yeah?"

"Do you know that Eden's grandma has a pet duck?"

I loosen my tie. "Yes, Jo. I've been to Nannabeth's a heap of times."

"I haven't. I've only been there twice, but her duck is amazing. Moby Duck. That's his name. Isn't that an *amazing* name for a duck?"

She sways a little, and I put my arm around her waist to steady her.

"Okay, take it easy."

She leans forward and whispers, "When I was little, my nanny took me to the pond in Central Park to watch the ducks. I used to think I could control them with my mind." She puts the glass down and grabs onto my lapels. "Like, I'd stare at them and think, *You should go have a swim, little guy,* or *You should waddle over to the grass now,* and they did it. But when I told my nanny, she said I wasn't controlling them. It just turned out that the ducks and I had really similar ideas about what they should do with their time."

I try to get her to let go of my jacket. "That's great, Jo, but we need to get you into bed, okay?"

She stands up onto her toes and touches my face "Toby, that is literally what I want more than anything in the whole world. Take me to bed. Please."

She loses her balance, and I end up scooping her up into my arms.

"Okay, clearly gravity is a challenge. Also, I'm not going to have sex with you. What you need is sleep."

"Pfft." She snuggles into my neck, and I close my eyes, overwhelmed by how my body reacts. "I need sex, too, but whatever. Be boring. That's fine."

Straightening my back and ignoring how my body would much rather go with her plan, I stride down the hallway toward her room.

"You're so strong, Toby." She puts her hand on my chest and digs her fingers into my pecs. "So big and tall and gorgeous and strong. I love how strong you are. Not just in carrying me, either. But in your heart. In your mind. There's nothing you can't do."

"You're wrong about that." *I can't carry you to your bedroom without imagining all the ways I want to make you come, that's for damn sure.*

"Toby ..." Her head is in my neck, lips grazing the skin there. "I know you think I pretended to like you for your hacking skills, but you're wrong. When I found out you were a hacker, I tried to stop liking you, because I thought you might disappear like Sergei did, but then ... you stayed. You helped me."

I clench my jaw as her breath tickles my jaw. "That's me. Helpful Toby."

"That *is* you. So helpful. So handsome. Such a beautiful man in every way." She sighs. "I always liked you for you, Toby. Not for what you could do for me. I hope you know that."

I swallow as I process that, and somewhere deep inside, my most insecure self breathes a sigh of relief that not everything between us has been a lie.

When I get to her room, I deposit her as gently as possible onto the edge of the bed.

She looks up at me with pleading eyes. "You're going?"

"Yes. I need sleep, too."

She lifts one of her feet and points to the delicate but complicated straps winding up her leg. "Can you help me first? I can't even see how to get them off right now."

I look over my shoulder at the relative safety of the hallway where I won't be assaulted by the smell and sight of her, but right now she needs me, so I have no option but to help.

I kneel in front of her and start on her shoes. She reaches out and runs her fingers through my hair as I work.

"The number of times I've fantasized about having you between my legs, and now here you are."

"Jo … please. You can't say stuff like that." It's hard enough to be this close without imagining giving her the best oral sex of her life. A lot of men won't even perform it, because they're selfish fucks who have no idea how to navigate a woman's anatomy. But nothing thrills me more than making someone come apart on my mouth. Saliva starts to flow just thinking about it.

"Why can't I say it?" She looks down at me. "You want me to tell the truth, right? Well, here it is. I've spent months stopping myself from saying sexy things to you. I've been so freaking strong in trying to keep my distance. But it didn't make any difference, did it? We still broke apart, because no matter how many languages I speak, or how good I am at making money, the one thing I can't do is make people love me."

My face burns hot. "That's not true. Lots of people love you."

"Do you love me, Toby?"

My hands freeze on her shoe. "Joanna …"

"No, I want to know. You can even just say you love me as a friend, because God knows, at this point, I'll take anything I can get." She shakes her head as her expression crumbles. "I've worked so hard to be strong and self-sufficient. I've done it my whole life, so the only person I ever needed to rely on was me. But then you come along, and none of it means anything anymore. I don't need you to control my rogue AI or destroy my father, Toby. I need you to breathe."

She looks at me, her face full of despair. "How am I going to breathe when you're gone?"

She doesn't cry, but tears fall down her cheeks nonetheless, and goddammit, how can I do anything but comfort her right now? For once, she's showing me who she is, and even though it's not the whole story, for the moment, it's enough.

I squeeze her ankle gently. "I'm still here, Jo. Right now, I'm here for you."

She stares down at me, pain filling her expression. "I'm sorry I didn't tell you everything. Over the years, I was so lonely, I built myself a whole new reality where my parents loved me, and nothing bad ever happened. I remade myself into the opposite of who my father wanted me to be. But even now, the one thing I can't pretend my way out of is fear."

"Fear of what?"

She shrugs. "Everything. Fear of not being enough, or of being too much. Of stupid nightmares that no amount of therapy can remove."

I finish taking off her shoes and sit on the bed beside her. "I don't understand."

"I know, because even now, I don't have the words to tell you. I want to, but I can't. Every time I think about it, I feel sick. Like every cell wants me to stop."

I rub her back, and she leans into me. "It's okay. Just keep breathing."

"Do you want to know something pathetic?" She pulls back and looks up at me, her cheeks wet and mouth trembling. "I had an amazing time today. It was one of the best days of my life, not because we spent it with my dad, because that part sucked. But because for the entire time, I was someone who *you* loved. You held my hand and hugged me and kissed me. And even though you were just pretending, it felt better than anything in my whole life. I dream about being loved like that."

I cup her face and wipe away her tears with my thumb. "Jo, you will be loved like that, but not until you stop hiding. You seem to think that people can only love the best parts of you, but that's not how it works. Loving someone means accepting their flaws and mistakes. It means taking the bad with the good, and the dark with the light. You can't just leave out the stuff that make you uncomfortable or embarrassed, because then they're not loving *you*, they're loving a lie." She drops her head and nods. "You always said that guys leave you, but you're wrong. No man has ever left you, because they've never known the real Joanna. They just left the woman you were pretending to be."

She wipes her eyes with the backs of her hands. "My life is complicated, Toby. My family is complicated. The way I feel about you is super complicated. But lying … it's easy. And lying to myself is the easiest of all." She sniffles. "Sometimes when you want something so impossible it eats away at you, a lie can make you numb for a second. Like ... the moment before you admit it's a lie, it could be the truth."

Her speech is becoming more slurred, and I'm still not sure I understand what she's saying. Or what it all means.

"Jo, let's get you undressed and into bed, okay? We can talk more about this in the morning."

"Sure."

With a deep sigh, she turns her back to me so I can unzip her, and then with as much decorum as I can summon, I stand her up, pull off her dress, and walk her around to the side of the bed so she can climb beneath the covers. Then I place her dress on the easy chair and put her shoes near the wall.

"Toby?"

I turn the lights down to low. "I'm here."

"Don't leave me. Please."

Her eyes are closed, but she's reaching for me. I run my fingers through my hair.

So much for keeping my distance.

"I'll stay until you're asleep, all right?" Judging from how far gone she is, that won't be long. I take off my jacket and remove my tie. Then I pull off my shoes and climb onto the other side of the bed, on top of the covers.

When she feels me there, she turns and snuggles into my chest. I put my arm around her and stare at the ceiling, knowing that keeping my attention away from her lacy underthings is the only way I'm getting out of this situation alive.

"Stay with me," she says, her cheek on my chest. "You're the only one, Toby. The only one I want to stay."

I tighten my arm around her and press my head into the pillow as her hand comes to rest on my stomach. I try to match my breathing to hers to calm my hammering pulse, but having her warm and soft against me is setting everything into overdrive.

I hated seeing her as miserable as she was tonight, and as much as I'd like to blame everything on her father, I think I'm a big part of it. Whatever dysfunction is in her past, she's been getting over it for years now. More than the bitterness she feels over her father, I'm the one who's hurting her now. One more reason for me to get out and let her get on with her life.

Just a couple more days, and we'll have the information we need. Then we can go our separate ways.

The thought should cause a sense of relief, but all I feel is a growing sense of dread.

28

SHUTTERED

When I wake, the sun is peaking over the tops of the buildings outside Joanna's massive bedroom window. Looking down, I see her sleeping peacefully on my chest. My arm is tucked into her side, and damn all the gods and saints of every religion for her feeling so right in my embrace.

I allow myself a few more seconds of stolen bliss before gingerly sliding out from under her. As I move away, she makes a disapproving noise and reaches out to where I used to be. When her eyes open, I freeze and watch as confusion spreads across her face. She looks at me, then at the bed, then at the window, and finally, back to me.

"What time is it?"

I check my watch. "Uh … early. Before seven."

She frowns and sits up. "How long have I been asleep?"

I collect my jacket, tie, and shoes. "You passed out pretty quickly after I put you to bed, so … six hours-ish, I guess."

She stares at me, confusion turning into something else I can't put my finger on.

"And you slept here? With me?"

"I didn't mean to. I was going to sneak out after you were asleep, but I passed out before that happened."

"I didn't … make any noise?"

"If you mean did you scream the house down and then go all Bruce

Lee on my ass, obviously not, or you and I wouldn't be having this nice conversation about your sleeping habits."

She lets out a short laugh, but it's not a happy sound. "Of course. That makes perfect sense."

I get the feeling she's gone off on a tangent from our conversation, rather than reacting to what I just said.

She climbs out of bed, and without saying anything else, goes into the bathroom and closes the door.

I look around and sigh. "Okay, then. Guess I'll be on my way." As I suspected, her being honest and emotionally vulnerable was only a temporary affliction and now, she's over it.

I go back to my room, confused and in need of a shower to bring me back to the land of the living.

I replay everything Joanna said last night in my mind as I shower and get dressed, and when I head out into the kitchen to make some breakfast, she's already there, wearing her running gear and sipping a coffee.

"Hey."

She doesn't answer. In fact, she doesn't look at me.

Okay, she's embarrassed about admitting she wants and needs you. Be cool about it.

I get out some cereal and pour it into a bowl. "So … about last night …"

"I don't want to talk about it."

I'm so damn tired of her obfuscation and deflection, a flash of anger hits me.

"About what, exactly, Joanna? The moment you admitted you've been having sexual fantasies about me? Or the part where you begged me to say I loved you? Or how about when you held onto me for dear life the moment you fell asleep as if I was a lifeboat in a hurricane?"

So, that's the exact opposite of being cool, Toby. Good job.

Jo glares at me before dumping the rest of her coffee down the sink and putting the mug in the dishwasher.

"I have to go."

I step in front of her. "Dammit, Jo, when are you going to stop running away? You can pretend you didn't say those things, but you did, and I'm tired of you pulling me toward you with one hand and pushing me away with the other. Every time things get too deep, or you feel like you're getting too attached, you shut down."

"That's not true."

"It absolutely is. Once may be an accident, two can be coincidence, but more than that is a goddamn pattern. What sets off this behavior?"

"Nothing." Her expression tells a different story.

"Is it needing people? Needing *me*? Is that what has you running scared?"

She just stares at me, and I wonder why I couldn't just keep my big mouth shut. Why do I keep trying to steer her into areas where she's clearly not willing to go?

It's because you somehow believe that if what's broken in her can be fixed, you might have a chance after all.

I sigh and put down my bowl.

"Jo, I'm really trying here, but I don't know what else to do."

"There's no use talking about a forgone conclusion, Toby. Talking won't change our outcome, so I'd just rather not." She moves away, but I grab her arm gently, to stop her.

"Please don't go. I don't agree that talking won't help. Let me make you some food."

"I'm not hungry."

I gesture to my bowl. "Then stay and talk while I eat something. Please."

She shifts her weight from one foot to the other, restless and frustrated. "I don't want to talk, Toby. And I don't want food, okay?"

"Fine, then for the love of God, tell me what you *do* want. At least be honest about that."

She stares at me for a few seconds, blinking. "Everything, Toby. That's my problem. I want *everything*. The romance, the toe-curling sex, the easy friendship, the passion that burns so hot it turns my body into a melted mess. *All* of it. But I'm learning more and more that not everyone is built for love like that, so I'm training myself to stand down." She stops and swallows, and I swear she's holding herself back from touching me. "And when I can't stand the longing that twists inside me every day, I get out of bed, lace up my Adidas, and run around Central Park, until I don't want anything but to stop. Then I go to sleep and wake up the next day *wanting* all over again."

Without waiting for a response, she heads out to the entrance hall, and I know she's gone when there's a soft ding of the elevator.

I shove my bowl into the sink, and it clatters loudly.

"Fuck." I rub my face in frustration. "Jeeves, what the hell is going on with her?"

"I'm sure I don't know what you mean, Toby."

"Cut the bullshit. Out of everyone on the planet, you know that woman the best, so please, for the sake of my confused heart and mind, tell me how to figure her out."

"She's a complicated person. Even with all my processing power, it would take a long time to calculate an accurate answer to your question."

I put my palms on the island and hang my head.

"Right. Of course. No easy answers from anyone today."

"Although I can't fulfill your specific request, perhaps I can offer one piece of information that might shed some light."

I look up at the ceiling, because that's where I always picture Jeeves lives, which is dumb as hell. "And what's that?"

"It's been a long time since Joanna has slept six hours straight."

I process that for a second. "How long?"

"Well ..." he goes silent, as if he's already said too much.

"Jeeves, come on. You started this. How long?"

"Years."

I frown. "How long does she normally sleep each night?"

"She doesn't."

"What do you mean?"

"I mean, that to the best of my knowledge from what she's told myself and Sergei when he was here, Joanna hasn't slept through the night since she was sixteen years old. Instead, she takes regular naps."

I ponder what he's told me. "So, she's achieved so much in the past decade, because she doesn't power down for eight hours like the rest of us mere mortals?"

"A lot of great people in history had similar sleep patterns. Most notably, Leonardo Da Vinci."

"That makes sense. If anyone in this world is a renaissance woman, it's Jo. So, why is she now pissed with me? Because she told me how she feels for once? Or because I enabled her to sleep without screaming?"

"That's something you'll have to ask her."

"In other words, you know the answer but don't want to betray her confidence."

He stays silent, and that's all the answer I need.

I clean up the kitchen and head to my room to do some work on my laptop, all the while, trying to push away thoughts of Joanna. That speech she gave about wanting wasn't all about me, that much I know. There's something much deeper at work, but if she won't talk about it, I can't help, and not-helping feels like crap.

Later in the day, Eden calls, and we talk for a while about how she's going with the cache of documents from Crest's study, as well as her progress on identifying the congressmen and city councilors from the event last night.

I give her whatever help I can, and when we're done, I head to the gym for a quick workout before dinner.

Just as I'm starting to get worried that Joanna hasn't come home, she walks out of the elevator as I'm perusing the contents of the freezer. She's drenched in sweat, as if she's been running for hours.

"Jo, hey. Have a good run?"

"Uh huh."

She doesn't even stop. She just goes straight to her room and closes the door.

"My day was great," I mumble to myself. "Thanks for asking."

I heat up one of the preprepared meals and sit on the couch, mindlessly flicking through TV channels, until I'm sure Jo isn't coming out of her room.

I head up the hallway and knock on her door. "Jo? Do you want me to make you some dinner?"

I hear muffled movement inside and then, "No, thanks. I'm not hungry."

I lean closer to the door. "You have to eat something. You didn't have breakfast. Did you eat lunch?"

"I'm fine, Toby. Please just leave me alone."

I walk back to my room, still concerned but unwilling to argue about it. If she's determined to keep me at arm's length, then I can't force her to bring me closer. It makes me sick to think this is how things are now, but at least I can say I tried.

I flop onto my bed, and even though I'm exhausted from the emotional turmoil of the past couple of days, I toss and turn all night.

In the early hours, I hear Joanna's door open, and when I poke my head out, I find her passing through the kitchen, dressed in a fresh set of jogging gear.

I sigh as the elevator dings to signal that yet again, she's gone.

29

CRACKS IN THE ARMOR

Sitting in Marcus Crest's office, I try to seem interested as he and sidekick-Brad point to a map on the giant screen behind his desk. It shows Manhattan with a collection of colored dots that represent Crest properties in various stages of construction.

"You see, Toby, everything marked in green has been finished and sold or leased. Yellow indicates bought and being developed, and red are those properties I'm going to acquire."

"That's a lot of properties, sir." *You greedy fuck.*

He looks proudly at the screen. "They don't call me the King of New York for nothing. When I'm dead and gone, all of this will be my legacy."

Joanna crosses her legs. "Yes, but at what price, Dad? You've had thousands of lawsuits brought against you over contract disputes or unsafe work practices. Doesn't that tarnish the reputation you're so proud of?"

Marcus pulls his shoulders back, clearly not used to people challenging him. "You always were a bleeding heart, Joanna. You can either care about people or build an empire. You can't do both. A bunch of nobodies suing me is a blip on the radar of history. Their petty grievances are fleeting. My buildings will last forever."

Joanna's expression flares, and I can tell how angry she is. But pissing off dear dad before we complete our mission won't help anyone, so I try to steer the conversation back into safer waters.

"Mr. Crest, did you always have a talent for real estate?" If I can get him to focus on himself, then Jo will have time to calm down.

"Yes, Toby. I always knew I wanted to change the New York skyline, and every year, I complete at least one major project." He points to a spot downtown, near the river. "And that right there is going to be the next jewel in my crown."

Brad goes to the desk and picks up a tablet. "Actually, the Tompkins Square Park site is no longer available." He taps something into the screen, and the red spot disappears.

Marcus frowns. "What the hell happened? That deal was about to go through."

"The seller said someone outbid us at the eleventh hour."

"Who? Not the LL Group again?"

"The seller wouldn't divulge a name, but I'm assuming that's who it is."

"Dammit, Brad, that's the third property we've lost this year. You still haven't tracked them down?"

"We're trying, sir, but all we have so far is an office in Brooklyn that seems to never be manned. The incorporation information lists a Russian national we've been unable to contact."

"Well, maybe we've had the wrong man on the job." Crest turns to me. "Toby, you're a computer wizard. How experienced are you with tracking people down?"

"Uh … well, I have certain skills that might be able to help you." *Not that I would, but I'd like to find these people, so I can shake their hand for pissing you off.*

He grabs a file off his desk. "We need to know who's behind this. They keep stealing properties I've earmarked, and it can't continue."

I flick open the file and see it's just basic information about a corporation. The name sparks something in my brain, but I'm too distracted by Crest standing over me to work it out.

"I see you've brought your laptop with you today." He gestures to my bag on the chair next to Joanna.

"Yeah, wasn't sure if I'd need it or not, but I guess I do."

"Great." He turns to Brad. "Find somewhere for Toby to work. And Joanna, if she's so inclined."

Jo smiles. "You know that real estate never interested me."

"No, but you always liked marketing and PR. It would be great for us if you came back to the fold. I need you to carry on my legacy."

Fire sparks in her eyes. "I have a job, Dad."

"What, being an assistant at a publishing company? There's no money in that."

"No, but I love my work, and that's all I need." She stands, and I shoot her a look. She composes her face. "Still, maybe I'd consider working here if I knew a bit more about the corporate structure. Can we get that tour today?" She looks at Brad. "Do you have time?"

Brad gazes at her with far too much enthusiasm for my liking. "Sure. If your dad doesn't need me for a while, we can go now."

Marcus nods his assent.

"Great." Jo looks at me. "Let's go, honey. Don't forget your bag."

Brad leads us to the elevator. "We'll head to PR first, and then we'll take Toby to IT to get started on his hunting expedition. It will really impress Marcus if you can unmask his real estate nemesis."

"I'll do my best." *You fiancée-coveting prick.*

For the next hour, we get the full Crest experience. Despite my dislike for the man, I must admit that Marcus's business certainly seems to be booming. Mind you, in the three floors we've toured, not many people seem happy to be working here. In fact, whenever Brad passes, the employees avert their gaze as if he's a basilisk who might turn them to stone.

"And here's our IT department," Brad says, gesturing to a collection of cubicles and offices. "Legal is also in the far corner, and security is down the opposite side."

"Toby." I stiffen as Jeeves's voice comes through my earpiece. He's been quiet this whole time, so I'm startled to hear from him now. *"Judging from the heat signatures of the building, the server room is close to your current position, behind the bank of elevators."*

I see a door with a security pad on the wall adjacent to where I'm standing.

"Is that the breakroom?" I ask. "Because honestly, I'd kill for a coffee."

Brad looks at the door. "No, that room contains our servers."

Bingo.

"Oh, wow. What are you running? TX59s? Nexiums?"

Brad laughs. "Do I look like the kind of guy who knows about geek stuff?" *No, Brad, you don't. You look like the guys from the football team who used to beat me up, so fuck you very much.*

"Sorry," I say, gesturing to the door. "Just geeking out. I'd love to see inside, if that's doable."

Brad shakes his head. "Sorry. No one's allowed in there except the geek squad and their security team."

Joanna frowns. "Oh. So, they don't even let the COO of the company in?"

I can tell she's baiting him, but apparently Brad is oblivious. He touches the security tag clipped to his breast pocket. "I can go in if I like, but visitors can't. Strictly authorized personnel only."

"No worries," I say. "Jo would have been bored by the tech anyway. Maybe after I've been here for a while, the guys will show me around."

Brad looks confused, as if me getting kicks from checking out a phat server array is strange. "Sure. That could happen." He glances down the corridor. "Hang here for a sec while I organize a workspace for you, Toby. Be right back."

As he walks away, Jo comes closer. She's been distant when we're alone, but as my fiancée, she's been warmer.

"Getting into that room is the goal," she says. "And it seems like Brad's key will do the trick."

"Just a reminder that if either of you gets your phone close to a security card, I can clone the frequency."

"Then I guess that's your job, Jo."

"Why?"

"Because Chuckles McGee there is dying to get close to you. All you have to do is let him."

She shoots me a look. "You weren't so keen on letting him near me the other night."

"Yeah, well, he didn't have his pass card on him then."

Brad returns and asks that we follow him down to one of the offices on the north side of the building.

He shows us into a large, luxurious space, far fancier than anywhere I've ever worked. "This is yours for the meantime, Toby. The floor staff has been notified that you'll be working here for a while, and the head of security will drop off an access pass later today."

I'm impressed. The office has a wall of huge windows on one side and a large desk on the far side.

"Wow. This is great. Thanks, Brad."

"You're welcome." He turns to Jo. "And would you like to stay here? Or can I convince you to come and shadow me for the rest of the afternoon?" *I suspect you can convince her, Brad, you tool.* "I know your dad would love for you to take over the company one day, and I think we'd make a great team."

Fuck you, Brad. She already has a team, and it consists of me and a super-intelligent artificial lifeform.

Jo glances at me and then back at him. "Well, I can't say I haven't thought about running the business one day, so sure. Let's go." She comes over to me. "You've got work to do anyway, honey. See you later, okay?" She lifts onto her toes, and I automatically lean down to give her a soft kiss. I admit, I might put a bit more passion into it than I would have if Brad wasn't watching.

Of course, I should know better than to take my chances kissing Jo. Despite how distant she's been, her feel and taste make fireworks go off in my head and chest, and it still boggles my mind that her merest touch can slam into me with the force of a particularly aggressive Mack truck.

When I come back to reality, I look up to see Brad staring in barely disguised disgust.

"Okay, Jojo, let's go. Later, Toby."

Jo looks back at me, color flooding her cheeks, before following him down the corridor.

I hate how tight my shoulders get watching them leave.

I go over and put my bag down on the desk before dropping into the sumptuous chair.

"Right. Guess I'd better get to doing some work I won't be paid for."

I unpack my laptop and start looking into the LL group while trying not to imagine what Jo's doing in order to get Brad's pass card.

It only takes half an hour for my heart rate to return to normal after our kiss.

By the time Joanna walks back into my office, four hours have passed, and most of the IT and law crowd has left for the day. Twilight colors filter through the windows, and Jo leans on the side of the desk, next to where I'm working.

"Having fun?"

I keep my focus on the screen, feeling more tense than I planned on being today. "Actually, yes. It's been quite an informative afternoon. Lots of interesting tidbits came to light."

I lean back in my chair and stare at her. "Care to tell me what I discovered?"

Uneasiness fills her face. "Well … I don't know …"

"Yes, you do." I turn my laptop, so she can see the screen. "I'll give you props for how thoroughly you covered your tracks, but when I saw the name 'Jeeves' in the source code of the website, I started putting the pieces together. The Russian national on the papers is S. Petrov. That's Sergei, right? He helped you with the digital camouflage, because this is sophisticated stuff. And the LL Group? Pretty sure that stands for Liza Lotte."

She looks at me with defeat. "Letting you discover it on your own seemed easier than explaining everything."

"That seems like a recurring theme with us. Leave Toby in the dark, until he gets blindsided. In case I haven't been clear, I really fucking dislike this game."

"It's not a game, Toby. I just …" She pushes her hair away from her face, more flustered than I've ever seen her. "I don't know how to share, okay? Every damn day I try to be different than I am, but it's like I'm stuck in the groove of the same broken record. I know I'm pushing you away by not changing, but it's the one thing I truly suck at."

It's like all the tension from the past couple of days is finally bubbling over, so I stand by and let her get it out.

"I hate that I can't do it. I'm so used to keeping everything to myself, I've forgotten how to trust people. And every time I think, 'oh, you know what? You should share that with Toby,' something stops me, and I have no freaking idea why."

I wait for something else … a clarification or determination, but apparently, she's done.

I rub my eyes. "That's fine, Jo." I pull my laptop over and start shutting down. "I'm used to your secrecy by now. Whatever the reason, you do what makes you comfortable."

"Toby …"

"What?"

I almost jump when she cups my cheek, getting me to look up. Her hand is warm and filled with sparks, and her eyes are the same. "What I'm trying to say, badly, is that … even though it may not seem like it, I do trust you. You're the only person I've trusted completely in a really long time."

"Jo, I'm all about evidence-based conclusions, and nothing in our entire relationship supports your assertion. You've hidden stuff from me so often, I feel like I'm in a story that contains only half the narrative."

"I know, but …" She takes a breath. "If I didn't trust you, I could never have slept next to you the other night. And knowing that … well, it freaks me the hell out. I'm aware I have problems with letting people in … and by people, I mean you. But I want to change. I just don't know if I can."

I pull back from her touch. "If you don't think you can do it, then I have no chance of helping you. But you have to understand that hiding yourself away … holding your secrets to your chest like they're a bullet-proof vest that will prevent you from getting hurt … that's not a healthy way to live. Believe me, I've been there and done that. You were the one who convinced me to stop, remember?"

She looks at the floor, and I realize I'm too tired to have this conversation right now.

"It feels like we're just talking in circles, so let's stop." I push my chair back. "All I want to do is get what we need off the server and get out of here without getting arrested. Beyond that, you can live your life however you want. If you ever decide you want to talk, you have my number."

I stand and shove my laptop into my bag, and when I turn to face her, she takes the bag from me and lays it on the desk before taking a deep breath. Her expression shows the same kind of fear as someone about to perform a high-wire act without a net.

"Do you know how many times my dad told me he loved me when I was growing up?" I shake my head. "None, Toby. Zero times. He's incapable of feeling it, so why should he say it? To him, the only emotions worth anything are lust, anger, greed, and revenge. Love is for Hallmark cards and idiots."

She has a determined look on her face, like she's going to share this stuff or die trying.

"Go on."

"When I was little, I learned that trying to earn his love was pointless. And if I couldn't gain his approval, then I was sure as hell going to get his attention." A bitter smile crosses her face. "There's nothing my father hates more than a woman he can't buy or control, so as I got older, he absolutely loathed me. I never cowered to his temper or let his ridiculous, uninformed opinions go unchallenged. Me not falling into line infuriated him more than anything else."

"So, he was a bully? Even to his own daughter?"

"He's a bully to everyone. It's the only thing he's truly good at."

"Is that why you left home?"

She hesitates, and something flashes behind her eyes. I'm guessing that even with all this honesty, there's still some secrets she's holding back.

"There were a lot of reasons I left. I just couldn't be in that apartment with him anymore."

"So, what was the plan?"

She laughs. "I didn't have one. I was a kid, but I hated him so much, I came up with a roadmap pretty quickly." She looks out the window, as if reminiscing. "I was fifteen when I left home. Sixteen when I applied to become an emancipated minor. Sixteen and a half when I changed my name from Crest to Cassidy. Seventeen when I decided to become my father's worst nightmare. Twenty-two when I'd amassed enough wealth to go toe-to-toe with him on business deals, and I'll be twenty-six by the time I destroy him."

"Jesus." She speaks with such conviction, it's almost scary. "So, the LL Group is what? Getting into his head? Shaking his stock price?"

She straightens her posture. "All of the above. My dad spent most of his life strutting around this city like he's the apex predator, but that's about to change. When we crack that server, I'll have everything I need to take him out. He's not the predator anymore, I am. And he has no idea what's about to hit him."

I nod, oddly exhilarated that perhaps for the first time, I'm seeing the real Joanna standing before me, and she's fucking magnificent. Yes, I can feel the bitterness for her father filling the room, but the honesty she's just exhibited is intoxicating, and the urge to kiss the hell out of her is rising like a tsunami.

I walk over and take her face in my hands. Then I lean down and kiss her gently, just long enough for the breath to exit my lungs. When I pull back, I lean my forehead on hers.

"That was some decent honesty, there."

She looks up at me. "Did I scare you?"

"A little, but in a good way."

"What does that mean?"

I smile. "Joanna, I thought you were incredible when you were pretending to be less-than. But now that you've shown me the full scope of who you are? You're hot as fuck."

Her eyes flash, and long moments stretch between us when neither of us moves, and for once, she doesn't shut down and turn away.

But we don't have time to get waylaid by our mutual attraction or commit acts in this very open office that would be viewed as obscene. We still have a job to do and little time to complete it.

To break the tension, I clear my throat and step away. "So ... did you clone the pass card?"

She holds out her phone for me to take. "Uh ... yes. Here."

We both look out the glass wall to the office beyond. By this time, it seems everyone except for the IT manager has left. He's still in his office on the opposite side of the space.

"You go to the server room," Jo says as I grab my computer bag. "I'll distract that guy." She strides toward his office, and when his attention is firmly on her, I slip out and head over to the door with the security pad.

"Okay, Jeeves," I whisper. "I hope you've done your job."

"*I have. The security cameras are now on a loop, so no one will see you enter the room.*"

"Okay. Let's punch this thing in the balls." I hold the phone over the digital reader, and there's a quiet buzzing before the light flicks to green. "May the hacking gods be with me."

I slip inside the room and breathe in the familiar smell of high-quality air conditioning and miles of plastic-wrapped cables. "Sooo ... if I were an air-gapped server, where would I be?"

I walk up and down the banks of servers, searching for my target. Smack-bang in the middle of center aisle I find it. Separated from the others, it blinks with an array of monitoring equipment.

I pull my laptop out and attach a cable and SD card. "Jeeves, are you ready to rock and roll?"

"*If you mean intervene in security alerts, then yes. Ready and waiting.*"

"Great. This thing might be triggered by unauthorized devices. Be prepared to shut it down to prevent the guards from busting up our party."

"*Understood.*"

I connect to the server and hold my breath for a few seconds, waiting for an alarm or running feet. When nothing happens, I get to work. The system is a bit more complicated than Crest's home server, but not much, and certainly not the worst I've cracked. Within fifteen minutes, I'm in, and I immediately start downloading the entire contents of the hard drive.

"How's Joanna doing, Jeeves?"

"*She's discerned the office manager is an avid maker of craft beer, and he's deep in conversation about his favorite methods of fermentation.*"

"Great. That could keep him talking for freaking hours."

There are a lot of compressed files on the server, which is excellent, because they take far less time and space to download. After nearly twelve minutes, there's only a quarter of the files to go.

"*Toby, there's a man walking toward your office.*"

I pull out my phone. "Show me."

Jeeves loops me into the internal cameras, and I see it's LeBron, Crest's head of security. He comes back out and looks around. When he sees Joanna, he goes over to her.

"*He's asking her where you are. She said you had some bad shawarma for lunch and had to go to the bathroom.*"

LeBron looks down the hallway before nodding at Joanna and walking away.

"Jeeves, please tell me he's not going to look for me in the bathroom."

"*As much as I'd like to oblige, it seems that's exactly where he's heading.*"

I check the timer. Two minutes to go.

"Come on, come on, come on." As much as I grind my teeth and wish it to go faster, I know it's going to take as long it takes. Unfortunately, LeBron will find out I'm not in the bathroom way before then.

"Jeeves, tell Jo she's going to have to stall."

"*Understood.*"

On the screen, I see Joanna running after LeBron. He stops, and she smiles at him.

"*Joanna's asking why LeBron's looking for you. He said he's got your new pass card. She said she can take it for you. He said that's against company policy, as you must sign for it. Now she's making derogatory comments about how disgusting your bowel movements are and is recommending he wait in your office."*

"Wow. Okay. That devolved quickly."

I see LeBron look towards the bathroom, and then back to Joanna. He nods and says something.

"He said he'll come back in five minutes."

"Yes! That's all the time I need."

I watch the progress bar slowly inch toward a hundred percent.

On the screen, I see LeBron go to the elevators and press the call button. Then he frowns and walks back to look at the server door.

"Oh, shit. Jeeves …"

He walks toward the door, pulling out his pass card as he goes.

"Jeeves, if you have a way of distracting this guy, now's the time, or we're going to be sunk."

"Understood. Stand by."

A huge screeching sound comes from the elevator shaft, followed by an alarm.

LeBron hurries back to the elevators and pulls out his phone.

"Playing with the emergency brakes won't distract him for long, Toby. You need to get out."

"Just a sec, I have to wipe the download logs."

"You don't have time. He's already established the elevator alarm is a malfunction."

"Can you do it if I go?"

"Not unless you leave your computer attached to allow me access, but then he'd discover it and trace it back to you anyway."

"Shit, fuck, shit." I yank the cable out of the server and shove it and my laptop into my bag before sprinting toward the door.

"Quickly, Toby."

"This is as fast I can go."

I yank open the door and slip out before closing it silently behind me. I've only taken two steps toward the elevators when LeBron turns the corner and practically runs into me.

"Oh, hey," I say, trying not to sound as breathless as I feel. "LeBron, right? How's it going?"

He looks at me, and then at the server door behind me. "Your girlfriend said you were in the bathroom."

"Yeah, that's right. Just came from there." I pat my stomach. "Not feeling great to be honest, so we're about to head home." I look over and see Joanna coming toward us. "Honey, you ready to go?"

She comes and takes my hand. "Absolutely. Let's get you into bed."

LeBron scans my face, and I know he's clocking the beads of sweat running down the side of my face. "You look nervous, Mr. Jenner."

I wipe the sweat away. "Not nervous, just crampy. Probably running a fever, too." I cough weakly. "Hope it's just food poisoning and not a stomach bug." I cough again, this time in his direction. "Would hate to give it to anyone."

That seems to have the desired effect, because he takes a step back before pulling an ID badge from his pocket. "Mr. Russell asked me to provide you with this." He pulls his phone from his jacket and points to the screen. "Sign here, please."

I do as he asks, even though my scrawled signature is barely recognizable.

"Great. Anything else?"

He looks at the server door again, and then back to me. "Not right now. You both have a good night."

"Thanks, LeBron. We'll try."

He steps back to let us pass, and we walk around the corner to the elevators.

"You okay?" Joanna whispers as she pushes the call button.

"Not sure yet," I say.

Once we're in the elevator and the doors have closed, I let out a tight breath. "Jeeves, where are we at?"

"*Your download was complete, but your software didn't complete wiping the logs. If anyone checks, they'll know they've been hacked.*"

"What's LeBron doing now?"

"*He's looking around your office. It's clear he doesn't trust you. Just a minute …*" There's a pause, and then he says, "*Bad news. He'll calling the IT manager over to come and check the server room.*"

"Dammit."

The elevator lets us out in the lobby, and I take Jo's hand and stride out into the street with her trailing behind me.

When I head toward the nearest subway station, Joanna squeezes my hand. "Where are we going? Gerald is waiting with the car."

"In a few minutes, LeBron's going to know we hacked the server and will be looking for us. In this traffic, he'd catch us on foot. Better we jump on the subway and get to somewhere safe."

"They'll look for us at the apartment."

"Exactly."

"Where do you have in mind?"

"Somewhere I hope they don't know about."

I pull out my phone and bring up Eden's number as we head down the stairs into the station.

"Toby, hey. Everything okay?"

"We've hit a snag. I need a favor."

I LOOK around as I knock on the door to Nannabeth's apartment. In a second, Eden has yanked it open to usher us inside.

"Come in. What's the situation?"

She closes the door and leads us into the living room where Moby Duck is sitting on the couch, watching Animal Planet.

I check if we're alone. "Where's Nannabeth?"

"On the roof watering her plants. We can speak freely."

"Okay. We didn't have time to cover our tracks, and Crest's security chief found us out. He's called in all of the security personnel, and they're scouring the city for us."

"They haven't called the police?"

Jo shakes her head. "Knowing my dad, he'll try to take care of this in-house before bringing in the authorities. He won't want to explain to them what information was stolen, considering it would implicate him in a whole bunch of illegal activities."

I pull out my laptop and remove the SD card. "This is everything we got today. Looks like years of legal filings and confidential memos. I also saw a big fat blackmail file of politicians and city officials that he's paying off. In other words, the motherlode."

I place the card on the coffee table, so I can put my computer away.

Eden looks between us. "So, what's the plan?"

Jo looks out the window onto the street below. "The only way to end this is to publish your article and detail all the evidence we have. Then we deliver the whole thing to the district attorney and stand back as my father and his company crash and burn."

Eden puts her hands on her hips. "That sounds great, but I haven't finished sorting through all of the safety reports from the construction sites yet, let alone trawling through this new cache of files."

Moby Duck hops off the couch and digs his beak into a bowl of meal worms on the coffee table. I pat his feathers as I try to figure out how to play this.

"Okay," I say. "I'll get Jeeves to help us sort and collate everything we've got. That will leave you free to write your article. Maybe Max can compile the photos from the function last night, and then by the end of this week, we should have enough evidence to go to print. Sound good?"

Eden nods. "Yeah, that's a solid plan."

"Do you think Nannabeth will be cool if Jo and I crash here for a while? It could take a few days."

"Absolutely." Eden points down the hallway. "You guys can have Asha's and my old room. We took our beds when we left, but Nan turned it into a pretty comfy guest room with a big old queen ensemble. I assume you two roomies are cool sharing a bed."

Jo and I look at each other, and I know she's thinking about the last time we shared a bed for a whole night. Apparently the memory still freaks her out, because her discomfort is clear.

"We'll work something out," I say as much for Jo as for Eden. "I can always crash on the couch."

Eden screws up her face. "Unlikely, large man. Look at that thing." She gestures to the old-fashioned three-seater with ornate wooden arms. "Half of you would fit on it, and the rest would be on the floor." She looks at Jo. "What's going on? You two can't lie next to each other?" She narrows her eyes. "Holy shit, have you guys had sex? Is that why there's a weird vibe going on here?"

"Jesus, Eden, no." I rub my forehead. "Why does a weird vibe always translate into people having sex with you?"

"Because sex makes people weird." She looks between us. "Also, not having sex makes people weird." She narrows her eyes. "Maybe that's what's wrong with this picture. Have you two considered taking a ride to bone town? God knows, you could both use a decent lay."

I'm about to find a way to argue with her when Jeeves' voice comes out of my phone.

"Toby, we have a problem."

"What is it?"

"I'm monitoring the phone signals of several Crest security officers, and they seem to be converging on your position."

"What? How?"

"I'm not sure, but it would seem they have some way of tracing you."

"How far away are they?"

"Four blocks. We have to find the tracker immediately."

Joanna looks around, and then a virtual light bulb goes off over her head. She strides over, shoves her hand into my left pants pocket, and pulls out the ID card LeBron gave me.

"This is what they're using. Shit!"

Without missing a beat, she runs down the hall to the bathroom, and a second later, we hear a flushing sound.

She comes back, worry still etched on her face. "Jeeves, what are they doing? Are they still headed toward us?"

"One moment. Waiting to see if they change course."

We're all silent for what feels like an eternity. Eventually, I swear I hear relief in Jeeves's voice when he says, *"It seems to have worked. They're now following one of Brooklyn's major sewerage lines."*

Eden pushes out a breath. "Okay, that was scary. Not sure I'm cut out for this spy crap." She shakes out her arms. "Before anything else happens, let's get started on uploading stuff to Jeeves, so this can be over ASAP."

"On it." I turn around to grab the SD card off the coffee table but stop short when I don't see it. "Where's the card?"

I look at Eden, but she holds up her hands. "Don't look at me. I didn't touch it."

I drop to my knees and scour the carpet. "It was just here. It can't magically disappear."

Jo joins me on the floor, and we frantically rub our fingers over the highly patterned carpet fibers, searching for the tiny card.

We both freeze when Moby Duck seems to cough and then quack loudly.

Jo and I look at him, then at the meal worms that have spilled onto the table, then at each other.

"You don't think he …?"

The duck coughs again, and Eden groans before getting down onto his level. "Moby, you tiny, fat eating machine! Can't you tell worms from digital storage devices?"

Moby quacks, slightly indignant, and then coughs again.

"Shit." Eden sighs and drops her head.

"How do you get a duck to throw up?" Jo taps something into her phone.

"Are you Googling that?"

"Of course. How else are we going to find out?"

"Well, you could ask me." We freeze on hearing the familiar voice from behind us. We all turn as one to see Nannabeth standing there, hands on her hips; small but intimidating. "But before I tell you anything about that gluttonous little troublemaker, I suggest someone fill me in about what the hell is going on."

30

OPEN HEARTED

Sitting around Nannabeth's kitchen table, we all take turns telling the long and complicated tale of Crest Construction and why we're working so hard to take them down. Nan listens as she makes tea and sandwiches, and by the time we're done, there's a feast on the table in front of us.

"So let me get this straight," she says, taking her seat. "Marcus Crest is *your* father." She points to Jo, who nods. "But you hate him, because he's a heartless bastard, and you've spent most of your adult life trying to find a way to destroy him."

"In a nutshell, yes."

"And you," now she points at me, "have a father who was crippled by Crest and have been searching for a way to get payback for the better part of five years."

I nod and chew on an amazing BLT. "Yeah."

"And you, darling granddaughter …" She points to Eden. "You've decided to throw your hat into the ring by writing an explosive exposé on one of the most powerful men in New York that could result in you getting sued out of existence."

Eden sips her tea. "Well, it sounds bad when you say it like that …"

"And now," Nannabeth leans back in her chair, "you're all here, dragging me into this entire mess and plugging up my duck with digital memory cards." She looks at each of us in turn. "Have I got the shape of things about right?"

"Technically, yes," Eden says, treading carefully. "But we didn't mean for any of this to happen, Nan. We especially didn't mean for Moby to think a plastic chip was a worm. I mean, really, that's on him."

We all look to where Moby is seated on his own chair, seemingly unperturbed by a foreign object in his body. When he catches us staring, he quacks loudly.

Eden takes her grandmother's hand. "If this is too stressful, we can go somewhere else. We just need to get the card out of Moby first."

Nan gives her a smile. "Oh, darling, it's not stressful. This is the most exciting thing to happen to me since I came out of a coma. I just wanted to make sure I have your stories straight, because honestly, you kids have some serious issues to work out." She looks at Joanna. "Especially you, young lady."

Jo swallows. "What do you mean?"

Nan puts more sandwiches on each of our plates. "Well, I mean you've made your entire life about destroying your father, and all going well, your mission will soon be completed. What are you going to do then? What will your purpose be? More importantly, who will *you* be when this is done? Have you thought about that?"

Jo puts her sandwich down and wipes her mouth with her napkin. "Uh … I guess not."

"Maybe you should. If you think taking your father down will magically make you whole again, I hate to tell you, it's not going to happen. Toby helping take him down isn't going to make his father whole, either. Eden telling the story isn't going to make the rest of Crest's victims whole. Don't get me wrong, what you all are doing is a good thing, but it's not a miracle that will fix the lives of the people he hurt. Just something to consider, that's all."

We all go quiet as we think about her words. I'm not sure what I thought would happen when the story came out. Maybe I figured Dad would finally get the compensation he deserves, but even that's not going to cure him. Crest getting bitch-slapped by karma would be the first step in a long journey for a lot of people, and judging from the look on Jo's face, she's the one who'll have the farthest to go.

"Anyway," Nan says, topping up our teacups, "there's not much more you can do tonight, because Moby's not going to pass that card until tomorrow at the earliest. So, you might as well get comfortable and try to relax. Eden, you'd better go pick up some extra clothes and toiletries for Joanna and Toby, since they'll be here for a few days. They can't risk going home. Agreed?"

She looks at me and Jo, and we nod. "That'd be great."

Jo pulls out her phone. "I'll make a list for you, Edie. Thanks."

We finish the rest of our meal in relative silence. Nannabeth chats away, but Jo in particular is quieter than I've ever seen her.

After dinner, we all help clean up, and then Eden heads out to grab us supplies. When she's gone, the rest of us take Moby up onto the roof for a swim in his pond. It's a cool Autumn night, so Nan loans Jo one of her thick cardigans. While Nan and I sit in folding chairs next to Moby's landscaped pond, Jo wanders through the incredible rooftop garden looking at the plants and sniffing the flowers.

Nan and I sit in amiable silence for a while, happy to watch Moby paddling away, but then she glances over at Jo, who by now is standing on the other side of the roof, looking out at the city. I follow her gaze, and there's so much about how she's acting that worries me. I know the events of the past week have been stressful, but I hadn't realized how much of a toll being reunited with her dad was taking on her until tonight. All I want to do is go over and make her feel better, but even if I tried, I'd probably find a way to make matters worse. Despite her breakthrough in the office today, I get the distinct feeling she's been fighting a losing battle since she slept beside me. It's like parts of her keep retreating, preparing for the day I leave. I know it's what I have to do, but thinking about being without her makes me want to simultaneously punch a wall and throw up.

"Toby, what are you doing?"

I turn to see Nan studying me.

"What?"

"Oh, you know what, young man. You've fallen in love with that girl, even though there's a hundred-percent chance she's going to destroy you."

I take a deep breath. "It's only a ninety-three percent chance, actually. Ninety-five if you factor in how goddamn attracted we are to each other."

Nan laughs her singular, old-lady laugh and leans back in her chair to watch Moby swim.

"How did you know?" I ask, also watching the duck.

"That you love her? It's written all over your face. You're making yourself sick with how you feel. That amount of passion is going to burn you out if it has nowhere to go. Best you start preparing for how to handle it as soon as you can."

I rub my knuckles over my jaw, uncomfortable with how much truth is being thrown my way. Nannabeth has always been scarily observant, but it's usually directed at her granddaughters. This is a new and uncomfortable experience.

I take a deep breath. "Does she look at me the same way I look at her?" Even though she's drunkenly admitted she feels the same way, a small part of me doesn't trust she's telling the whole truth.

Nan laughs again and leans forward. "Young one, she looks at you with *exactly* the same lovesick expression, and that's the problem."

"I don't understand. If we love each other, then why are the odds telling us we can't be together?"

"You can be," Nan says, looking at me like I'm a little slow. "But not now. Not until she figures out her issues."

"I know she's struggling, Nan, she's been honest about that. But I have no clue what's at the heart of her issues."

Nan looks over her shoulder at Jo, and then back to me. "Have you ever wondered why she runs around doing a million things all day long? Why she works so hard to accomplish so much? Why she bends over backwards to help people, putting their needs above her own most of the time?"

"Part of it has to do with her being a good person with a good heart, but … yeah. I know there's more to it than that."

"Toby, there's something in that girl's past she hasn't told anyone. Something that hurt her so much, she's never recovered. Take it from someone who knows the signs. Everything she's doing now, everything she's done since that mysterious event … she's trying to prove she's worthy."

I lean forward, trying to keep my voice low. "Of her father? Because that ship has sailed. She told me she's given up trying to gain his approval."

A light breeze ruffles Nan's hair, and in the low light of the few lamps up here, she looks like a wise woman from a story book.

"A lot of times we do things and pretend they're directed at others, but that's a garbage lie we tell ourselves. That little girl has a giant hole in her heart that can only be healed when she realizes her father not loving her wasn't her fault. She needs to understand that she's *always* been worthy of love. Until she convinces herself of it, she'll keep pushing away the people closest to her. She'll never be truly honest with her friends, or you. It's the oldest saying out there, but it's the God's honest truth. If you don't love yourself, how in the hell are you going to love someone else?"

I look over at Jo, seeming so small and lonely on the other side of the garden. "How do I get her to love herself?"

"You don't. That's the trick. She has to do it on her own. All you can do is be there and support her. Make her understand that you're her person, no matter what. You can encourage her, sure, but all the hard choices about who she wants to be? Well, they're up to her."

This isn't what I want to hear. I want to know what the problem is and how I can solve it. That's my modus operandi. Find the equation, identify the variables, and then figure out the freaking solution. Telling me I can't help is like kicking me in the balls and walking away. Telling me I can't help Jo in particular? That's a special kind of pain.

"Toby, you're a good man, and I know this isn't what you want to hear, but I'm saying it for your own benefit. You probably have some romantic notion about how the bond you two share is so special, it's powerful enough to overcome the odds. But that's just not true."

"Wait. Didn't you say we could be together if she figures things out?"

"Yes, but that's not defying the odds. It's *changing* them."

Something clicks in my brain, and I'm pissed with myself for not figuring it out sooner. Nan's implying that the math will work in our favor if Jo decides to live her life differently. That's one possibility I hadn't considered. Jo's instinct to push people away may have been reflected in her questionnaire answers, which may be why our scores bombed. Truth is subjective, and if someone changes their outlook, their truth may change, too.

"Toby?" Nan smiles at me. "Whatever's going on in your head, slow it down. Changing someone's destiny is likely to be a marathon, not a sprint." She pulls her jacket more firmly around her. "Did you know that before I got Moby, I had a cat?"

"No," I say.

"Her name was Cinnamon." She grabs the thermos she brought up with her and pours herself some coffee. "She was this scrawny, flea-bitten thing that lived in the alley behind the building. I used to take her food every day, but she was skittish and wouldn't eat until I left. But I was patient. Each day, I'd just wait a little closer, and eventually she trusted me enough to eat while I stood there. Then, while I sat next to her. And finally, while I petted her. It took months to get her to trust me, but then she followed me right up the stairs one day and made herself at home. And that's when I knew that we were going to be okay. I let her into my heart, and then she let me into hers. I couldn't rush it. I had to let her set the pace. And that's what you need to do with Joanna."

I can't help still being skeptical. "So, you don't think soul mates should just click together effortlessly? Or do you not believe they exist?"

She sips her coffee, then looks at me as she cradles her mug. "That' a tough question. I do believe they exist, but do I think every happy couple is fated? No."

"Was your husband your soul mate?"

She laughs. "Oh, George was a wonderful man, and I'm grateful for all of the good years we had together, but there was never that churns-your-stomach, all-encompassing love between us."

"Then why did you get married?"

"We might not have had A Great Love, but we still loved each other more than we loved anyone else, so it seemed like a good idea." She takes another sip of coffee and stares at something off in the distance. "Some people get married because … well, they're lonely. We're not meant to go through this great journey of life alone. Sometimes when we reach a hand out in the darkness, we want someone to grasp it. To make us feel safe. To make us feel like a 'we' and not a 'me.'" She brings her gaze back to my face. "George might not have set my world on fire, but he always made me feel safe and loved, and considering I didn't have anyone else, that was enough for me."

I tilt my head back and stare up at the stars. "I designed an app to help people find their soul mates, but it only proved that Jo wasn't mine, despite it feeling like she was. Now you're saying she might be, but not at this point in time. How the hell do I know what to do?"

She glances over at me. "What do you want to do?"

"You know the answer to that."

She sits forward. "The trouble with people who set your soul on fire is that sometimes, your soul doesn't survive. Someone can be your soul mate and still be bad for you." Her expression becomes more intense.

"And someone who isn't your soul mate can be the best thing to ever happen. You understand?"

I nod. "So, you're basically saying go for it, and if I get destroyed, at least I gave it my best shot."

She leans back and gives me a smile that's full of patience and just a touch of condescension. "Toby, nothing in this life is a hundred-percent certain or a hundred-percent doomed. Compatibility isn't some immovable, pre-destined thing. Sometimes it's fluid and mysterious, like trying to grip onto an oiled eel. Being compatible isn't a God-given right. It's the result of the choices we make. But every relationship in your life … every one that's important … is like a garden. If you want it to thrive and bloom, you need to tend it every day, in dozens of ways. You can have the most perfectly placed garden beds in the world. It doesn't mean they won't be plagued by weeds. It's not destiny that keeps people together. It's a lot of hard work."

She stands, and Moby must know his time is up, because he swims to the side of the pond and climbs out before shaking himself dry.

"Come on, little man." She picks him up and cradles him under her arm. "Now I'm going to take this gremlin downstairs and put him to bed, because he has a lot of pooping to do in the morning. I suggest you spend a little time tending the garden before you go to bed."

"I will. Thanks." I bend down and kiss her on the cheek. "Has anyone ever told you that you're amazing?"

"Not recently, but it's always nice to hear. Goodnight, Toby."

"Good night, Nan."

I watch as she goes over to the stairwell and disappears inside. Then I walk over to where Jo is, still standing like a statue, looking out at the city lights.

I stand beside her. "Whatcha doing?"

"Staring."

"How's that working out for you?"

"Not bad."

I shove my hands into my pockets and follow her gaze. She's looking out toward the river, and I must admit, from up here, the city looks beautiful.

"You're quiet." I move closer. "Want to talk about it?"

She rolls her neck. "Believe it or not, I'd like to, but I can't. I don't know what I'm feeling, so I don't have the words to describe it."

"Okay. But when you do, I'm here for you."

She turns to look at me, and then with only a moment of hesitation, she steps forward and envelops me in a hug. "You're the best friend I've ever had. I wish I'd made that clearer, sooner."

"You know best friends can tell each other everything, right?"

"Yeah. I just have to find a way to do it."

"Okay. I'll be waiting."

We step away from each other, and she goes back to staring. "Thanks."

"And Jo?"

"Hmm?"

"Just to be clear, I'm in love with you."

She turns to me, confused. "What?"

"I'm in love with you. Thought you should know."

I turn and head back toward the stairs.

"Wait a minute." She catches up to me and grabs my arm. "You can't just tell me you love me and then walk away."

"Why not?"

"Because it's … well, it's …"

"What?"

"Rude."

"Is it? Despite my best efforts to keep my distance and not do something stupid, I have to face up to the fact that I'm hopelessly, irrevocably, desperately in love with you. Why is that rude?"

"Because … you …" She pulls her cardigan around her, like it's going to protect her from what she's feeling. "We agreed we can't … and our score … and my track record … and you … you …"

I step into her and cup her face in my hands. "Jo, pardon my French, but fuck our agreement. This is my truth, and I'm not going to run from it anymore. Fuck our compatibility. Fuck all the doubts and reasoning. Fuck the logic of why we shouldn't be together. I love you. I'm *in love* with you. I want you with every fiber of my being, and if you said the word, I'd carry you downstairs right now and make sweet love to you until the sun comes up. But you have to speak your truth for that to happen. You have to find whatever wall you're hiding your heart behind and dismantle it, brick by brick, because that's the only way this is going to work. You have to want me more than you want your secrets. More than you need to hide your shame. You have to want me more than you want to deny yourself happiness. It's not an easy choice, I know … but it's one you have to make. So, whenever you're ready, I'm here for you."

I lean down and kiss her softly, testing every ounce of patience in my body as I struggle to not let it devolve into something strong and urgent. I want her to trust me. I need her to set the pace. To see that even if her heart is still closed, I'm letting her into mine.

"Whenever you're ready, come and find me." I kiss her again, trying to infuse it with all the tenderness I feel; all my love. She hesitantly kisses me back, but I know she's not ready. All this honesty is already too much for her to handle. Even before we break apart, I feel her retreating.

"I'm heading downstairs," I say with a sigh. "Eden will be back by now with some fresh clothes, and I'm going to shower and go to bed. You should join me. Sleep with me. No sex, just actual sleep. You need more rest, Jo. You look tired. Whatever you're afraid of, I promise I'll keep you safe until you wake."

I give her one last kiss, soft and lingering, and then I turn and go downstairs to the apartment, leaving her alone in the moonlight to ponder her choices.

I'M in bed dozing in the T-shirt and boxer briefs Eden brought back from her shopping trip, when I become aware of someone moving around in the bedroom.

"Jo?"

I open my eyes and see her in the dim light from the lamp on the nightstand, tidying up wearing a tank and sleep shorts, hair damp from the shower.

I close my eyes again, trying to will myself to sleep. I laid it all out to her tonight, and if she rejects me, then I'm in no hurry to hear it. I'm too tired to deal with heartbreak right now.

She moves around a bit more, and then I feel the covers move and the bed dip as she climbs in. I smell soap and sense warmth, and even though I made sure to perch myself on the far edge of the bed to leave her plenty of room, within seconds she's right up against me, her head snuggling into my chest, arm draping over my waist.

"Hey." Her voice is soft and hesitant, as if she's unsure if touching me is okay.

I wrap my arm around her shoulder to reassure her, and she relaxes against me. "Hi. Welcome to Nannabeth's guest room where there's absolutely no extra charge for the large warm man in your bed."

She lies there for a few seconds, breathing. I look down and see her face, half in shadow. She's staring up at me, a frown line sitting between her brows.

"You're the only guy who's ever made the nightmares go away, you know," she says quietly. "Every time I closed my eyes for nearly a decade, I've had the same recurring nightmare, which is why I stopped sleeping ...but with you ..." She touches my face. "There's nothing. Sweet, dreamless unconsciousness. What the hell is that about?"

"Are you asking me? Or is that purely hypothetical?"

"Both. There's so much about you that sets my whole body on fire, but then you're also the only one who can make all my inner voices totally quiet."

"I don't understand."

"Of course, you don't. I've spent so much time keeping you in the dark, I'm surprised you haven't given up on me. All the lies. The half-truths. The flat-out omissions. You deserve better." She pats my chest. "But there are still things I didn't tell you, because ... I didn't have the words. They're things I've never wanted to tell anyone ... until you came along."

"I'm listening. If you want to tell me now, I'm here for you."

She takes a deep breath. "Okay. Here goes." She looks up at me. "When I was fifteen ..." She pauses, and I squeeze her arm to let her know she's safe. "When I was fifteen, a group of men broke into the penthouse at the Crest Condo and kidnapped me. They didn't hurt me, but ... they took me from my bed and abducted me."

I'm not sure what I was expecting. Maybe some tale of physical abuse from Crest, but certainly not this. "Jo, what the fuck?"

She pushes up onto one elbow. "They were people my dad had ripped off. A bunch of contractors who dad had been stringing through the courts for years. They were on the verge of losing their businesses and felt they had no other choice but to do something desperate to get the money they were owed."

"So they kidnapped you for ransom?"

"Yes. But at first, I had no idea what was going on. I was a frightened teenager, and even though they didn't hurt me, they kept me locked in a tiny room for more than a week before they let me go."

"So, that's the recurring dream?"

She shivers. "Every time I fell asleep, I'd feel half a dozen hands holding me down, another hand over my mouth. I'd relive the terror as they taped my hands and feet and gagged me ... how I could barely breathe when they loaded me into a steamer trunk to carry me out of the building."

"Jesus." I can feel her anxiety ramp up.

"Being locked in that trunk ... while they drove out of the city ... then that tiny prison room." I stroke her back to soother her. "That's ... that's when I developed claustrophobia."

"Of course it is. God."

She sits up and crosses her legs, and after taking some deep breaths, she lets out a nervous laugh. "I feel stupid carrying so much trauma for all these years, considering they were mostly decent to me."

"The fuck they were." I sit up and lean against the headboard. "Big, scary men abducted you in the middle of the night. You were a kid. Of course you were going to be traumatized." I realize I'm getting way too loud in the quiet apartment and dial it down a few notches. "What happened to them?"

She pushes some hair away from her face and tucks it behind her ears. "Nothing. One day they came into the room and blindfolded me, and the next thing I knew, they were letting me out near a subway station in Queens. I rode the subway home, and that was the end of it."

"They weren't arrested?"

"No. In the car ride I heard them talking about what went wrong. When they called my father to demand a ransom of two hundred thousand dollars, he hung up on them."

I sit up straighter, a burst of anger filling every artery with magma. "He ... what?"

She nods, and it's clear from her expression that the memory is a painful one. "They told him they had his teenage daughter, and ... he refused to speak with them. Even when they threatened to hurt me, he wouldn't negotiate." She looks out the window, purposefully averting her gaze. "He didn't even call the police. Didn't want the papers to get ahold of the news, in case it affected his precious share price."

She blinks a few times, struggling to talk. I want to hug her and tell her to stop, but I know it's important to get everything out, so it can't poison her anymore.

She gives me a bitter smile. "The cheap asshole who owns billions in assets wouldn't even pay a measly two-hundred grand to get me back." Her tone gets more emotional. "What kind of father does that, Toby? What kind of *person* does that?"

"He's not a father or a person. He's a monster. No wonder you've spent your life trying to take him down." So much about her makes sense now. Why she held such a grudge. Why she wanted to hurt him to make up for how she'd been hurt.

She looks down at her hands as she fidgets with the edge of the sheet. "When I walked into the penthouse, he hugged me and asked if I was okay, but he wasn't really listening to my answer. He put his hands on my shoulders and said it would be best if no one knew. Said it would be embarrassing for us both. After that, even though he beefed up security, I couldn't sleep in my bedroom anymore, and I couldn't stand being around him."

The muscles in her jaw work overtime for a few seconds, and I take her hand and squeeze it.

"He'd drop little comments here and there, about how his instinct to do nothing was right, because they let me ago without getting a cent out of him. When I said that it was a big gamble to make, considering I could have been raped or killed, he stared at me as if I was a fool for questioning his decision." She looks at me. "That was the moment I knew I had to leave. I packed as much as I could fit in a suitcase, took the five-hundred dollars I had in cash, and got the hell out of there."

"What did he do when he found you were gone?"

She laughs, tears in her eyes. "Nothing. It was two weeks before he even called, and even then, it was only because my piano tutor showed up, and I wasn't home. He hadn't noticed I was gone. When I told him I wasn't coming back, he was angry, but only because it would look bad to his friends and employees." She takes my hand in both of hers. "I found out later that he told everyone I'd gone to an exclusive finishing school in Austria. That's how easy it was for him to lie away my disappearance."

She climbs off the bed, as if moving will stave off the emotions that are fighting to get out. I go to her and grasp her hands. "I'm sorry, Jo. He was a piece of shit for treating you like that."

She takes in a shaky breath. "I mean, I knew for years that he didn't care about me, but the way he reacted to the abduction … I still don't understand what I did to make him hate me so much."

Her face crumbles, and I pull her into my chest as she breaks down. "You didn't do anything. He's the deficient one, not you. God, Jo. Anyone else would have felt blessed to have you as their child and moved heaven and earth to get you back. None of what happened was your fault."

She pulls back. "Then why does it feel like if I'd been better … a better person, a better daughter … that it wouldn't have happened? I've tried to direct all of my hatred toward him over the years, but there's always a voice in the back of my mind whispering that I d-deserved it."

"Joanna … no. Please don't think that."

Sobs interrupt her words, and I wait for her to continue.

"I'm s-so ashamed it still gives me n-nightmares. I should be over it by n-now."

I wipe away her tears, and if I had the power to take all her pain inside me, so she wouldn't have to feel it anymore, I'd do it in a second. "Trauma has no timeline. You can't help how you feel."

"And you …" She sniffles. "You come along, and I'm terrified all over again."

I stroke her hair. "You have to know I'd never hurt you like that."

"I know, but …" She gestures to me. "I'm scared of what I'll do to you. Every man who gets close. Every man I feel something for …" She looks up at me. "I hurt them, until they have no other choice but to leave. And I didn't want to do it with you, but … I don't know how to be any other way. I've tried so hard to be different, but I can't. This is me, and if I can't make it work with you, the most amazing man I've ever met, then I'm done. I deserve to end up alone."

"That's not going to happen. Come here." I pull her into my arms. She puts her hands on my chest, fingers tense, digging into muscle. "Look, I'm here. I'll always be here. You can't push me away."

"I can." She glances up at me, pain and frustration bright in her eyes. "I feel myself doing it all the time, and I freaking hate it. I want to do it now." The pressure of her hands on my chest increases, but I don't let go.

"Then stop. Every time you want to push me away, pull me closer. Every time you want to escape, run toward me." I push her hair away from her face and urge her to look me in the eyes. She does, but I can see how difficult it is. "Jo, your dad damaged you, and he'll continue to damage you every time you sabotage a relationship that might give you happiness. Don't let him win. Let *me* win, because I'm the opposite of him. He couldn't love you? That's his fucking loss. I couldn't stop loving you if I tried. And despite what you might think, you're worthy of all the love in the world. You just have to believe that. Let yourself be loved. Let *me* love you."

She stares up at me, fear still sparking behind her eyes. "What if I fail?"

I rest my forehead on hers and close my eyes as I breathe her in. "What if you don't?"

I stay there, holding my mouth just above hers, muscles wire-tight and chest full of so much emotion, it feels like my skin is going to explode off my bones. She's soft under my hands, but her tension is palpable, and right now, the odds are about even between her kissing me within an inch of my life or running into the night and never looking back.

"Toby …" The plaintive tone of her voice is begging me to kiss her, but I can't. Whatever happens next needs to be her decision, and I pray to all the gods that she chooses me.

She winds her fingers in the hair at the nape of my neck and pulls me down, and I close my eyes as she presses her lips softly against mine.

"I want you so much," she whispers. "From the moment we first met, I've wanted you."

"I feel the same way. Even when I told myself I couldn't have you, I wanted you so much it hurt."

She kisses me again, more insistent this time, capturing my lips as every cell in my body fills with fire. She kisses me once more, and now there's not even a hint of holding back. She crushes against me, as if she's trying to climb inside my skin, and when she opens her sweet mouth, I groan in relief as the powder keg of our passion that's been smoldering for weeks finally gets to ignite.

"God … Joanna."

I wind my arms around her and pick her up, kissing her fiercely. At the same time, she wraps her legs around my waist, and I walk us over the wall. I press her into it, trying hard not to make noise but failing.

She moans as I slide myself against her, and I'm so damn hard the friction is excruciating. When I circle my hips and press harder, her moans get louder and more needy.

"Shh," I say. "We have to be quiet."

She writhes in my arms. "You're not making it easy."

I keep kissing her as I lower her to her feet, and when I feel warm hands push under my shirt to explore my skin, my breathing goes haywire.

"I love your body," she whispers, breathless. "I need more of it."

She pushes my shirt up, and in a second, I reach over my shoulder and pull it off. The fabric has barely touched the floor before she's kissing my chest, exploring me with her lips and tongue.

"Fuck." I throw my head back and press my hands flat against the wall to brace myself as she kisses down my stomach, driving me crazy. When her hand closes around me through my boxer briefs, I let out a loud moan, and my legs almost give out.

"Oh … God. Joanna … wait."

I pull her up and kiss her, eager to give her more pleasure before she makes me lose my ever-loving mind. I push my hand beneath her tank, and I'm about to ask permission to remove it when she steps away from me to do it herself. After she pulls it off, I'm dumbstruck for a second as she stands before me, half naked. I stare, and she smiles before taking my hands and placing them onto her beautiful breasts. As soon as I touch her, whatever meager brain power I still possessed disappears in a wave of pre-historic, animal lust.

I caress her velvet-soft skin as I bend over and pepper her with kisses, first on one breast, and then the other.

"So … fucking … gorgeous."

I close my mouth round a nipple at the same time I slide my hand into her shorts.

"Oh, sweet Jesus … Toby."

She pushes her head back into the wall as I take my time finding out what she likes. How much pressure to use. How fast to circle my fingers. She pants and grips my shoulders, fingers digging in every now and then, giving me signals as to how much she's enjoying herself.

When she starts making small, tight noises, I kneel in front of her, gripping her shorts. "May I?"

"God, yes."

I yank them down, and when she steps out of them, I hook one leg over my shoulder as I taste the part of her I've been dreaming of for so long.

"Ohhhhhh …. Oh, God, Toby. Ohhhh, God."

I close my eyes and savor her taste, her incredible noises, the way she slides her hands into my hair and grips me when I'm doing something that feels good. She bites back a moan when I grab her backside and pull her more fully onto my mouth.

"Oh … oh … Toby."

I increase my suction, tongue and lips working in tandem, and when I look up, her face is stunning, contorted in pleasure and total abandon.

'Oh, God, wait …" She pants and grips my hair. "Wait … not yet."

She pulls me up, and I wipe my mouth on the back of my hand before she kisses me, hard and desperate.

"Toby …" She pushes me back toward the bed. When my legs hit the side, she hooks her thumbs into my boxer briefs and pulls them down. They're kicked away, and I stop dead as I register her reaction to seeing me fully naked. Her expression is so full of tenderness, so full to the brim with awe, that my chest swells. She urges me to sit on the edge of the bed, and then, she's kneeling between my legs, kissing down my stomach, gripping me gently at first, then more tightly as I hiss a string of whispered curses.

I'm mesmerized watching her - the most beautiful woman I've ever seen, kissing my body. Loving me as much as I love her.

As I watch, transfixed, her hot mouth moves over me, and then the blinding sensation of light suction robs me of even the simplest thoughts.

"Oh … fuuuuck …"

I lean back on my hands and throw my head back, desperately trying to hold on as she licks and sucks, her hand still gripping me, twisting and pumping.

"Oh, God …" I squeeze my eyes shut, blood thundering through every vein, muscles trembling, heart pounding like a runaway train.

"Jo … oh, God, Joanna …"

Just when I think I can't take anymore, she climbs up into my lap, kissing me, giving me air and a chance to catch my breath. We press together, chest to chest, and I gaze at her as she positions herself above me, stunning in the moonlight, looking down on me like Aphrodite.

I grip her hips and look into her eyes. "Are you sure about this?"

She bends down and kisses me before whispering against my lips. "I'm sure that in this moment, I've never wanted anything in my life as much as I want you. Tonight, I need every part of you, Toby. Please."

The kind of need I've never felt before is reducing me to my most base instincts, and yet, one small hurdle stops me from giving in to it.

"Jo, what about protection? I don't … I don't have anything."

She strokes my face. "It's okay. I'm covered."

Grateful and relieved beyond words, I pull her down to kiss her again. We get lost for long minutes, but when she lowers herself onto me, we break apart and stare at each other, shocked by a whole world of new, ecstatic sensations.

"Oh … Toby." She rocks a little, taking me deeper with each tilt of her pelvis. I don't know what she's feeling, but if it's even a fraction of what I am, her heart is a thousand times too big for her chest.

She looks down at me as she moves, bracing herself on my shoulders. "Tell me again that you love me."

I put my hand behind her head and pull her down for a kiss. "Joanna, I'm so fucking in love with you, I can barely breathe."

When she starts circling her hips, neither of us can speak anymore, and we cling to each other as the threads of our pleasure tighten and stretch. We move as one, sometimes she leads, sometimes I do, and in all my years on this earth, I've never felt anything as indescribably right as being inside this magnificent woman. I lie back and watch her move above me, and from her expression, it's clear she feels the same way. There's no coming back from this. It's like this is what our bodies were made for. More importantly, it's what our souls were made for. This is love-making in its purest form, and for the life of me, I don't know why I've ever wasted time on anything less.

It's because you didn't have her. Don't ever doubt that you belong together ever again.

I flip her onto her back and keep building our pace. She looks into my eyes as everything builds to a breaking point, and we're trying to be as quiet as we can, but every hard breath and stifled moan sounds deafening to me.

When her noises become more urgent, I reach between us and find her with my fingers as I continue to thrust.

"Toby … God, yes. Just like that. Oh, God!"

When she throws her head back, and everything tightens around me, I can't hold on anymore. I thrust a few more times when my orgasm rips through me, and then I press in as far as I can go as her waves of ecstasy spur my own. I grip her shoulders, and we both hold our breath. Then after long, pleasure-filled seconds, we collapse onto the bed, a tangle of sweaty, exhausted limbs, completely breathless and sated.

We lie there for a long time, panting and boneless, unable to fully process what the hell just happened, and when I finally muster the energy to look over at her, I discover she's already asleep in my arms.

31

WARNING SIGNS

I 've always heard that an amazing night of sex with the person of your dreams can change your life, but I've never truly understood the concept until now. Lying here with Joanna wrapped around me, I get it. For me it's like up until this point, my cells have been vibrating at the wrong frequency, and now they've finally aligned. I feel both completely serene and like I could run into traffic and lift a car.

Considering the number of orgasms I had last night, I also feel extremely dehydrated.

I ease out of bed and pull on my boxers before sneaking across the hall to the bathroom. Once inside, I close the door and lean down to drink my fill from the tap. The water doesn't taste great, but it does its job, and when I'm done, I turn on the shower and climb in.

I wash myself in a daze, still blissed-out and exhausted, but not tired. When there's a soft knock at the door, I know it's Jo before the door opens a crack, and her beautiful face appears.

"Good morning."

If my smile were any bigger, it would break my face. "Yes, it is."

"May I join you?"

"Of course."

She hurries inside and strips off before climbing over the edge of the tub. I pull her close and kiss her, and then things get heated for a good few minutes before we get back to the original task of washing up.

When we're done, we wrap ourselves in our towels and use our new toothbrushes. Neither of us can stop smiling, but when we pull open the door and find Nannabeth standing there wearing a bemused expression, our faces drop.

"Good morning, young people." She says it as if seeing us together in the bathroom is the most natural thing in the world.

"Uh … good morning, Nan," I say, horrified she's seeing me in this state.

"Oh, relax, Toby." She waves her hand. "I've seen more semi naked men in my lifetime than I've had hot dinners. I'm not going to faint at the sight of your manly chest."

"Good to know."

"Morning, Nan." Jo adjusts her towel, and I don't miss the look Nan gives her.

"Well … Miss Joanna. Seems like you had an interesting night, hmmm? How are you feeling?"

Jo glances at me and suppresses a smile. "Um … great."

Nan gives her a knowing look. "I bet. You both hungry?"

We nod, and already I can detect the distinct aroma of frying bacon wafting from the kitchen.

"Good." Nan steps back to let us through. "You go get dressed, and I'll finish up with the breakfast." We go to cross the hall, but Nan holds up her hand. "Oh, and before I forget …" She reaches into her overalls pocket and pulls out a small, black SD card. "I thought you might want this. Moby kindly ejected it during his morning walk." She holds it out to me. "Don't worry, it's been thoroughly cleaned."

I take it from her. "Fantastic work, Nan. Thanks."

"Don't thank me. Thank his feathery highness. He was so damned pleased with himself, you'd think he'd laid a golden egg."

Moby waddles into view at the far end of the hallway and pauses when he sees us.

I wave the SD card at him. "Thanks, Moby."

He stops to give me a self-satisfied quack before continuing on his way into the living room.

Nan heads toward him. "I'd better go put on his shows, or I'll never hear the end of it."

When we get back into the bedroom, I immediately grab my laptop and plug the card in while Jo gets dressed.

I set it to upload to the AI server. "Jeeves can sort through these files while we have breakfast. Then we can …" When I look up, I'm immediately shocked into silence by the sight of her dressed in unbelievably sexy underwear. It's a pale purple color, and for a second, I can't even remember what I was about to say.

"Toby?"

I close my mouth and swallow. "Sorry. You, there. Underwear. Just … wow."

She puts her hands on her hips. "You've seen me naked for hours, but this is what stalls your brain?"

"Yep. Sorry. No explanation."

She rolls her eyes and smiles before pulling on jeans and a T-shirt. "Finish what you're doing and get dressed. I'm going to help Nan in the kitchen.

When she exits the bedroom, my brain comes back online, and I set the computer down before digging through Eden's shopping bags for comfortable clothing.

"Jeeves, are you getting those files?"

"*Yes, Toby. I'll start analyzing them as soon as possible. Also, last night I finished the other cache you uploaded. I went through each file to find identifying information and cross-checked the building sites with reports of accidents that resulted in injuries or deaths. Then I searched through court records to find corresponding legal proceedings. I've compiled a list of what I've found and sent everything to Eden.*"

"Great. Out of interest, was my dad's accident in there?"

"*Yes. I'll cross check his case with the lawyers' records that are uploading now and try to find evidence of them admitting wrongdoing. Also, Max has uploaded photos from the Chamber of Commerce event, and I'm in the process of matching government officials with information from Crest's blackmail file.*"

"Excellent." I button my jeans and pull on a T-shirt and cardigan. "Let me know when you have something interesting."

"*Understood.*"

I head down the hallway into the kitchen, where I find Nan and Jo already sitting at the table with plates of food.

"Help yourself," Nan says, gesturing to the pans on the stove. "Bacon, eggs, garlic mushrooms, and toast. There's also fresh juice on the table."

My salivary glands go nuts. "Awesome. Thanks, Nan." I didn't truly understand how hungry I was, until I saw the food. Now my stomach rumbles like a Grizzly waking from hibernation.

I load up my plate and join the ladies, who are now discussing Asha and her new author.

"I'm telling you Nan," Jo says, "they're going to end up together. I feel it in my boobs."

"I agree. I've known they were soul mates since they were kids. They just needed some time apart to realize it for themselves. Of course, you can't tell Asha I know about Jake. I don't want the fact that he's been in contact with me for all these years gumming up the works."

Joanna sips her orange juice. "No problem. I don't understand how they didn't sort things out before now."

Nan pats her mouth with her napkin. "Well, finding the right person isn't as easy as it sounds. Sometimes, you have lessons to learn before the pieces click into place. That's what happened to Jake and Asha. They were both so incredibly pigheaded, it took them too darn long to realize it."

She looks over at me and Jo. "You know, it's hard for us to find our place in this world and even harder to find our person. But when you do, you don't let them go, and you don't run away. You make them your new sun and moon. You start and end the day by worshipping them. You understand?"

She glances at Jo as she says the last part, and I don't miss how tension instantly creeps into Joanna's posture.

"Nan? Toby? Jo?" Eden's voice echoes down the hallway, and in unison, we call out, "In here."

Eden enters the kitchen with her laptop bag slung over her shoulder and smiles. "Good morning, lovely fugitives. How was your night?"

I have no idea what expression passes over my face, but instantly, Eden puts her hand over her mouth and gasps. "Oh my God, you had sex!" She looks at Jo, who seems horrified. "And *you* had sex!" She makes a squeaking sound. "Holy flaming shitballs, my two best friends had white-hot animal sex with each other!"

I'm about to crack like a duck egg when Nan makes a scoffing noise. "Of course they didn't, Eden, and don't tease them like that. They were perfect house guests who went to bed before ten and kept their bedroom door open all night. Now, take this." She passes Eden a bowl of lettuce with oats on top. "Go give Moby his second breakfast while these two help me clean up."

Eden's face drops. "Dammit. Nan, you keep telling me I'll inherit your incredible intuition one day, but it never happens."

"Patience, darling. All good things come to those who wait."

Eden disappears into the living room where we hear her carrying on a one-sided conversation with Moby.

Nan leans into Jo and me. "Best keep things about your relationship on the downlow for now. People think I'm pushy about relationships, but I'm nothing compared to Eden. You should avoid saying anything until you're sure … *really* sure … that you're both in this, boots and all. You hear? I don't want Eden getting her hopes up about this pairing, only to have them dashed a few weeks later. Her moping would be insufferable."

We nod, and although I hate the thought of lying to Eden, I agree that disappointing her would be worse. For the time being, Nan's plan seems the best.

Jo gives me a small smile, but there's something behind her eyes that makes me nervous. It's like she's already started second-guessing what happened between us, and the fear that's peeking out makes everything I've just eaten sit like a brick of lead in my stomach.

We spend the morning liaising with Jeeves about what he found in the server files, and Jo and I oversee printing out anything Eden feels is relevant to her story. By lunchtime, the living room is covered in files and bits of paper, and Eden has resorted to mapping out the elements of her story on different colored Post-Its that she sticks to the wall.

She stands back to look at all the colored squares and sighs. "You guys, this story is massive. So much bigger than I first thought. The amount of city officials Crest has in his pocket is insane. Aren't there any non-corrupt people working in our government, for God's sake?"

I lean back on the couch and rub my temples. Last night's exertions, coupled with my lack of sleep, are starting to take their toll, and the rumblings of a headache start up in my frontal cortex.

"Eden, do you think we should take this stuff to the attorney general before we go to the press? What if we're corrupting the chain of evidence?"

She puts her hands on her hips. "What if the attorney general is on Crest's payroll? Toby, at this stage, the only power we have is putting all of this out into the world, so Crest can't pay someone to cover it up. That's been his game in this city for decades, and it has to stop."

"I agree. I just want to make sure we're not doing more harm than good."

Jo stands and stretches. "If I need to go on record as a whistleblower, I will. I made sure Brad registered me as an employee yesterday in case we needed that kind of protection. Toby, since you were given a security badge, you'd also be on the books. We need to make sure as many publications as possible pick up this story. If only *Pulse* publishes it, my father can say you're biased and sue for defamation, and believe me, he'll throw every lawyer he can find to bury you in lawsuits. If all the news outlets run the story, he's powerless. He can't sue everyone, even though he'd like to."

I lean forward and put my elbows on my knees. "That's a great idea."

Eden frowns. "What? Give the story to everyone? What about my exclusive?"

"You can drop the first bombshell, but we set up a public server with all the information from Crest's files and make it accessible to every news outlet in the city. Hell, every outlet in the world. We open it up when your story is almost ready to go. By the time they've done their own research and written their pieces, your story has been published, and then everyone else will join in a huge pile on. That will force law enforcement agencies to get involved, and by the time Crest realizes his house is on fire, he's standing in the crumbling ruins of his life."

Jo stares at me with lust in her eyes. "My God, your brain is hot."

Eden nods. "She's not wrong, and if Max was here, he wouldn't mind me saying so." She pulls out her computer and sits in the big easy chair near the window. "If it can work for Ronan Farrow, it can work for me. Okay, I need some alone time to get started on this bad boy, so why don't you kids join Nan and Moby up on the roof for a while? Oh, also, can you order some food? I'm going to be starving in about an hour."

"Sure. We're on it."

We leave the apartment and head into the stairwell that leads up to the roof. We've only taken a few steps up when Jo pushes me against the wall and kisses me. I'm taken off-guard, but within seconds, I'm kissing her back like I'm drowning and she's oxygen.

"I've wanted to do that all morning," she says, breathless.

"Really? You hid it well."

"I had to. Eden's more intuitive that I give her credit for, and I think Nan's right about keeping our new status on the down-low for a while."

"I've been keeping a lot of stuff from Eden recently. Clearly I suck at being her best friend."

"You're an amazing bestie, Toby, but there's a lot going on right now. Do you think we should cool things down, until this whole thing with my dad blows over?"

That lead brick in my stomach makes an encore performance. "Is that what you want? To cool things off? Because kissing me like you just did is the wrong way to go about it."

She thinks for a few seconds, and in that time, my heart shrivels to the size of a peanut and throbs with so much pain, I fear for my cardiac health. "Jo … be honest. Do you want us to hit pause? Or stop?"

She goes up one step, so we're almost eye-to-eye. "No, I really don't, because even contemplating staying away from you just made my entire body hurt. I only want us to be cautious. No telling Asha or Eden. No public displays. Not yet."

"For how long?"

"Until it feels like the right time."

"And if it never feels right?"

She ignores that question and takes my hand before leading me up the stairs. The sense of foreboding I felt earlier returns. A secret relationship may seem exciting, but it's also a bit like a thief in the night. It can come and go without anyone knowing it was ever there.

32

———

TRYING

I stretch and squint against the sunlight coming in the bedroom windows. It's still early, but I didn't sleep well, and when I reach over to find the other side of the bed empty, I realize why.

I sit up and sigh. For the third day in a row, Jo hasn't slept with me. We went to bed and made love for several mind-blowing hours, but when I'm unconscious, she gets up and leaves, and I don't know why.

Have her nightmares come back? Am I not the dream whisperer she thought I was?

Or is there something deeper at play?

The sex between us has been off the charts, but when it comes down to it, sex is easy. People do it all the time. However, letting someone into your heart? Opening up to them about your shame and fears? That's the hardest thing in the world.

After her incredible confessional the other night, I thought Jo had conquered her fear of intimacy, but it's clear that's not the case. I get the feeling that sleeping in my arms makes her feel too vulnerable. It makes her need me too much, and for a woman who's spent her whole adult life training to be one of the most self-sufficient people on the planet, that kind of dependency must chafe to her very core.

She's pushing me away, just like she said she would, and for all my big-brain, genius-level thinking, I don't have a fucking clue how to get her to stop.

"Jeeves, do you know where Joanna is?"

"Yes, Toby. She's on the roof watching the sunrise."

I move over and sit on the edge of the bed. "Why?"

"I assume because it's visually appealing, and humans like that sort of thing."

"No, I mean why is she on the roof and not here with me?"

"I'm afraid I don't know."

"Then have a guess. Use your immense processing power to analyze what the fuck I'm doing wrong, and tell me how to fix it, because honestly, I'm at a loss. I can't lose her, and for whatever reason, it feels like I am."

There's a pause, and I swear Jeeves is trying to figure out a way to let me down gently.

"Toby, do you like neglected animal videos?"

I drop my head into my hands. "What sort of question is that? What are you even talking about?"

"I mean videos that people share where a neglected dog, for example, is found and rescued, and no matter how terribly it's been mistreated, with enough patience and love, that dog turns into a sweet, loving animal again."

"Oh. Yeah, I guess. It proves love heals everything."

"Precisely. That's the reason those videos are so popular. They posit the theory that no creature is so damaged it can't be healed by the power of love. Of course, that theory is false. It's true for dogs, because their brains are simple and easily rewired to forget past trauma, so they can embrace present happiness. Humans are almost the exact opposite. Your brains are complex and incredibly fragile, and you start creating pathways of negative thinking after a trauma. The more time that passes without the trauma being addressed, the more entrenched those thoughts become."

"Yeah, I know how neural reinforcement works, Jeeves. What's your point?"

"Joanna's negative processes can't be changed without a major mental upheaval. Over the years, her brain has been programmed, time and again, to think a certain way, and forgive me for saying it, but several nights of very enthusiastic sex with you isn't going to change that programming."

"So, what do I do?"

"Nothing. You're not qualified. But I've heard of several methods of treatment that may help. Shall I research them further?"

I climb out of bed and get dressed. "If you think they could help, then yes. Let me know what you find out."

"I will."

I pull on a pair of jeans and grab a knitted blanket off the chair in the bedroom before heading out of the apartment and up to the roof. Jo is at the far end, leaning on the balustrade and watching the sunrise, just like Jeeves said. I go over and hug her from behind, wrapping the blanket around both of us. The morning sun is bathing everything in a golden light, and we both stare at the stunning vista.

"Morning," I say, my mouth next to her ear. "You didn't sleep?"

She leans back against me, her head on my shoulder. "A little. I'm kind of out of practice."

"Is that all it is?"

I expect her to give me some vague platitude, but she doesn't. "It's not just the sleeping, but I guess you already knew that." She grabs my arms and pulls them tighter around her. "Eden's nearly done with the article, the server is set up and ready to go, and … I don't know. I kind of feel weird that my life's work to take down my father is almost over."

"Is that a bad thing?"

"No, but …" She shakes her head. "Nannabeth has a way of seeing things no one else does. Like what she said about me and my dad the other night." She steps up to the concrete barrier and puts her hands on it. "I didn't even realize how I'd oriented my whole life to be about him. Every day, in a million ways, he affects my decisions, even when I'm not aware of it." She turns to face me. "If I don't have my hatred of him dictating my every move, what's my purpose? Who am I anymore?"

I put my hands on the barrier, on either side of her. "You're still Joanna, you just have less revenge on your to-do list. You're the daughter of a soon-to-be-disgraced businessman," I kiss one cheek. "The best friend to two amazing sisters from Brooklyn," then the other, "a remarkable publishing assistant," I kiss her forehead, "and the owner of one of the most incredibly diverse resumes in the history of the world." I stop just short of her lips. "And you're the woman who owns me, mind, heart, body, and soul." I brush my lips across hers. "Isn't that enough?"

She kisses me back, but I feel how unsure she is behind the passion. "I want it to be."

"Then we're halfway there."

I don't truly believe what I'm saying, but I want to, and I suspect Jo is in the same boat. If good intentions were gold bars, we'd be rolling in cash. But it's going to take more than that to make things work between us. Jo has come so far in unburdening herself of her secrets, but that doesn't erase the damage they've left behind.

I LEAN BACK in the chair and close Eden's laptop.

She's standing in the doorway to the living room, staring at me and gnawing on her thumbnail.

"Well?" she says, expectantly.

I shake my head in awe. "It's amazing, Eden. Truly. The best thing you've ever written."

She punches the air. "I knew it! And you understood all the connections I made?"

"Absolutely. It helps that you've couched your accusations with a liberal smattering of 'allegedly,' so Derek and his lawyers won't freak out."

"Are you still cool to make up the interactive graphics for the website?"

"Yep. Almost done. Jeeves is going to render everything for me and package it up before sending it to you and Derek."

"Great." She slumps into the couch. "It's taken five days, but we finally got there. Here's hoping that when it drops, you and Jo won't be cooped up here anymore."

I haven't minded being cooped up with Joanna, but I don't think she feels the same. She's been crazy restless for the past couple of days. I think it's partly because she's not used to inhabiting the same space twenty-four hours a day and would love to go for a run in the park, but the other part is that she can't run at all. She's used to her freedom, and being trapped here with me ... well, she's not the kind of person who likes having her wings clipped.

"Speaking of Jo," Eden looks down the hallway. "Where is she?"

"On the roof, exercising. She and Moby ran laps for a while, and now I think he's swimming while she does yoga."

Eden stands and starts pulling Post-Its off the wall before tossing them in the trash. "Have you noticed how tense she's been? I would have thought she'd be happier knowing her dad was about to get body slammed."

"Her relationship with her dad is complicated."

Eden makes a scoffing noise. "Yeah, I have no idea what that's like."

I'm well-acquainted with Eden's father issues, so her sarcasm isn't lost on me.

"Toby, do you realize you're the only one in our circle of friends whose parents are still together? I mean, me and Asha: Mom died, Dad's an absentee loser. Max: Mom died, Dad's a felon. Jo: Mom died, Dad's a sociopathic douche nozzle. You're the only one who doesn't have severe parental issues. And still has a mom."

"True, but I did get beaten up every day at school for years, so that's something you don't have."

"Yeah, and the irony is, now that you're a man-mountain, people would be insane to take you on." She finishes with the wall and starts gathering up the research files and shoving them into a storage box. "I guess we've all suffered in our own ways. And we all carry damage from it. When I think about my previous defense mechanisms, it's a miracle Max and I got together. I nearly screwed things up, because of my daddy issues."

"Yeah, about that …" I put her laptop on the table. "How did you go from swearing off men for life to shackling yourself to Max's side? What changed for that to happen?" *Asking for a friend.*

She ponders that for a second. "I think when Nan had her accident and ended up in a coma, I realized that even though I could do everything by myself, I didn't want to anymore."

"Okay, so a stressful event was the catalyst." *Good to know.* "Did Max encourage you to make that decision?"

"A bit. Mostly he just urged me to stop pushing him away."

Been there, done that.

"But you were the one who made the decision in the end, right?"

"Yes. He kept his distance while showing me he cared and being there for me. One night, I'd had enough of being alone and went to him, and the rest, as they say, is history."

"Hmmm."

"Why the twenty questions, bestie?"

"No reason. Just interested about how relationships work." *Or don't, in my case.*

"Yes, well listen and learn. As soon as this story is out there in the world, I'm making it my mission to pair up you and Joanna."

"What? Why?"

"Not to each other, doofus, because obviously, you're not right for each other."

Obviously.

"But I need to find you both partners who are worthy of your awesomeness. Did you know there's a guy on the HEA database that scored a ninety-one with Jo?"

Know about it and hate it. "Yeah, I'm aware."

"Pretty sure I need to get those kids together."

"Uh huh." *I will find his profile and delete the fuck out of it before I allow that to happen.*

Nan walks in with a tray of snacks and puts it on the coffee table. "What are we talking about? Relationships? Sounds interesting."

"Yeah, Nan, I was just saying that I need to find Jo and Toby amazing people to date."

"Were you, now?" She gives me a knowing look behind Eden's back. "And what does Toby think about that?"

"He showed a definite lack of enthusiasm."

"I'm shocked."

Eden puts the lid on the storage box and picks it up. "Okay, I have to head to *Pulse* and run the gauntlet with Derek about publishing this story tomorrow, but talk to Toby, would you Nan? I want to see him happy, and right now, he's not."

"Sure, darling." Eden bends to kiss Nan's cheek and waves to me before heading out.

Nan offers me a bowl of pretzels. "So, Toby, tell me why you're not happy. I would have thought that with the amount of sex you two are having, you'd be floating ten feet off the ground."

I push my fingers into my eye sockets. "Nan, please tell me you can't hear us."

"Not really, but the floors are old in this place. They squeak." She waves me off. "It's not a problem. You're consenting adults, and I'm glad you're having a good time. But why do I get the feeling not everything is as rosy as it seems?"

I stretch out my legs and cross them at the ankles. "God, I don't know. We're having an incredible time together, but sometimes, she shuts down. It's like she can only stand intimacy in short bursts. Every day I feel more and more like Marie Antoinette waiting for the guillotine to fall." I rest my head on the back of the chair. "All I want to do is love the hell out of her for as long as possible, but that may not be in the cards."

"Toby, sometimes you overthink things."

"Only sometimes?"

"Well, it's good you can recognize your own flaws. No matter which way you slice it, this thing with Joanna is going to be a risk, but you have to decide if it's one you're willing to take."

"She has to decide that, too."

"Yes, but you're only in charge of your own decisions, not hers. You want to go all in? Do it. However, you need to be aware she might still choose to walk away. That's the danger of love. Even with the greatest relationship predictors in the world, it's *always* going to be a risk. Love can't be owned and tamed like a stray cat. Sometimes it's going to be a huge hulking lion that rips out your heart and eats it for breakfast. But you can't have great love without understanding that and walking into the cage anyway. You just can't."

"So, that whole story you told me about the stray cat …?"

She rolls her eyes. "Toby, regular love is a cat, obviously. What you have with Joanna isn't regular. It's epic. Big love is a giant freaking lion."

"Well, sure, but you keep changing your similes, so it's very confusing."

She fake glares, but then smiles before handing me a glass of iced tea from the tray. "Stop giving an old woman a hard time and go give your lioness a drink. She's working hard up there. And you two need to figure out whether you're willing to roll the dice or walk away from the table."

"There's a table now? Where did the lion go?"

She laughs and chases me out of the apartment, so I head up to the roof. I may be joking, but it's only to cover up how fucking terrified I am that we're not going to make it.

Jo's on a yoga mat, arms over her head, standing on one leg. When she hears me approaching, she turns and smiles.

"Hey." She comes over and wraps her arms around my neck, and I grip her waist with my free hand as I kiss her. The kiss is a little more forceful than I intend, but she kisses me back with equal passion. These kinds of moments reassure me that she's as invested in this as I am. I just wish they weren't so fleeting.

"Nan made you iced tea."

"She's the best."

"Yeah, except when it comes to relationship similes."

Jo frowns. "Huh?"

"Never mind."

We walk over to the duck pond and sit. Moby quacks at us and starts swimming faster, showing off for our benefit. Jo sips her drink while I watch, mesmerized by her mouth on the cool glass.

"So, Eden says the article will probably come out tomorrow."

"Yeah, I figured."

"Which means we should be able to go home, right?"

She puts the glass down on the upside-down crate between us. "God, I hope so." She realizes what she's just said and tries to backtrack. "I mean, not because of you. Just … you know. Our own space again. I miss my stuff."

I nod. "Yeah. I get it." I glance over at her. "But it's going to be strange, going back the apartment as a couple rather than roommates." As I feared, she basically does a full-body flinch when I say the word 'couple'.

I turn and watch Moby. At least he seems happy with his situation.

"Toby …"

"It's fine, Jo."

"No, it's not."

"You're right, it's not. But what are we going to do about it? Please tell me, because right now, I'm all out of fucking ideas." I stand and pace to alleviate my frustration. "When I told you I loved you, I gave you a choice: You could choose me or continue to have let your defense mechanisms ruin your romantic relationships. I thought you sharing yourself … your story … meant you'd made your choice, but that's not the case, is it?"

"It's not that simple."

"No, it's not. Before we made love, I had an infinitesimal chance of surviving losing you. Now that chance is gone. Do you think I can just go back to not loving you? Do you think I can ever go out with another woman and not compare her to you? Because let me tell you, you're a pretty fucking hard act to follow."

She comes over and pulls me into a hug, and I sigh as I wrap my arms around her as if I'll never let go.

"I'm trying, Toby. I really am."

"I know you are." I bury my face in her neck. "I'm sorry. I just didn't think being with me would be so difficult for you."

She squeezes me tighter, hands pushing into my hair. "You silly genius. Being with you is the only thing that feels right. That's the problem."

~

THE DAY the story breaks on Crest Construction, everyone at *Pulse* in on high alert. I made it into the office without seeing anyone following me, but Derek has hired extra security, just in case. As soon as the story broke, Jeeves opened the research server to any and all media the world over, and now there's a feeding frenzy as news outlets report on Eden's story while frantically writing their own.

Of course, Crest began his denial tour early, holding a press conference in the foyer of his building and calling the entire story a fabrication. But there's now a mountain of evidence in the public domain to contradict him, and judging from everyone's reaction, there's no way he's going to weasel out of this. So far, Jo and I have been kept out of the spotlight, but that may change down the track if Crest decides to reveal it was us who raided his servers.

Regardless, I'm mentally preparing myself for whatever happens next: Crest crucifying us; Jo leaving me; a giant meteor crashing into the earth. I've decided that the key to surviving all of them is the supreme, overwhelming power of not giving a shit. I've tried caring. Let's give this new thing a try for a while.

Right now, Derek, Eden and I are standing near the front windows of *Pulse,* watching as our extra security guards keep a throng of reporters and paparazzi from entering the building. I don't know why they're bothering to come here. The real story is public and ripe for the taking. Any journalist worth their salt would know that and move along.

"Here's another fine mess you've dropped us into, Tate," Derek says, folding his arms over his chest.

Eden rolls her eyes and smiles. "Oh, don't even pretend you're not loving this. Contrary to your predictions, advertisers are flooding in, readership and subscriptions have skyrocketed, and there's a bunch of photographers out there giving you more free brand exposure than you could ever afford to buy."

Derek smiles, and honestly, it's a sight so rare, it's a little off-putting. "Not a word of a lie in your statement, Tate. I have to admit, if you weren't already taken and completely repulsed by me, I could kiss you."

He walks back into his office, and Eden and I stand there and watch the spectacle for a few more minutes.

"Do you think you and Jo are safe from LeBron and his cronies now?"

I shrug. "When we went back to the apartment this morning, there was no sign of them. I think Crest will avoid doing anything that draws more attention to him at this point. And he certainly doesn't want to be harassing people who might be called to testify against him in court. Apart from blustering about how the whole thing is a web of lies, I suspect he'll be keeping a very low profile for a while. And even if he doesn't, I have Jeeves monitoring him. We'll know his next move before he does."

Eden links her arm through mine and rests her head on my shoulder. "I can't thank you and Jo enough for your help, Tobes. I mean, this was a real team effort."

"You know I'd do anything for you. Of course, for the next hundred years it will be your treat at the Tar Bar."

"As long as you're cool with an average eighteen-dollar glass of whiskey, I'm okay buying."

"You're on."

We walk back to my cubicle, and as I take a seat, she stops to look at me.

"Tobes?"

"Hmmm?"

"You're okay, right? I mean, all this cloak and dagger stuff has been a lot, and you and Jo have borne the stress of it all. Is there anything you want to talk about?"

Well, I'm hopelessly in love with Joanna, and live in mortal fear of her leaving and breaking my heart into a million pieces, but other than that, I'm cool.

"No. I'm good."

"See you at the bar later?"

"Yes, you will."

We go our separate ways, and considering I'm way behind on all my articles for next week due to my unplanned sabbatical, I spend most of the day sorting through my inbox and getting a few hundred words down. It's almost five-thirty when I finally pack up my stuff and head back to the apartment.

I call Jo's number while I walk to the subway station. For the third time today, she doesn't answer. I know she's also got a mountain of work to catch up on, especially with Asha and her new author being a major handful, but I feel like a drug addict strung out for a fix. After being with her twenty-four/seven for an entire week, eight hours without any contact is torture.

When I get back to the apartment, it's quiet, but as soon as I'm halfway down the hallway, she comes out from her bedroom and sees me. From the look on her face, it's clear she's feeling just as deprived as I am, and I stride over before kissing her with every ounce of passion I possess.

"God, I've missed you."

"Same."

I keep kissing her as I scoop her up and take her over to her bed. As soon as I place her back on her feet, she's clawing at my clothes, trying to remove them as quickly as possible. I do the same, but it still feels too long until we're naked, skin pressing to skin.

"Toby ..." The need is clear in her voice, and my need is throbbing through every overworked artery and tight muscle.

She slides back onto the bed, and I can barely contain myself as I crawl over her and settle between her legs. Right now, neither of us is interested in foreplay. Our bodies are screaming to be joined, and as I push into her, we both let out a long moan of relief, as if spending our time apart was an affliction, and this is the only cure.

"God, Jo ... I love you ..."

We move together, each in perfect sync with the other. She touches my face and looks into my eyes, and there's so much emotion there, I can't believe I ever doubted her. She watches me as if I'm the most fascinating thing she's ever seen, and they only time she closes her eyes is when her body is wound so tight, she can barely take it.

She comes seconds before I do, and after we ride out the muscle-trembling aftershocks, we just lie there, still joined, not ready to become separate people again so soon.

Eventually we make it into the bathroom and shower together before getting dressed separately. When I get back into her room, she's applying makeup, and I sit on the bed, waiting.

"I take it you had a crazy day," I say, feeling bad that we're only now having a conversation.

"Yes. My father tried to call me about fifty times, and we're going in all guns blazing at work with the Professor Feelgood book."

"You feeling okay about the story coming out?"

"As good as I can. I thought I'd feel more satisfaction seeing that bastard burn, but so far, it's more like a vague sense of accomplishment."

"Well, I think we both deserve to celebrate tonight. Eden's buying the drinks, and there are a whole bunch of people from *Pulse* going, too. Even some folks from Romance Central."

She turns to look at me. "Toby …"

There's an edge to her voice that stops me in my tracks. "What?"

It's only then I notice the very large suitcase packed and sitting next to the door.

"I'm not going to the Tar Bar."

I go over to the suitcase. "Jo, what's going on?"

We just had what is possibly the most incredible sex any human has ever experienced, and now she's leaving? Judging from the size of the suitcase, it's not a short trip, either.

"Toby …"

I grip the handle of the suitcase so hard, the plastic creaks. "Jo, seriously, what the fuck is going on?"

My pulse is racing, and panic is pounding behind my eyes. So much for not giving a shit.

She takes a tentative step forward. "I'm going away for a while."

I take a breath, trying to keep my voice steady. "What do you mean 'away?'" *Running away. From me. That's what she means.* "Was this a kiss off? A sympathy fuck, and then you're out of here?"

"Toby, no …" She comes over and takes my hands. "That's not it at all."

"Then please, tell me what this is before I lose my mind."

I feel sick. Even though I knew her bailing was a possibility, I'm not remotely prepared for the reality of it. She's become a part of the fabric of my life. I'm going to unravel without her.

She kisses me to get my attention. "Calm down." It works. Panic is quickly replaced by intense arousal. "I'm not running away, I promise."

"Then what's going on?"

She laces her fingers between mine and looks down, color blooming in her cheeks. "I'm going to get some help. Treatment for my trauma." She glances up as if to gauge my reaction. "Jeeves told me that you two had been discussing it, and … I think it's a good plan. I don't want to keep repeating the same self-destructive patterns in my life, and if we're going to have any chance at all of working, I need to do this."

She looks terrified, and I know why. Exposing that part of herself to me was hard enough. Now she has to do it in front of strangers.

"There's a place in Denmark. A cutting-edge clinic in the middle of nowhere that's having amazing results for people suffering from addiction and PTSD. They said I was a great candidate for their program."

"How long will you be gone?"

"The program lasts two weeks. While I'm away, I'll still be working for Asha, but only part-time."

"Can I call you?"

"No. Apart from my few work calls each day and limited computer time, I'll be off the grid. They want me to have as little contact as possible with the outside world."

My body is already aching at the thought of letting her go. "Jo, I barely got through today without seeing you. How the fuck am I going to last two weeks?"

"I know. I feel the same way." She touches my face. "But if I don't do this …" She shakes her head. "That ninety-three percent chance of us failing? That's me. It's *all* me. I feel it every day. And even though I know in my bones that you're the one for me, I could still screw things up so epically, neither of us will ever recover. I want to put the past behind me, so I can have the incredible future I want. With you."

I nod and pull her into a hug. She clings to me, fingers digging into my back, and I know she's thought everything through except how the hell I'm supposed to let her walk away.

With effort, she pulls back and grabs her purse. "You should take some time off, too. Go see your dad. I know you missed his operation, but you can see him in recovery. Also, your sister would love it if you made it to her opening night." She comes over and kisses me softly.

"You've spent months taking care of everyone else. Take some time for yourself for once."

It's a tempting thought. I'd always planned to go home after the app launched, and with Jo out of town, the last thing I want to do is stay in an apartment that will do nothing but remind me of her.

Still, before we part, I need Joanna to understand what she's leaving behind.

I cup her face and kiss her with everything I have, and by the time we break apart, the memory of our kiss is seared onto my soul.

"I love you, Toby, more than anything."

"I love you, too."

After a final hug, I wheel her suitcase out to the elevator, and when the doors close, I stand there for long excruciating minutes, fighting the urge to go after her.

33

THERE'S NO PLACE LIKE HOME

"Do it again!" My sister giggles as she runs to the other side of the garden. Mom watches on, smiling bigger than I've seen her in a long time. I guess she's got a lot to be happy about these days. Dad's back surgery was a total success, and even though he's still in the hospital recovering, he's regaining more mobility every day. Of course, when I got here, I discovered Joanna had set him up with an incredible rehab team who are working miracles. He still struggles to speak, but he's getting clearer, and he's even been able to support himself walking with bars on either side. To say his physical therapists are pleased with his progress, would be a massive understatement.

"Mom!" April calls out. "Sing the song!"

Mom laughs, then starts humming the theme song from *Dirty Dancing* as April runs toward me at full tilt.

"Nobody puts April in a corner!" I say, before catching her when she jumps. I lift her above my head, and she laughs and holds her arms out by her sides as I spin her around. From the corner of my eye, I catch Mom pulling out her phone to video the moment.

"Okay," I say panting as I lower her gently to the ground a minute later. "That's it. I'm done. Ten times lifting you up is my limit."

"Awwww!"

"I'll do it again tomorrow, I promise." I roll my neck and massage my shoulder. "But right now, I'm going to need you to prove how much you love me by grabbing a soda from the fridge. Nothing with sugar, please." I collapse into the chair next to Mom. "I need to keep my dancer's body in peak condition."

April giggles and kisses my cheek. "Yeah, right. At least you don't need to work out at the gym today."

"Exactly. Bench pressing you is all the exercise I need."

She runs inside, and Mom smiles at me.

"You have no idea how good it is to have you home, sweetheart. We've all missed you."

I lean over and kiss her cheek. "And I've missed you. And your cooking."

She laughs, and I sigh when I think about how much better I feel after spending time with them. There's nothing like my family to recharge my batteries. Apart from the constant simmering tension of Jo's absence, I haven't felt this good for ages.

"So, not long to go until Joanna gets home, right?"

I nod as April places an iced glass of diet cola in front of me. "Yep, just a few days to go."

"Do you miss her?" April asks, sitting down before sipping her own drink.

"So much." Just thinking about her makes my stomach do a cliff dive.

"So, Joanna's your girlfriend," April asks, "but no one knows about her? I mean, you haven't told Eden or anyone?"

I shake my head. "It's still new, and we wanted to wait for the right time."

"But you're going back to New York on Wednesday, right? That's, like, nearly a week after Jo gets back?"

"Yes."

"Why aren't you going to see her sooner?"

"Well," I say, leaning forward, "there's this show opening on the weekend starring someone I've heard is an incredible young actress, so I thought I'd swing by and check it out."

April already knew that was the reason I was staying, but nevertheless, she beams. "And you're going to buy me flowers, right? Every leading lady needs flowers opening night."

"Yes, I'll buy you flowers. Or are they not cool anymore? Maybe I'll get you some free range, organic pavement weeds instead."

"Toby!" She slaps my arm. "I want lilies, please. They smell nice."

"Alright. I suppose I'll get you some uncool, regular old lilies instead."

Mom laughs. "And then Toby's staying a couple of days after your opening, so he can bring dad home from the hospital.

April does a semi eyeroll. "Are you going for the Best Son and Brother award or something?"

"Actually, yes, and I feel like this is my year." I cross my fingers. "I hope I can rely on your votes."

My phone rings, and I check the screen before standing. "Sorry, it's Eden. I'll be right back."

"Say hi to her for me!" April says.

I walk inside and answer the call. "Well, hi, best friend. Calling to say you miss me? Again?"

"You know I do. How dare you spend time with someone other than me? It's so selfish."

"I know, and I apologize. How's New York?"

"Busy. Did you get the interview requests about the HEA app?"

"Yep. I did a few over video chats this week, and I've finished the written interviews."

"Great. It seems everyone wants a piece of Doctor Love right now. We're getting dozens of requests every day. Raj offered to step in for you, but no one thought that was a good idea." She lowers her voice. "I found him moving things around in your office the other day, and when I asked why, he told me he was trying to improve the Karma Sutra."

"Oh, God. Please lock my door."

"Already done. Any news about Crest?"

I sit on the couch and put my feet up on the coffee table. "Not really. Jeeves said the AG is gathering everything they need to issue subpoenas, but you know how slowly the wheels of justice turn. It will probably be years before anything exciting happens. However, in some other good news, when his stock price plummeted, a corporate raider swooped in and bought a controlling share in the company."

"Wow. So, he's lost his business?"

"That's the rumor. It won't be official until the board of directors meets and formally removes him, but from what I've heard, he's going to get booted very soon."

She makes a triumphant noise. "Couldn't happen to a nicer asshole. Ooh, before I forget … you're back here on Wednesday, right?"

"Yeah, why?"

"Nan is throwing a surprise birthday party for Asha, and she wants you and Jo to be there."

"Uh … is that a good idea? Isn't your sister notoriously anti-birthday?"

"Yes, but it's time she got over it. So, are you in?"

"Of course. What time?"

"You need to get there by seven, so we can hide you."

"I'll do my best." I won't get dad home from the hospital until three, and knowing what traffic is like getting back into the city, it will be a push, but I'll make it work.

I clear my throat and put on my most casual tone. "Have you talked to Jo since she's been away?"

"No, but Ash talks with her briefly every day. Apparently, the health retreat she's at is amazing, but she's eager to get back."

My chest flutters and aches, and I'd give my left arm just to hear her voice. She'll be in NYC before me though, so I hope that the second she's back on the grid, we can spend several hours on the phone. Maybe I can convince her to Facetime me. Naked.

"Well, it will be great to see her … uh, and you, and everyone else, when I get back." *So smooth, Jenner.*

"Can't wait to see you, too." There's a sound, and I hear the rumble of Max's voice in the background. "Oooh, gotta go. Max is home, and he has costumes."

"For work, right, Eden?" There's a conspicuous silence. "For *work*, right?"

"Sure, Toby! Love you! Byeee!"

She hangs up, and I go over and lean against the frame to the French doors. April is using the garden rake as a makeshift microphone and singing a song in a language I don't know, but guess is probably Korean. She's halfway through when her phone rings, and she immediately drops the rake to answer it. "Britney, hi! … Yeah, you wanna come over tomorrow? … Of course! I've only watched it twenty-seven times." She waves to Mom and me and then hurries inside to her bedroom and closes the door.

I shake my head and go to sit next to mom. "How did you raise such a shy daughter? She really needs to come out of her shell."

Mom smiles. "Don't ask me how I got her or a brilliant, genius son. Just lucky I guess."

She takes April's abandoned soda and sips it. "So, tell me more about this amazing woman who's captured your heart."

I cross my ankle over my knee and lean back. "Well, it's a long story, but we met in the men's room of a bar after she'd been groped, and a short time later, we found out we had practically zero compatibility."

"Oh. Wow. That'll be a story to tell your grandkids one day."

I sigh. "Yes, indeed."

34

LOVE LIGHT

I sit on the horn of the rental car as the traffic leading back into NYC crawls along at a snail's pace. I can feel my blood pressure rising with every passing minute.

"Don't block off the intersection, you jackass!" My windows are up, but I really hope the asshole sneering at me from his Mercedes can read lips. "If you make me late to meet my woman, I'm going to find you, hack your bank accounts, and reduce your credit score to zero."

He flips me the bird before pulling into another lane, and I veer around him with the ferocity of a Formula One driver.

I must get home to see Joanna before we go to Asha's party, because if I don't get to make love to her before I see her in a public setting, things are going to get real awkward, real fast.

By the time I make it back to our building and park the car in the underground garage, it's after six. I quickly grab my bags before getting in the elevator and jabbing the penthouse button relentlessly, until it opens on our floor.

"Jo?!" I run through the front door that Jeeves has conveniently swung open for me. "Joanna?!"

I nearly sprint down to her bedroom, and when I find she's not there, I drop my bags onto the floor and grab my phone to call her.

"Toby, Joanna tried to call while you were in the garage but couldn't get through. She asked me to let you know she'll have to meet you at the party. Her last meeting of the day is running long. She'll get there as soon as she can."

I exhale and wipe my forehead. "Are you kidding me?"

"No, I'm not."

"You couldn't have told me that before I busted a lung running in here?"

"I could have, but watching you run and yell was quite amusing."

I sit on the edge of Joanna's bed and drop my head in my hands. "I can't believe I'm not going to see her before the party. I broke land speed records to get here in time."

"I noticed. Between your parents' house and here, you've accrued two speed camera infractions and three reports from red-light cameras."

I flop back on the bed. "Cool. Can I trust that you'll find a way to delete those tickets?"

"Already done."

"You're the best, Jeeves."

"Indeed. I'm the only Jeeves."

I reach above my head to grab one of Joanna's pillows, press it to my face, and sniff.

"Oh, God." My sense memory sets my whole body on fire, and I groan in frustration. "You're really missing out, Jeeves. If you could only understand how incredible this woman smells …" I get up and throw the pillow back onto the bed before striding into my own room.

"I take it you'll be showering before you leave."

"You bet your sweat ass I will be. A lot."

"Starting Toby's Private Shower Time program now."

For a change, I let Gerald drive me to the party, and sitting in the plush comfort of the Escalade, I can't help but think back over the conversations I've had with Jo since she got back from her retreat. Even though she still sounds like the same woman I know and love, she also sounds different. There's a new openness in how she speaks, like somehow, all her borders have been expanded. To date, she's slept every single night, with not even a hint of a bad dream.

I'm beyond happy for her.

She describes the treatment course as if it rebooted her brain. Participants took part in daily meditation and therapy rituals, and in Joanna's words, they all "took a ton of hallucinogens" that were used in a clinical setting to purge negative habits and build new, healthful connections. She also said she worked through the issues she had with her father, and she was more than ready to close the book on that painful part of her life. There was something in her voice that set off my Spidey-sense, but I have to trust that she means it.

In any case, she seems to believe that the therapy has helped her in deeply meaningful ways, but I won't feel totally at ease until she's standing in front of me, declaring that her love for me was the one aspect that didn't get rebooted.

After a slow crawl through traffic over the bridge to Brooklyn, we finally pull up in front of Nannabeth's building. I'm feeling excited and anxious, wondering if Jo's already here.

Gerald turns in his seat. "Mr. Jenner?"

"Gerald, please, you know that weirds me out. Call me Toby."

"Of course, Toby. Miss Cassidy left this for you. It's a present and card for Miss Asha."

I take the envelope and heavy box from him. "What's inside?"

"I believe it's a first edition of a book series Miss Asha enjoys."

"Of course it is. Trust Joanna to get her the perfect gift."

I bid Gerald goodnight and hurry upstairs to Nan's apartment. When I knock, she ushers me inside with a sense of urgency. To my immense disappointment, there's no sign of Jo.

"Thank God you're here," Nan says, urging me down the hallway. "Put your gift in the spare room. I need your help."

I do as she asks and hurry back. "What do you need, Nan? My computer skills? Technical prowess? Encyclopedic knowledge of everything wrong with the latest batch of *Star Wars* films?"

"Not exactly." She leads me upstairs to the roof and points to a long string of fairy lights lying on the ground. "I need your height. Those lights need to be strung along the poles on the side there, and the others can be draped all over the bushes and garden beds." She pulls a thumb drive from her pocket. "Oh, and can you upload these songs into that jukebox I rented? Start with the jazz playlist, and I'll change over to other songs later."

"Uh … sure. No problem." I must admit that after all the pressure of the HEA app, followed by the extreme stress of the Crest espionage, being asked to do some basic grunt work is a nice change.

Nan leaves me to get on with it, and within thirty minutes, the entire garden is draped in sparkling lights. I step back and appreciate the view. It really does look amazing. I head over to the jukebox, where I quickly upload everything and bring up the playlist Nan suggested. Gentle jazz filters out of the speakers, and it enhances the romantic scene.

Jo is going to love all of this. I just wished she was here to see it. A pox on the damn meeting that's keeping her away from me. Does no one understand how badly I need to see her? How much I've missed holding her?

I'm about to head back downstairs when Nan returns.

"Oh, wow, Toby, good job. Everything is almost ready." A tall man comes out of the doorway, and I recognize Asha's author and childhood friend, Jake, from the night we met at the HEA launch.

"Toby, have you met Jacob Stone? Jake, this is Eden's best friend, Toby."

"Yeah," I say. "We met a few weeks ago. Hey, man." Jake and I shake hands. "Good to see you again."

He nods. "You, too."

Jake's carrying a box under his arm, and I gesture to it. "Birthday present?"

He looks down at the box, seeming nervous. "Yeah, I just hope she likes it."

"Oh, don't be silly," Nan says with a wave of her hand. "We both know you're her present, Jake. Everything else is just cream."

Jake smiles, but he still seems unsure. He turns back to me. "I appreciate you helping out, Toby, and thanks for coming. Asha's going to love this. If I can manage to pull everything off without freaking out, it should be a fun night."

"Absolutely."

He walks over to the center of the garden where there's a bench seat and carefully places the box onto it.

I turn back to Nan. "Looks like you guys have a plan. Is there anything else you need me to do?"

"No," she says. "But Eden and Asha will be here shortly, so you can hide behind the stairwell if you like. We're going to have dinner downstairs for about half an hour, and then Asha will come up to discover Jake. Wait for my signal, okay? Jake needs to deliver his presents before we reveal ourselves." She has a gleeful look in her eyes that makes me feel like she's not telling me the whole truth. Still, I play along.

"Sure. No yelling and scaring anyone prematurely."

She pats my arm and looks as excited as a teenager as she heads back downstairs. I smile and walk around to the far side of the stairwell, out of view. Nan uses this part of the roof to store her garden supplies, and I see a range of empty pots and garden implements underneath a makeshift lean-to beside the water tank. I go over to the side of the building and look out over the city. It really is magnificent. I check my watch, then my phone. I'm about to text Jo to see if she's on her way when I hear a noise behind me.

"Toby?" I turn to see Max walking toward me. "Hey. I guess this is our secret hideout, huh?"

I smile and nod. "For the time being. Are the Tate sisters in the building yet?"

"Yep, they just arrived. I snuck in after them. Did Nan give you the full story?"

"No, but from her excitement, I'm assuming Jake's proposing."

Max leans his elbows on the concrete balustrade and clasps his hands. "Yep. And if Eden and Nan manage to not give the game away beforehand, it will be a minor miracle."

I laugh. "You need to give them acting lessons, man."

"I did. They failed miserably. Ah, well. We'll have to see what happens."

"Toby?"

Joanna's voice sends a cascade of shivers up my spine, and I feel like I turn in slow motion to see her standing a short distance away. She's staring at me, beaming like she's been granted three wishes, but then she realizes Max is next to me, and her face falls. "Oh, Max. Hey."

Max laughs. "Wow, Jo. My heart is warmed by the enthusiasm of your greeting."

She gives him a smile. "Sorry. Just didn't see you in the shadows there."

After she gives him a quick hug, she turns to me. "Hi."

My heart is pounding so furiously, I swear to God half of Brooklyn can hear it. "Hi."

She leans in to hug me, and I try to play it as cool as possible considering Max doesn't know about us. Still, I end up squeezing her with way too much intensity, and she clears her throat before pulling back.

"Good to see you, Toby."

"Yes, Joanna, you, too."

Jesus. Talk about needing acting lessons. We're as unconvincing as the 'actors' they get for infomercials in the pre-dawn timeslot.

"Busy day?" I say as Max frowns at us.

"Yes." Jo glances at Max, then back at me. "Very busy. Much … work."

Max gets a bemused look on his face and shoves his hands into his pockets. "Fascinating."

"What?" Jo says defensively.

Max glances at each of us. "You two acting like you're not completely into each other. Does Eden know about this?" He shakes his head. "Of course she doesn't, because if she had any clue that her two best friends were falling in love, she'd already have talked my ears off about it."

Jo clasps her hands in front of her. "Max, please don't say anything."

"Why are you trying to hide this? It's amazing news. Eden will be over the moon."

"I know, but this night is about Asha, and I don't want to do anything to detract from that. I promise, I'll tell everyone tomorrow."

"You will?" I ask.

"Yes," Jo says, emphatically. "Or rather, *we* will." We grin at each other. I think some part of me didn't believe we'd get to the 'going public' phase, but I'm over the moon to learn I was wrong.

Jo turns to Max. "Let Eden concentrate on Asha tonight. If she gets any more good news of the romantic kind, she's going to explode."

Max nods and looks over toward the stairwell. "You're right. Let her deal with one milestone at a time. Not only is your secret safe with me tonight, but I'll go one better and chat with Jake for a few minutes, so you two can have some … alone time. God knows I can feel the sexual frustration coming off you in waves."

He strolls over to the other side of the roof, and as soon as he's out of sight, Jo and I stare at each other, the air between us all but shimmering with electricity.

All I want to do is kiss her, but I need to make sure her new awakening is real, and not just a transitionary phase.

"How are you feeling?" I sound fucking desperate, but I can't help that right now.

She takes a small step forward, then stops. "I feel incredible, Toby. Like a brand-new me."

"Not totally new, I hope. I mean, I was extremely attached to the old you." I move forward, but only a little. Holding back from touching her is excruciating. "You look beautiful, by the way." I take a breath. "I've forgotten how just looking at you can stop my heart in its tracks."

"Toby ..." The way she says my name sends shivers up my spine. It's full of pain and pleasure, like being with me again is so intense, it hurts. I know how she feels.

"Joanna." When you're so in love with someone, you can't imagine living without them, everything changes. You look at them with new eyes. You even say their name differently. It's like it's suddenly a precious word that needs to be spoken with the utmost care. A personal, private prayer.

"We have to talk." She says it calmly, but the deeply paranoid idiot inside me who's heard that phrase in way too many break ups, is immediately on edge.

"Okay. Do I need to raid Nannabeth's liquor cabinet in preparation for this bad news?" *Please, Jo. You're holding my heart in your hands. Treat it gently.*

"I don't think it's bad news, but I need to know if you do."

I nod. "Okay." I may seem calm, but I feel anything but. I clench my hands at my sides, trying to breathe steadily, so my heart doesn't burst through my ribcage.

"Did you hear that Dad lost the controlling share in his company?" she asks.

"Yes. I also heard he's on the way out."

"He is out. It was confirmed this afternoon."

I raise my eyebrows. "Wow, okay. I didn't know about that yet."

"No one knows. That's why I'm telling you first. New honest me, and all." She takes a breath. "My stockbroker had a standing order to buy up Crest stock any time it dropped in the market. The person who bought Dad out is me."

"Uh ... holy shit." Not the very last thing I expected to hear today, but damn close to it. "That's good, right?"

She nods. "The meeting I had this afternoon was with the Board of

Directors. They voted my father out and me in. I'm the new CEO of Crest."

"Joanna, my God. That's amazing!" I want to run to her, but I settle for two steps forward.

"Is it? I'd hoped you'd think that, but I wasn't sure if you'd think it was me not closing the door on the past. That I was still lost in my vendetta or whatever."

"Is that what's happening?"

"Not at all. For too long, Dad hurt the people he should have been helping and destroyed lives. I couldn't watch it happen anymore. He had so much potential to do good in this city, but he squandered it on his stupid, petty legacy of hoarding wealth. I'm going to change that."

She's so fucking magnificent, I get butterflies in my stomach. "What's your plan?"

"To use Crest Construction in two ways." She holds out her fingers. "One, to build luxury condos that I'll sell for obscene profits to rich people, and two, using those profits to fund affordable housing projects throughout the boroughs in New York."

Butterflies again. Hell, moths, now. "That's amazing."

"I know, right? I had a lot of time to think while I was away, and the therapists kept pushing me to figure out what my purpose was now that my father was no longer my focus. I realized that what I enjoy doing more than anything is helping people."

I step closer, almost touching distance, so proud I want to beat my chest and tell the world that this incredible woman is mine.

"So, you'd give up your Whiplash job and be a real estate mogul full-time?" I touch her fingertips, and she takes in a sharp breath.

"I haven't figured that out yet. I think I'd get bored doing just one thing."

I slide my fingers between hers, and my breathing gets shallow as my body reacts. "You're incredible, Joanna. You know that?"

She puts her hands on my chest. "You're the one who inspired me. If you hadn't given me that ultimatum when I was feeling lost—"

"Ultimatum?" I chuckle. "See, I saw that more as a pep talk."

She laughs. "Oh, no, it was a big, fat, scary ultimatum, but that was exactly what I needed to hear. And the only person I would accept talking to me like that is you."

"So …" I hover my lips above hers, floating in a sea of goosebump-inducing hormones. "We're good?"

She strokes my jaw, making even more goosebumps. "Oh, no. We're not good, Toby Jenner. We're freaking spectacular."

We finally give in to the magnetic force pulling us together, and for long minutes, we get lost in the most extraordinary kiss I've ever experienced.

"God, I've missed you."

She kisses me like we haven't seen each other for months. "Not as much as I've missed you."

We kiss furiously, trying to make up for our time apart, but at some point, we realize we need to stop, because if things go much further, the apartment buildings overlooking the rooftop will see far more of both of us than is wise or legal.

I pull back and put some space between us, not only to straighten my suit and tie, but also to cool off before I have to interact with people again.

"Okay … wow … just give me a minute." I pace in one direction, and Jo paces in the other.

She takes some deep breaths and makes a pained noise. "Toby, I'm so turned on, I'm aching. This is unacceptable."

"Right there with you." Being this aroused with no way of finding release is a special kind of torture. When I glance over and see her lips are still swollen from our kiss, my situation isn't helped at all.

"Damn … fuck." *Come on, Toby, deep breaths.* I look away from her and instead gaze at the potting shed, but knowing she's just a few feet away is still at the forefront of my mind.

"Got anything incredibly non-arousing to talk about?" I ask. I can still hear her pacing behind me.

"Uh … well, I got a bikini wax yesterday."

I squeeze my eyes shut. "*Non*-arousing, Jo. Jesus."

"It was non-arousing for me. It hurt like hell."

We keep pacing, and we figure out not talking is probably for the best. Eventually, the cool night air works wonders, and when I can breathe again, I turn to face her. I'm surprised to find she's on the other side of the roof.

"Being as far away from you as I could get seemed like the thing to do," she says.

"Yep. Solid plan."

"Do I have any lipstick left?"

"Not even a little."

She pulls out some lipgloss from her pocket and applies it. "That's it. No more kissing. We're here for Asha, not ourselves."

"Right. No more kissing." Of course, saying that makes me want to kiss her more than ever. Thankfully, Max walks back into view and takes up a position right behind the stairwell.

"Eden just texted me. Asha's coming. Get over here, so she doesn't see you."

We both head over to Max's position and press ourselves against the wall on either side of him.

"Did you get it out of your system?" he whispers to us.

I shake my head. "Not in the slightest."

He smirks. "Why do I get the feeling you'll be cutting out of here early?"

Joanna presses her head back into the wall. "No one has ever been more right in the history of the world."

Max chuckles softly, and then we freeze as we hear footsteps coming up the stairs.

"It's her," Jo whispers. "She's going to freak when she sees Jake."

I smile that she's so happy for her friend. If there's ever someone you want to have in your corner to cheer for your eternal happiness, it's Joanna.

After a few minutes, we hear voices. I can't tell exactly what they're saying, but it seems Jo can, because she tears up.

"Oh, my God. So beautiful."

After more talking, I glance around the corner to see Jake on one knee and Asha holding her hands over her mouth. I guess it's the big moment, and as soon as Asha nods and Jake sweeps her into his arms, Eden and Nan come and grab us, urging us to sneak out.

As we come around the corner, I notice the stairwell is filled with a bunch of people. Some I guess are Asha's work colleagues, but there are also people from Romance Central, as well as Nannabeth's neighbors. They all tiptoe onto the roof, and Jo and I are positioned in front of them, along with Eden, Max and Nan.

By this time, Asha is crying, but after Jake slides a ring onto her finger, Nan leads the applause, and she turns, totally surprised to see us all there.

"You're not allowed to be mad at me," Nan says through her happy tears. "You vetoed a birthday party. You didn't say anything about a surprise engagement."

Asha cry-laughs and gestures for us to come over. After Jo and I hug her and congratulate Jake, we help turn the area in front of Moby's pond into a dance floor, and Nan goes over to the jukebox to change the playlist to love songs.

I turn to Jo, who seems almost as emotional as Asha. "Dance with me?"

She glances over at Max and Eden, who are already making use of the dance floor. "Can you dance with me without letting everyone know you love me?"

I pull her into my arms and press my lips against her ear. "Probably not, but let's give it a try."

We dance for a while, and I don't think I've ever been this happy. My dad is on the mend, my mom and sister are living their best lives, my career is on the rise, and I'm in love with the most incredible woman in the world. And to think, a few months ago, none of those things were true.

Jo plays with the hair at the nape of my neck, and I groan softly.

"How long do we need to stay before we can take off?" I murmur. "Hours? Minutes?"

Jo looks around. "I think seconds. Everyone here is so blissed out, they won't even notice we're gone."

"Really?"

"Absolutely. Look, even Nan's dancing with Mr. Lester from the third floor."

I turn to see it's true, and honestly, Nan and Mr. Lester look pretty good together. I wonder if Nan might get a second chance at love. If anyone deserves it, it's her.

I glance over at Eden, and when I see her snuggled into Max's chest with her eyes closed, I take Jo's hand and pull her toward the exit. "Come on. This is our chance."

We run down the stairs and exit the building, and considering the traffic is still terrible, we head to the subway station to get back to Manhattan. The trip home is filled with loaded looks and stolen kisses, and by the time we reach the safety of the elevator, I can't hold back anymore and push her up against the wall as I kiss her. All too soon, the doors open, and I take her hand and lead her into the entrance hall.

"Wait, Toby …" She pulls me to a stop. "I want to show you something."

"Here?" I ask. "Won't the neighbors get an eyeful?"

She smiles as she takes my hand and leads me to the balcony. Confusion hits me when I see that the table is laid with crisp linens and fine silver, and the whole area is lit with hundreds of tiny candles.

"Joanna … wow …"

"I wanted to do this earlier, but I got held up at that stupid board meeting. Wait here."

She goes back inside and returns a minute later with two plates full of gourmet food. My stomach rumbles.

"I knew you wouldn't eat before you left. Hungry?"

"Starving in every way, but sure, let's do food first."

We sit at the table and eat, and even though the air is heavy with the need to be together, for a few minutes, I'm just content to take time to sit and watch her for a while.

"Did I mention that I missed you?" I say, as I reach over and take her hand. I lift it to my mouth and kiss her knuckles. "Please don't ever leave me again."

She presses the back of my hand to her cheek. "Definitely not planning on it."

After staring at me for a few seconds, she pulls out her phone. "Toby, you know how I said that since I had the treatment, I'm far more in control of my negative reactions?"

"Yes, and that's amazing to hear."

"It is, because for the first time in my life, I feel like I don't have something to prove. I accept that you love me, and I deserve that love, and that …" She smiles. "That feels better than anything I've ever felt."

She brings up the HEA app on her phone. "Anyway, when I got back, I felt like I was finally my best self. Someone who didn't need to second-guess her decisions. Someone who didn't need to hurt people before they hurt me."

"Jo, what are you saying?"

She points to her phone. "I did the questionnaire again with my new state of mind, and do you know what?"

My heart jumps into my throat. "What?"

"It gave us a new compatibility score."

Oh, God. It's the moment I've dreamed of. "Okay." Now I get affirmation that we've been right for each other all along, we just needed a little work. At last, Jo is going to be revealed as my one-and-only soul mate, and we can ride off into the sunset, secure in the knowledge that out of everyone on the planet, we belong together.

She hits a button, and there's a quiet ding as a number comes up in gold on the screen. She turns the phone so I can see it.

When I register what it says, I frown so hard, my eyebrows hurt. "What the hell?"

It's forty-two percent. A massive increase, yes, but hardly soul-mate level compatibility.

Jo smiles and puts the phone away. "That's exactly what I thought when I first saw it, but then I realized, the number doesn't matter." She pushes away from the table and comes to sit in my lap. "Toby, I don't have a crystal ball, and I know that according to the math, we don't have a snowball's chance in Hades of working out. But I also know that I love you more than I thought I could love anyone, and as complicated as love is, it can also be incredibly simple. Because love isn't perfect. It's hard, and stressful, and scary, but despite all that, I *choose* you. I don't care what the math says. No matter what life throws at us or how it tests us, every day I wake up with breath in my body, I will choose you, over and over again, until a whole lifetime is behind us." She leans down and kisses me, and it's the sweetest, most intimate kiss we've ever shared. "I choose you, Tobias Matthew Jenner. And us being happy together can be as simple as you choosing me back."

Emotion fills my chest, and I struggle against it as I look at this magnificent woman who has changed my life in so many ways. "Of course I choose you, Joanna. Every day for the rest of my life."

We kiss and hold each other, and after a few minutes I lift her off my lap and stand before reaching into my jacket pocket for the small gold band I put there earlier. It's my grandmother's engagement ring. After I'd raved to my family about Jo for the entire time I was there, Mom had given it to me without a second's hesitation.

I must have hidden my intentions well, because when I pull it out, Joanna gasps.

"I swear to God," I say. "I decided to do this weeks ago, not long after you left, with the hope that once you'd completed treatment, you'd still want me as much as I wanted you. I'm not just jumping on Asha and Jake's engagement bandwagon here."

"Toby ..."

"Jo ..." I take a breath. "I learned about love from my parents. They always gave me the best example of what it's like to love someone with all your heart and soul, but I doubted I'd ever find it for myself. When I was little, mom told me that we're all born full of love, but sometimes people steal it, and others waste it. But the most important decision we'll ever make is deciding who to give our love to. My love belongs to you. All of it. And I can't imagine that ever changing. Please make me the happiest man alive and spend your life with me."

She reaches into her pocket and pulls out an engraved gold band, not dissimilar to mine. "If you'd given me a few more minutes, I was going to propose to you."

I pull her into my arms, and for the hundredth time since I met her, my heart feels too big for my chest. After sliding the rings onto each other's fingers, I look at her in awe.

"You realize that Eden may have a coronary when we tell her."

"She'll recover. She has to if she's going to be my Best Woman."

Jo laughs, even though tears are streaming down her cheeks. "Oh, my God, and Asha is going to be my Maid of Honor. Now we just need to get Max to propose, and we can have a triple-decker wedding that New York will talk about for decades."

We kiss, until we can barely breathe, and then I turn her, so we're both looking out onto the city, my arms around her waist and my head on her shoulder. "There's just one more thing I want you to see. Jeeves ..."

The lights in the buildings opposite us flash, and Jo gasps as the lit offices across the way spell out, "Toby Loves Jo."

"That was Jeeves's idea."

Jo looks at it in awe. "Jeeves, are you turning into a romantic?"

"*Possibly, Joanna. Why? Do you know any cute AIs to whom you can introduce me?*"

Jo smiles and takes my hand. "Come on. It's getting cold out here, but my bed is extremely warm."

She leads me back into the apartment, and we don't even get to the living room before she's kissing me and pulling at my clothes. We slowly make our way to the hallway, leaving a trail of garments in our wake, and I make it as far as my bedroom doorway before I lose patience altogether and throw her over my shoulder.

"Toby!"

She laughs as I carry her into the bedroom, but that only lasts as long as it takes me to strip her bare and kneel between her legs. Her noises then devolve into curse words and moans.

We make love all night, in nearly every room, and when the sun comes up, we sleep for a few hours before starting all over again.

That night, while she lies on my chest and sleeps without a single nightmare, I stare at her beautiful face and get choked up from the utter perfection of this moment in time. It's like I've had this recurring dream for my whole life, full of images and feelings I've never understood until right now.

And then I realize what a miracle it is that we're here together.

When I was in college, I read a quote that said, "Sometimes the universe gives us exactly what we want, and most times, because we're self-destructive monkeys, we spit it right back in its face," and that could have been our fate.

If Jo hadn't had the courage to face her demons, we would have been over before we began.

I used to believe that suffering made us fragile, but that's not true. The strongest souls in the world have scars on their scars. They may not have gotten through their battles unscathed, but in terms of overcoming whatever life has thrown at them, they've come out victorious every time. That's true strength, and that's what I've found in Joanna. And I know that no matter how much she loves me, I love her more. I don't mean 'more' as in a quantifiable amount. I mean more than any hard times we have ahead. More than any fight or silly misunderstanding. More than the darkest night or the dimmest dawn.

And that's what life is about.

When you meet someone you know in your soul is yours, and they love you back, run toward each other with the force of asteroids colliding in space. Let rules, opinions, doubts, and logic crumble around you in order to be with them. Because that kind of love is rare and precious, and only exists for those brave enough to fight for it.

To put it plainly, the most powerful force in the universe is love.

Take it from a man who knows.

Anyone who says true love is easy has
never felt it, because there's nothing
easy about loving a person who's as
necessary to your life as breathing.
There's nothing easy about being
so terrified of losing them,
you'll make a thousand wrong decisions
before you figure out that
risking everything
is the only right one.

PROFESSOR FEELGOOD

ALSO BY LEISA RAYVEN

THE *STARCROSSED* SERIES

BAD ROMEO

BROKEN JULIET

WICKED HEART

BAD ROMEO CHRISTMAS

THE *MASTERS OF LOVE* SERIES

MISTER ROMANCE

PROFESSOR FEELGOOD

DOCTOR LOVE

For more information, please visit

WWW.LEISARAYVEN.COM

ACKNOWLEDGMENTS

Darling readers, it's been a while.

I'm so sorry this book is reaching your eyeballs (much) later than expected. The last few years have been trying for all of us, so I truly appreciate the grace and patience you've all shown as I traveled a difficult path in getting Toby and Joanna's story out into the world. Every author believes they have the world's best readers, but I truly think I do. I can't tell you how touched I've been by the near-constant messages of love and support that you have all sent. You will never truly understand how important they were to me in my most challenging times. Please know that I am eternally grateful for every single one of you.

As usual, getting this book finished was a group effort, and I couldn't do it without an amazing team behind me.

To my agent, Christina, as well as Hannah and my whole Jane Rotrosen Agency family, thank you for your constant support and patience. I truly appreciate you all.

To my editor and friend, Caryn – is it too cheesy to say you're the wind beneath my wings? Screw it, I'm saying it. Couldn't do this without you, my love, and what's more, I wouldn't want to.

To my gorgeous bestie Andrea – thank you for your boundless enthusiasm for my characters. You make my heart happy every day.

To my fabulous pre-readers who still catch things in chapters I've read through dozens of times – Ngaire, Kendra, Marty, Anne, and Sara – you're all total rock stars.

To Regina Wamba who has made all my Masters of Love covers – you're incredible. Thank you for bringing my gorgeous guys to life.

To Jenn and the whole team at Social Butterfly PR – thank you for getting me back out into the book world after being away for so long.

To all my foreign publishers who have been so patient in waiting for this book, I'm eternally grateful for your grace and faith.

To all the bloggers and reviewers, all the beautiful readers, and members of my private reader group who have infected me with their enthusiasm for this book – I'm in awe of all of you. Your constant love and support are a marvel and a blessing.

And finally, an enormous thanks to my incredible family. My darling husband, Jason, who continues to be the best husband on the planet, (I will fight anyone who says otherwise), and my beautiful boys, Xander and Kyan, who are two of the most remarkable young men I know. The past couple of years have been tough for us all and involved incredible amounts of hard work, sacrifice, and resilience, and I'm eternally grateful that I have you and your father as my true north and safe haven.

Thank you all so much for reading.

Come find me on social media for a chat sometime.

All my love,
Leisa x

Leisa Rayven burst onto the romance scene in 2014 when her Starcrossed Series was optioned by Macmillan New York in a three-book deal. As a former actor, her debut novel, *BAD ROMEO* revolved around the world of Broadway, and was published to critical acclaim in December 2014.
Since then, all her subsequent novels have regularly featured on international bestseller lists and she has received glowing praise from high-profile authors such as Colleen Hoover, E.L. James, Christina Lauren, and Jennifer Probst.
Her latest series, The Masters of Love, includes *MISTER ROMANCE, PROFESSOR FEELGOOD*, and *DOCTOR LOVE*, and is available through publishers all over the world.
Leisa lives in Brisbane, Australia with her husband, two large teenage sons, and four judgmental cats. When not writing books, she's eating guacamole.

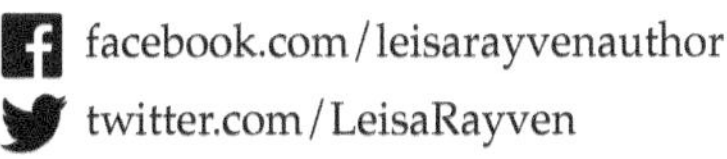

facebook.com/leisarayvenauthor
twitter.com/LeisaRayven
instagram.com/leisarayven

www.ingramcontent.com/pod-product-compliance
Lightning Source LLC
Chambersburg PA
CBHW021716110726
47902CB00005B/1221